THE
LONGEST
FRAUD

THE
LONGEST
FRAUD

MAGGIE GIBSON

POOLBEG

Published 1996 by
Poolbeg Press Ltd,
123 Baldoyle Industrial Estate,
Dublin 13, Ireland

© Maggie Gibson 1996

The moral right of the author has been asserted.

A catalogue record for this book is available from the British Library.

ISBN 1 85371 549 2

Cover photograph by Michael Edwards
Cover design by Poolbeg Group Services Ltd
Set by Poolbeg Group Services Ltd in New Baskerville
Printed and bound in Great Britain by Cox & Wyman Ltd, Reading, Berks.

For Katy, Mart and Damien

Prologue

A sudden urge to panic gripped ex-garda Grace de Rossa by the throat as she stood outside Harcourt Terrace Garda Station for the last time, clutching the cardboard box that contained the accumulated contents of her desk and locker. The carton was too small and she could feel the bottom straining to give way against the palms of her hands, so she lifted her knee to support the box whilst she struggled to edge her arms further underneath.

Jack Mulloy wandered down the steps towards her.

"Need a hand?" he asked half-heartedly.

Grace shook her head. "No thanks . . . I can manage."

"Suit yourself," he said and strolled off down the street hands in pockets.

Goodbye Grace, all the best Grace, sorry to see you go Grace, she thought, watching him disappear round the corner. *Still . . . what did I expect. Half of them still think I'm bent.* Surprisingly this thought

1

cheered her up a little, or at least strengthened her resolve that she was doing the right thing.

She looked into the top of the box. *Is this all I have to show for ten years in the Garda Siochana,* she thought and headed off despondently towards her car.

Dermot leant against the bonnet, arms folded, waiting for her. "All finished up?" he asked smiling.

She nodded. "Yes. I think so. I suppose so."

Acting Detective Inspector Dermot McEvoy had been a member of the Gardaí for twenty-five years, most of it spent in and around the capital. He was a widower with three daughters all just about grown up. Grace had learnt a lot about police work from him in the four years that they had worked together. He had a volatile temperament but she sometimes found his attitude a touch jaded, even a little callous, a fact she put down to the number of years he had been in the job.

He and a couple of others were alone in believing she was totally innocent of the corruption complaint that had been maliciously lodged against her and she was grateful for his support. The complaint had been dropped through lack of corroborating evidence and, although she knew that her former Inspector Howard Hatchett was the guilty party, he was now dead, and to make matters worse, the investigating officer was his brother-in-law who wouldn't hear a word against his sister's exemplary late husband. Grace knew all about the sticking power of slung mud, and decided to resign. Her career was dead in the water anyway.

She rested the box on the car bonnet next to Dermot and fumbled for her keys. "Are you coming to the pub?" he asked.

Grace snorted in response. "I don't think I want to find out just how few will show up, thanks all the same."

Dermot gave a heavy sigh. "Cut the paranoia, Grace. You can be such a pain when you're feeling sorry for yourself. Anyway, you may be surprised."

"Who said I was feeling sorry for myself?" she snapped, straight away on the defensive. "And anyway you know how I hate surprises . . ."

"Shut up, Gracie, and get in the car or I'll arrest you for wasting good drinking time," he said, laughing.

She relented. "Oh all right. But just the one . . . and don't even think of trying to talk me out of anything."

"It's a bit late for that now, woman, you've burnt your bridges, but far be it from me to come between an ex-cop and her dubious business partners."

They drove in silence for a while then Grace said, "What d'you mean dubious?"

It was Dermot's turn to snort. "What do I mean dubious? . . . an ex-hooker and a psychopath . . . are you kidding me?"

"Dermot, you can get right up my nose at times, particularly right now. The operative word in this is ex-hooker."

"And is Mungo an ex-psycho too," he said, but he was grinning and she realised he was winding her up.

"I'll have you know Mungo is as gentle as an eighteen-stone lamb," she said and burst out laughing.

"Well, as eighteen-stone lambs go I suppose he is," he conceded. "But d'you think the agency will work? D'you think you can make a go of it?"

Grace shrugged. "I don't see why not. Mungo was in Intelligence in the American army."

"Now there's a contradiction in terms."

"Shut up, Dermot. Phoebe has had to duck and dive most of her life and she has a good few contacts."

"What? You mean the wives of her clients paying to have them followed?" cracked Dermot. Grace gave him a sharp dig in the ribs with her elbow and he grunted and threw up his hands in submission.

"No, smart arse! I mean influential business contacts who might just possibly be ex-clients as well."

"OK . . . OK . . ." he said, grabbing the steering wheel again to avoid hitting a parked car. "I hope it works out for you, I really do, but I think you're in for a few headaches with those two."

"I'd have been in for a lot more without them," she said under her breath.

4

Chapter One

"You can't be serious!"

Phoebe Lamplighter shrugged her elegant shoulders.

"Why not . . . What's wrong with her?"

Exasperated, Grace said, "Where d'you want me to start?" And flung her hands in the air.

"Oh don't be such a boring old fart! She's perfect." Grace was about to launch into the reasons why not, so Phoebe cut her off at the pass. "Listen, Grace, just talk to her, you can't judge by just seeing her . . . don't be prejudiced." She knew this would get to Grace's guilt factor. It did.

After a pause Grace said, "Oh all right."

The casual observer wouldn't have wondered at Grace's reaction on seeing Alice in reception, anything less like a delicate Alice was hard to imagine. She stood a little under five feet tall, looked about seventeen (though Grace later discovered that she was in fact twenty) and her ten-and-a-half stone frame was encased in a pair of pink embroidered Chinese mandarin pajamas a little the worse for wear. Her face was matt white and elaborately made-up with exaggerated slashes of vivid pink blusher and deep burgundy, black-outlined lips fashioned into the shape of a geisha rosebud. The pancake finished in a tide-mark below the chin and the skin below it was almost transparent with blue veins visible beneath the surface. Her eyes were a veritable work of art and Grace wondered how long it would take her to get ready for work in the morning. The whole ensemble was topped with jet-black hair braided into a million tiny plaits tied off with pink wool. Her temples were shaved and the girl's elaborate eye make-up stretched back behind her multi-pierced ears. Mungo leaned against the windowsill, arms folded, making no comment, face impassive as usual.

Phoebe went to the door and called Alice in. "This is my partner Grace de Rossa, Alice."

Alice strolled over and shot out a chubby hand to Grace.

"Charmed," she said and gave Grace a dazzling smile. Her handshake was firm if a little clammy. "Me real name's Alice bu' I prefer Xin. It's me

Ninja name," she added. Then before Grace could get a word in edgeways she said, "I expect you think I'm not suitable, righ'?" Grace swallowed and Alice pressed on, "Bu' I'd be great. I can type an' use yer computer, which incidently has crap sof'ware, I could get better stuff from me brudder for yeh for nothin'. Righ'?" She addressed this last remark over her shoulder to Phoebe. "Me ma loves Philip Marlowe an' I want to learn to be a real detective like you. An', as I said, I'm a qualified Ninja," she added almost as an afterthought.

"What!"

"A qualified Ninja. I'm an exponent of the Martial Arts." She paused and smiled the dazzler up at Grace again. Phoebe knew Grace was almost lost. Alice's enthusiasm was overwhelming.

"I'll do anythin', work as long as you want . . . and FAS'll pay half me wages on a scheme." Phoebe knew for definite that this last point would be the clincher. "I'll start in the mornin'?"

Grace could only bring herself to nod.

Phoebe said, "Right. We'll see you in the morning, nine-thirty sharp Alice . . . em sorry . . . Xin," and ushered her out before Grace could come to her senses. Mungo smirked, still leaning against the window-ledge.

"A qualified Ninja?" Grace said to nobody in particular. "Xin! . . . Is she for real?"

7

It was a bright late August morning and the office smelled of fresh paint. Phoebe had somehow managed to acquire the three-storey-over-basement building on Baggot Street for a peppercorn rent from an ex-client. Grace didn't inquire too deeply into the circumstances leading up to the arrangement other than to make Phoebe swear that she had retired completely from Executive Recreational Services and that nothing as shoddy as blackmail was involved.

The building was in good condition structurally but had been in dire need of decoration. The offices, comprising reception, one large office and a smaller one at the back of the building, were to be accommodated on the ground floor. Phoebe and her twelve-year-old son Ronan were to live on the first floor (when he was home from his boarding-school). Grace insisted on the top floor because there was a flat roof at the back where she could sit out in fine weather, and Mungo took the basement.

They had the whole interior painted a crisp white and the front door a cheerful red but as yet only Phoebe and Mungo had moved into their respective apartments.

Grace was still in the process of moving out of the house she and her husband Andrew had shared before he flew the coop with Kiera, her ex-best-friend, who was now seven months pregnant with Andrew's child. Grace had felt more humiliated and betrayed by Kiera than by anything else. She knew that she and Andrew had grown apart long before his departure. The upshot was that Andrew and Kiera bought out her interest in the house, giving Grace the capital she needed to go into partnership with the ex-hooker and the hardman in Sleuths Investigation and Security Specialists.

Phoebe came back into the office. "She'll be fine, you'll see. By the way I asked her to wear something a little less eh, outstanding for work tomorrow."

"How did she react to that?" Mungo asked, still smirking.

"No problem. I told her she'd need to blend into the background if she was doing any surveillance work."

"Oh well! Different clothes really ought to do the trick!" Grace cut in sarcastically. "I just hope she doesn't frighten away the clients."

"What clients?" observed Mungo drily and the two woman gave him a withering look.

The Telecom man came to connect the phones at that point so Grace said, "I'm going home to finish packing, I'll see you later."

As she opened the front door a well-dressed

woman in her mid-forties stood on the footpath looking at a scrap of paper and up at the building in turn. When she saw Grace she hesitated for a moment, then smiled and turned up the step. "I'd know you from Hope," she said. "You must be Grace. You look so alike. My name is Tessa Peace, your sister Hope suggested I contact you about my little problem."

My God a real client, Grace thought, but said aloud, "I'm pleased to meet you, Tessa. Would you like to come in to the office and we can discuss your problem in private." As they walked through the hall she added, "You'll have to excuse the mess, we're not quite ready for business yet, and we're still waiting for the signwriter."

Tessa Peace was slim and very well-dressed, as Grace expected any friend of her sister Hope would be. Hope was the eldest of the four girls. Charity came next, at thirty-six she was two years older than Grace. Faith, the youngest girl, was two years younger. Hope lived in Killiney with her Paediatric Consultant husband and the two point four kids. She and Grace had little in common.

Grace asked the Telecom engineer to work in the small office and introduced Phoebe and Mungo to Tessa. She looked a little alarmed when Mungo put out his huge paw to shake her hand.

10

Grace felt relieved that Xin, aka Alice, wasn't starting until the following day. Tessa settled herself on the edge of the black leather sofa looking slightly uncomfortable.

"How can we help you, Tessa?" Grace prompted.

"It's rather embarrassing," she began and then rushed on, "I think my husband is seeing someone and I need . . . want you to follow him. I need to know if he's being unfaithful."

"What makes you think he's having an affair?"

"A woman always knows these things," Tessa answered with a strained smile.

Grace thought, *How? I didn't have a clue.* "I understand that," she lied. "But is there any evidence?"

Phoebe butted in, "You know, credit card bills for hotels you've never been to, flowers, restaurant bills, lingerie bills, that kind of thing?"

Tessa looked down at her lap for a short while gathering her thoughts.

"Nothing like that. He's been . . ." she searched for a word and only managed to come up with "Strange."

"Strange?"

"Well yes. Strange. Odd phone calls, going out late at night. That kind of thing. He's very . . . " she searched again for the right word. "Tense . . .

yes, tense. He's very tense. He's hiding something from me."

"Has he done this kind of thing before?"

Tessa shook her head. "No he's never been like this before. I thought we had the perfect marriage."

Grace patted her arm. "Well, you may well have . . . there could be an entirely different reason."

"That's what I want you to find out," Tessa said. She opened her bag, picked out a cheque and held it out to Grace. "I was speaking with my solicitor and he advised me that this should cover your expenses and fee for two weeks. Let me know what you find out on a daily basis."

Grace was about to protest when Phoebe snatched the cheque from her hand. "No problem, Tessa. If you'll just give Grace some details and a photograph of your husband we can start this afternoon."

Later after Tessa had gone Phoebe sat on the corner of Grace's desk. "*Never* ever refuse money up front, Grace. First rule of business. Now how do we go about this surveillance thing?"

Mungo took Phoebe on the first shift to show her the ropes and Grace set off belatedly to finish her packing. When she arrived Andrew was in the hall going through some of the boxes she had already packed.

"I'm sorry," he said when he saw her. "I didn't think you'd be here."

"Obviously!" she answered frostily. "What's the matter? Are you afraid that I'm taking your stuff?" She snatched the book that he had just removed from the box.

"Don't be like that, Grace, but as a matter of fact that book is mine." Grace looked at the title.

"No it isn't! The John Irvings were all mine."

Andrew shrugged and raised the palms of his hands.

"Fine, fine. I don't want to argue with you, it's yours, you can have it. Now can we at least try to be civilised about this? Please."

As usual the exchange left Grace feeling foolish and petty, but she couldn't help herself, Andrew had that effect on her these days. They stood in silence until he broke the ice. "Can I help you move some of this stuff, I've got the Range Rover outside."

Grace had noticed it on the way in. "When did you get that?" she asked and bit back the urge to add an acid comment.

"Kiera thought it would be handy to have something bigger for carting the baby stuff around," he said. "Mother sends her love by the way. She said you don't phone her much these days."

13

Grace never phoned Kathleen, in fact she spent her days getting just about anyone else to field her calls for her, but the mother-in-law from hell was nothing if not persistent and had spent the last year trying to restore the status quo. Grace fervently hoped that the birth of a first grandchild would make her see sense, accept the inevitable, and leave her alone.

"How is Kathleen?" she said for something to say.

"Fine. She misses you though."

She could have done without the guilt trip. Most of the kitchen stuff was packed ready for moving. She opened and closed cupboards aimlessly, wishing he would leave, his presence made her uncomfortable.

"Do you need the food processor? Kiera thinks it would be useful for the baby's feeds . . ."

He caught sight of Grace's expression and said, "Well, perhaps not."

She ripped the appliance from the carton and thrust it at him.

"Take the bloody thing. I don't need it. Now do you think you could give me some peace and privacy so I can finish packing up my few belongings? I promise I won't steal anything of yours or anything that your precious Kiera thinks *the baby might need*."

14

Dignified as ever, Andrew picked up the food-processor and stalked out through the hall. He stopped at the front door and said very calmly, "You know, Grace, I don't know how I stayed with you as long as I did. You're totally unreasonable, bordering on unbalanced and it's about time you grew up a little and stopped behaving like such a spoiled brat." He closed the door quietly behind him and a minute later she heard the Range Rover start up and drive away.

Mungo called her on the mobile at about seven and she drove over to the Peace homestead to take over. She parked and slid into the back seat of Mungo's car.

"What's been happening?" she asked.

Mungo handed her a clip-board.

"Nothing much, as you can see. Drove here from the housing development in Kimmage and he's been inside the house ever since."

"This isn't so boring," Phoebe said.

"It's early days yet," said Grace. "I'll take over and stay here until they turn in for the night. I'll call in if I need you."

All the lights went out at about eleven-thirty so Grace gave it an hour and went home. Phoebe, by some miracle, got up and out by six-thirty to do first shift. Grace supposed it was just the novelty value of the operation.

At nine-thirty sharp Xin arrived in the office. True to Phoebe's instructions, she wore a set of plain black cotton Mao pajamas but didn't look any less startling. On closer inspection it was obvious that the make-up had been retouched from the day before.

"I'll load the new sof'ware on t' the computer first," she said. "If I'm goin' t' be usin' it, it's best I have a package I understand." Grace couldn't argue with that. "I did me City an' Guilds y'know," she said over her shoulder as she deftly loaded the floppy discs into the computer. "Office management, word processin', triple entry book keepin' an' communication skills."

"Really," said Grace, a little stunned.

Xin opened the bright fluorescent plastic attache case that was sitting on top of her desk and neatly laid out a Bart Simpson calculator, a box of felt tip pens, a Far Side calendar and a dictionary. Then she opened the desk drawer.

"Where's the stationery?"

Grace pointed towards a carton standing behind the door.

Xin nodded. "I can see y'll need some organisin' here," she said and started to move stuff around and put things away. "A place fer everythin' an' everythin' in its place," she said to herself.

Grace grinned and retreated to her office. She was beginning to think that Phoebe had been right about Xin after all. Appearances were, in this case, definitely deceptive.

That afternoon Xin begged Grace to take her on surveillance, arguing that she'd done all that was to be done in the office, and if she knew what surveillance involved she'd be, as she put it, multi-skilled and could help out in cases of emergency. Grace took her, glad of the company, and after a couple of uneventful hours Xin suddenly said, "Why did y'call it Sloats." It took Grace a couple of minutes to realise what she was talking about.

"It's called Sleuths."

"Yeah. So why'd y'call it after a slow moovin' furry animal. I'd a thought that was a negative image." Grace was at a loss until she suddenly she realised what Xin meant.

"No, no. It's Sleuths not Sloaths. A sleuth is an archaic term for a detective."

"Oh," Xin said gravely nodding her head, "Sloots."

At the end of two weeks Warren Peace had shown no signs of adulterous behaviour. When Tessa arrived at the office Grace handed her a report beautifully typed up by Xin, along with photos of him leaving the house, leaving building sites and so forth. Phoebe was all for persuading her to do another week but Grace disagreed, saying that really it would border on unethical when it wasn't necessary and they needed to build up a reputation at this stage of the game. How sorry she would be.

Chapter Two

Dermot McEvoy hated mortuaries. He hated the sickly antiseptic smell that clung in his nostrils and to his clothes. He hated the glaring white light that reflected off the floor-to-ceiling tiles.

Dermot was a career policeman, but his bulky frame made him seem shorter than the regulation height. He was, in fact, five feet ten inches tall and balding, with black eyes and a prominent nose which gave him a slightly Jewish look. He'd taken the job in his stride for twenty-five years, coping with villains, robbers, drug dealers and pimps. The one duty he could never come to terms with was attending post-mortems and he avoided doing so whenever possible. He had no trouble with corpses, as such, however beaten up, as long as they were entire. The weakness in his stomach erupted only when visceral material was in evidence. Today he had to attend. No one else was available.

He had been called to the scene of a suspected suicide earlier that morning. The postman had noticed the Daimler parked with the engine running and a hose attached to the exhaust. A middle-aged man was slumped behind the wheel, the car was filled with noxious fumes. Now Dermot stood outside the morgue killing time, waiting for the grisly bits of the autopsy to be over before finding out Leo Yentob's opinion as to the cause of death.

He checked the time on his watch then stubbed out his half-smoked cigarette and pushed open the heavy swing door. His footsteps echoed down the corridor and he shivered slightly despite the stifling heat of the building. Yentob was just finishing up as he entered the room and he looked surprised to see Dermot. The two men had known each other for some years, their wives had been childhood friends, their children had attended the same schools and he was well aware of Dermot's weak stomach.

"What have we got, Leo?"

"Well, I thought it was a suicide at first."

"At first?"

Yentob picked up a kidney tray from a trolley. "I examined the body tissue and, as you know, carbon monoxide should leave the organs with a bluish tinge." He lifted the sheet covering the body.

"As you can see that isn't the case, the tissue looks normal suggesting that none of the gas entered the lungs." Dermot looked away. He would take Yentob's word for it. He was sure he saw the ghost of a smile on Leo's lips.

"Then I found these."

He handed Dermot the kidney tray. Two thin masonry nails lay in the bottom. "Where did you find them?" Yentob lifted the left shoulder of the corpse and pointed to two small puncture marks below the shoulder blade.

"He was shot dead with a nail gun. The nails entered here," he pointed at the marks, "and lodged, one in the heart, killing him instantly, hence the lack of bleeding. I found the other in the rib cage."

"Shouldn't the force have made them pass right through the body?"

"I'll bet the technical team will find where these went through the back of the driver's seat. Much of the force would have been absorbed that way. The nail in the heart definitely killed him." Dermot put the tray down.

"What time would you estimate he died?"

Leo Yentob scratched his grey beard. "Hard to say exactly. The heater was on in the car which kept the body temperature up, but I'd guess at between two and five this morning."

"Where's his stuff?"

"Over there." He pointed to a pile of transparent plastic evidence bags. "Forensic are coming for it shortly."

"I'd better get over to the next of kin and organise formal identification," said Dermot. He walked out of the front door and met Luke Ryan on the way in.

Luke had been in the Garda Siochana ten years, and had joined Harcourt Terrace shortly after Dermot had been made Acting Inspector. He had a pleasant easy-going manner and got on with most of his colleagues. His height made him easily recognisable in a crowd and, though he was by no means drop-dead handsome, his quirky smile and floppy blond hair left him with no shortage of women friends.

"I thought you were in court," Dermot said.

Ryan was out of breath. "The Justice threw it out."

"Why?" Dermot asked, surprised. "I thought you said it was open and shut?"

"The defendant's solicitor introduced pages and pages of medical evidence." They were standing by the car now. "Apparently she suffers from intermittent bouts of amnesia, so she claims she forgot to pay for the leather jacket, four bottles of perfume and six pairs of tights that the store detective found in her bag!" Luke's tone was more than somewhat sarcastic.

"I don't suppose she mentioned it either when you questioned her?" Dermot smirked, knowing what Luke's answer would be.

"She must have forgotten," Luke said with a grin.

"What have we got here?" Dermot told him. "Why would someone shoot him, then try to make it look like suicide?"

"Maybe it was an accident and they panicked."

"Hmmm . . . Who was he?"

Dermot got out his notebook. "Warren Peace. He has an address in Killiney. I was on my way to interview the widow."

By the time Dermot and Luke Ryan arrived at the home of the late Warren Peace, his widow had already been informed of her new status, but was not yet aware that her husband had been murdered. The entrance was concealed by high shrubs but it was easy to guess where the house was because of the gaggle of journalists gathered round the gate.

They pushed forward when they saw the car approach but Dermot just flashed his warrant card at the Garda on duty and drove through the gate.

The house was an imposing Georgian mansion called The Oaks. The drive swept in a semi-circle past manicured terraces overlooking Dublin bay and there was a half-erected marquee on the front lawn. The two main poles and top canvas were in place, but the side awnings were missing and only half of the wooden floor was laid.

"Looks like they were planning a party." Luke Ryan had a knack of stating the obvious.

"Can I help you?" asked the buxom woman who answered the door. Dermot identified himself and asked for Tessa Peace. "Mrs Peace is in the morning-room. Please could you wait here," she said. They waited.

After a few minutes she returned and led them into an airy room at the rear of the hall. Tessa Peace sat by a window which looked on to the garden. She rose from her seat when they entered. Her face was pallid from shock and her cheeks tear-stained. Dermot showed her his warrant card and introduced Luke.

"My sympathies," he said extending his hand.

She took it limply then dropped it.

"Why, Inspector . . . Why would he do that?" she asked, shaking her head. There was a catch in her voice.

"I'm afraid I have some more bad news, Mrs Peace." She was staring at him now. "We have reason to believe that your husband was murdered." Dermot had learned through the years that there was no easy way to break this kind of news. She opened her mouth to speak but no sound came out. She sat down heavily.

Dermot gave her time to regain her

composure. "I know this is difficult, Mrs Peace, but if we're to find the person responsible we need some information."

She rose from the armchair, walked over to a side table and poured a very large brandy which she swigged in one swallow. Dermot watched her shoulders rise and fall as she took several deep breaths. She turned to face them. Some of the colour had returned to her cheeks.

"Very well, Inspector. I feel a bit better now." She sat again. "What do you want to know?"

"Firstly, when was the last time you saw your husband?"

"Just before ten last night. He had a phonecall and said he had to go out."

"Do you know from whom or where he went?"

She shook her head. "No, but he seemed upset."

"Weren't you worried when he didn't come back?"

"I went to bed and took a sleeping tablet."

"Were you planning some sort of party?" asked Dermot.

"Party?" She looked confused, then she remembered. "It's our . . . would have been our Silver Wedding tomorrow. And our son Eoin's eighteenth birthday. We were going to have a joint celebration." She started to cry again.

"I'm sorry to have to ask you this, Mrs Peace,

but can you think of anyone who could have been responsible for your husband's murder?"

"No, Inspector. Warren was . . . he was a wonderful man." She jumped up from her seat again.

"Eoin must be told."

At that point the door to the morning room burst open and a tall man in a city suit barged in. "Tessa. Darling."

She threw herself into his outstretched arms.

"Bob, they say Warren was murdered."

The man looked startled. "What! but who? Why?"

Dermot looked at the man and said, "And you are?"

"I'm sorry," said the Widow Peace. "This is my brother Bob Berry." She had her handkerchief out again and was dabbing at her nose. He looked about fifty and was heavily-built.

"I wonder, Mr Berry, under the circumstances, if you could come to the mortuary and formally identify the body?" Dermot made a gesture at Tessa Peace.

Berry nodded. "Oh. Fine Inspector. Now?"

"As soon as you can."

"My wife is on her way over to stay with Tessa. I'll come now."

As they turned to leave, Dermot said, "We can talk later, Mrs Peace. Try to remember anything which could be of help. Goodbye for the present."

Dermot and Bob Berry went to the morgue. They dropped Luke Ryan at Harcourt Terrace on the way. The posse of newsmen pushed forward again hoping for a quote, but Dermot still didn't oblige. He asked Berry about his brother-in-law. "How long have you known Warren Peace?"

Berry gave a shrug.

"Years. He and my sister were married twenty-five years ago. Since then, I suppose."

"It seems he was very well off. What did he do?"

"Warren had a very successful building firm, Clough Peace. You may have heard of it."

Dermot had seen Clough Peace hoardings on a number of building sites round the city.

"Successful men can make enemies on the way up, Mr Berry. Do any spring to mind?"

Berry pursed his lips and shook his head.

Dermot went on, "Would you know if he had any money problems?"

"No. Not that I know of." He shook his head again. "You should speak to his partner Curtis Clough about that, but I have no reason to think so. I can't believe that someone would want to kill him."

They had reached the mortuary. Berry seemed reluctant to get out of the car. Dermot sat for a moment, then said, "Shall we go in?" Berry hesitated, then opened the car door.

The body of the late Warren Peace looked like

a wax-work dummy. Leo Yentob had made a good job of tidying him up after the autopsy. Berry gave the body a cursory glance, then nodded his head, and turned to leave. His face was pale and strained.

He was silent for most of the journey back, but just before they reached The Oaks he said, "He looked as if he was sleeping. It's hard to believe that he met a violent end."

Several cars were parked in the driveway outside the front door. "Where can I contact you if I need to speak to you again, Mr Berry?"

"Well, unfortunately I have to go to Japan in the morning." He saw Dermot's eyebrows shoot up.

"I know, I know, it couldn't have come at a worse time but the truth is I can't afford to miss the opportunity, CTT and I have been trying to set up this deal for two years."

"What deal would that be, Mr Berry?" Dermot asked, aghast that Berry would swan off and leave his sister at such a time.

"I re-export imported cut crystal from Romania, I've been working on this . . ."

"For two years. Yes, you said. I'd like to speak to Mrs Peace again if she's feeling up to it," he said as they entered by the front door.

"Of course," agreed Berry as he ushered him into the drawing-room. "I'll get her."

Dermot walked over to the window and looked across the lawn. The marquee still stood forlornly flapping in the breeze. It had started to rain and small puddles were forming in the unstretched canvas.

He remembered another rainy day twelve years before when he had buried Matty, his wife. He wondered if Tessa Peace was feeling as desolate as he had felt that day or if she had reason to suffer the same depth of guilt that he had suffered. The guilt of having taken her for granted for so many years. Of not knowing how ill she had been, of the neglect. The neglect of never being around for the kids' birthdays, never remembering anniversaries, never telling her how much he cared about her.

Not that she had suffered in silence, she had nagged for years about the job coming before the family, etc. He couldn't remember when the nagging had stopped. The brain plays tricks and events don't always inhabit the memory in chronological order but he felt sure it must have been when she discovered that her illness was terminal. She hadn't confided in him so he carried on in blissful ignorance, fuelling future guilt. His shirts were always ironed and his meals in the microwave but she withdrew. It was only after she was killed by the hit-and-run driver, after the post-mortem, that Leo had told him about the cancer.

Susy was fourteen when her mother was killed and they had been very close. Susy was a mirror-image of Matty, they had the same blonde hair, the same tilt to the chin. After the funeral she attacked him, letting go of all her feelings and grudges. He could hear Matty's voice speaking the words. She accused him of being unfeeling.

"Didn't you notice that she was dying before your eyes? Everyone else could see it," she raged. "Everyone who loved her, that is."

He couldn't argue, every accusation she spat at him was justified. Then she collected her belongings and moved out to live with her Aunt Annie, Matty's youngest sister, and hadn't spoken to him or been home since. Her two sisters Jane and Maura, who were ten and eight at the time, stayed with him.

He heard the door open behind him. Tessa Peace came in. She had changed her clothes and was now dressed completely in black. She was calm and composed.

"My brother said you wanted to speak to me again, Inspector." They both sat on a chintz covered settee looking out through french windows which were closed against the drizzle.

After a moment he said quietly, "Are you sure

you haven't any idea who your husband went to meet last night?"

"No, Inspector. I told you. He didn't say."

"And you didn't ask?"

She looked uncomfortable. "No I didn't."

"Did your husband have any business problems?"

"My husband and I never discussed business. You'll have to speak to Curtis about that."

"That would be Curtis Clough?"

She looked past him through the window. "Yes, that's right. In fact that's him pulling up now." Dermot turned and saw a small balding man getting out of a Range Rover. A large Alsatian bounded up to him and started to bark and snarl. Curtis Clough hurried towards the front door but the dog darted between him and the safety of the entrance. The dog was now crouched, snarling at Clough on the step.

"Oh dear!" sighed Tessa. "I'd better rescue Curtis, the dog can sense that he's terrified." She hurried from the room and he saw her emerge behind the dog.

"Tolstoy! Sit." Tolstoy sat and Clough gingerly sidled round him and made a run for the house.

Shortly afterwards he bustled into the room accompanied by Tessa. "Tessa, Tessa. What can I say?" He stood with his feet planted apart and the palms of his hands outstretched. "Who could have done this awful thing?" He looked at Dermot.

Tessa Peace said, "This is Inspector McEvoy. He needs to ask you some questions about the business."

Clough looked surprised. "If I can be of any help. Of course."

Curtis Clough was short and stout. He reminded Dermot of Toad of Toad Hall. Mr Toad sat on a straight-backed chair facing Dermot.

Tessa Peace was still by the door. "I'll leave you, Inspector. I'll be with Bob and my sister-in-law in the kitchen if you need me again." She left the room and quietly closed the door.

"How long had you and Warren Peace been doing business together, Mr Clough?" asked Dermot.

"For about ten years. We knew each other for two years before that though."

"So how come you decided to go into business together?"

"Warren was a property speculator, and I'm a builder. I used to do up old properties for him. It just seemed like a natural progression. We each had know-how to offer the other. It's been a profitable alliance."

Dermot looked around the opulent room. "So it seems." Clough sighed.

"Warren could smell a good deal at twenty

paces, Inspector. In 1986 we branched out into building shopping malls and housing estates. Warren had parcels of land on the outskirts of the city and when out-of-town shopping became the thing, we were lucky that most of the land was rezoned and we got planning permission, no problem."

"And he had no money worries that you know about, or enemies?"

Mr Toad got up and wandered over to the french windows and Dermot noticed that he was wearing a yellow check waistcoat under his sports jacket. His gaze travelled down to his little feet and he was surprised. Curtis Clough wasn't wearing spats.

"Money wasn't a problem, the company is very healthy," he said after a pause. "About enemies. Who can say? But I doubt it." He let the sentence trail off.

"His wife said that he had a late night phonecall. Do you know anything about that?"

Curtis Clough shook his head. "A phonecall? No. I've no idea."

"And he never mentioned anything about receiving threats or anything of that nature?"

"Threats!" He looked shocked. "I'm sorry, Inspector, I'm afraid I can't help you. Is that all? Do you mind if I go and see if there's anything I can do for Tessa?"

"Where can I contact you if I need to speak to you again, Mr Clough?"

Clough gave Dermot his card and scuttled out of the room to look for the widow. Dermot had to stifle an overwhelming urge to say, "Don't leave town."

Chapter Three

"God! if only we'd talked her into another week, he'd probably still be alive."

"Perhaps," said Phoebe. "Perhaps not. We should go and sympathise or something, shouldn't we?"

"I suppose so," Grace said

"Isn't tha' yer man we were watchin'?" Xin shrieked as she caught sight of the image on the front page of the lunch-time edition of the *Evening Herald*. The coffee slopped on the tray as she slapped it down on the desk.

"Yes, that's Warren Peace all right," said Grace.

"Jaysus!"

"I wish she wasn't so loud," Phoebe observed when she had left the room.

Grace phoned Harcourt Terrace looking for Dermot but he was out so Luke Ryan took the call.

She hadn't taken to Luke Ryan. He'd joined Harcourt Terrace two months before she had resigned and she thought he was too full of himself. She also got the impression that he agreed with the general consensus and wasn't particularly sorry to see her go.

"He's out," he said coldly.

"Well, could you ask him to call me at the office please," Grace asked.

"OK," he said shortly.

Grace and Phoebe drove out to Killiney to see Tessa Peace. The housekeeper showed them into the morning-room and they found Tessa sitting on the sofa writing a letter. She put it aside when they walked in.

"If only I had kept you on another week he would still be alive," she said. Grace looked at Phoebe, but neither said anything in reply. "The Gardaí were here this morning. I thought he'd committed suicide," she trailed off. Grace started to speak but the widow didn't seem to hear. "In a way I'm glad he was murdered." She noticed the look on Grace's face. "Oh, I don't mean I'm glad he's dead, I mean I'm glad he didn't kill himself. I couldn't bear it if he had left me like that. If he felt so bad about something and couldn't confide in me, ask me for my help, you know . . ."

Grace nodded. She didn't know what to say.

"Well, at least you know he wasn't unfaithful," Phoebe said lamely.

"Do I?" Tessa snapped. "How do I know? All I know for sure is that he wasn't unfaithful for the last two weeks."

"If a man is being unfaithful he doesn't take a couple of weeks off, Tessa," Phoebe said. "Trust me on this, I know what I'm talking about."

"Perhaps," said Tessa. "Perhaps."

Grace was beginning to feel uncomfortable. She cleared her throat. "We just came to offer our condolences, Tessa, if there's anything we can do?"

Tessa said, "Yes. You can do something for me. You can find the person who murdered my husband."

"Well the Gardaí are doing that, you don't need . . ."

"Don't tell me what I need!" Tessa burst out. "Everyone is telling me what I need. Right now what I need is to feel that I am doing something. I want you to find who did it, I *need* you to find who did it!"

"But what about the Gardaí . . ." Grace started to say.

Phoebe took her arm. "Could I have a word, Grace?" she said, steering her into the far corner of the room.

"Look," she hissed. "This woman is throwing work our way. We're supposed to be running a business here."

"I know," Grace whispered. "But it's not our job."

"Of course it's our job. If Tessa Peace wants to spend the money, who are we to stop her?" Grace said nothing, Phoebe squeezed her arm again.

"Look, if we take it on, she'll feel better, look on it as therapy for the grieving widow. Anyway I don't know if you've noticed but at the moment she's the only client we have."

She turned to Tessa. "Don't listen to Grace, Tessa, of course we'll take the case on. We'll find your husband's killer."

Tessa smiled for the first time. "Thank you," she said and heaved a sigh of relief. "I'm very grateful to you."

"Thanks a bunch," Grace hissed under her breath to Phoebe. She smiled at Tessa and said, "I'll need to ask you some questions."

Later back in the office Grace called Pattie Doyle. "I was wondering if you had anything on the Warren Peace murder." Pattie was a forensic scientist who worked for the Garda Technical team.

"Jesus, Grace. Give me a break!"

"Come on, Pattie, I'm working for the widow, I

just need to know what you found. You know I won't drop you in it."

There was a silence at the other end of the line, then Pattie said, "Look, I can't talk now. Meet me in The Beggars Bush at five this evening and I'll see what I can do."

"Thanks, Pattie. I owe you one."

"Maybe not," Pattie said. "Don't count your chickens, I'm not working on that case, but I'll do my best."

As soon as Grace put down the receiver Dermot called.

"So your new rottweiler passed on the message," she said when she heard his voice.

"Now, now, Grace. What can I do for you?"

"Why do you assume I want something? I was just wondering if you'd like to go for a pint, that's all," she said trying to sound innocent.

"OK," he said. "I'm just going off duty, I'll meet you in The Bush in half an hour."

He got there ahead of her and had the drinks on the table before she sat down. "How's it going?" he asked.

"Fine, we're quite busy, in fact you might know one of our clients."

"Oh?"

"Tessa Peace." She waited for his reaction. His eyebrows shot up to his hairline. "And?"

"She asked us to put a tail on her late husband. She thought he was having an affair."

"And?" Dermot said again as he leant across the table.

"And what have you to trade?" she said, smiling.

Dermot frowned. "Come on, Grace, you know you can't withhold information. Was he?"

"Was he what?"

"Grace!"

Grace drummed her fingers on the table. The silence lengthened. Finally she leaned across the table and said, "Look, Dermot. The widow wants us to look into her husband's death, she wants to feel she's doing something. I didn't want to take it on but we had no choice. All I want is to trade information, you know I won't get in your way. We can help each other here."

"OK," Dermot said. "What have you got?"

"You'll trade?"

"Maybe," he shrugged. "OK. I'll trade."

She relaxed back in her seat. "He wasn't having an affair but he withdrew three grand out of his personal bank account two weeks ago, and again the day he was killed. Tessa doesn't know what it was for. She also said he had some odd phonecalls and was acting strangely. That's what made her suspect he was having an affair."

"I knew about the calls, but she didn't tell me about the money."

"She didn't know until I made her pull the statements. She had the bank fax them. What have you got?"

"No more than you," he said. "And I'd have found out about the money sooner or later, we put in for a warrant to see the bank statements."

"Come on Dermot! You found out sooner and you didn't know she suspected him of having an affair. Now, what have you got?"

He grinned at her. "OK. He was shot with a nail gun and the perp tried to make it look like suicide."

"A nail gun?"

"Yes."

"And that's all you have?"

"That's all I have."

"No motive, no suspect?"

He shook his head and grinned again. "No motive, no suspect."

She didn't believe him, but she saw Pattie walk in and sit at a table in the corner. When Pattie saw Dermot, she got up and walked quickly to the Ladies.

"I have to go to the loo," Grace said and stood up. He stood up also.

"And I have to go home. Mind yourself," he said and drained his glass and left the bar.

Grace hurried into the Ladies where Pattie was waiting.

"Jesus, Grace, what are you trying to do to me!"

"Sorry, you're early, what did you find out?"

Pattie handed her a piece of paper. "You know he was shot with a nail gun from behind while he was sitting in the driver's seat of his car?"

"Yes about the nail gun, but I didn't know he was shot from behind. What else?"

"Well, we lifted some blue acrylic fibres from the back of the victim's jacket and some clay from behind the driver's seat of the car."

"What kind of clay?"

Pattie shrugged. "Probably from an excavation, a building site perhaps. It would normally be found about three feet underground. Oh, and they took a cast of a motorbike tyre marks, and I believe some of the residents near the scene heard a bike engine running about the same time."

"Thanks, Pattie, I owe you."

"You certainly do," she said.

Grace went back to Baggot Street and found Phoebe and Mungo eating a Chinese takeaway in Phoebe's apartment.

"Where are we up to?" Mungo asked.

Grace sat down at the table and pinched one of Phoebe's spring rolls. "Well, Warren Peace was shot in the back with a nail gun while sitting in his car. The murderer or murderers then tried to make it look like a suicide by putting a length of hose on the exhaust, pretty futile really, but there you are. And he or they probably escaped the scene on a motor bike. Six grand missing from his bank account, in two lumps, the last the day he was killed. Oh, and there was clay, probably from a building site, behind the driver's seat."

"Motive?" grunted Mungo.

"Don't know. He was probably being blackmailed, but why would a blackmailer kill the goose that laid the golden egg?"

"Have we any idea why he was being blackmailed?" Phoebe asked.

Grace shook her head. "No."

"Suspects?" (Mungo again).

Phoebe sniggered, "A mad environmentalist probably! Have you seen the shopping complexes he puts up?"

"As far as Tessa knows there's no business trouble, but I'm seeing Curtis Clough tomorrow. He's the business partner."

"There must be skeletons in the cupboard," Phoebe ventured. "How well does your sister know them?"

Grace shrugged. "I don't know but I can call her tomorrow and see. Now, what have you been up to?"

"I got Xin to do a mail-shot for Security clients," she said, sounding pleased with herself. "And I made a few calls to spread the word."

Chapter Four

Dermot met Jack Mulloy on his way out of the office.

"What's happening in the incident room?" he asked.

"Not a lot. The house-to-house isn't finished yet."

"OK. I'm going to see Tessa Peace again, come with me. You can drive."

He settled into the passenger seat and when they were underway said, "The business partner says that they had no money worries. What d'you think? Jealous husband?"

"Do we know if he was playing away?"

"We've yet to find out," said Dermot. "His widow hired Grace de Rossa to put a tail on him. Apparently she suspected he might be, though she didn't mention that suspicion to me. Grace also found out about the two three-grand withdrawals from his personal bank account."

"How did she do that?"

"She just asked the widow to phone the bank and fax them," Dermot said. "I'd like to speak to Curtis Clough again to see if he knows if Warren Peace was faithful to Tessa."

"What's Clough like? D'you think he could have a motive?"

"I doubt it. I get the impression that Warren Peace was the energy behind the company from what Clough told me. Blackmail is always an option we should bear in mind, of course. The house is in here on the right."

Only a handful of reporters remained doggedly at their posts. They made a half-hearted lunge at the car, but when they saw that it was Dermot they slunk back and lounged against the wall, talking amongst themselves. The tent contractors were in removing the marquee when Mulloy and Dermot drove up to the front door. Curtis Clough's Range Rover was parked beside a silver BMW.

"Nice place," said Mulloy.

The housekeeper ushered Dermot in to see Tessa Peace and Mulloy stayed in the hall to talk to her. The widow was a lot calmer than she had been the previous day and rose from the window seat where she had been sitting when Dermot entered the room.

"Inspector. What can I do for you?"

"Hello, Mrs Peace. Do you feel up to a few more questions?"

She sat down again and he stood by the fireplace. "I don't know what else I can tell you."

Curtis Clough wasn't in evidence despite the presence of his vehicle. Dermot handed her the relevant part of the bank printout. "This is a printout of your husband's bank account. We have a theory that he may have been blackmailed. I wonder if you have any idea what these two large withdrawals could have been for?" He leaned over and pointed at the printed page.

She looked surprised that Dermot should have her late husband's bank statement. "How did you get this?" Her tone was annoyed. Dermot explained why they needed the statements and that they had obtained a warrant.

"You needn't have done that," she said as she took the sheaf of papers from his hand. "I would have given them to you if you'd asked me." She studied the print-out. After a little while she shook her head, and with a dismissive air of irritation said, "No, I've no idea."

"Would he normally have told you if he were to make a withdrawal of that size?"

"I expect he would mention it. It is his private account, not a business account, after all."

"Do you know if your husband had any other phonecalls like the one the night he died?"

Tessa Peace sat on the edge of the window-seat twisting a handkerchief in her hands. "Only one, about three weeks ago. But I've already told you all this."

"I know, but I was hoping that you may have had time to remember more. Did he seem unduly worried about anything? Anything at all?"

Tears slid down her cheeks. She dabbed at them with her crumpled hanky. Unable to speak she just shook her head. The door opened and Jack Mulloy came into the room. Dermot introduced him and he sat down. Just then his pager started to beep. "May I use your phone?" he asked. Tessa Peace nodded mutely and pointed out in the direction of the hall.

Dermot closed the door behind him and dialled Harcourt Terrace. He got through to Luke Ryan.

"We had a call from a pub landlord in Ringsend, Jack Dwyer from The Dockers Arms. Apparently he remembers seeing Warren Peace and another man in his pub. He recognised his photo from the morning papers."

"Go and see him, Luke. I'll meet you back at the office later."

"OK, was Tessa Peace any help?"

"No. Not so far."

As he was speaking Dermot sensed a presence. He looked round the hall but could see no one. Then a movement reflected in the oversized mirror on the wall opposite caught his eye. He was certain it was Curtis Clough who stood listening to his call. But the figure retreated out of sight.

While Dermot was out in the hall, Jack Mulloy was talking to the Widow Peace. She had regained her composure again so he went in with both feet.

"Is there any possibility that your late husband might have been involved with someone else?"

Tessa took a sharp intake of breath and her eyes filled up again. "What makes you say that?" she snapped. "Why would you think that? Do you know something I don't?"

Mulloy thought about dropping Grace in it by telling her why they thought that her husband might be having an affair, but then thought better of it. Dermot would skin him alive if he broke the confidence. He was getting the impression that Tessa could switch her tears on and off at will.

She rose gracefully from her seat as Dermot re-entered the room.

"I'm forgetting my manners, Inspector. Would you or your colleague care for some tea?"

"No thank you, Mrs Peace. We have to be going." Jack Mulloy stood and put his notebook away.

As they were going through the hall Tessa Peace said, "Inspector. When can we have my husband's body? I have to organise his funeral."

"The Coroner's inquest is this afternoon so we'll allow the body to be released directly after that."

"Thank you," she said. "Thank you." As they were going down the steps she shouted after him, "Inspector." He stopped and looked around. "What about the reporters? Can you make them go away?"

"They'll give up soon, don't worry about them. You don't have to talk to them if you don't want to."

As they drove back down the drive Dermot looked through the rearview mirror. He saw her standing at the door watching them leave, then she turned abruptly and went back in before they had reached the gates.

Tessa watched the police car disappear down the drive. Dermot McEvoy made her feel uneasy. She closed the front door and went back through the hall where she met Curtis. They walked together in silence back to the morning-room. Tessa's emotions had been on a roller-coaster since the previous morning when the police turned up at her door.

They were talking to her but she couldn't comprehend the words. Warren would never take his own life, there had to be a mistake. No, they had said, no mistake. Why? How could he leave her like that without a word? Tears rose to her eyes again. It had been like that all day, tears one minute, cold calm composure the next.

Paradoxically, she was almost relieved to learn later from McEvoy that Warren had been murdered. At least that meant that he hadn't betrayed her. But what now? What if the police started digging into the past?

Curtis must have been reading her thoughts. "What if they start checking up on a few things?"

"We'll have to cross that bridge when we come to it, Curtis." She sat by the fire and lit a cigarette, inhaling deeply.

"Have they asked you any worrying questions?" She looked down at the cigarette and wrinkled her nose, then she threw it in the fireplace.

He shrugged. "Such as what?"

"Your lack of imagination does you no credit, Curtis." She could feel the anger rising in her chest.

He thought for a moment. "No, not so far, but I think they're bound to."

"Don't be paranoid. They're not bound to at

all." She immediately regretted being so sharp with Clough. "I'm sorry Curtis, I didn't mean to snipe at you like that, it's just . . ."

He patted her on the shoulder, "I know. I know."

She noticed the clock on the mantel. "Oh God . . . can you pick up Eoin from the station? I have to get ready for the inquest." He just nodded gravely and left the room.

★ ★ ★

"Luke's gone to The Dockers Arms in Ringsend to question the landlord. He puts the victim with another man there."

"The blackmailer?" asked Jack Mulloy.

"Possibly. If it was blackmail. What do you think of the widow?"

Mulloy shrugged, "Bit hot and cold."

"I thought that. But then grief can affect people different ways. I wonder why Curtis Clough didn't want to see us?"

"Was he there?"

"That was his Range Rover parked in front of the house."

"Maybe he's got a guilty conscience about something," said Mulloy. "D'you think there's anything between him and Tessa Peace? That would be motive if they wanted the husband out of the way?"

"I think that notion's a bit previous. For all we know the Peaces were the perfect couple, but it wouldn't hurt to check it out. Did you get anything from the housekeeper?"

Jack Mulloy shook his head.

They drove on in silence and passed Grace at the bottom of Killiney Hill. She was driving in the opposite direction.

"Was that Grace?" Jack asked.

Dermot craned his neck to see out of the rear-view window.

"Yes. It's Grace all right. I wonder what she wants with the widow now?"

Grace was not en route to see Tessa Peace. She was on her way to see Hope, her elder sister and friend of the family Peace. There was no reply to her ring at the front door so she walked round the side of the house and found Hope swimming up and down the length of the outdoor pool. The early autumn day was quite cool and the clear blue water didn't look very inviting. She stood by Hope's towel and waited.

"Hello, Grace, what on earth brings you out here?" Hope asked, and heaved herself up on to the side.

Grace handed her a towel. "Hello, Hope. I suppose you heard about Warren Peace?"

"Dreadful business!" she said, dabbing herself dry.

Hope, though a couple of inches shorter than Grace, at first sight appeared to be quite tall due to her skinny frame. She was dark-haired and sallow skinned unlike Grace and her younger sister Faith. She and the fourth sister Charity took after their father, Paul de Rossa. Grace had little to do with her as they shared no common interests, friends or aspirations, and they met mainly at any family gatherings that Grace could not avoid.

"How well did you know him?"

Hope shrugged. "Him, hardly at all. I know Tessa through my charity work. We lunch sometimes. I think I first met her at the banquet for Somalia."

"A banquet? Isn't that a tad inappropriate"

"What do you mean inappropriate?" Hope was at a loss.

"Never mind." Grace shook her head. "I got the impression that you were bosom buddies." Hope didn't comment, so Grace went on. "How come she confided in you about the husband?"

"I don't think she meant to. I found her in tears in the loo at the Shelbourne after a Hospice fund-raiser," Hope explained. "She just blurted it out. So I sent her to you. I mean, how many investigators do I know?"

"So you wouldn't know if she had any

suspicions about the murder herself then?" Grace asked.

"I'm afraid not. I only told her about you so she'd stop whining, she was an embarrassment."

"Gee thanks, Hope . . . You're all heart."

★ ★ ★

Luke Ryan drove over to Ringsend to the Dockers Arms. The interior of the pub was in keeping with the general ambience of the neighbourhood, Victorian Seedy, and was empty except for a few lunchtime customers. A thin middle-aged man behind the bar looked up when Luke entered. "Mr Dwyer?"

"Who's asking?" Luke took out his warrant card which Dwyer examined. "Oh that's grand," he said. "Would you like a drink?" Luke declined.

"About your call, Mr Dwyer, are you sure the man you saw the other night was Warren Peace?"

Dwyer was nodding enthusiastically. "No doubt at all. I recognised him from the *Evening Herald*."

"And the man that he was with. Could you give me a description?" Dwyer scratched his head to assist his memory. "Tall, young, about twenty-one, two. Fair hair."

"Did you notice his clothes?"

"Donkey jacket and jeans. Looked like a joiner,

he had a tool box with him." Then he added as an afterthought, "He had an English accent."

"What kind of accent, Northern? London, what?"

Dwyer shrugged. "I dunno. Northern I think, maybe Liverpool or Manchester, it's hard to say."

Luke thought for a minute. "What time did they come in?"

"The fella in the paper came in first on his own. He sat over there." Dwyer pointed to a table in the corner. "About twenty past ten or a little after. The other guy came in just before closing. They were talking, you know, with their heads close." He pushed the palms of his hands together leaving a gap of three inches to illustrate the point. "I had to nearly let the dog out to get them to leave."

"They left together?"

Dwyer nodded.

"Had you seen either of them before?"

Dwyer made a face and shook his head. "Not that I noticed. Though the young one could've been in and I wouldn't have remarked, if you know what I mean."

Luke knew what he meant. Warren Peace would have stuck out like a sore thumb in his Louis Copeland suit and handmade shoes. The younger man would have just blended in with the scenery.

"Thank you Mr Dwyer. You've been a great help. Could you come over to Harcourt Terrace when you have time, before the end of the day, to do a photofit?"

Dwyer was nodding again. "I'll come when the barman comes in after the dinner."

Dermot went straight to the Coroner's Court after lunch for the inquest on Warren Peace. Both Tessa Peace and Curtis Clough were sitting at the back of the room. A young man Dermot took to be Eoin sat with them. He was lanky and had very blonde hair which reached his thin shoulders. They were talking quietly together. He was surprised at how full the courtroom was. He looked around to see who was there but he didn't recognise anyone except the press, so he just settled down and waited to be called to give his evidence.

Leo Yentob rushed in, out of breath, just before the Coroner arrived and flopped down on the bench beside Dermot.

"Didn't notice the time," he said by way of explanation.

The proceedings got under way. Both men in turn gave their evidence after a distraught Tessa Peace, who established the time her husband had left the house for the last time. Her evidence took some time as she kept on breaking down.

Eventually the Coroner returned the not unexpected verdict of unlawful killing by person or persons unknown. The Court adjourned and everyone filed out. Dermot saw Curtis Clough talking to a man he didn't know. He walked over, and their conversation ceased abruptly.

"Excuse me, Mr Clough. Could I have a word?"

Clough looked disgruntled. "If it's necessary," he said with bad grace. His companion walked away and Dermot led Clough to to an empty solicitor's room.

"I need some information about Warren Peace's personal life, Mr Clough. Did he and his wife have a good marriage?"

"Not that it's any of your business, Inspector, but they were very happy as it happens."

"We are trying to establish a motive for Warren Peace's murder, Mr Clough. We have to cover every possibility. Where did the Peaces live before they moved to this area?"

Clough's body language was defensive though he tried to appear calm. Dermot wondered why.

"Somewhere down South. Cork or Limerick I think, though I can't say I ever asked."

"And as far as you know he was faithful to his wife?" Dermot thought Clough was going to explode.

His face went bright red and he burst out, "I

really don't think there's any call for that kind of talk, Inspector, and the man not cold yet."

Dermot tried to calm him down. "Mr Clough, you have the advantage of having known the victim. We have to start from scratch to try and build up a picture of his life. It is the only way we have any chance of bringing his murderer to justice." This speech seemed to placate Clough a little.

"I'm sorry, forgive me." He shook his head. "It's the loss you know. He was my friend."

"I understand, Mr Clough. I also take it from your answer that he was faithful to Tessa."

Clough just nodded.

"Now . . . was Tessa Peace faithful to her husband?"

This question really struck a nerve.

"How dare you, you've no right. You've gone too far!"

"Calm down. I wasn't making any accusations." Let him take that whichever way he wanted. "I'm afraid I have to ask these questions."

Clough took out a handkerchief and mopped his brow.

"Tessa is, was a wonderful wife to Warren. They were devoted. Warren was a pillar of the community."

"Thank you, Mr Clough."

Clough looked surprised. "Is that all?" he

asked. Dermot was already on his feet. "Thank you. We'll be in touch." He left Clough standing looking pensive and drove back to Harcourt Terrace.

Chapter Five

Grace called to see the housekeeper, Mrs Danvers, who lived quite near The Oaks. She was a widow in her early sixties. She was quite heavily built and had a habit of folding her arms beneath her ample bosom. Grace was an ardent old movie fan and thought her name thoroughly inappropriate as this Mrs Danvers was warm and friendly.

"Sit down, love. Like a cup of tea?" Grace accepted and Mrs Danvers came back a few minutes later with tea and homemade fruit cake.

"How long have you worked for the Peaces?"

"Six years. After they moved into the house. I worked for the previous owners, Mr and Mrs Kelly. They recommended me." She poured the tea and handed Grace a cup. "Sugar?" Grace shook her head.

"What do you think of them?"

"He was all right, a gentleman in fact. She's a bit upstairs, downstairs, you know, treating me like a servant. If you ask me, it was far from servants she was reared. Do you know, she wanted to call me Danvers. Just Danvers. No way I was having that. My name is Missus Danvers, and that's an end to it, I told her. But apart from that she was OK."

Grace fought hard to hide a smile and grabbing the opening said, "Do you think that they were faithful to one another?"

"What kind of a question's that? How would I know?"

Grace let it pass. "You must have heard them talking from time to time. Do you know if Mr Peace had any money troubles?"

She pursed her lips, "If he did, it didn't show."

"How about Curtis Clough and his wife? Were they social friends with the Peaces?"

"I suppose so. He knew Mrs Peace from years back. I don't know if the two wives liked each other. Portia Clough grew up at The Oaks years ago and her father sold it to Mr Kelly in the seventies. Old Major Crockett, that's Portia's father, he was a Protestant you know, [she mouthed the last phrase] was a sort of squire figure in the area, you know, old money." She tapped the side of her nose with her finger and winked at Grace. "If you ask me there's a certain amount of jealousy there. I reckon Portia thinks

Tessa's a bit, you know, got notions." She nodded slowly and meaningfully to lend weight to the last statement, then went on to say, "But Mr Peace and Mr Clough were good enough friends."

"Did you see anyone hanging round the house in the last few weeks?"

"Not that I noticed. But there was a lot of coming and going this last week on account of the big party. Shame about that. Their twenty-fifth you know. And young Eoin's eighteenth."

"Lovely cake. How about phone calls, did you answer any strange phone calls?"

"What? You mean like heavy breathers?"

Grace's face broke into a smile. "No, no, I mean threatening calls. Or did you hear the Peaces discussing anything like that?"

"I don't listen in on other folks' private conversations," said Mrs Danvers indignantly.

"Do you think Curtis Clough and Tessa could have been more than just good friends?" Grace was afraid that she might be treading on thin ice. She was right.

"AB-SO-BLOODY-LOOOT-LEE NOT." Mrs Danvers was now in high dudgeon and two pink spots appeared high on her cheekbones. "She and Mr Peace were devoted." With no more information on offer Grace thanked her for the tea and made her way back to Baggot Street.

"I see there's still no sign of the signwriter," she

said to Xin as she walked into reception. "Is Phoebe in?" Xin, who was reading the paper, just pointed at the back office. Phoebe was sitting with her feet up on the desk reading *Vogue*. Grace flopped down in a chair beside her. "Well, the general consensus is that our Tessa and Warren were a model couple with no money problems, so it looks as if we're back to the skeletons. What d'you think?" Phoebe looked up. "Everybody has something they want to hide," she observed and went back to reading *Vogue*.

Chapter Six

Two days later Grace and Phoebe sat at the back of the old stone church. Mourners were trickling in in twos and threes. Most sat in the body of the church or down towards the back, and a harmonium played soulfully somewhere up near the front. Mungo was outside in the church yard discreetly taking photographs of everyone in attendance. Earlier that morning the Companies Registration Office at Dublin Castle had sent him the information that he had requested. Warren Peace and Curtis Clough were joint directors of Clough Peace. Warren and Tessa were directors of Peace Land Holdings which was the company Peace used to buy and sell parcels of land. Both companies appeared kosher, submitting annual tax and VAT returns, and were to all appearances very solvent.

Dermot come in and slid into the seat beside

them. Being a lapsed Catholic, Dermot rarely visited churches, the odd wedding maybe, but mostly it was in the line of duty. Sadly the Catholic service he was most familiar with was the burial ritual.

"How are you getting on?" he asked.

"Fine, no thanks to you," Grace hissed. "I haven't forgotten how you stitched me up the other night."

Dermot grinned. "I didn't stitch you up, I was just . . ."

"Economical with the truth?" she said raising her eyebrows and grinning back. She found it hard to be angry with him for long. She saw Mrs Danvers, who was sitting halfway down the body of the church, turn and look towards the door. She smiled and nodded at Grace. Grace smiled back.

Dermot noticed and said, "Been chatting with the servants?"

It was Grace's turn to be economical with the truth.

"Hmmm."

The little church had filled up by this time. All those in attendance were very affluent looking, if not particularly grief-stricken, and she noticed Hope and husband hadn't bothered to put in an appearance.

The parish priest came out of a door at the side of the altar and stood waiting at the top of the church beside the flower-covered coffin. At that moment Tessa and Eoin Peace made their entrance accompanied by Curtis Clough and a woman Grace took to be Portia Clough. She was an unremarkable-looking woman and, though expensively dressed, did not possess the style of the widow. She did have a definite air of poise and breeding about her though. They sat behind the family. Tessa Peace was heavily veiled and Eoin supported his mother's elbow as they made their way up the church.

After the priest delivered a homily, Eoin read the twenty-third psalm. He was very composed for a lad of his age, Grace thought. Then the choir sang, "All in the April evening."

Dermot, Phoebe and Grace slipped out of the church before the end of the service to watch the mourners file out. The priest led the coffin, the chief mourners followed and the rest of the congregation formed a procession behind them.

At the graveside only the Peaces and the Cloughs stood with the priest, the rest of the small assembly standing some way back in small groups. Grace noticed Mungo lurking behind a gravestone taking pictures of the mourners. Luke Ryan was also taking pictures of the mourners, and of Mungo taking pictures of the mourners.

It had started to drizzle, though Tessa Peace and her son didn't seem to notice. Grace watched them closely. What did she really feel? she pondered. Tiny droplets of rain clung to the veil over her face. Eoin, who stood a good head and shoulders over his mother, was a good-looking lad, tall though quite slightly built, with the fine bones of his mother.

The priest handed Tessa a few grains of earth which she tossed on top of the coffin. At that point she broke down and, with Eoin supporting her, she half staggered away from the graveside towards the lane and the waiting car. The Cloughs followed. Dermot pulled up the collar of his rain coat.

"I'm off," he said. "I hate funerals." And he walked across the grass to where Luke was standing.

Phoebe and Grace made their way back to the narrow lane where Mungo had parked. Tessa Peace and Eoin sat in the back of the funeral director's limo. Curtis Clough was leaning, talking to them through the open window.

Portia Clough picked her way through the puddles on the verge to the Range Rover which had parked directly in front of Grace's car.

"Did you notice anything strange about the service, Grace?" asked Phoebe when they were sitting back in the car waiting for Mungo.

"Not really. Why?"

"There didn't appear to be any relatives.

Neither Tessa nor Warren Peace appear to have one relative between them."

Grace said, "She has a brother, but he buggered off on some business trip."

"OK. But what about Warren Peace?"

Grace shrugged. "Maybe they're just estranged."

Phoebe mulled that over. "They're definitely hiding something. You said the housekeeper says that Clough and Tessa Peace knew each other way back. Her words, yet when you spoke to Tessa she said that he'd only known Warren for twelve years."

"That could be true. I didn't actually ask her how long she's known him."

Phoebe saw Portia Clough sitting alone in the Range Rover. She said, "Why not seize the opportunity, try talking to Portia."

"Good idea."

The sun came out from behind the grey clouds and the drizzle ceased as she picked her way, trying to avoid the large puddles that had formed on the side of the lane. She tapped on the passenger side window of the Range Rover. Portia looked round, a little startled, then wound down the window.

"You're with the Inspector, aren't you?" she said.

Grace just smiled. Portia had a cultured well

modulated voice. Close up she was far more attractive than Grace had thought on first sight. Her complexion was flawless and peaches and cream in colour and, unlike Tessa Peace, she wore only the lightest of makeup.

"Yes, Mrs Clough," she said, bending the truth. Portia opened the door and climbed down, stretching her long shapely legs. "How can I help you?"

"I was wondering how long you've known the Peaces?"

Without hesitation she said, "Warren, about twelve years, though Tessa and Curtis were at school together."

"Oh really," said Grace, trying not to let her surprise show. She hadn't realised that "way back" meant that long ago. "And where would that have been?"

Again, without any hesitation she said, "They lived next door to each other as children in the wilds of Galway. They went to the local primary school together, then Curtis went on to the Jesuits, I don't know where Tessa went." Grace let a silence hang, hoping that Portia Clough would elaborate. After a pause, she obliged. "Her family moved away then, I think to Liverpool."

A further silence ensued so Grace said, "So you both only met Warren when they came back here?"

"I didn't know Tessa until then either."

"Do you like her?"

Portia looked a little taken aback by the question.

"Well, as you ask. Not a lot."

"And do you think the Peaces had a happy marriage?"

"Who can say what is a happy marriage, my dear? Is there one ideal?"

She saw her husband return. He looked annoyed when he saw to whom she was speaking, but Grace threw him off balance by saying, "Lovely service, Mr Clough." Clough spluttered a little and then agreed, and Grace beat a tactical retreat.

"We were right," she said to Phoebe. "Clough and Tessa grew up together, and for some reason don't see fit to admit it."

"I can hear the skeltons rattling from here," Phoebe said.

When they got back to the office, Xin handed Grace a large brown envelope. "It's from Pattie somebody or udder, she said not to call her at work." Grace ripped it open and pulled out a photofit of a young man with blond hair. On the back it had details of his physical characteristics and a scribbled note at the bottom. *He was with Peace in a pub the night he died. Might have Liverpool or North of England accent.*

"That's two I owe Pattie," she said.

"We should try lookin' round the building sites," Mungo said. "I mean, we have the clay and the nail gun, I think it's worth a shot." He took the photofit and ran off three copies on the copier and handed one to each of them.

They decided to concentrate on Clough Peace sites to start with and left Xin to hold the fort.

They had no idea where the Clough Peace sites were situated and so the operation was decidedly unscientific. They just drove round until they saw a Clough Peace sign and went to the office. By dusk, Grace, who was rapidly losing heart, was navigating the traffic on the quays and was about to call it a day, when the now familiar logo came into view. She swung in through the gateway and parked outside a portakabin which seemed to be the general office. She pulled her jacket collar up against the chilly wind that swept in from the river. A few men were standing round a burning brazier, drinking steaming mugs of tea. She got the usual comments and cat-calls that navvies feel obliged to make as she made her way up the wooden steps to the door.

Two women were sitting at desks inside, one at a computer terminal. They looked up from their work as she entered and the elder of the women put her hand on some loose papers to prevent the draught from the open door blowing them to the floor. The air was blue with cigarette smoke. Grace shut the door and showed the two women the photofit of the suspect. She asked if they recognised him, fully expecting them to say no. The younger of the two left her computer and sat on the corner of her co-worker's desk looking at the picture. She had long blonde hair and she twiddled it round her finger as she concentrated. After a while she sniffed.

"These photo-yokes all look like serial killers to me." She giggled nervously as she said it.

The older woman was more serious. She picked up the picture and held it closer to the desk lamp. A long worm of ash fell from her cigarette onto the paper-littered desk. She looked up at Grace and frowned and asked, "Who did you say you were?"

Grace said, "Grace de Rossa, I'm a detective."

The woman said, "Oh, that's all right then. It could be a lad we started here a few weeks ago. Remember him, Tracy? The one who went sick."

"Oooh yessss," said Tracy. "It could be." She took the picture from her friend and examined it more closely.

Grace took out her notebook. "Do you have his name and address?"

Tracy went to a grey metal cabinet and started flipping through the files. Eventually she found a buff folder and handed it to the older woman.

"Here you are. Carl Rose. 22 Sabbath Lane, Finglas. I think he's in digs."

"When was he last at work?"

Tracy sat down at her desk. "I'd have to look that up," she said and looked blankly at Grace.

After a few seconds when she hadn't moved, Grace said, "Well. Could you?"

Tracy rummaged in a plastic case and put a disc in the drive of her computer. After a minute or two she pointed at the screen and said, "Not since last Monday week. His landlady phoned in to say he was sick. He'd only worked four weeks before that."

"He's a nice lad. What d'you want him for?" asked the older woman. "He's not in trouble, is he?"

"It's gotta be about Mr Peace, Molly. It's gotta be," said Tracy excitedly, tugging at Molly's arm.

"Well, yes. It's to do with that investigation," conceded Grace. "Do you know where he came from before here?"

Molly read through the sheet of paper from the folder. "It doesn't say, but he had an English accent. Strong Liverpool."

"And you've no previous address?" Molly shook her head. Grace copied Carl Rose's details into her notebook. "Did he have any friends on the site?" she asked. Both women looked blank.

Molly shook her head. "Not that I noticed, but

you could ask the men, they're on tea break just now."

The cold hit Grace in the face as soon as she opened the door. A few of the men who were standing round the burning brazier recognised the picture of Carl Rose. Others disagreed. But after all the banter and back-chat, it seemed that no one knew Carl Rose very well, and that he kept himself to himself.

Grace sat back in the car and tried to get warm. Her feet were wet, and clay caked her runners. She was glad that she had changed into her jeans after the funeral.

She blew on her hands and rubbed them together to get the circulation going again. Her dilemma was, what she should do next. If she phoned Dermot he'd want to know where she got the photofit, but if she took Mungo to Finglas to see Carl Rose and he found out, he could make life difficult for her for withholding information. The classic "rock and a hard place" syndrome. She decided to take the bull by the horns and called Mungo on the mobile.

"I've found him!" she said. "He has an address in Finglas."

"So what d'you wanna do?" he asked.

"I want to talk to him, will you meet me there?"

Mungo agreed. The heavy traffic delayed Grace and it was nearly an hour before she pulled up in front of 22 Sabbath Lane, Finglas. Mungo arrived shortly after and climbed into the passenger seat. "You're sure this is the right address?"

"As far as I know, but there's only one way to find out." As she was speaking she recognised Dermot's car pull up in front of her.

"Shit! Look who's here," she said. Dermot was just as pleased to see her. He got out and came over. She wound down the window.

"What the fuck are you doing here?" he stormed.

"Following up a lead," she snapped.

"What lead? How did you get this address?"

"Information received."

Luke came over and, when he saw her, looked as thrilled as Dermot. "What's she doing here?"

"She's just leaving," Dermot snapped.

"The hell I am!"

Mungo oozed out of the passenger seat. "It seems to me that standin' here ain't doin' a whole lot."

"Look, Dermot, if you'd traded information with me in the first place, we'd be a lot further on by now. Let's just call a truce and see what Rose has to say."

Dermot seethed for a couple of minutes. "All right. But I'll ask the questions," he said grudgingly. She heard Luke start to say, "Oh for fuck sake!" She ignored him and the four of them walked across the road to the terraced house.

The rows of houses on Sabbeth Lane were mostly occupied by families who had resided there for some years. A few, like number twenty-two, let out a room or two. It was a respectable working-class neighbourhood. A light shone in the downstairs front room so Luke pressed the doorbell. They could hear a man's voice calling for someone to answer the door. Eventually a red-faced woman opened the door, drying her hands on her apron.

Dermot produced his warrant card and said, "Detective Inspector Dermot McEvoy. I have to ask you a few questions."

The woman peered at the warrant card.

"What's up?" She was anxious looking. "Has our Kevin bin up to mischief?"

Luke reassured her. "No, Missus . . . ?"

She stared at him for a moment before she realised that he was asking her name. "Ward. Lilly Ward. What is it then?" He showed her the photofit.

"We're looking for Carl Rose. We believe he stays with you?" The fact that Her Kevin wasn't implicated in anything left her much relieved.

"Carl! Yeh he stays here. Nice lad. He's not been well though. He popped home for a few days. What d'you want him for?"

Dermot ignored her question. "Do you have his home address?"

She shook her head. "No. But he'll be back in the morning."

"When did he leave?"

Without hesitation she said, "Last Sunday."

Luke looked at Dermot. "Could we see his room?"

She didn't seem too sure about that and scratched her head. "I don't think that'd be right, with him not being here and all."

Dermot tried to reassure her. "We just need to eliminate him from our enquiries, Mrs Ward. You can be present while we take a look. If we have to wait until he comes back, it could seriously hamper our investigation."

She squinted at the four of them while trying to make up her mind.

"We could come back with a warrant . . ." Luke let the sentence hang.

"Oh! Go on then. I don't suppose it can do any harm," she said, and leaned past them to look up and down the street to make sure that none of the neighbours was watching.

His room was at the back of the house on the second floor. As she climbed the stairs ahead of them, a voice from behind the closed door of the front room shouted, "Who is it, Lil?"

"Nothing, y'nosey bastard," she shouted back.

The bedroom was neat and tidy with a single bed up against the wall and a whitewood dressing-table under the window. The recesses on either side of the fireplace had been converted into fitted wardrobes. Luke opened the white painted louvred door. A couple of jackets and a shirt hung on wire hangers. Neatly folded on the floor of the cupboard were a few pairs of jeans and three sweaters. None of them was of blue acrylic. The small room was crowded and Lily Ward backed out. "I'll be out here," she said.

Grace opened the drawer of the dressing-table. It was empty except for some underwear and socks. Luke Ryan glared at her, so she smiled sweetly back. On the bedside table stood a picture of a middle-aged couple. It was a grainy photo, and the clothes had a nineteen-seventies look about them. Beside it was a ghetto blaster, and audio tapes were stacked in a cassette holder. Luke flipped through them, Tears for Fears, Bruce Springsteen, Simply Red and U2. Nothing revolutionary there. An empty suitcase was stowed under the bed.

"Looks as if he's coming back," said Luke.

Mungo sniggered at him. "I doubt it."

"Did Carl Rose ride a motorbike, Mrs Ward?" Dermot asked.

"Yes, and real proud of it he was too," Lilly Ward said.

Outside again Grace took Dermot's arm. "Look Dermot, if we pool our information we won't get in your way. This state of affairs is stupid."

He sighed heavily. "What's bloody stupid is you working on this case."

"Maybe, Dermot, but it's a fact of life. If Tessa Peace wants to feel that *she's* doing something who am I to argue if she's paying us?"

"Well, I suppose it would be better than having you and the hit-man over there crashing about like a couple of loose cannon," he said eventually. "But if you get in the way . . ."

Grace squeezed his arm and gave him a peck on the cheek. "You know it makes sense!" she said in a serious voice.

The four of them crossed the road together.

"He doesn't seem to have anything personal lying around like letters or books or stuff like that, does he, apart from the photo and the tapes?" Grace said.

Luke sniffed. "Well, if he is our man he wouldn't, would he?"

Dermot was deep in thought. Rose had disappeared a few hours before the murder. What was the connection between Warren Peace and Carl Rose apart from Liverpool? Or was that just a coincidence? "Let's show Tessa Peace the photofit and see her reaction," he said finally.

"Now?" asked Luke, looking at his watch and

thinking about his date with Jenna Pierce. It had taken him weeks to persuade the gorgeous creature from collating to go out to dinner with him.

"Yes, now. And he must have been staying somewhere since last Sunday. Get the photofit circulated to all the B&B's. See if we can get a bite."

Grace and Mungo tagged along behind. They found Tessa Peace home alone when they arrived, Eoin had gone back to school earlier that evening. She wasn't pleased to see Grace and Mungo in the company of Dermot, and said as much. Grace took her to one side. "Look, Tessa, it's the only way we're going to be able to get the guy that killed your husband. We need Dermot on our side, he can blow us out as easily as not if he feels like it." Tessa was uncertain, but when she saw that she had little choice, she agreed to cooperate. She looked blankly at the photofit and then she shook her head. His name didn't seem to provoke any reaction either.

"I'm sorry, Inspector. I've never seen him before," she said. "Is this the one? Is he the man?"

"We don't know that yet. We just want to speak to him at the moment. He's probably the man your husband had the phonecall from." Dermot watched her face intently as she spoke. Her expression showed none of the signs of the stress that he would have expected if she were lying.

"Apparently Carl Rose is from Liverpool." That struck a nerve. "I believe you met your husband in Liverpool." He didn't wait for her to answer but went on, "Is there any chance that Carl Rose could have known you or your husband while you were living there?"

Tessa Peace had gone pale. "He would have been only a child when we were in Liverpool," she stammered. "It was a long time ago. Twelve years or more."

"Why would Curtis Clough lie about how long he has known you?"

"Lie?" She looked alarmed.

"Curtis Clough said that he has only known you for twelve years. Why would he say that when you knew each other as children?"

"I don't know. Are you sure he said that? He's only known – " she corrected herself, "knew Warren that long. That's probably what he meant. You'll have to ask him." She was getting upset. "You'll have to ask him."

"Don't get upset, Mrs Peace. We're just trying to understand the connection between Carl Rose and your late husband," said Luke.

"There *is* no connection!" she screamed. "There is no connection. Now please, leave me alone." She was crying.

Grace put her arm round her shoulders. "Are you sure you don't recognise the picture, Tessa?" she coaxed.

The older woman shook her head violently from side to side, "No. No. NO! How many more times do I have to say it? I've never seen him before. Now go away and leave me alone. I'm terminating your contract, I don't want you bothering me again."

"Now hang on a minute, lady," Mungo said. "You hired us to find your husband's killer."

"Well, I just fired you," she screamed. "I'll put a cheque in the post." She stood up. "All of you. Get out of my house."

"Well, something certainly rattled her cage," Mungo said as they stood outside.

"She knows who the photofit is. She has to," said Grace.

"Well, it's of little interest to you now," said Luke smugly. "You just got fired."

* * *

Tessa dialled Curtis Clough's number. She had difficulty as her hands were shaking and she misdialled at the first attempt. Portia answered and grudgingly went to get her husband.

"Curtis! Why did you lie to the police?" Tessa blurted out as soon as she heard his voice.

"I panicked. They took me by surprise. What did they say to you?"

She told him what Dermot had said. "I told him you must have been referring to Warren. I hope he believed me."

Clough was silent at the other end of the phone.

Tessa said, "What's it about Curtis? Who is this Carl Rose and why did he kill Warren?"

Clough gave a sigh. "I really don't know, Tessa, but I suspect it has something to do with Liverpool."

"Oooh God! I don't want that dredged up now. Not now."

"Maybe you should go away for a while, just until this dies down," he coaxed.

She thought about that for a moment. "Maybe," was all she said.

When he put the phone down Portia, who had been sitting listening to his end of the call, said, "I told you if you lay down with dogs you'd get up with fleas."

"Don't start, Portia, that dog put Gucci on your feet and Chanel on your back."

Chapter Seven

"It looked the same as the other one," said Hugh O'Boyle, who had arrived at the Drury Street multi-storey car park just before them. He was standing by the side of a grey Jaguar XJS. The area was cordoned off and the police surgeon had just finished examining the victim, pronouncing him dead at the scene.

The same sort of hose led from the exhaust through the side window of the car, and the engine was running when he had been found. The man was a little older than Warren Peace, balding and quite well-dressed. He differed from Warren Peace in two respects. He was sitting in the passenger seat, and the back of his skull was missing. There was very little blood, skull bone or brain tissue in evidence, suggesting that he had been killed elsewhere and the body driven to the point of discovery on the top level of the car park.

"Who was he?" asked Dermot as he pulled on a pair of rubber gloves and tried to avoid looking at the back of the victim's head.

"A Mister Shanks. Armitage Shanks."

Dermot looked round at Hugh. "Are you winding me up?"

Hugh handed Dermot the victim's wallet. "No. Straight up, that's his name."

Dermot looked at the contents of the wallet. Driving licence, organ donor card, both in the name of Armitage Shanks, four fifty pound notes and credit cards. There was a Bray address on the driving licence.

Luke interviewed the woman who had discovered the body. She had been doing her late-night shopping and four plastic carriers lay on the ground, the contents spilling out where she had dropped them. Her white battered Fiesta was parked near the Jag but the rest of the level was empty of vehicles.

"I saw the hose. I knew it couldn't be normal. Then I saw him behind the wheel. Is he dead? I never saw a dead body before." Her voice was rising to the point of hysteria.

"What's your name?" asked Luke, trying to calm her down a little. The question had the desired effect.

"Monica Houlahan."

"Did you see anyone hanging around when you got out of the lift, Monica?"

She shook her head. "No. But then I wasn't looking. This place gives me the creeps, I get in and out as quickly as possible. I only parked up here because I was late into work today and the lower levels were full." Luke took her address and then they both started to repack her shopping.

"Did he top himself?" asked Monica, trying to peer through the back window of the victim's car. She had forgotten that she was upset.

"We don't know at this stage," lied Luke and reached under the rear bumper for a wayward grapefruit. The last of Monica's groceries packed, he called to Dermot, "Can I let the witness go?"

"Got her statement?" he asked and Luke nodded. "OK. Tell her we'll need her at Harcourt Terrace tomorrow sometime to sign it."

After he had escorted Monica through the barrier, Luke examined the mat on the driver's side. He took out a small plastic evidence bag and scraped up a few particles of dried clay from the ridges in the rubber.

"What's that, Luke?" Dermot was leaning over his shoulder.

"It looks like the same clay that was in Warren Peace's car," he said.

"OK. Leave that to the technical team. Get on

to the Bray gardai and get them to inform the next-of-kin."

It was late by the time the garda photographer and the technical team had finished with the victim and his body had been eventually wheeled away to the morgue in a black body-bag.

Still unaware of the latest turn of events, Grace and Mungo got back to Baggot Street a little after nine. Phoebe's light was on so they went up.

"Where did you two get to?" she asked and appeared to be in a bit of a sulk. They told her. "Well, that wasn't very smart, was it?" she snapped. "You didn't need to go to see her with the bloody gardai. You had the picture of Carl Rose, you could have taken it round any time if you wanted to see her reaction. We're supposed to be working for her, not the guards."

"She went bananas when she heard that Rose was from Liverpool," Grace said. "But she'd have fired us anyway, it was more to do with the photofit than the fact that we were there with Dermot."

Phoebe stared at them as they stood by the door like two schoolkids up before the headmistress. "She fired you? Oh great! Our only client and you two get us fired." After a pause she added, "It's a good job one member of this company can bring in a crust."

"Did you get us some new clients?" Grace asked, incredulous.

"Don't sound so amazed, actually they came because of the small ad in the *Herald*."

"So what's it about?" Mungo asked.

"Well, it was Xin really. When I got back here she told me that an old biddy had come in and asked her to find a board."

"A what?"

"That's what I said. Seemingly the woman lost a yellow board and Xin found it. She threw a hundred quid into my hand and rushed out to her Mitsubishi class, or whatever qualified Ninjas do."

"What? like a surf-board?" Grace asked.

"I don't know, but the old biddy gave her a hundred quid for two hours' work, so who cares?"

★ ★ ★

Dermot phoned not long after Grace got into bed. "I thought you might be interested to know that we've had another body, same MO as Warren Peace."

She sprang up in bed. "Any connection?"

"We don't know yet, but the MO makes it possible. His name's Armitage Shanks."

"Are you winding me up?"

"That's the name on his driving licence. His address is in Bray."

"Why are you telling me this?"

She heard him clear his throat at the other end

of the line. "An attack of conscience," he said. "But we're even now."

Grace laughed. "When did you acquire a conscience?"

"I've always had one," he said. "But don't spread it around, it would be lethal for my street cred!"

"Was the victim married?"

It was Dermot's turn to laugh. "That's for me to know and you to find out," he said. "I told you, we're even now."

They bantered on for a couple more minutes before he hung up, then Grace jumped out of bed and grabbed the phone book. She found Armitage Shanks's address in Bray and ran down to Phoebe's flat. She and Mungo were up watching the late movie so she told them about Dermot's call.

Mungo got up and made for the door. "If he was connected to Warren Peace he'd probably have been at the funeral," he said. "I'll go get the pictures of the funeral."

"Fine, except we don't know what this Shanks guy looks like," Phoebe observed drily.

"We will as soon as we see the morning papers," said Grace.

Chapter Eight

There was no picture of Shanks in the morning paper so they collectively decided that Grace and Mungo should go to see the Widow Shanks, and Phoebe should call on Tessa Peace to see if she could talk her into re-employing them.

There was no Widow Shanks. Armitage Shanks had lived alone in a modern ranch-style split-level bungalow with a large double garage at one end of the frontage with open doors revealing an American-style pick-up truck. Through a stone arch at right angles to the garage, the blue water of a swimming-pool was just visible.

Sarah Hargan, the housekeeper, was in tears as she let them into the hall, prompting Grace to suspect that her relationship with the late Armitage Shanks was probably more than that of just employer and employee. An attractive woman in her late thirties, she was slender and of medium height, and her russet skirt was exactly the same colour as her shoulder-length hair. As she led them to the rear of the house and down a shallow set of slate steps to the kitchen she said, "Would you like tea?" as if looking for something to keep her hands occupied. They accepted her offer.

"What time did you last see Mr Shanks?" Grace asked gently.

Sarah blew her nose loudly on a ball of damp tissues and stuffed the soggy remnants in her pocket. "About four yesterday afternoon. He had a phone call and said he had to go out. I told him I'd leave his dinner ready to pop in the microwave." She pointed at a covered dinner plate sitting on the worktop. "It's still there." She started to weep quietly again. Grace waited for a few moments while Sarah tore off some kitchen roll and dabbed at her eyes.

"Did he say where he was going or when he'd be back?" Sarah just shook her head. "Did he seem worried about anything?"

Sarah sat at the table opposite to where Grace was standing, and looked up at her. Grace could see deep sadness in her eyes. "He was quite jumpy this past week, ever since Warren Peace was . . . " She couldn't finish the sentence. Mungo looked over at Grace, then said to Sarah, "He knew Warren Peace?"

Sarah looked puzzled. "Yes of course, didn't you know? And he was only at his funeral yesterday before . . . " She started to cry again. After much coaxing they discovered that the late Mr Shanks had retired. He had owned a group of DIY shops which a large superstore had bought outright making him an overnight millionaire. He had lived quietly since the buy-out four years previously, filling his time with golf and his passion for fishing.

Sarah had worked for him for about nine years and lived with her elderly mother close by. He had no children. She didn't know where Shanks had come from before he moved to Bray, but she thought he had been in the Bray area about twelve years.

The phone rang and Sarah went out to answer it. After she left the room Mungo said, "D'you think he was being blackmailed too?"

"There isn't much chance of finding out unless we get to see his bank statements, and there's not much chance of that."

They walked through to the hall where Sarah was just hanging up the phone. "We'll be off now, Sarah." Grace shook her hand and said, "I'm sorry about your loss."

Sarah Hargan nodded and opened the hall door for them. As they stood by the car Mungo said, "I could wait for the housekeeper to go out and see if I can find his bank statements."

"Absolutely not!" Grace said firmly just as Luke Ryan drove up. He got out of his car. "What the hell are you doing here?" he snapped, and Grace's hackles rose.

"The last time I looked, this was a free country," she said and got into the driver's seat.

"Why's he so hostile?" Mungo asked as they were driving back to Baggot Street.

"He thinks I took the shilling," she said.

There were no cars parked outside when Phoebe drove up to the front door of The Oaks. Mrs Danvers answered the bell. Tessa Peace was not at home.

"When do you expect her back?" Phoebe had asked.

Mrs Danvers shrugged and turned the palms upwards. "Dunno, love. She'd gone by the time I came in this morning. Sometime later I suppose."

"Did you know Armitage Shanks?" Phoebe asked on the off-chance.

"Who's he?" A pause then, "You mean Lou?"

Phoebe looked puzzled. "Lou?"

Mrs Danvers nodded. "Yes, Lou Shanks. That's what they call him. Older than Mr Peace? Lives in Bray? He drives one of those daft American trucks with all lights on the front?"

"I don't know about the truck," Phoebe said. "But he lived in Bray."

"Yes, he comes here from time to time. He was at the funeral yesterday." She obviously hadn't heard.

"I'm afraid he was found dead last night."

"Dead! What happened? Heart I suppose?" she

94

said. Then it dawned on her. "Oh Christ! Not like Mr Peace?"

Phoebe nodded. "I'm afraid so. Do you know if they had any business connections?"

"I wouldn't know, but I don't think so."

"Do you know if he knew Curtis Clough?" Again Mrs Danvers shook her head. "Maybe, I couldn't say. They might have met at one of Mrs Peace's parties, but I couldn't say for sure."

Phoebe could see that she wasn't going to get anything else from the housekeeper, so she told her she'd call back later when Tessa was in and headed back to Baggot Street and lunch.

* * *

It was two hours since he had spoken to Sarah Hargan and Luke Ryan was standing with his back against the tiled wall watching Leo Yentob perform the autopsy on Armitage Shanks. Luke didn't have a weak stomach like his boss and had no difficulty watching Leo Yentob go about his task. The only aspect he did have difficulty with was the overpowering stench. Yentob, a pathologist of twenty years standing, didn't seem to notice it and worked away, speaking from time to time into a small cassette, recording his findings ready to be typed up in a report afterwards.

After he had finished and was washing his gloved hands, Luke cleared his throat to attract his attention. He looked round and noticed Luke for the first time.

"Hello, Luke. Where's Dermot today?"

Luke laughed. "He sends his regrets."

"I'm sure!" said Yentob. He turned and nodded towards the cadaver which was lying on the stainless steel table. "Basically your victim had his head bashed in." Then added, "Not being too technical for you, am I?" Luke grinned and, hands in pockets, sauntered over to watch as Yentob lifted the late Armitage Shank's head. "He was hit from behind with some force, I would guess with the back of a big axe or something like that." He pointed at a large indentation on the skull. Pink brain matter was visible through the shattered bone. "There only seems to have been one big blow. He must have fallen on his face on grass." Yentob laid the head back and lifted the victim's upper lip. The two front teeth had been knocked inwards and there was mud and grass in the mouth. "I think the force of the fall knocked in his teeth." He pointed to the purple bruising inside the upper lip. "The face is virtually unmarked. I found these fibres inside the skull." He handed Luke a small plastic evidence bag. "It looks as if the murderer wrapped something round the open wound to minimise the mess." Then he added as an afterthought, "He's had an appendectomy and his liver shows signs of malignancy. I haven't tested for toxins yet, I'll let you have the full report by tomorrow morning."

★ ★ ★

Grace, after persistent nagging from Xin, allowed her to tag along when she went to see Curtis Clough. The Clough household resided in a Jacobean mansion set in about ten acres.

"They don't look as if they're short of a few bob," Xin commented as they pulled up on the gravel drive. The Cloughs certainly appeared to have done well out of their alliance with Warren Peace. On closer inspection, the house turned out to be a Victorian folly, but was nonetheless impressive. Two black and tan rottweillers bounded round the side of the house on hearing Grace's approaching car. They didn't look particularly friendly.

"God, I hate dogs," Grace said. "Especially large ones with big teeth." The dogs circled the car, barking and snarling. After about half a minute, when no one had come out of the house to rescue them, Grace shoved the car into reverse.

"Where're we goin'?" Xin asked.

"Where do you think," Grace said. "I'm not about to risk being torn limb from limb by those two monsters."

"Don't be daft," said Xin. "I can handle them." She reached down and opened the car door. The dogs bounded to her side of the car and crouched, ready to attack.

"Don't be stupid!" Grace said, panicking. She didn't want to be the one who would have to pick bits of Xin off the driveway.

"Chill out Grace. Bein' a Ninja, I have a way wit' all livin' creatures," Xin said haughtily. "Leave this t'me." She climbed out of the passenger seat and cooed at the animals. They eyed her suspiciously for a moment, hackles raised, teeth bared. Then, all of a sudden, they relaxed and started to wag their tails and pant. Grace watched in amazement as Xin tickled their ears and blew softly into their nostrils.

"C'mon," Xin called to her. "Yer safe now." Grace climbed apprehensively out of the car, keeping the door between herself and the dogs.

"It's OK, Grace. They're a couple of pussycats," Xin said, but Grace was sure she saw the ghost of a smile on Xin's lips as she said it. "Come on. Give 'em a pat."

"What?"

"Give 'em a pat on the head. Don't let them see yer afraid."

"How the hell am I supposed to do that?" Grace snapped, as the larger of the two animals looked in her direction and licked his lips.

Xin sighed, then pointed her chubby index finger at the dogs. "Sit!" she said, in a firm tone. The dogs instantly sat.

"Piece a cake," she said. "Shall we go in?" Oozing fear from every pore, Grace edged past the dogs and hurried to the front door. The gravel crunched under her feet. Xin followed and the dogs stayed put, sitting as she of the ancient wisdom had commanded.

The bell was an oldfashioned brass ring which Grace had to tug with some force before she heard the distant jangle in the depths of the house.

A uniformed maid opened the door and had a fit of apoplexy when she saw that the dogs were lose. She threw her hands in the air and babbled incoherently in Spanish until a gardener came round the side of the house and led the dogs away.

When she had calmed down, the maid led them to the library. Grace wondered where Portia Clough could have found a maid willing to wear the awful black dress and frilly doily hat.

The walls of the room were lined with bookshelves filled with leather-bound volumes. Some were battered and worn and others looked as if they had been restored. They consisted of classics and poetry, but there were also a number of very old botany volumes and well-thumbed zoology reference books. The slightly musty smell of the room flashed comforting memories fleetingly into Grace's mind. A short time later Portia Clough glided in, her patrician features and body language betraying her tension.

"I'm so sorry if the dogs startled you," she said. "Curtis is terrifed of them too, but there have been some break-ins in the area lately and . . . Well, I just feel safer." She offered them tea which Grace accepted. She wanted to put Portia Clough at ease.

"This is my associate, Xin Mountjoy." Xin stepped forward and held out her hand to Portia. Portia cringed slightly, but then recovered and shook hands with her.

"Do you or your husband know Armitage Shanks?" Grace asked.

Portia wrinkled her flawless brow. "The name sounds familiar," she said.

"He was also known by the name of Lou." Grace watched her face closely. Suddenly Portia seemed to grasp the past tense that Grace had used.

"Was!"

"I'm afraid he was found murdered last night. Do you know if your husband knew him?"

She bypassed the last question and said, "Oh my God. What is going on?" Her hands were shaking as she tried to light a cigarette. She succeeded after the third attempt and inhaled deeply. Grace coaxed her again. "Did your husband know Armitage, Lou, Shanks, Mrs Clough?"

"Yes. Yes he does . . . Did." She paused then a thought struck her. She said, "Do you think that the two deaths are connected?"

"We think so at this stage," said Grace. "Though

it's important that, if they are, we can establish some sort of motive, or even a connection between the victims which could lead us to a motive. Then maybe to the murderer." Grace tried to read Portia's face. It wasn't easy.

The sound of a racing engine skidding to a halt on the gravel announced the arrival of Curtis Clough. A moment later he burst into the room looking hot and bothered. He was nonplussed to see the two women sitting drinking tea with his wife.

"Curtis! Miss de Rossa tells me that there has been another murder."

"I heard," he said. "Do you know if the gardai have any suspects yet?"

"I'm not sure," Grace said. "I believe you knew Mr Shanks?" she said, staring into his bloodshot eyes.

"Yes. I knew Lou quite well. Did business with him on a few occasions."

"With you or with Clough Peace?" she asked.

"With me."

"How did he know Warren and Tessa Peace?"

Clough shrugged. "They were just in the same social circle I think. I'm not sure." He looked uncomfortable.

Grace tried to take advantage of his discomfort. "Can you think of any reason why Mr Shanks or Warren Peace may murdered?"

"Why don't you ask Tessa?" His brow was bathed with sweat and Grace wondered whether he was concerned for his own safety.

101

Portia Clough said sharply, "For God's sake, Curtis, tell her."

"Tell me what, Mrs Clough?"

Curtis glared at his wife.

She ignored him and said, "Warren and Lou knew each other a long time ago in Liverpool. It's supposed to be a big secret, I don't know why."

"Perhaps you could tell me, Mr Clough." Grace looked at Clough.

He shook his head and mopped his brow with a large white cotton hanky. His colour had gone from red to grey. He looked unwell and swayed slightly, so Grace asked if he was all right. He didn't answer but staggered, clutched at his chest and collapsed onto the carpet, hitting his head on the corner of the coffee table. As he fell he sent the teatray and Royal Doulton crashing to the floor. Portia Clough screamed in fright.

"Call an ambulance," shouted Grace as she felt for a pulse in Clough's neck. It was weak, but still there.

"Where's the phone, Mrs Clough?" Xin yelled, but Portia didn't answer, She was rooted to the spot. Grace loosened Clough's collar and was pushing a cushion under his head when she saw that Portia was still standing frozen.

"Where's the phone, Mrs Clough?" Still no reaction from Portia. Grace grabbed her mobile phone from her bag and threw it to Xin, who dialled 999, telling the operator to send a cardiac ambulance.

Grace felt Clough's pulse again, it was weaker. She started pumping his chest.

One, two, three, four. One, two, three, four. Trying to keep the rhythm even.

"Here, let me help," Xin said, and started giving him the kiss of life as Grace continued to pump his chest. She felt for his pulse again. It seemed a little stronger. Portia Clough was still standing transfixed, staring at her husband. She was white as a sheet.

"Do you have a rug or blanket or something to cover him with, Mrs Peace?" That seemed to bring her out of her trance.

"Yes," she said and left the room, returning a couple of minutes with a cashmere shawl which Grace placed over the patient. He was breathing more evenly by this time. His pulse was much stronger and his colour better. After what seemed like an age they heard the nee-naw of the ambulance arriving. It crunched to a halt on the gravel outside. Xin had already run out to open the door.

* * *

Curtis Clough was put on life support in the Cardiac Care ward. His prognosis was good provided he didn't have any further attack for forty-eight hours. Grace looked into his room after speaking to the registrar. She thought that he looked somehow shrunken with all the tubes attached to his body, and she was aware of the bleep bleep of the cardiac monitor.

A movement in the corner made her start. She hadn't noticed Portia sitting quietly by the wall in the shadows watching her husband.

"They said that you and your little friend probably saved his life," she said. "I wonder if it was worth it."

"What do you mean?" said Grace. But Portia just shook her head, leant back on her chair and disappeared into the shadows again.

★ ★ ★

The office was a hive of activity when Grace arrived back. Eight or nine very large men were sitting, standing, or just lounging around reception. Reviewing the group, Grace thought they all shared a look implying generations of in-breeding. She looked enquiringly at Xin who just said non-commitally, "Mungo's interviewin' them."

Grace went on into the big office where Phoebe and Mungo were talking together.

"What's going on outside?" she asked.

"We've been hired to sort out security for the Screeming AbDabs."

"The what?"

"The Screaming AbDabs. The Aussie rock band. They're having a huge gig at the Point next week," Phoebe said with studied casualness. "How's Clough? Xin said something about him having had a heart attack."

"He did, but so far he's OK."

Phoebe looked alarmed. "Really! What brought that on?"

"Portia pressed him to tell us about *The big secret*. I think the stress was too much for him."

"And what's *The big secret*?" Mungo asked.

"What we suspected. Shanks knew the Peaces, and Tessa met Warren Peace in Liverpool. Portia pressed him to tell me why it was such a big deal and he just keeled over."

"Will he survive?"

Grace shrugged. "The registrar said if he gets through the next forty-eight hours without another attack he'll probably be fine."

"I suppose talking to him again just now's out of the question then," Mungo observed.

"Did you get Tessa to reconsider?" Grace asked hopefully. Phoebe shook her head. "I can't get hold of her. She was out when I called at the house, and I've being trying to get her on the phone ever since." Xin buzzed on the intercom. "A Mister Andrew Dillon t'see you, Grace." Grace groaned. "God! What does he want now?"

Andrew was standing in reception waiting for her. "Could I have a word?" he said, indicating the hallway outside. "In private." They went out through the glass door into the hall and he handed her a sheaf of papers. "If you sign here," he said pointing with his pen to an X at the bottom of the top sheet, "I can give you a cheque for the balance owing on the house."

Grace took the paper, and leaning it on her knee, signed her name. After she had handed it back, he handed her a cheque.

"Thanks," he said and turned to go. Grace looked at the cheque. "Wait a minute," she called after him. "This is a thousand quid short." He stood at the top of the steps. "No. I think you'll find that it's correct. The one thousand is for legal fees."

"Legal fees? But *you're* my solicitor."

"That's right," he said. "But not after today." With that, he turned and trotted down the steps into Baggot Street. Grace was livid and stormed back into reception letting the door slam loudly, nearly shattering the glass. "What's black and tan and looks good on a solicitor?" she raged at no one in particular. Xin looked up from her keyboard. "Wha'?"

"A fucking rottweiller!"

There was four seconds of total silence before one of the mutants gave a loud guffaw.

Chapter Nine

The following morning Phoebe took Mungo to see if Tessa Peace was back in the hope that she had forgiven them, and that she had only fired them in anger. There was no police guard at the entrance to The Oaks and the gate was open so they swept up the drive. The press had other fish to fry with the new victim. Warren Peace was old news.

Mrs Danvers answered the door holding Tolstoy, who was snarling at Mungo, tightly by the collar. She looked harassed and Mungo noticed, as she led them through the hall to the kitchen, that she had left the phone off the hook.

"Are the press bothering you?" he asked.

"No, they gave up last evening," she said seeing that he had noticed the receiver lying on the hall table. "I just didn't feel like talking to anyone."

The kitchen was functional and neat,

suggesting that Tessa Peace didn't spend much time there herself. "Would you like some tea?" she said. Phoebe shook her head, then asked where Tessa was.

"Dunno, love. She's gone away fer a few days."

"Gone away? Are you sure?" Phoebe said, shooting a look at Mungo. "I thought you said she'd be back yesterday?"

Mrs Danvers looked annoyed. "Of course I'm sure! I had a note through the post this morning. And why shouldn't she go away if she wants some peace and quiet."

"She should have told us," said Mungo. "We're supposed to be trying to find her husband's murderer after all, and we may need her."

"Do you know where she might have gone?" asked Phoebe.

Mrs Danvers was shaking her head. "No idea," she said. "Maybe Mr Clough can tell you."

"Haven't you heard?" said Mungo. But before he could go on the housekeeper gave a yelp. "Not him too. Oh my Gawd!"

"No, no. He just had a heart attack," said Phoebe, "He's in hospital."

"This is all too much," said Mrs Danvers and sat down heavily at the kitchen table, putting her head in her hands. The kettle hissed on the Aga. Mungo looked around until he found the teapot and made them all a pot of tea. He opened a cupboard looking for some cups and Tolstoy started to snarl at him again.

"Shurrup Tolstoy," snapped Mrs Danvers. "Go to bed." Tolstoy slunk into a large box by the Aga and lay down. "Stupid animal. Where were you when yer master needed you?"

"Can I see her note?" Phoebe asked. Mrs Danvers rummaged in her pocket, pulled out a crumpled scrap of paper and handed it to her.

Dear Mrs Danvers, Please feed Tolstoy, I will be back in a few days. Please find enclosed wages. Sincerely, Tessa Peace.

Phoebe handed the note to Mungo, who after reading it, motioned her over to one side and said in a low voice, "D'you think she went of her own accord?"

Phoebe shrugged. "Who knows, but I think we should act as if she didn't. Just in case." Then she turned to the housekeeper who was nursing her cup of tea between her hands, still sitting at the pine table. "Did the Peaces have a holiday home?"

"They had a time-share in Portugal," she said thoughtfully. "Oh, and the cottage."

"Cottage. Where?"

"Dunno exactly. Somewhere in the west, I think."

Phoebe was uneasy and when she got back to the office she passed on her anxiety to Grace. "D'you think she could be a victim too?"

Grace shrugged. "I doubt it. We'd have heard."

"I sincerely hope she isn't dead," Phoebe added. "If she's dead we don't get paid."

"You're all heart, Phoebe."

"Well, somebody has to think about the finances of this company," Phoebe said huffily.

They sat around in the small office while Mungo finished interviewing prospective bouncers for the rock gig in the larger room. After a lull in conversation, Phoebe suddenly said, apropos of nothing, "Don't you think that they're very makey-uppy names?"

"What?" Grace frowned. "What d'you mean makey-uppy?"

"Well, I mean, Armitage Shanks. Who ever heard of anyone named after a toilet? And Warren Peace . . . "

"What's wrong with Warren Peace?"

Phoebe cast her eyes heavenward. "Come on! Warren Peace. Say it quickly."

"Warren Peace. Warren Peace. Warranpeace. Warrandpeace. War and peace." She burst out laughing. "And his dog's called Tolstoy for God's sake! The cheeky sod."

Phoebe said, "So the change of name definitely clinches the deep dark, probably illegal, past theory."

Grace just said, "Hmmmm," and looked in her bag for her address book. "I think I'll phone a contact I've got in the Liverpool police."

110

And she made the call to Rachel Toolin at Liverpool Central CID. The two women had met a couple of years before when Rachel had asked Grace for help. A rape suspect had fled Liverpool to the Republic and Grace arrested him. There was a glitch in the extradition process and Grace had to let the suspect go. But she rearrested him on a pretext and strung out the interview process to give Rachel time to sort it out. After she had spoken with her and faxed her pictures of the victims and of Carl Rose, she sat and waited for Rachel to get back to her. Phoebe went out to the hairdressers.

Time hung heavily, and after what seemed like an age but was only about half an hour, Xin came in with coffee.

"Was I magic or wha'?" she said. "Philip Marlowe couldn't 've done better."

Preoccupied, Grace didn't understand at first, then realising she was talking about her client said, "Oh yes, Xin. Magic."

Xin beamed proudly. "She said she'd lost the board so I go round to her place. It was easy really. I seen this big cat comin' outta the shed so I went in. And there it was, dead as a door-nail."

"Dead? What do you mean dead? How could a board be dead?" Then, after a moment's thought. "What kind of board was it?"

Xin looked irritated, "A yella singin' one."

Grace grinned. Xin's pronounced Dublin accent had confused her for a moment. "You mean a bird?" she said.

"Yeh. That's wha' I said. A board."

"And the woman gave you a hundred quid for finding her dead canary?" she asked, unable to hide the note of disbelief in her voice.

"No not then. I went down town an' bought anudder identical one in George's Pet Shop. Then I *found* it in the shed. That's when she gave me the hundred quid."

Before a very gobsmacked Grace could make further comment, Xin bounced out of the room.

Phoebe was long back when Rachel Toolin's call came through. Grace put her on the speaker phone so she wouldn't have to repeat everything to her partner.

"Sorry to have taken so long, Grace, but the good news is you're in luck. A guy on my shift was talking to me when the stuff came through on the fax. He was with the fraud squad twelve years ago and recognised George Warren as soon as he saw the picture," she said. "Your victims are fugitives. The Liverpool fraud squad have been looking for these guys for over twelve years."

"Who are they?" asked Grace.

"Wait a minute," she said. "I'll put you on to Mike Slaughter. He's up to speed on the case."

"Hello, Grace. You found my villains then?"

"I hope so," Grace said. "Who are they?"

"Your latest body is positively ID'd as one Lou Armitage, aka Armitage Shanks. Then there's George Warren and Gary Grant," he said.

"What was your interest in them? Who were they?"

Slaughter snorted, "They're my very own bête noir." His scouse accent made it sound like *Bate Noo-are*. "They were three amateurs who ran rings round us. Twelve years ago the three of them pulled off the biggest LF ever on this manor. Got away with over two million."

Grace and Phoebe both said together. "LF?"

"Long Firm Fraud." He went on to explain. "That's a fraud that goes on over not less than say, two years."

"How does it work?" asked Grace.

"A legitimate trading company is set up and small orders are placed with suppliers. In this case it was proprietary goods and textiles. The company sells the goods on at less than cost to associates for cash, thus giving them cash-flow to pay the invoices on time.

"Over the months they increase the size of the orders, having gained creditworthiness. The whole sting relies on the goods being turned over quickly to keep the cash flow buoyant and the invoices paid on time. Phase two comes when the company gets involved in importing goods from abroad. In

WAG's case (that's the name of the company), they imported cotton goods from Italy, sheets, duvet covers, towels and the like. With impeccable credit references, the orders start big and just get bigger. The extra advantage with the imports is that they can gain at least another ten days credit on invoices."

"Who would buy all the goods?" interrupted Grace.

"Usually market lads and the like. They would have built up a list of customers, who would get invoices for the recommended wholesale price, so they gained in two ways. The stuff wasn't bent, and their unofficial profit for the few that declared accounts was up at least ten percent. Anyway, near the end of the two year period, before the revenue and VAT start to shout, one last lot of very sizeable orders are placed. Take into account that the invoices would be on thirty days, so giving time for the first suppliers to notice that their accounts haven't been settled, the lads have at least fifty days to get the stuff in and out and vanish with the proceeds. These three got away with two million one-hundred and forty-eight thousand pounds. Cash."

"Wow!" said Grace, not without admiration in her voice. "You said that they were amateurs. What did you mean by that?"

"We only got interested because about eighteen months into their operation, we got a tip from a snout about something going down, so we checked them out. Although we had doubts about some of the people they were selling to, all the paperwork was in order, so we had no grounds to get heavy. None of the principals had form for as much as a parking ticket. We started surveillance, but they sussed us and cried harassment, so we were called off. It seems as if it was a one-off. What were they mixed up in in Ireland?"

"That's just it," said Grace. "They both appeared to be pillars of the community. Well off respectable business men. Until they were murdered."

"There must have been others involved in the company," said Phoebe. "What happened to them?"

Over the speaker phone they could hear Slaughter flip over pages of one of the files. "Well the other partner, as I said before, was a guy named Gary Grant. The office was run by George's wife, Tessa, and the warehouse by a manager and four warehouse lads. The manager was an unfortunate sod called Frank Dodd. He went away on his two weeks summer holiday and came back to find the warehouse empty and the fraud squad waiting for him."

"How did you get involved so quickly? How did the suppliers cop on so quickly if there was thirty days credit?"

"Angelo Steffani, of Delmarco Steffani the Italian supplier, got on to us. Apparently he wasn't happy with the deal from the start but he was overruled by his board. He nearly throttled Frank Dodd. We had to pull him off."

"And Dodd wasn't involved?"

"We couldn't believe that he was completely innocent at first, but we hung on to him, hoping that if we managed to get only one of the others, we could at least have them for conspiracy. But his brief went to judge in chambers and got him bail."

"What was the outcome?"

Slaughter sounded uncomfortable. "Two days before he was due in court for committal he topped himself."

"How?" asked Phoebe, looking at Grace.

"What?"

"How did he top himself?"

Slaughter said, "Gassed himself in his car, I think."

"So who's Carl Rose? Is he known to you?"

"Yes. That's Carl Dodd, Frank's son. He was only twelve when all this was going on. After Dodd topped himself the mother, Maureen, changed back to her maiden name of Rose. I lost touch with the case after Dodd topped himself and the others went missing, it was just left on file. But I asked around when Toolin heard from you. Apparently the mother fell apart and the lad went off the rails. Nothing serious, just the usual juvenile stuff." They could hear Slaughter rummaging again. "It says here he joined the army for three years until he was twenty."

"Is that all you have on him?"

"'Fraid so. Wait a minute, it seems the mother is from Dublin and that she went back to live there. Maybe he went too."

"Well, at least all the pieces are coming together," Grace said. "Even if we don't know where he is."

"Have you had any sight of Gary Grant?" Slaughter asked.

"I don't know," said Grace. "We don't know what he looks like or what his alias is. If you fax a picture we'll look out for him for you." Then a thought struck her. "He qualifies as another victim unless we can find him and Tessa before Carl Rose."

Slaughter said, "I suppose so." Then, "Did you say Tessa Peace was missing?"

"Yes. Though she may have heard about Shanks. She may be just lying low."

"Well let me know if Gary Grant floats to the surface," Slaughter said. "I'll hand you back to Toolin now."

When Rachel came back on the line Grace said, "Listen, Rachel. I think I should tell you, I'm not in the Job anymore, I'm working privately."

She heard Rachel laugh at the other end of the line. "I kind of sussed that when your receptionist answered the phone, Grace. I'm not a detective for nothing, you know! Anyway I owed you one. But remember, you didn't get this stuff from me or Slaughter, OK?"

They were now left with a dilemma. There was no way Sleuths had the resources to find Gary Grant in the short space of time which seemed to be imperative, or Tessa for that matter. Carl Rose could be on to them already. Grace realised the only course of action was to hand on the information to Dermot. He wasn't at Harcourt Terrace and she found herself talking to Luke Ryan.

"He's in Court all day. What do you want?" he asked with his usual lack of charm.

Grace ignored his coolness. "I've information from a contact in the Liverpool Police about Warren Peace and Armitage Shanks," she said. "You have to trace a man called Gary Grant who was involved in an LF with them, he's probably Carl Rose's next . . ."

"Wait a minute," he cut in. "What are you talking about? What's an LF?"

"A Long Firm Fraud," Grace said with a certain sense of satisfaction. Luke Ryan didn't know what it was either. She explained to him the workings and passed on the rest of the information Slaughter had given to her.

"Where did you get this? We were onto Liverpool Police and they had nothing on either of the victims." He sounded more than a little irritated.

"A contact recognised Warren Peace, I was just lucky, that's all," she said. "If you drop by later I'll give you a copy of the photo of Gary Grant. The only problem is we've no idea what alias he's using. I thought I might recognise him from the funeral pictures but so far I can't pick him out."

"I'll be over in about half an hour," he said and Grace hoped he wouldn't give her any grief. She was tired of having to fight with just about every man she knew.

"You know," said Phoebe after a while. "What Slaughter told me got me thinking. There's another possible suspect now."

"Who?"

"This Angelo Steffani guy. The Italian. What if he and Carl Rose are working together?"

"What if?" acknowledged Grace.

Xin put her head around the door. "I'm off," she said. "I switched the phone through. See yeh in the mornin'." Grace looked at her watch. She was surprised to see that it was well after six.

"See you in the morning, Xin. You did well today," she said. Xin beamed with pride.

True to his word, Luke Ryan arrived thirty minutes later at about seven. His usual frosty manner had thawed a little and he had some blown-up photographs of the funeral with him. They spread them out across the desk and started examining them through magnifying glasses, trying to pick out the possibly soon-to-be late Gary Grant. There were two possible candidates, one standing next to Armitage Shank, the other a little apart

"We could ask Tessa if we knew where she was," Phoebe said, hoping that if Luke Ryan knew of her whereabouts he might tell them.

"Isn't she at home?" he asked, surprised.

"Not since yesterday. The housekeeper said she's probably gone away for a few days, but we're not so sure. If this Gary Grant is a possible victim on account of his involvement in the fraud, who's to say Tessa Peace isn't too?"

"That thought had struck me," Luke said just as his bleeper started. "D'you mind?" he said pointing at the phone.

"Go ahead," Grace said and Luke dialled Harcourt Terrace.

"Grace!" Phoebe hissed. "Look at this." Grace peered through the magnifying glass at the enlarged photo. A shadowy figure could just be seen half-concealed behind a large stone angel. The man had fair hair and, though his features were blurred, the general shape of his face and what could be seen of his build conformed to Mr

Dwyer's photofit of the man Warren Peace had met in the pub the night he died. The man whom they now knew to be Carl Rose.

"There's our man, now all we need is to find him," she insisted. Grace craned her neck to hear what Luke was saying on the phone, but she couldn't make it out until he turned round to face her again and said, "OK. I'm on my way," and replaced the receiver. Then to Grace he said, "I think we may have found Gary Grant. It's just a hunch but there's another body. Same MO as Peace. His name's Archie Leach. D'you want to come?"

Stunned, Grace didn't wait for him to change his mind and, in the car on the way to the murder scene she said, "I'd say there's no doubt that it's Gary Grant, judging by the other aliases anyway."

"Why d'you say that?"

"Gary Grant. There was a very famous Archie Leach who changed his name to Cary Grant. Why shouldn't Gary Grant change his name to Archie Leach, it sounds par for the course."

"I knew that," Luke said defensively.

The blue flashing lights of the police cars pinpointed the spot where the victim had been found in Herbert Park. As they got out of the car it started to lash with rain. Grace pulled up her coat collar and followed Luke past the cordon. He left her for a moment and spoke to a uniformed

Garda whom Grace recogised. He nodded in her direction and she smiled back at him.

"Who are they?" she asked looking over at a young couple who were standing near the grass verge. The young man was comforting the girl. He had one arm round her shoulder and was holding an umbrella over them with the other.

"They found the victim. Apparently they were on their way home after work and were going through the park. They though it was a suicide and tried to save him, then the girl went hysterical when she saw the screwdriver sticking out of his back."

"Do you blame her?" said Grace as they walked over to the late Mr Leach's car. "I'm sure I saw him at Warren Peace's funeral." The car was a Saab Turbo and, once again, the same type of hose led from the exhaust through the side window. The duty police surgeon had just arrived and was examining the victim for signs of life, although the first officers on the scene had already ascertained that Archie Leach was well and truly dead. They gave him a few minutes, then went over to him.

"What do you think?" Luke asked.

Dr McHugh sucked his teeth. "Not the same as the others," he said.

"In what way?" Luke asked, surprised.

"Too much blood. I'd say, this time, the fumes killed him and that he's not that long dead. May

even have been alive when those two found him."
He gestured over at the young couple who were
now hugging each other.

"Would the wound in the back have killed him
anyway?" asked Luke.

"I can't say. Leo Yentob'll tell you that after
postmortem tomorrow." He snapped his bag shut.
"Right. I'm off. Why people can't choose to be
murdered at a civilised hour I'll never know," he
said and walked briskly away to his car, leaving
Grace and Luke standing looking at the late
Archie Leach. Luke looked through Leach's
wallet. Apart from a driving licence, a small
amount of money and a photo it was empty. The
driving licence had a Killiney address not far from
the Peace's and the photograph was of an
attractive woman and two children, all smiling at
the camera.

"Must be the next-of-kin," said Luke, handing
the picture to Grace.

"Nice looking woman," she said. "Are we going
to talk to her tonight?"

Luke shook his head. "*We* aren't going to talk to
her at all. I'll talk to her tomorrow. Uniform have
already broken the news."

"I thought your *Mister Nice Guy* routine was too
good to last," she said, but not with malice and he
actually grinned at her.

The young couple looked restless. "I'll take

their statements," he said. "If you wait in the car, I'll give you a lift back."

It felt strange to Grace to be at the scene of a crime and not to be involved in the investigation. She wandered back to the Saab. It had been parked with the nose in towards a neatly trimmed grass verge about three feet deep. Plastic sheeting had been rigged up over the immediate area to protect any evidence from the weather, and also to shield the murder scene from the ever-present media. The ground was very wet, and by the light of the arc lamps she could see the tracks of a motor cycle and a set of footprints. She called to Luke, "Look at this. We, sorry *you*, ought to get casts of the treads and the footprints. The residents heard a motorbike at the Warren Peace scene, didn't they?"

"How did you know that?"

Grace said, "Information received."

Luke called to the technical officer who had just arrived, "Martin, can you get casts of these?" Martin shouted back that he would. Luke peered into the back of the car, shining his torch on the floor, but there was no sign of any clay either in the back or the front.

The rain was coming down heavily now and battered off the plastic. The photographer had finished and the body was being placed in the body bag, so Grace went to sit in the car and wait for Luke.

124

On the way back to Baggot Street, she said, "I assume Shanks was being blackmailed too."

"Yes, Carl Rose had him for one payment of six grand."

"I wonder how much Leach had to pay."

"Well, we know Rose is at least twelve grand up, not counting Leach, so he's plenty of cash to help him to vanish."

"You know, they must have planned the vanishing act as meticulously as the fraud," said Grace. "They would have needed passports and driving licences at the least, not to mention good, well-rehearsed cover stories."

"Two million buys a lot of documents," said Luke. "But where does Curtis Clough come into it? And now we know Carl was definitely making a statement when he gassed the victims, but why did he wait so long? I think I'd like to talk to the mother if I can find her. She might know where he'd go."

After a pause Grace said, "Unless of course he stays around to take a pop at Tessa. Then there's still the possibility that Angelo Steffani could be involved in a conspiracy with Rose."

"I'd say that's unlikely. I mean how would they have got together?"

"Coincidence?" Grace ventured.

Luke parked outside Sleuths. "I'll get on to Liverpool CID and put in an enquiry for Georgie

Warren this time." Then seeing the look on Grace's face added quickly, "Don't worry, I won't drop your friend in it."

"Careful, Ryan," Grace said as she got out of the car. "People will begin to think you might be a human being after all."

* * *

As Grace was taking her leave of Luke, Dermot was pushing open his front door. He was in a foul humour because the GBH case that he'd involved in had been thrown out of court due to the chief prosecution witness's failure to turn up. He was irritated further at the prospect of having to decide what to cook for his evening meal. He was surprised to see a crack of light under the kitchen door. The sound of laughter filtering out from behind the closed door puzzled him further. He had expected the house to be empty. He opened the door and the chatter ceased abruptly. Standing by the cooker stirring a saucepan was Jane, and Susy was sitting on the worktop. He stood in stunned silence for a moment, hardly daring to believe his eyes. Susy slid off the counter and broke the silence.

"Hello, Dad."

He held his arms open unable to speak, and circled her with them when she came to him. She hugged him back hard. He could smell scent in her hair.

"I'm sorry, Dad," she said into his chest. He patted the back of her blonde head with one hand,

"No Princess, I'm sorry," he said, his voice breaking. He held her out at arm's length and looked at her. She was a little thinner than the last time he had seen her on the day of Matty's funeral, and very tanned.

They ate as a family for the first time in twelve years, after Susy and Maura had laid the table and Jane had finished cooking her curry. Susy told them what she had been doing since she left. She told them that after she had finished college she had gone straight out to Israel to work on a kibbutz.

"For this I paid college fees!" he joked, turning up the palms of his hands and shrugging like a rabbi. Later, after they had washed the dishes and the two younger girls had gone out, they sat at the kitchen table and talked. Susy told him about her time in Israel and Dermot was stunned when she told him that she had been married to a Polish-American Jew. It took a few moments for the past tense to register.

"Been. You mean you're divorced?" Dermot pushed his chair back and stood up. He couldn't take this in. He leaned over her, resting his weight on the palms of his hands. The colour rose up his neck. "Married and divorced, living halfway across the world and I'm the last one to find out." He was hurt and angry. Susy could always make him rise. She might be her mother's double in looks and build, but temperamentally they were like peas in a pod.

"Calm down," she said. He opened his mouth to say more but she put her hand to his lips. "Josh is dead."

"Dead?"

Slowly nodding her head, she went on. "He was a soldier. We lived in Jaffa. Me, Josh and Simon."

"Simon?"

"Our son." He sat down again heavily and put his head in his hands. His princess had been married and had a child. "Where is he? Where's my grandson?" She looked up at him with tears running down her cheeks. "He died in the car crash with his father." She held up her hand to stop him speaking. "After they died I discovered what real grief was. I knew what you must have felt after Mum. I'd been so angry when she died that I blamed you." She rose from the table. They were both crying. He for Matty and the lost years; she for her husband, son and mother in that order. They hugged each other across the table, each trying to comfort the other.

Much later Dermot went to bed exhausted but happier than he had been for years.

Chapter Ten

Tessa Peace sat huddled by the fire in the small sitting-room of the cottage she and Warren had bought a few years before on the west coast in Mayo. His bolt-hole he had called it. They used to escape there from time to time whenever Warren had had a particularly busy or stressful spell.

The room was stuffy and hot but she was shivering, her arms wrapped tightly round her body. Through the rain-splattered window she could see daylight creeping above the cliffs overlooking Clew Bay and, if there had been no mist, she would have been able to see the outline of Clare Island out in the Atlantic.

A gust of wind blew a puff of smoke down the chimney and she leaned back from the fire until it had cleared. Then the door crashed open and she nearly jumped out of her skin. Leaping to her feet she clapped her hands to her mouth to stifle a scream, but the door just flapped in the wind until another gust banged it shut again. Her heart beating, she went over and slipped the bolt on to prevent the storm from bursting the rickety lock.

She wasn't sure why she was so afraid. She had no idea who Carl Rose could be or why he had been blackmailing Warren. Suddenly a wave of loneliness overcame her and a terrible longing for Warren. She felt as though her other half had been cut away. A great sob racked her body and she rocked back and forth, sitting on the rug in front of the fire, her arms wrapped round her knees, until she had cried herself to sleep.

She awoke cold and disorientated. Her legs and back were stiff and her arm had gone dead. The fire was out, but it was brighter outside and the storm seemed to have passed. For just a moment she had the flicker of hope that she had been dreaming and that the events of the past few days had been a horrific nightmare, but reality hit her like a ton of bricks when she recognised her surroundings.

"Pull yourself together," she said aloud. "Get a grip. Think positive." After showering, she decided to walk into Murrisk to buy fresh milk and bread for breakfast. The air was crisp and bracing but had that calmness that always follows a storm. She was beginning to wish that she had brought Tolstoy and regretted having left in such a panic.

Maura Keane was standing stooped over the counter of the general store reading the paper when Tessa walked in. She looked up when the door opened and her expression turned sympathetic when she recognised her customer.

"Oh, Mrs Peace. Is it yourself?" she said. "I'm sorry for your trouble." Tessa smiled, grateful for the friendly word. "Have they got the, you know?"

Tessa shook her head. "Not yet, Maura, soon I hope." They stood in silence for a moment before Maura went on to say, "Mam and Dad, well, we just couldn't believe it when we saw it on the TV." The plump teenager took Tessa's hands in hers, making her feel slightly embarrassed. "But look. How are *you*?" She looked straight into Tessa's eyes. Her own were filled with concern for the older woman.

"Bearing up. I just felt I needed to have a little time on my own." Maura nodded solemnly. Tessa said, "Now how about some milk and bread and the paper." She was trying to sound cheerful and almost succeeded.

Back at the cottage she put the kettle on the gas and popped two pieces of bread in the toaster. She was beginning to think that she had overreacted and felt a little foolish. Her mood changed however when halfway down the front page she recognised Lou's name. Tessa tried to read the copy but her brain wouldn't take it in. Her head was buzzing and confused. The smoke alarm's high-pitched beep brought her back to her senses and she grabbed the grill-pan and threw the charred toast into the sink, burning her hand in the process. She swore and ran it under the cold tap. Then she read the piece again. Lou had been found just after ten-thirty the previous night in his car, just like Warren.

The kettle whistled insistently and it took all her concentration to make a pot of tea without scalding herself due to the near uncontrollable tremor in her hands. The feeling of panic receded a little when she remembered that no one knew where she was, so she must be safe. After much soulsearching she decided to lie low until the police found Carl Rose.

Later, when she had calmed down, she started to look through her old photo album. She had been rummaging for some extra blankets in the blanket box at the end of the bed and came across it by accident. She sat cross-legged on the bed and flipped absently through the pages as one does, smiling at the memories that drifted in and out of her head.

The summer of sixty-seven was very prominently recorded in the dilapidated volume. That was the long hot summer when she had met Warren. He was known as Georgie then, of course. Her girlfriend, Vonnie, had set her up with him on a blind date. Tessa, who had never been on a blind date before, was expecting a disaster, so she couldn't believe her luck when Warren had shown up in his little green MG Midget to pick her up. He was the most handsome man she had ever seen. They had driven out into the country to a little pub for dinner, and they sat and talked well into the night until the restaurant manager had thrown them out. They were both in their final year at Liverpool Poly and, unknown to Tessa, Warren had arranged with Vonnie to set up the date. He had seen Tessa round the campus, and was terrified of rejection by the woman of his dreams. Warren had a wicked sense of humour and would do anything for a laugh. They had married the week after their finals and hadn't been apart for more than two nights since.

After they left college Warren had gone on a management course with a supermarket chain and Tessa studied teacher training. They bobbed along happily for seven years and then she gave up her career to have their son. She loved being home all day looking after her baby and spoiling Warren when he came home from work in the evenings. One day Warren brought home a colleague, Lou Armitage. She took an instant dislike to him for no understandable reason, but kept the fair side out. He stayed for dinner and soon became a regular visitor. Shortly afterwards Warren told her that he Lou and Gary, an old college friend of both Tessa and Warren, were going into business together. She was naturally excited at the prospect. They were on the verge of the prosperous eighties and Lou, Gary and Warren assured her that they would all make their fortunes. It was only six months later, when the three associates needed her to run the office, that Warren dropped the bombshell about the true nature of the business. At first she was terrified and wanted him to get out, but he promised her that there wouldn't be any repercussions and that, after all, companies had insurance to cover those sort of losses.

How was she to know that Frank Dodd would kill himself, that wasn't supposed to happen. Delmarco Steffani wasn't supposed to go belly up either. She felt particularly bad about that. Claudio Steffani and his wife Sophia had been so hospitable when she and Warren had visited them in Milan. She hoped that she would never have to face them again. She continued to flip the pages and came across a group shot of all the staff of WAG. Supply Company. She shuddered. They were all there, Warren, Lou, Gary, the four warehouse lads and Frank Dodd standing at the end of the row, all smiling at the camera, frozen for posterity. Frank Dodd stared out at her. She snapped the book shut. A sudden gust of wind slapped the branches of the rhododendron against the window-pane and she nearly jumped out of her skin. "Don't be foolish," she said aloud. She clambered off the bed and switched on the radio for some noise. She shivered, the room had grown cold. She walked back into the kitchen where the warmth of the Aga was comforting. Outside it was dismal and quite dark, considering that it was only just after two in the afternoon. She felt very alone.

Chapter Eleven

The following morning Grace went down to the office and found Phoebe already there.

"What was the name of the Italian company that lost nearly a million?" Phoebe asked absently, as if her mind was on something else. Grace rooted through the file of companies that WAG had defrauded and read down the list.

"Delmarco Steffani. Their head office is in Milan. It was a family owned firm. They went under when WAG failed to pay them. The son of the founder, Angelo Steffani, went to Liverpool Fraud Squad before anyone else. Apparently he was uneasy with WAG from the start, but his old man wouldn't listen. He called at the WAG warehouse when his telexes went unanswered and found that the birds had flown, along with his million. How many lire do you think there are in a million quid?"

"Lots I should think," Phoebe said, and reached over the desk for the file. "Why don't we see if we can trace Angelo Steffani? It says here that he's in London, working for the Italian Trade Centre."

"So phone him. I know it's a long time, but he may have some information or may even be involved with Carl Rose." Grace looked up the number and dialled, but was told that Steffani was now in the Dublin Embassy.

"Better still," Grace said and rang the Embassy. "But I think you should see him. You're more likely to loosen the tongue of a hot-blooded Latin than I am."

Dermot meanwhile had just received the forensic report on Archie Leach. All it had to tell him was that the screwdriver was a standard size and make, on sale all over the country, and the capsules were Mogadon, the twist being that they were Leach's own prescription drugs. So that raised the possibility that they could have been self-administered. Dermot mused on this. What if, after hearing about the murder of his two associates, he was driven to despair at the thought of losing everything if the past were to come to light? And so resolved to take his life, only to be disturbed by Carl Rose who, not knowing what Leach had decided to do, killed him. No, he thought. Too far-fetched. His thoughts were disturbed by the phone. It was the duty sergeant.

"I thought you might be interested, sir. We just had a call from The Oaks. There's been a break-in reported."

He and Hugh O'Boyle arrived at the same time as the technical team, and a Garda on duty by the gate let them through. Mrs Danvers was sitting in the kitchen drinking a glass of sherry. She jumped up when she saw them and started to babble.

"I only came in an hour ago and found it a shambles. I was afraid that whoever had done it was still here."

"Calm down, Mrs Danvers. No need to get upset," said Dermot. "I'd like you to walk round the house with me and see if you can determine if anything's missing."

"I'll do my best," she said.

Suddenly a thought struck Dermot. "Where's the dog?"

She started to cry and pointed out of the window. Dermot looked out and saw the dog lying in the yard, stiff and very dead-looking.

"Is he dead?" he asked, knowing the answer. She just nodded and unable to speak mouthed the word, Poisoned.

When Mrs Danvers said the house was a shambles she was grossly exaggerating. Only the ibrary had been disturbed, and only the desk ind a chest of drawers had been tampered with. Whoever was responsible had been looking for something specific. An address perhaps, a name?

Dermot walked over to the french windows. The glass had been taped and cut neatly with a glass cutter. The tape had prevented the glass from falling to the floor. The technical officer was dusting the glass for prints, but it was clean. Hugh, who was outside, called to Dermot, "There's a clear footprint here sir. Looks like the others." He was kneeling on the ground by the flowerbed.

Mrs Danvers was standing by the door wringing her apron between her hands. "Mayo," she said suddenly apropos of nothing.

"Sorry?" said Dermot.

"Mayo, that's where Mrs Peace has her cottage."

"Could you be any more specific?"

Dermot could see that she was close to the edge. "Near Westport or Mulranny, I think."

"Hugh! Call in and get dispatch to call Westport Garda Station and Mulranny. Tessa Peace has a cottage somewhere between the two. We need them to make sure that she's OK and then to get back to us." He suddenly remembered Eoin. "The boy! Mrs Danvers, where is Eoin at school?"

He was livid with himself for having forgotten

about him. Mrs. Danvers had walked out of earshot and hadn't heard him so he hurried after her. He found her back in the kitchen with her glass of sherry.

"Saint Jude's College. It's outside Athlone," she remembered after some thought. Dermot went to the hall and found the number of the college on the phone-pad. He dialled and got through to the headmaster who in turn went to call Eoin. After what seemed like an age a very flustered Head came back on the line. "I'm afraid I can't locate him just at the present."

Dermot was silent for a moment. "What do you mean?"

"Well. He doesn't seem to be here, but I'm sure he'll be back soon."

Alarm bells started to ring in Dermot's head. "When was the last time he was seen, Brother Kevin?" Brother Kevin was slow to answer. "Think, man. He could be in danger!"

That kicked the Head into gear. "About an hour ago. His form had a free study period. Then, I suppose."

"Think carefully. Have you any idea where the Peaces' holiday cottage is in Mayo?"

Brother Kevin hummed and hawed and waffled, but in the end he had no idea.

Dermot got straight on the radio to put out a general call to all areas in the State for Tessa and

Eoin Peace. He hoped his memory lapse wouldn't be the cause of any harm coming to either of them. His worst fears were confirmed when a black Harley Davidson, registered to Carl Rose, was found abandoned outside Athlone and a Toyota Starlet was reported missing in the same area. Both incidents had occurred within thirty yards of each other. He called Hugh, and the two of them drove straight off at speed towards Athlone.

Fifty minutes later they skidded to a halt on the gravel drive of Saint Jude's College. It was an imposing ivy-clad Gothic structure dating from the eighteen-thirties.

"Bet this place costs a few bob," said Hugh as they waited by the massive front door. They were shown to the headmaster's office and Brother Kevin sent for Eoin's two room-mates.

The first boy was Eoin's best friend, a pleasant-looking confident lad called Forrest Grimes. He and another boy, called Paul Zombieu, shared a study with Eoin, and they had been studying together just before he went missing.

"One of the younger boys, I think it was Egan minor, came up and said that someone was asking for him at the lodge," said Forrest. "He just dropped what he was doing and went down."

"What time would that have been?"

Forrest thought for a moment then said, "Just after eleven, I think."

"Did Egan minor see the visitor?" asked Dermot.

"I don't think so. You'd have to ask him. But the porter would have answered the bell."

Paul Zombieu had the same story as Forrest, so Dermot asked him to send in the porter. A maid came shortly afterwards while they were still waiting for the porter, with a tray of coffee and biscuits. Hugh looked at the plate. "I hate Bourbon Creams," he said and poured two cups of coffee. Dermot looked round the Headmaster's office. It was the room of a true academic, book-lined from floor to ceiling with scholarly well-thumbed volumes. He got up from his chair and walked over to the window. It was dull outside and he could only see his own reflection in the glass. He felt Eoin's disappearance was due to his incompetence and was angry with himself, though he didn't share his thoughts with Hugh, munching the Bourbon creams despite his declared hatred of them.

There was a tap on the door and the porter walked in. Peter Adams was in his late fifties, and, according to Brother Kevin, had worked for the College for twenty years. He had no difficulty remembering Eoin's visitor.

"He was youngish. About twenty-three or so," he said. "He just came to the lodge and asked for

Mr Peace. Said he had a message for him from his mother."

"And that was about eleven?" Dermot asked.

Adams nodded. "About that, or a little after."

Hugh asked, "Could you describe him?"

"Medium height, fair hair, pleasant looking. He had on a biker's jacket, but he didn't look like a biker, if you know what I mean. He was too neat and tidy."

"Can you remember anything else about him? Accent, anything like that?"

"Yes, now you mention it. He talked like Ringo Starr." Dermot showed him the photofit of Dodd, aka Rose. He took it and peered closely at it. "Yeah. That's him."

It was pretty certain Carl would want to dump the car and get as far away from the area as quickly as possible. Dermot wondered if it had been an opportunist spur-of-the-moment crime, or if Carl had planned the operation beforehand. If it was the latter option he was going to be much harder to trace. The men called at the local Garda Station. Brother Kevin had phoned them as soon as he had realised that one of his pupils was missing, telling them about Dermot's fears for his safety.

Sergeant Kelly met Dermot and Hugh at the front desk and took them up to CID.

"We set up road blocks as soon as Brother

Kevin phoned, but I'd say the bird had long flown. We put out a call for the car though."

Dermot nodded. "Good. Good," he said.

"What makes you think the lad's been abducted anyway?" asked Kelly. "Maybe he's just gone off."

"I doubt it," said Dermot irritated. "He's hardly likely to go off voluntarily with his father's murderer." He got on to the Westport Gardaí again to see if they had located Tessa Peace.

* * *

Tessa was unaware that Eoin had been abducted by Carl Rose. She didn't know who Carl Rose really was. Neither did she realise that the Westport Gardaí were checking the area trying to locate her.

She watched every TV news bulletin in the hope of hearing that Carl Rose had been apprehended so that she would feel safe enough to go home. When Archie's murder was reported it came as no surprise. She knew it was inevitable. In some ways that was the least of her problems. What would happen to her life now, particularly if the past was dredged up? Would she lose everything? Would she be implicated in the fraud? Would she go to prison? Then another more horrifying thought struck her. What if the killer was looking for her right now?

Terror and panic overtook her. She ran to the bathroom and vomited in the toilet. Oh God! Why is this happening to me? What am I going to do?

She splashed her face with cold water and felt a little better. Get a grip, she said out loud, looking at her reflection in the mirror over the sink. After several deep breaths her heart rate slowed down enough so that her stomach stopped trying to defy gravity. Then she sat on the edge of the bath and tried to think.

Suddenly with a chilling certainty she knew who Carl Rose was. She ran back into the bedroom and grabbed the photo album, frantically flipping through the pages. Then there it was, the Christmas party nineteen-seventy-nine. Warren with Lou. Warren with Gary and Frank. Sitting on Frank's knee was Eoin, then aged six, and standing behind his father was Carl Dodd, tall, blond and gangly as only a twelve-year-old youth can be.

Was this the face of Warren's killer, this young fresh-faced innocent-looking boy? Tessa still felt guilty about Frank's suicide. Her anger with Warren had taken a long time to pass. *But you promised that no one would get hurt,* she had screamed at him. *You said that it was like a practical joke with a big punchline.* And he had yelled back at her, *It's not my fault that he lost his bottle.* Warren had always maintained that Frank knew the score and had been well paid for his trouble. That it was his own stupid fault that the law caught up with him. Tessa wasn't so sure anymore, and what else had Warren lied to her about? Curtis had said that the police were asking him if Warren had a mistress. Why did they ask such a question? Had he betrayed her after all?

A loud rapping on the door of the cottage made her jump. She sat paralysed for a moment then leaped up and looked out of the window. A white garda car was parked outside. She felt a wave of relief and ran to answer the knocking. A tall garda was standing under the porch, trying to shelter from the rain.

"Would you be Tessa Peace?" he asked.

"Yes. What do you want?"

"Inspector Dermot McEvoy of Dublin asked us to trace you. He was concerned for your safety."

"Oh," said Tessa. "Why? I'm fine."

"Inspector McEvoy asked us to take you to the station for your own protection. He's coming down to take you back home."

"But why?" she insisted.

"Carl Rose has been sighted at your son's school, and your son is missing."

Her hand flew involuntarily to her mouth. "Oh God. Not Eoin."

"It looks as if he's been abducted by Carl Rose. The Inspector thinks that you should be at home in case he tries to make contact with you."

When Tessa didn't move he said, "Mrs Peace?"

She snapped back to consciousness. "Yes yes. I'll get my things." Tessa collected her belongings together like a robot. *If he harms one hair on Eoin's head I'll kill him.* Then she realised how futile a thought that was. Carl was only avenging his own father's death. The boy must have been harbouring the thought of revenge for the past twelve years. How did he find them? If McEvoy had identified Carl Rose, he must know about the WAG affair. The game was up.

As she drove behind the Garda car towards the country town, she had a dread in her heart that her own very precious son might also be a victim of Warren's practical joke. But unlike the others he would be an innocent victim.

Two hours later Dermot and Hugh walked into Westport Garda Station after a dash down from Athlone. All things considered, they had made excellent time. Dermot's eyes had been shut for most of the way and Hugh had used the siren from time to time, prompting very careful and polite driving from a lot of surprised motorists.

Tessa was waiting for them in an interview room nursing a cold half-empty cup of tea.

"Have you found him?" she asked, jumping up the minute Dermot and Hugh entered the room. "Is Eoin all right?"

"Not yet, Mrs Peace, but we hope it won't be long. Please, sit down, we have to talk." He tried to sound comforting.

Tessa was shaking her head, very agitated. "No. No. You should be trying to find him before something happens, not hanging round here. Please, please find my son."

She stood very close to Dermot, looking into his face and had knocked her cup of tea off the table onto the floor. The shards of the cup crunched under their feet but she didn't seem to notice.

"Sit down, Tessa. We have to talk." His voice had an edge now that made her realise he didn't just want to talk about Eoin.

Dermot and Hugh sat side by side across the table from Tessa. "Would you like some fresh tea?" Dermot asked. She shook her head. "You know what I want to talk to you about, don't you, Tessa?" She stared down at the table, making patterns in the spilt tea with her index finger. After a moment she nodded. Dermot took out his note-book and flipped through the pages. "What can you tell me about Carl Rose, Tessa?"

"You know about WAG don't you?" she said.

Dermot nodded. "Yes, but if we'd known sooner Gary Grant and Lou Armitage might still be alive. Why didn't you tell us about WAG and Carl Rose?"

After a long pause she said, "I didn't know who Carl Rose was. I only just realised tonight that he must be Frank Dodd's son, so I didn't think WAG was relevant."

"I bet you didn't," said Dermot. "How did you find out who Carl is?"

"I found his picture in an old photo album and put two and two together."

"You must have realised that after all the misery that the four of you caused, there was a possibility that the WAG business must have had something to do with your husband's murder?"

She banged her hands on the table. "We didn't cause misery. We didn't," she yelled. Dermot stared passively at her across the table. She was half sitting half standing with her hands flat on the table surface, her face livid.

"Get real, Tessa! What about Frank Dodd? What about Carlo Steffani? What about the dozens of small companies who went to the wall when you and Warren and Lou and Gary buggered off with two million pounds?"

"They said no one would get hurt," she said, and slowly sat, resting her head on her arms.

"They said that the companies had insurance. Anyway Frank Dodd knew the score, he wasn't an innocent victim. He was just stupid."

Dermot looked at Hugh and cast his eyes up to heaven. "Do you really believe that, Tessa? Do you really think he would have walked into the arms of the fraud squad that morning if he had really known what was going on?"

"What did Curtis Clough have to do with it? He was involved, wasn't he?" asked Hugh after a pause, giving her time to take in what Dermot had just said.

Tessa wearily raised her head. "We ran short of cash and the whole pyramid was in danger of toppling. It was just before the last huge orders were going to be placed, it was critical. Anyway, Curtis was an old friend and I knew he was quite well off, so I contacted him. I think he still had a thing about me, so I played on it and he finally agreed to invest."

Dermot took that in. "You realise that that makes him also a potential victim?"

"I think he realises that himself," she said. "He'll keep out of the way, he'll be on his guard." Dermot told her about Clough's heart attack.

"I know. But he'll live," she said. She didn't appear to be too concerned.

"Perhaps, if we can keep him away from Carl Rose."

Dermot drove Tessa back to Dublin in her car and Hugh followed. They arrived back in the early hours of the morning. Dermot left Tessa at The Oaks with a police guard and went home to get some sleep.

Chapter Twelve

Grace met Luke on the door step of Archie Leach's house the following morning. He sighed when he saw her approach. "I don't suppose there's much point in asking you to leave?" he said.

She shook her head emphatically. "No, and please don't give me a hard time about it. Besides, she may open up to me more than she will to you."

"Are you casting doubt on my natural boyish charm?"

Grace snorted and rang the doorbell. Alison was a good deal younger than she appeared in the photo and Grace guessed she was about thirty. Her spectacular body was encased in a skin-tight leopard-print jump-suit which left little to the imagination. Grace noticed Luke's gaze travel slowly up and down her body. Her hair was very blonde and cut extremely short, accentuating her tan and very high cheekbones. Too many gold bracelets jangled on her wrists and she wore gold stiletto-heeled mules. Her enormous brown eyes were bloodshot from crying and mascara was smudged under the lower lids onto her cheeks. The children weren't in evidence.

Like the previous victims, Archie Leach and his family lived in splendour. His home was a seventeenth-century stone rectory. The interior design was exquisite and entirely furnished with good antiques. Grace recognized a Chippendale settle and a couple of Stubbs on the walls of the hall. Judging by Alison Leach's sense of style the house had clearly had been decorated by an interior designer. There was a smell of beeswax polish and old wood.

She seemed reasonably composed when they arrived and offered them coffee which they refused. Grace asked her about the last time she had seen her husband.

"About six the night he died. He had a phonecall and said he had to go out. I was annoyed because we were supposed to be going to dinner with some friends."

"Did he say where he was going?"

She shook her head vigorously, making her heavy gold earrings clank. "No. He just said it was out of his control. We had a row and he just drove off." She was becoming distressed. "The last thing I said to him was *piss off.*" She put her head in her hands and started to sob.

After she had calmed down a bit, Luke said, "Have you any idea who the call was from?"

"No. But he had an accent."

Grace looked at Luke. "You spoke to him?" she asked. Alison Leach nodded. "In a way, I mean I just answered the phone, gave the number and when he asked for Archie I asked him to hold the line."

"Oh," said Grace. "Do you know if your husband knew the caller?"

This time Alison shook her head and said nothing. After some coaxing they discovered that Archie Leach had owned four health clubs and a residential spa. They had met six years before when she had gone to work at one of the clubs as an aerobics instructor. She was his second wife, but the two children were from his first marriage. She was vague about his previous history including the discarded wife, and Grace didn't know if her reticence was genuine ignorance or something else entirely. All she appeared to know was that her late husband had bought his first two clubs twelve years previously.

When they got outside again Luke told her about Eoin's apparent abduction and about Tessa having surfaced.

"How is she?"

"Not the best," Luke said. "Dermot's put a guard on the house but as far as I know Carl Rose hasn't been in contact yet."

"I think I should go over to The Oaks," she said, as she got into her car. "See you around."

Luke drove off ahead of her, and she tried to reach Phoebe on the mobile at the office to give her the news. Xin told her that Phoebe had already left the office to see "some Italian fella."

★ ★ ★

Phoebe found a parking meter quite close to the Italian Embassy and arrived five minutes early for her appointment. An athletic-looking Australian girl showed her to Angelo Steffani's office.

When she saw him standing up behind his desk to greet her, her first reaction was that Angelo was a thoroughly appropriate name for this angel, for he was tall, dark and drop dead handsome! Regaining her breath, she introduced herself, and he invited her to sit.

"I don't know how I can be of help. That WAG affair was a very long time ago," he said.

He had only the slightest trace of an accent, which Phoebe found very attractive. She judged that he must be in his early forties. He had a few flecks of grey at the temples and deeply tanned unwrinkled skin.

"Well, the enquiry isn't directly connected with the fraud investigation Mr Steffani. It concerns the murder of the three principals, George Warren, Lou Armitage and Gary Grant."

He looked stunned. "I didn't see this reported in the media," he said.

"The victims were all living under assumed names. They were known as Warren Peace, Armitage Shanks and Archie Leach."

He gave a bitter laugh. "It is my loss that someone found them before I." He paused, looking down at the polished surface of his desk. "You have heard of vendetta, Miss Lamplighter?" Phoebe nodded. "In my country we take the vendetta very seriously. If I had found these pieces of shit first, I assure you they would have suffered a much worse fate."

"What's worse than dead?" Phoebe asked.

"The manner in which that end is achieved," he replied.

The Australian girl came in with a tray of coffee and laid it on the desk.

"Graze," he said and she left the room. There was a silence while he handed Phoebe a cup of coffee. Then he looked at her and said, "I wouldn't look too hard for the killer of those unspeakable people, Miss Lamplighter. They have done a public service." He paused, watching her reaction, then went on. "I didn't trust George

Warren from the start, there was something about him. My father unfortunately thought otherwise and it led to his death. He and my mother entertained Warren and his wife in their home. They thought he was a friend. When the facts proved otherwise and the company failed as a result, the shame killed him."

"I'm sorry to have to ask you this, Mr Steffani, but can you account for your movements at the time of the murders?"

Steffani burst out laughing. "Yes, I'm sure I can," he said. "Do you have a list of the times and places?" Phoebe was puzzled by his attitude. She gave him a list of the dates.

"What do you find so funny?" she asked.

He wiped his now streaming eyes with a silk handkerchief. "I'm sorry," he said. "I'm sorry. I am just surprised that you would ask such a question. Do you think I would be so stupid as to actually do the deed myself?"

Phoebe cleared her throat. "Well. Did you?"

Gently mocking her he said, "It is my eternal regret to say that I'm afraid the answer is no." He looked at the list of dates she had given him. "On two of these days I was involved in the Food Fair at the RDS. But then I would have an alibi, wouldn't I." He gave her a crooked smile and she felt herself redden.

"Can anyone corroborate that?" she asked.

He started to laugh again, it was unnerving. "Yes. Ask your President Robinson, she opened the exhibition. I met Gay Byrne on the second day and on the third date I was in Turino. You can check with my Embassy staff."

"Do you know a man by the name of Carl Rose, also known as Carl Dodd?"

He wrinkled his gorgeous brow. "Dodd? Was that not the name of the unfortunate manager of WAG?"

"Yes," said Phoebe. "Carl is his son."

"Is he a suspect?"

"The Gardaí want to speak to him," said Phoebe, not committing herself.

"I don't know Carl Rose, but if I meet him I will certainly shake him by the hand."

Phoebe could see that she was, sadly, going to get no further with Angelo Steffani. "Thank you for your help, Mr Steffani. And I'm sorry about your father."

He shrugged. "It was all a long time ago. But you understand why I cannot give even a pretence of sorrow for the fate of those men?"

Phoebe nodded. "Yes," she said. "But that doesn't make what happened to them right."

"I didn't have anything to do with it, Miss Lamplighter," he said. And she believed him.

* * *

Grace met Dermot for lunch in Smyths and she told him about Phoebe's interview with Angelo Steffani.

"She doesn't think that he's involved in any conspiracy with Carl Rose."

"Neither do I," said Dermot. "We still haven't had any word from Rose about Eoin Peace though. I hope he's looking for a ransom and doesn't just mean to kill him too."

"How did Luke Ryan get on with the mother?"

"He's not back yet."

"It's a mess, isn't it? I have to say it feels weird to be working for Tessa Peace."

"I thought she fired you," he said trying to hide a smirk.

"That was a temporary glith," she said and hoped that she was right. "What did she have to say about the LF?"

Dermot gave a wry laugh. "She pretended to be naive. Says that there was no harm in it, that no one got hurt. I think she has some idea that they were all Robin Hoods or some other bullshit. I mean, do you believe that?"

"Funnily enough," she said. "I do."

★ ★ ★

The neat tree-lined avenue in Finglas was still quiet when Luke and Jack Mulloy parked outside number seven Ardlane Park. Jack Mulloy stayed in the car while Luke got out and looked over the privet hedge. He saw that the garden was well kept, one single pint of milk stood on the doorstep and a newspaper was sticking out of the letterbox. He pressed the doorbell and after some time he heard footsteps coming down the stairs. A middle-aged woman in a candlewick housecoat opened the door a few inches and peered out at him.

"Yes?" she said, inclining her head to one side.

Luke held up his warrant card, introduced himself then said "Mrs Dodd?"

She squinted at the print on the warrant card. "Rose. My name's Rose. What do you want?" she asked without any attempt at charm.

"I need to ask you a few questions about your late husband."

"Why? Why after all this time?" she asked squinting up her eyes to get a good look at him. The door was still open only six inches and Luke noticed that it was secured with a safety chain.

"It's in connection with a murder enquiry we're involved with. You could be a great help . . . "

She slammed the door in Luke's face, nearly hitting him on the nose. He stepped back and was about to ring the bell again when he heard the rattle of the chain. The door was opened again.

"You'd better come in," she said, turning on her heel and went through a door to the right. Luke followed.

She lit the gas fire and sat on the edge of an armchair waiting for him to speak.

"Are you aware that Georgie Warren, Lou Armitage and Gary Grant have all been found murdered within the past week, Mrs Dodd?"

She stared at him, open-mouthed. "I didn't see anything on the TV."

Luke realised that the victim's real names hadn't been given to the media. "The three victims were known by aliases. They used the names Warren Peace, Armitage Shanks and Archie Leach."

Slowly it dawned on her, and her face hardened. "It wasn't half good enough for those bastards," she said spitting out the words. "That filth killed my husband. They ruined our lives. I hope they rot in hell." Her voice was rising.

"What do you mean they killed your husband?"

"As good as." The silence hung. Luke looked around the room and his gaze stopped at a group of three framed photos on the television. One was a print of the photo they had seen in Carl's digs and another bore a close resemblance to Dwyer's photofit.

"We're looking for Carl, Mrs Dodd, do you know where he is?"

"Why do you want him?" she snapped.

"He's involved in the murders. He's using the name Carl Rose now, did you know that?"

"Of course. We reverted to my maiden name after Frank died," she said. "The boy took it all very hard. But why do you think he's involved? He's never been violent." Her fists were clenched

160

in her lap as she spoke and she was leaning forward in her chair, full of tension.

"Where is your son now?" Luke asked gently, ignoring her question. Suddenly she slapped her hand to her mouth, a look of horror on her face. "Oh my God. He's in Dublin, isn't he? But he couldn't . . . " She left the sentence unfinished, and sat frozen on her chair.

"Could I borrow this picture?" Luke said, picking it up off the TV. "I'll get it back to you by tomorrow."

"It's not him, he wouldn't be capable of it." Her eyes were pleading, willing him to agree with her, and Luke felt a deep pity for her. She had lost her husband because of the three men, now it seemed to her they were going to be the cause of her losing her son.

"We just need to talk to him, Mrs Dodd. He may well be innocent, but if he is, we need to question him in order to eliminate him from the enquiry."

She wasn't convinced and jumped to her feet. "You want to take him from me. Eliminate him? I've heard how you lot work. Once you get your hands on him, you'll fit him up, just like you fitted up my Frank." Luke tried to speak but she shouted him down and started to beat her fists on his chest.

"I'll never help you get anywhere near him. Never. Now get out of my house and leave me in peace."

Luke grabbed hold of her wrists. "Calm down. Calm down," he said. "No one is going to fit up your son. We need to ask him about a meeting he had

161

with Warren Peace, Georgie Warren. That's all."

"I don't believe you." She sank down onto the chair and he let go of her. She wept quietly. Luke left her be. After a few minutes she mumbled, "He was so pleased to get that job."

"What job?" said Luke.

But she ignored the question and went on, "He'd been made redundant and we'd nearly lost the house. Then Georgie bloody Warren offered him that bloody job." She stared past him at nothing. "Georgie bloody Warren. Life and soul of the party." She looked up at Luke, who let her talk. "He thought everything was a joke. I bet he split his sides when he thought about my Frank getting back from holiday to find the warehouse crawling with police." She looked up at Luke again, tears welling in her sad eyes. "It was the first time we'd been abroad. When Frank got to the warehouse on that Monday he thought there'd been a robbery at first. It only dawned on him that he was in bother after he'd spent two days in a police cell." She was staring at the carpet now. "If I'd found the bastards first. I'd have done for them, but not my Carl."

"Do you know where he is now?"

"No. I don't." In the end she let him take the photo on condition that he returned it the next day. Luke felt a deep sympathy for her and asked her to try to persuade Carl to give himself up if he contacted her. She didn't answer, but he felt sure that she wouldn't.

162

Chapter Thirteen

Eoin was sitting on the floor where Carl had left him a couple of hours before. He was tightly fastened to a hefty pipe which ran along the wall. His hands and feet were tied with lengths of plastic coated wire. Carl had met him outside the lodge and told him that his mother had asked him to collect him from school and take him to her. That she was in hiding from his father's murderer. Eoin believed him and got willingly into the car. Then Carl got into the back on some pretext that he couldn't remember. The next thing Carl slapped something strong-smelling over his mouth and nose from behind, and he passed out.

When he came to, he was lying on the floor of the car under a blanket with his hands tied behind his back. The drive was bumpy and he felt sick. He didn't know how long they had been driving, but eventually Carl stopped the car and got out. Eoin lay there for what seemed quite some time before he heard footsteps and the car door opened. Carl pulled the blanket off. He grabbed Eoin under the armpits, dragged him into a sitting position and undid his bonds.

"Behave yourself and walk into the house quietly. Nothing will happen to you if you do as you're told."

"Who are you? Why are you doing this?" Eoin asked.

"I'm Carl Rose," he answered, assuming that the statement would explain everything, but Eoin was none the wiser. Carl roughly hurried him towards a door which led down a flight of steps to a basement.

"What do you want with me?" persisted Eoin. Carl said nothing and, when they were standing by the wall, whipped Eoin's feet from under him with a swipe behind the knees. Eoin landed on the cold floor a little dazed. Carl tied his hands to a pipe a little above his head, and then fastened his ankles together with the wire. All this he did in silence. Eventually he said,

"I don't really know what I'm going to do with you. Perhaps your precious mother will pay to get you back. Who knows, eh?" With that he turned and ran up the stairs, snapping off the light and banging the door shut.

Eoin was cold. When Carl had given him the fictitious message from his mother, he had wanted to go back to his study to get a jacket but Carl said that there was no time. As a result, now he was sitting on the cold floor in just his jeans and a sweatshirt. About an hour later Carl returned. He had a big cushion and blanket with him and Eoin noticed the smell of chips. He dropped the cushion beside Eoin and said, "Shift over onto that."

"Thanks," Eoin said. Carl unbound his hands and let him eat the chips out of the paper. He gobbled hungrily. He hadn't had anything since breakfast and he was starving. He looked up at Carl, who was holding a sawn-off shotgun under his arm.

"Have you decided what you're going to do?" he asked. Carl stared down at his captive. "No, not yet. I haven't decided, but don't try to tell me that you don't know what this is about," he said.

Eoin shook his head "I don't." Then, "Did you kill my father?"

"Yes," said Carl, a little surprised by the directness of the question. "Though it was an accident. I only meant to take the money but the nail gun went off and that was that." He said it without any trace of emotion. Eoin didn't know if the shiver that went down his spine was caused by the cold or Carl's detached attitude.

"What about Uncle Lou?"

Carl laughed. "That was no accident. That bastard was the worst of them. He said that my father was stupid to go back, but how was Dad to know what those bastards had set him up for?"

"What do you mean?"

Carl stared down at him, then shook his head slowly. "You really don't know. Do you?" he said and sat opposite Eoin on a wooden crate. "I hope that you're sitting comfortably because I'm going to tell you a story."

Much later Eoin sat stunned. He couldn't believe that his parents could have been responsible for all that Carl claimed, but it would explain a few things. Why they had moved so suddenly from Liverpool. Why they had had to change their names. At the time his mother had told him that it was because someone was after them, that had seemed plausible, a little exciting even. He had never questioned who was after them, like any six-year-old he took what his parents said on trust. Eoin thought about that for a while. How stupid can you get?

They had lied all these years, being holier than thou when he got into bother for smoking dope at school and was gated for three weeks. It seemed so hypocritical after what they had done. If what Carl said was true, then his own father had been responsible for Frank Dodd committing suicide. He remembered Frank, though he hadn't recognised Carl at first, and didn't recognise the name Rose. After all, he had only been six the last time that they had met. He had liked Frank who used to carry him round the warehouse on his shoulders.

Eventually he fell into an uneasy sleep, wrapped in the blanket against the cold. He was woken the next morning by Carl who brought him a cup of coffee.

"I've decided to ask your old woman for a ransom and see what happens," he said.

"How much are you going to ask for?"

Carl shrugged. "How much do you reckon that she's good for?"

"I don't know. Quite a lot I should think. But I don't know if she'd be able to get a lot of cash at short notice. You'd have to give her time to get it together."

Carl bent over Eoin and loosened his hands, they had gone a little blue and he rubbed them between his own to get the circulation going.

"I'm sorry, I'll put a longer bit of wire on so you'll be a bit more comfortable."

"Thanks," said Eoin and tried to pick up the cup of coffee but his hands still had no feeling. Carl, seeing his predicament, held the cup to his lips and Eoin drank the hot liquid gratefully.

"You know we're the victims, not our parents," said Eoin after a while. "We didn't have any say in how they screwed up our lives."

"I don't see how your life's so screwed up," sneered Carl. "Boarding school, pots of money, every chance."

"Oh sure. I never asked to go away to school. And as for pots of money, that's not everything. Try being pushed into achieving and not making the grade. Try having your old man's constant disapproval because you're not the best at everything. You can have all that as far as I'm concerned. All he was interested in was 'appearances'. He went loopy when I wasn't made captain of this or head of that, and he totally humiliated me by coming up to the school and bawling out Brother Kevin because I wasn't made head boy."

"There was no love lost between you then?"

Eoin replied bitterly, "Not a lot."

"I wondered why you were so cool at the funeral."

"You were there?" said Eoin, surprised.

"Sure. That's where I clocked Armitage and Grant, I thought all my Christmases had come at once," Carl said without a trace of humour in his voice.

"Did you get him?" Eoin hadn't heard about his Uncle Archie.

Carl nodded. "I followed him the night before last and he stopped in Herbert Park. I saw him just sitting in the car in the dark so I got in beside him. I think he was expecting me. Anyway, he told me that he'd taken an overdose. I didn't believe him but then he keeled over so I stabbed him with a screwdriver just to make sure and did the hose job again."

"Why did you bother with the hose?"

"It was a message. That's how my old man topped himself." Carl was staring down at his shoes. "I found him you know, stiff as a board, his face all blue. I can still see him in my dreams."

"I'm sorry."

"Yes," said Carl. "I think you probably are."

Chapter Fourteen

Tessa was glad to reinstate Sleuths. Phoebe persuaded her that at least they would act in her and Eoin's best interests, rather than the Gardai, who would be more concerned with apprehending Carl Rose. Tessa requested that one of them be at the house at all times until the whole nightmare was over.

She was beside herself with worry, pacing up and down, incapable of staying still. The phonecall had been very brief. Just a voice, obviously Carl's, saying that he had Eoin, and two hundred grand would get him home safely.

"Where can I get that kind of cash," was all she could say over and over. Carl told Tessa that he would call the following day with instructions for the hand-over. She had started to protest, saying that she would need time, but Carl had hung up the phone quickly, presumably afraid of the call being traced.

"We don't usually encourage people to pay ransoms, Tessa," said Dermot. "But under the circumstances I think you had better seriously consider it. Carl has nothing to lose, he's killed three times already."

"I know. I know, but where am I going to get the cash? I don't have two hundred thousand!" She was nearly hysterical. Grace asked, "How much can you raise?"

Tessa thought for a while, "About a hundred thousand I suppose, maybe a bit more."

"Would that be liquid cash?"

"Yes. Curtis may be able to lend me some more against Warren's shares in Clough Peace."

"Then I think you'd better start to organise it. Can you get on to your bank to arrange a withdrawal?"

Tessa nodded and went out to the hall to make the call. "I don't think she'll have much luck with Clough, he isn't in any condition to help. We'd better try and get her to negotiate on the amount of ready cash that she can get her hands on," said Dermot. As he was speaking the doorbell rang. Phoebe went out to answer it.

Angelo Steffani was standing on the doorstep in the company of another man whom Phoebe didn't know.

"Miss Lamplighter," he said. "How pleasant to see you again."

"Mr Steffani. What can I do for you?" she said, fully aware of the innuendo in the question. She smiled as she spoke.

"We would like to see Tessa Peace," he said. "And I don't have any concealed weapons on my person." He smiled back at her and opened his hands to show that they were empty. "This is Alec Gilchrist, my solicitor, we just need to speak with Tessa."

Tessa was standing behind Phoebe in the hall, still on the phone to her bank. As she replaced the receiver she turned towards the open front door and Phoebe heard her gasp as she recognised Angelo Steffani.

Angelo looked past Phoebe into the hall. "Hello, Tessa. I think the English phrase is *long time no see*," he said.

Tessa just stood open-mouthed, staring at him as if he were a ghost. Dermot came out into the hall at this point.

"What's going on?" he asked.

Phoebe introduced him to the beautiful Italian and his lawyer and Dermot suggested that they all go into the drawingroom. Tessa was still standing stunned and horrified so Phoebe took her by the arm and guided her through the door. Once they were all in the room, Alec Gilchrist took out a folded document from his crocodile skin briefcase and handed it to Tessa.

171

"What's this?" she asked looking at the paper in her hand.

"It's a notice of intent. My client has started civil proceedings against you personally to recover a debt of long standing."

"What?"

Phoebe said, "I think what Mr Gilchrist is trying to say is that Mr Steffani is suing you for the money that WAG failed to pay Delmarco Steffani."

"That and the compound interest," said Gilchrist.

"Suing me?" said Tessa, unable to take it in. "You can't do that. WAG was a limited liability company, I'm not liable."

"I'm afraid you are, Tessa," said Angelo. "Limited liability does not apply to fraud. We are perfectly within our rights to recover the debt, with, as Alec has pointed out, compound interest."

"That comes to approximately two million, three hundred and fifty five thousand," Alec paused. "And change."

Tessa stood her ground. "I don't have that kind of money. I can't pay."

Angelo looked at Alec who delved into his crocodile briefcase and took out a computer printout. "According to The Companies Registration Office you are a major, in fact now that your husband is dead, the only shareholder in Peace Land Holdings. You also now own your late husband's shares in Clough Peace." He handed her the printout. Then Angelo said, "So you do have money, Tessa, and I intend to take it from you, legally of course, unlike the way you took my father's money from him."

"But that money isn't mine. I have to pay the ransom for Eoin."

"Excuse me?" said Angelo.

Dermot, who was watching this scene from the hall, butted in. "Mrs Peace's son has been abducted by the same man responsible for the deaths of Georgie Warren, Gary Grant and Lou Armitage. He's just demanded a ransom of two hundred thousand pounds."

Angelo and Alec Gilchrist muttered together for a moment, then Angelo said, "That is not our problem."

"But you don't understand, I need that money to get my son back alive. I can't pay you. You can't get blood out of a stone." Her last statement was a mistake.

"You can't touch any of that money, Tessa. Alec has already taken out a sequestration order against it."

"What does that mean?" she asked.

"It means, Tessa, that until this case is settled, you can't touch a penny of the money in Peace Land Holdings, or sell any of your shareholding in Clough Peace at the risk of being in contempt of court."

"But what about Eoin?"

Angelo and Gilchrist turned to leave. "As I said, Tessa, not my problem." The two men walked out of the room leaving Tessa, Dermot, Phoebe and Grace staring after them.

As the front door slammed, the phone rang again. Tessa rushed to pick it up. When she came back into the drawing-room, her face was the colour of chalk. "That was the bank. They won't release the money. What will happen to Eoin now?"

Dermot said, "Carl doesn't know about Angelo Steffani's sequestration order, and anyway I doubt that he'd believe you, so I think we'll just have to bluff it out."

"What do you mean?" Tessa asked frantically.

"I mean that you should make arrangements for the handover of the money regardless, and rely on us to grab him when he goes to collect it."

Tessa was horrified. "But that's so dangerous for my son!"

"He'll be in no more danger than if you don't go along with it," said Grace. "Face it, Tessa, what other choice do you have?"

Tessa had to concede that Grace had a point so she agreed to deal with Carl as if she had the cash, but to stall him as long as possible in the hope that he would give away his whereabouts.

Chapter Fifteen

"I phoned your old lady. I told her I want two hundred grand. What do you think?"

Eoin didn't know what to answer. "What will you do if she won't pay?"

"She'll pay."

"But what if she won't?" he persisted.

Carl shrugged. "Let's cross that bridge when we come to it." He untied Eoin's wrists and ankles. "Would you like a wash? You can use the bathroom if you don't try to escape. I don't want to have to use this," he said lifting up the double barrels of the sawn-off.

"Thanks," said Eoin. "I'll be good." He was warming to Carl.

Carl led him upstairs to the bathroom and let him have a wash and use the toilet, though he insisted that the bathroom door be left open. Later in the small kitchen they sat down to spaghetti bolognese, the type that can be heated up in the microwave, but none the less filling and tasty.

"Is this your house?"

Carl shook his head, his mouth was full of food. "No I'm just renting," he said. "Just a short let." Then "D'you get on with your old lady?"

Eoin pulled a face. "I suppose so. She's OK. Bit clinging and over-protective though. How about you?"

"My ma's grand. She had a tough time after Dad killed himself. I wasn't a lot of help for a while, went off the rails a bit, you know, nicking things and stuff. I thought it wasn't fair that if I stole a packet of fags I got hauled up to the juvenile court, yet they stole two million quid and got away with it."

"What straightened you out?" asked Eoin.

"I joined the army for three years."

"Why did you leave?"

"I'd only signed up for three years anyway. No one knew me and I suppose the chip fell off my shoulder. I learnt a trade and life was good again, I could send my ma money."

"I wish my mother had stood up to my father a bit more, that's the only thing. She'd never back me up against him, you know. Like the time I wanted to go to dance classes, he wouldn't hear of it, said it was for poofters. He made me go to boxing instead, said it would toughen me up."

Carl stopped eating. "And did it, toughen you up I mean?"

Eoin started to laugh. "No," he said. "They

knocked seven kinds of shit out of me. Dad nearly did the same when he got me home. He was livid, it was nearly worth it to see his face!"

They were both laughing now, enjoying the shared joke. Carl got up from the table and stacked the plates on the draining board. Eoin made coffee.

"What'll you do when you get the money?"

Carl stopped what he was doing. "It's not about the money. It's about revenge."

Eoin looked at him, puzzled. "I don't understand."

"Your, if you'll pardon the expression, shit-bag of a father and his cronies hadn't crossed my mind for years, then a month ago I saw him. I'd got a job on the shopping mall site. I'm a chippy by trade. Anyway, there he was. I couldn't believe it was him at first, then I saw him with Clough and I knew. I'd only seen Clough the once, but seeing the two of them together confirmed who they were."

"Why didn't you just go to the police?"

Carl sat on the edge of the table and folded his arms across his chest. "I wish I had now."

"Did he recognise you?"

"Recognise me? Not at first, but when I told him who I was he was terrified. I have to say that gave me a lot of satisfaction. The feeling of power, of having his fate in the palm of my hand." Carl held out his hand and curled the fingers into the palm. "Just like he had my Dad years ago." He stared out of the window at nothing, deep in his own memories. Suddenly he came back down to earth. "Then things happened, like a roller-coaster, out of control. I only grabbed you on the spur of the moment, but now it's too late to stop."

"But if you get the money you can just get away."

"Where?" said Carl.

"I don't know, abroad maybe. You could change your appearance, dye your hair, grow a moustache. I'll help you."

"Why should you help me?"

Eoin thought carefully before he answered. "Because I think I owe you."

"Owe me?"

"You killed the bastard who ruined your life and was making my life a misery. Believe me, I owe you!"

Carl didn't know what to say and stayed silent for what seemed to Eoin like an age. At last he said, "How would we get away with the money without being caught?"

Eoin smiled. "Well. They don't know that we're working together. That has to give us a head start."

Shortly afterwards Eoin and Carl walked down to the local supermarket and bought a basket of groceries, also a packet of hair colour and a pair of sharp scissors. Carl saw a joke shop and bought a false moustache and a couple of other items.

Around the same time, Tessa decided to visit

Curtis Clough in hospital to see if he could help her raise some money. She was very unhappy about Dermot's plan of going to the rendezvous empty-handed.

He was alone in his room when she arrived, Portia had gone out to a hair appointment or something. He looked wretched, with tubes and drips attached all over his body, and the constant beep-beep of the heart monitor. He attempted to smile when he saw her.

"Curtis," she said, grasping hold of his hand. It was cold and clammy to the touch. "How do you feel?"

"I've felt better," he said. "But how are you?"

She just shrugged. "Not the best, Curtis, but bearing up." She unpacked the fruit she had brought him and made room for the bright orange Pelargonium on the window ledge.

"What's the matter, Tessa?" he asked suddenly. "I can always tell when something's worrying you."

Tessa sat on the edge of the bed and took his hand again. "I don't want to trouble you, Curtis, you have your own problems." He persisted as she knew he would and eventually she said, "Angelo Steffani came to see me. He's suing me for everything and more besides."

Curtis gave a low whistle. "I suppose the police dug him up." Tessa nodded. "Yes, but it's worse than that."

"How worse?"

179

"He's put a sequestration order on all my assets, so I can't even take the money and run."

"That's bad, but it could be worse," said Clough trying to look on the bright side and knowing that he was officially in the clear as far as the WAG affair was concerned.

"No it couldn't. Carl Rose, Frank's son, has taken Eoin, and he's demanding two hundred thousand ransom, or God knows what he'll do."

"You were right, it couldn't be worse."

Tessa looked into his bloodshot eyes, pleading. "I need to get money, Curtis, please help me."

Clough gave a heavy sigh. "I seem to remember hearing that plea before."

"You didn't do too badly the last time, Curtis," she said.

"What about Bob, can't he help?"

She shook her head. "He hasn't got the kind of money I need."

"How much do you need?"

"All of it. Two hundred thousand."

Clough nearly had another attack. "I can't just pluck that amount out of thin air," he said, exasperated.

"Well, how about one hundred thousand? Maybe I could bargain with him. Look, Curtis, I can't go empty-handed. He's killed three times already."

"Three times? Who else?" She'd forgotten that Clough hadn't heard about Archie, aka Gary.

"He got Gary, but the police think he may have taken an overdose anyway."

"Rose?"

"No! Gary, they think he took an overdose and Rose, not realising, stabbed him. But it comes down to the same thing, he's capable of killing and he's got my Eoin."

"When do you need the money?"

"He's going to call me to arrange the payment tomorrow some time."

"Then you'll have to stall him, I can't get the money that soon."

"How soon?" she asked, desperate now.

"Day after tomorrow. Maybe," he said, stressing the last word.

"The police will get the money back, Curtis, when they catch Carl Rose. You'll get it all back."

"What will you do then, Tessa?"

She threw her head back and looked up at the ceiling trying to stop the tears. "I don't care. I just want to get my son back in one piece."

"Leave it with me Tessa. And I'd prefer you didn't mention this to Portia." Tessa pressed her lips together and mimed pulling a zip across.

"My lips are sealed," she said.

"Sealed about what?" said an all too familiar voice from the doorway. Portia had returned to check up on her husband. She looked slightly disappointed that he was still alive.

"About WAG." said Clough before Tessa could

181

answer. Portia glared at Tessa. "I think you should go now," she said. "Curtis needs rest."

After Tessa had gone, Portia sat by her husband's bed with a sour expression on her face. "What did she want?"

Clough sighed. "Did it ever occur to you that she might just be concerned about me?"

"No. And if you had any perception you'd see that they're users, only interested in taking advantage."

Clough was getting irritated. "Don't forget that Tessa was the one who persuaded Warren to start Clough Peace. We'd have been in dire straits if it hadn't been for that."

"Rubbish. You were doing very well as it was. Anyway, you needn't tell me that he didn't need you more than you needed him. Don't delude yourself that Warren Peace ever did anything for you out of friendship."

"Whatever the reason we've done very well out of Clough Peace, so just shut up and tell the nurse that I need to use the phone." He could see that she was about to protest so he raised his voice to a shout. "JUST DO IT WOMAN! For once in your spoiled privileged life, just do what I ask."

Portia was so stunned at his uncharacteristic outburst that she mutely rose from her chair and went to get the nurse.

★ ★ ★

Dermot told Luke to stay with Tessa and wait for the call from Carl Rose. Grace was taking the early shift, Phoebe had gone to lunch with Angelo Steffani, and Mungo was down at the Point sorting the security for the Screeming AbDabs gig the following week. Xin was holding the fort back at the office. Gardaí Kevin Bulger and Jane Walsh from the unit at Harcourt Terrace had fitted a recording device to the phone and a trace line had been requested from Telecom Eireann. The trace would only be certain to work if Carl Rose called her from a digital exchange, and then he would need to be on the line for about a minute at least. They all sat round the kitchen eating bacon sandwiches and drinking tea, which Grace had prepared. Mrs Danvers had taken the day off. Tessa just picked at her food, and listlessly sighed a lot. It was getting on Grace's nerves. She hated babysitting at the best of times and had little sympathy for Tessa, who struck her as spoilt and indulged. Her impression was coloured somewhat by Angelo Steffani, and Luke's account of his visit to Mrs Dodd.

Luke on the other hand did feel a little sorry for her on account of Eoin, who was, after all, the only innocent victim in the whole affair.

The three of them sat in silence, each wrapped up in their own thoughts. Tessa was slipping into a deep depression, fuelled by guilt about Eoin and fear of the future if Angelo's court action were to be successful. She had phoned Sean Whelan the company solicitor earlier in the day. His manner chilled when she admitted to him that Angelo Steffani's accusations weren't without foundation. He frostily put her on to Alan Hughes, one of his associates who dealt with litigation. Tessa was incensed, talk about rats leaving the sinking ship. Sean had enjoyed their hospitality and fat fees for the past six years, and they had thought him to be a personal friend. I wonder how many of them will prove to be fair weather friends, she thought. She had a fair idea that it would be approximately one hundred percent. No, that wasn't fair. Curtis had always come up trumps, despite Portia.

Grace, on the other hand, was thinking about Andrew. She began to question her reasons for getting married in the first place. Andrew had always complained that her job came between them, but if she'd really loved him she knew that her job wouldn't have come first. He would. Maybe that was the answer. She just hadn't loved him enough in the first place, and it was really only family pressure that had taken them up the aisle. Perhaps he and Kiera were better off together.

Phoebe had accused her of still caring for him. She argued that if Grace didn't care, he couldn't wind her up so easily. She didn't subscribe to that theory herself. Andrew had always been able to wind her up. And when Grace had complained to

Phoebe that she shouldn't be going out to lunch with Angelo Steffani, that it was a conflict of interest, all Phoebe had said was, "Get a life, Grace." Perhaps it was time that she did.

The subdued tick-tock tick-tock of the casement clock on the mantle was the only sound disturbing the silence. The clock struck three.

"Would anyone like more tea?" asked Tessa.

"Please," said Grace. "I'll make it, it'll give me something to do." She emptied the teapot and made the tea with bubbling water from the kettle which was sitting on top of the Aga. The loud jangle of the phone made them all jump. Tessa made a run for the hall but Luke stopped her.

"Give Jane and Kev a chance, Tessa," he said. Jane put on her headphones, switched on the machine and gave Tessa, who was standing white-faced by the phone, the thumbs up. Tesssa picked up the receiver.

"Hello," she said, her voice strained. Then she relaxed. "Curtis! did you manage it? Can you get the money."

"Tomorrow, Tessa, not till tomorrow. Just one hundred thou' I'm afraid." Clough could have raised the full amount, but he didn't want to take the chance of the police losing Carl Rose along with his money, when there was little chance that Tessa would be in a position to pay him back. He was also afraid that if he gave her two hundred thousand she

185

might do a runner with the second hundred thousand after paying the ransom with the first.

"Thank you, Curtis. Thank you," said Tessa with sincerity. "When exactly can I have it? I have to make arrangements with Carl Rose when he calls."

"A Securicor courier will bring it to you at The Oaks tomorrow at three. I hope that's OK."

"OK? Curtis. I can never thank you enough."

Clough rang off and they all went back to the kitchen to wait. Luke cleared away the dishes from the table and put them in the sink and Jane pulled out a pack of cards and started to play Patience. Time dragged on. Tick-tock tick-tock.

"Black six under red seven and red Queen on black King," said Luke, leaning over Jane's shoulder and moving the cards. Tessa drummed her fingers on the table top and Kevin and Grace were doing a crossword together.

"Nine letters, second letter Y, last letter Y, meaning pretence of having standards?" said Grace aloud, biting the end of her pen.

"Hypocrisy," said Luke, and they all looked at Tessa. There was an uncomfortable silence. The phone rang again. Tessa ran to it but this time waited for Jane's signal before picking it up.

"Hello." Again her voice was shaky.

"You know who this is?"

"Yes. But I have to talk to you."

"That's what we're doing."

"I can only raise one hundred thousand, I can't

get any more." There was silence at the other end of the line. "Are you still there?" she asked frantically.

Carl Dodd's voice came back on the line. "I don't believe you, lady."

"It's true. Really, and I've had to borrow that much." Her voice was desperate. "I just can't raise the rest."

Again there was silence at the other end of the line then a muffled sound as Carl covered the receiver with his hand. He lowered his voice and spoke to Eoin, who was standing in the phone box with him.

"She says she only got a hundred grand. What do you think?" Eoin went pale, he couldn't believe that his own mother would bargain for his life, and his stomach felt sick. Carl could see that this had knocked the stuffing out of Eoin and could also see that he was incapable at that point of saying anything.

"Try again, lady. You'll get a message in the post in the morning," said Carl. "You have one last chance or your son dies."

Tessa gasped. Luke motioned to her to keep him talking. Quickly she said, before he could hang up, "How do I know that he's still alive? How do I know you haven't killed him already?"

Carl grinned at Eoin and handed him the receiver.

"Please get the money, Mother, please hel . . . " the sentence ended with a high pitched scream and Tessa dropped the receiver. Luke dived and picked it up. She was standing with her hand slapped to her mouth so he had to hold the receiver to her ear.

"Like I said lady, think again. You'll get a reminder tomorrow." Then the receiver was slapped down. Carl and Eoin stared at each other in the phone box and then both collapsed in hysterics.

"The mean old bat," said Carl. "Come on, we'd better get out of here in case they had a tracer on the line." They were still laughing as they walked back to the house. Suddenly Eoin stopped.

"I can't believe she'd do that. I can't believe she'd pretend she hadn't the money."

Carl felt sorry for his new friend. "Is there any chance she was telling the truth?" Eoin slowly shook his head from side to side. "No chance," he said. "No chance at all."

As soon as Tessa had put the phone down Luke looked at Kevin, who shook his head.

"It wasn't a digital exchange," he said. "He wasn't on the line long enough."

"Is there any chance you can raise the rest of the money?" Grace asked.

"No," Tessa said. "No chance at all."

Chapter Sixteen

Luke arrived the following morning at the same time as the postman, and took the small package and two envelopes up to the house to save him the trip. Tessa wasn't up. She hadn't been able to sleep the previous night, so Xin, who had relieved Grace, answered the door.

"Who're you?" she asked, eyeing Luke up and down suspiciously.

"Detective garda Luke Ryan. And who are you?" said Luke. He was equally circumspect. *What are you?* he thought. Xin, although dressed in sombre black, hadn't made any concessions with her Geisha make-up. She looked her usual startling self.

Xin sniffed and stood back so that he could get past her. "I'm Xin Mountjoy. I'm a private investigator and qualified Ninja."

"You work for Grace de Rossa?"

Xin, catching the disbelief in his tone, stiffened

189

defensively. "We're colleagues. She's trainin' me," she said, pulling herself up to her full five feet height, while at the same time adopting an imperious glare.

"Oh," said Luke, bemused, and edged past her into the hall. "Where is everyone?"

"Yer woman's in bed, an' them other two guards are in the kitchen." They joined "them other two guards" in the kitchen. Tessa came down at about eight-thirty, just as Mrs Danvers arrived for her day's work. Her reaction to Xin was predictable, but confined to a sharp intake of breath and no comment. Mrs Danvers shooed them out of the kitchen so they sat in the drawing-room.

Kev and Jane were checking the equipment and Xin picked up the Philip Marlowe mystery she had been reading before Luke arrived. Luke started to read his morning paper. Tessa nursed a cup of coffee and smoked a cigarette. Kev looked over at her and noticed that her hands were shaking, spilling coffee on her skirt. She didn't seem to notice so he took the cup from her and she smiled up at him. After a while she picked up the post and started to open it. Quiet settled on the room.

Suddenly Tessa started to scream hysterically. The three officers and Xin to leap to their feet. She was holding a small box at arm's length, cringing away from it at the same time. Luke grabbed hold of the box and Xin slapped Tessa on the cheek to stop her hysterics. She crumpled up on the chair drawing her knees up to her chest and started to sob.

Luke and Xin looked at the box, it was about four inches square and filled with red-stained tissue. Luke gently lifted back the tissue and revealed, lying underneath, a severed ear. He grimaced and looked at Xin, who gently lifed the ear with the end of her finger.

Suddenly they both relaxed. "It's a bleedin' rubber one," she said. They put the box on the table and Luke picked up the discarded wrapping from the floor.

"What's the postmark?" asked Kev. Luke squinted at the smudged frank mark. "It looks like Ballyfingal, though it's hard to say," he said.

"I think you're right," said Kev. "The rotten bastard."

"I dunno," said Xin. "It could've been worse."

"How?" said Luke.

"He could've sent the bleedin' real thing." Tessa yelped, and Luke glared at Xin. He contacted Dermot and told him about the package and the postmark on the wrapping paper.

"Right," said Dermot. "That narrows down the area for the phone tap. I'll sort that out and alert the local Gardaí. How's Tessa?"

"She went hysterical when she opened it, but she's fairly OK now," he said. "I think she's pretty near the edge though and the Steffani business hasn't helped."

"I believe Clough's going to lend her the money."

"Half of it," said Luke. "I expect he doesn't want to chance the whole lot."

"OK. Get back to me when you hear from yer man."

"How's Tessa?" Grace asked Xin when she arrived at the Oaks.

"OK, under the circumstances," Xin said. "She threw a bit of a wobbler when she opened the post though."

"Why?" Xin filled Grace in on the drama of the morning.

"Good grief! That was a bit over the top," Grace commented. "Poor Tessa."

Tessa had calmed down by the time Grace saw her. Luke had convinced her that the severed ear was a hoax, albeit a cruel one. Grace went to see Mrs Danvers in her kitchen, who insisted on making her a cup of tea. She sat at the now familiar table.

"Terrible business," Mrs Danvers said. "Rotten thing to do to anyone. Even to Mrs Peace."

Mrs Danvers had been told about Eoin's

abduction, but asked to keep it to herself, as publicity at that stage could jeopardise his chances of freedom. Grace knew that she was very fond of Eoin and wouldn't break the confidence.

"Will Master Eoin be OK?" she asked Grace, who was quite amused at Mrs Danvers' use of the archaic title.

"With luck," was all she could say.

* * *

Carl and Eoin sat at a different kitchen table eating a late breakfast. Carl looked quite different. Eoin had cut his longish hair short and spiky and had coloured it dark brown. They had fallen about when he stuck on the false moustache.

"You look like a Mexican bank robber," said Eoin. So they trimmed it and he began to look more normal.

They had worked out a plan for the hand-over of the money the previous night. Carl knew the area quite well, having lived in Ballyfingal after he had moved out of his mother's house a few years previously. They went over and over the plan looking for flaws.

"You'll really need a trail bike once you get the cash. It's more manoeuvrable than the car."

"Yes," said Carl. "I'll pick one up second-hand from somewhere."

"I wonder if she'll put up all the cash? If she cares what happens to me enough?"

"I'd say after the postman gave her the ear she got the idea."

"Hopefully," said Eoin.

They sat thoughtful for a while after finishing their meal, both nervous and excited, anticipating the next twenty-four hours.

"Well," said Carl pushing back his chair. "As Telecom would put it, I'd better *make that call*!"

"Shall I come with you?"

"No need," said Carl. "Anyway, I want to get the bike, so I think it'll be safer if we're not seen together again. I'll be back in a couple of hours, I want to run round the route and time the stops."

Carl Rose made that call. But by the time he did, Tessa was in a state of near collapse. Clough's promised cash had arrived one hour late and she had been unable to contact him in the meantime. Eventually she relaxed when the dark blue Securicor van pulled up in front of the house. Grace was surprised to see that the money was packed in a baked bean carton, she had expected at least a leather briefcase chained to the courier's wrist. They counted the money, signed for it and then settled down again to wait for Carl Rose to make contact.

★ ★ ★

"Did you get my message?" Carl said and started to

laugh. Tessa, not realising that he was talking about the rubber ear, was at a loss.

"Are you there?" he said.

Luke poked Tessa in the back, shaking her out of her trance-like state.

"Yes," she stammered. "I'm here."

"Have you had a rethink about the money?"

"I still can't raise any more, honestly. I can only get the one hundred thousand." Her voice was desperate. Carl thought about this. "You wouldn't be trying to stall for time, would you?"

"NO, no really, on my son's life!" She had said it before she realised the implication.

"Well, it is, isn't it," said Carl. "Be ready at five tomorrow evening. I'll phone you then with instructions about where to go. Don't involve the police or you'll get the real thing next time. I'll be able to see if you're followed, or if you've anyone with you, so just follow my instructions to the letter."

"Where do you want me to bring the money?"

"Tomorrow. I'll give you instructions tomorrow." His voice was impatient, obviously anxious to get off the line. He just said, "Tomorrow" again and hung up.

"What did he mean about being able to see if I'm followed? How could he see?"

Grace said, "He probably means that he'll be sending you on a wild-goose chase so that he'll be able to see you from various points without your knowing."

"What do you mean wild-goose chase?" Tessa was very tense again. Her fists were clenched and her face white. She was afraid of Carl Rose and didn't want to have to meet him on her own. What if it was just an elaborate plan to get her to go to her own execution?

"He'll probably send you to a phone box and call you and send you to another phone box. You'll only have a set time to get there, so he'll know if you stop on the way or try to contact us."

Tessa was horrified "Then how will you get him? How will you stop him hurting Eoin?" She couldn't bring herself to say the word "Killing."

"Don't worry. I'll be in the back of your car on the floor, and we'll have a tracking device fixed to the car."

"But he said he could see . . . "

"He won't risk being that close to the house, so he won't see us leaving. Don't worry, he's only trying to put the fear of God into you."

Grace could see that he had succeeded. They would have to call the doctor and get him to give Tessa something to calm her or she'd never be able to make the hand-over.

Luke called Dermot and told him about Carl Rose's phone call and their intention of getting a sedative for Tessa. "Fine," he said. "You and Grace get back here and let the others stay with Tessa. I want to go over the strategy of the hand-over with you both. Did Kevin trace the call this time?"

"It was from the Ballyfingal exchange all right, but he wasn't on long enough for us to pin-point the phone." After Tessa's GP had given her a sedative shot, Grace and Luke left her with the other two officers and headed for Harcourt Terrace. Dermot had a map of the area on the notice board when they got to the office and he and Jack Mulloy were studying it.

"The local nick is giving us assistance, one of their lads is on his way here now. Do either of you two know the area?" asked Dermot.

"I've been to a pub quiz there," said Grace.

"We'll have to have five or six cars spread round the area, and one tailing Tessa. Then, when we know where she's being sent, you can radio in, Grace, and we may have a chance of getting to the final rendezvous before Tessa and grab yer man as he picks up the cash."

"Plan A," said Grace under her breath, wondering what would happen to Eoin Peace if Carl Rose gave them the slip.

"What was that?" said Dermot glaring at her.

"I was just wondering what plan B will be." she said.

"We'll seal off the area and hope for the best," he said flatly, still glaring at her.

The rest of the team, including DS McGuire from Ballyfingal, started to drift into the office and they discussed various possibilities and what-ifs. At about seven-thirty they called it a day.

Luke asked Grace for a lift, and told her his car had gone into the garage for a service.

"Are you going home?" she asked.

"Yes. Why?"

"Oh, no reason, I was just going to get a takeaway that's all."

"Good idea," he said. "We could stop for the takeaway and a bottle of wine and go back to my place to eat it if you like."

"I suppose so," Grace said without much enthusiasm.

On the drive to his flat Luke said, "D'you think Carl Rose intends to kill Tessa and Eoin Peace too?"

"I hope not. Phoebe pointed out to me that if he does we don't get paid."

Luke didn't respond for a while, then he said. "Why do you have to appear so fucking hard-nosed?"

"And why do you have to be so fucking arrogant?" she snapped back. The atmosphere in the car was frosty for a few hundred metres then she stopped at a red light.

"OK," he said suddenly, "How about a truce. Until after we've eaten the takeaway and drunk the wine anyway." She saw him grinning at her out of the corner of her eye so just said quietly again,

"I suppose so."

"You suppose so?"

"I suppose so."

Eoin had cooked a shepherds pie and they sat down to eat.

"How did it go?" he asked. Carl gave a deep sigh, "Your old lady still reckons that she can only raise a hundred grand." Eoin looked crestfallen. "I was afraid that she was just stalling so I more or less agreed to that."

"What happens now?"

"I'll call about five tomorrow. I want it to be dark, it gives me a better chance of getting away with it."

"You got the trail bike?" Carl nodded, his mouth full.

"Then that's it. I suppose," said Eoin. He still couldn't believe his mother. She could have easily afforded the two hundred thousand. It would serve right if Carl did kill him, but then would she care one way or the other? They finished their meal in silence.

* * *

Dermot found his house in darkness when he got home. He was disappointed until he caught a delicious aroma coming from the kitchen, and saw that the kitchen table was set with three places. Ten minutes later he heard a key in the lock and Susy bounced in.

"Hi pops. Dinner won't be long." He kissed her on the forehead. "You're spoiling me. What is it? It smells good."

"Tofu and bean casserole."

"Very nice," he said, sounding anything but sure about it. He rooted in the fridge to find a can of lager.

"How's your case going?" she asked, and sat down at the table.

"Nothing much can happen now until Carl Rose phones tomorrow. I hope we don't get it wrong. He sounds pretty much a psycho. He could do for Tessa Peace, and for all we know may have done for the son already."

"Really?" she said, not really interested, but pleased that her father was talking to her. He had never talked like this to her mother. Maura came in at that point, so Susy served up the tofu and bean casserole, which as it turned out was delicious.

* * *

Tessa stood by the window of her darkened bedroom. She could see the patrol car parked in the drive and the intermittent glow of a cigarette from within. Two other officers were downstairs in the kitchen playing cards, and the strange girl with the heavy make-up was lurking somewhere in the house.

She couldn't sleep despite the shot of Valium the doctor had given her a couple of hours earlier. The phone started to ring and someone picked it up downstairs but didn't call her. A shiver ran down her spine. She walked over to the bed and climbed under the duvet but sleep wouldn't come. She lay there looking up at the ceiling. What would happen if the police didn't get Carl Rose after she had handed over the ransom? What if he'd harmed Eoin already? Worse than that, she realised that a different sort of survival problem would still remain after all this business was over.

She tried to remember the last time she and Warren had made love but she couldn't. She felt more alone than ever so she started to cry.

★ ★ ★

The Chinese takeaway was delicious, especially washed down with the bottle of red wine that Luke had found in the kitchen cupboard and the lager that Grace had picked up from the off-licence on the way.

They sat in front of the fire watching TV and finishing off the beer. There was an old Pink Panther movie on BBC Two and the laughter and the drink relaxed them both.

Luke asked her about Andrew and she told the story of her marriage without emotion.

"So it's well and truly over then?" he said when she had stopped speaking.

"Well and truly," she said. "I just wish the mother-in-law from hell would realise that." And, anxious to change the subject, she got up, snapped the light on and started to pick up the debris of foil cartons and empty beer cans.

"This place looks as if we just had an orgy," she said, feeling a little drunk and unsteady on her feet. Luke helped her to tidy up and they took the rubbish into the kitchen.

"Like a coffee?" he asked.

"Good idea." She opened the fire escape door to get some air as he put on the kettle to boil.

"Only instant, I'm afraid."

"There's another kind?" The cold night air cleared her head and she felt more at ease than she had felt in the past twelve months. She watched Luke making the coffee and, on impulse, leaned over and putting her hand under his chin, turned his head and kissed him on the mouth. She kept her eyes open to watch his reaction. Luke's eyes were open too and for an instant he didn't react at all, then gently he slid his arms round her waist and returned her kiss. With heart thumping, Grace wound her arms round his neck. He pulled her close and they started kissing feverishly. Luke was walking her backwards through the kitchen door when, coming up for air, she said, "Is this a good idea?" He silenced her with his lips and, as they fell backwards onto the Chesterfield, he said, "Absolutely!"

Chapter Seventeen

Grace opened her eyes, instantly regretting it as a pain exploded in her head. Her mouth felt fur lined. She rolled over and bumped against Luke's broad, very bare, shoulders.

Oh God. What have I done, she thought. Luke stirred and she shut her eyes, pretending to be asleep. She felt him turn over in the bed, and the draught, as he heaved himself up on his elbow.

"Hello," he said.

She opened her eyes and said sheepishly, "Hello."

Seeing her face Luke grinned and said, "Grace, I enjoyed myself a lot last night, and correct me if I'm wrong, but I got the impression you did too."

"Hmmmm," she said. "So what happens now?" and pulled herself up, sitting with her back against the head-board and pulling the duvet up over her bare breasts.

"Happens? Two Solpadine and a cup of tea would go down well." Grace's expression didn't change so he said, "Grace, I've harboured secret fantasies about you from the first day I moved to Harcourt Terrace."

"Really?" She was surprised.

"Really."

"Then why were you so evil to me?" she said thumping him on the arm.

"I thought you were bent. But it didn't stop me lusting after you."

"So what made you change your mind? I assume that you have changed your mind now and you don't think I took the shilling."

"That's right," he said. "I suppose I just got to know you a little better."

"Well, thanks a bunch," she snapped, adding after a pause, "The first time I saw you I thought you were an arrogant bastard."

"That's a bit harsh!" He rolled over and lay on his back again, he sounded a bit miffed so she leaned over and kissed him hard on the mouth.

"I still do as a matter of fact!" she said, but she grinned and he could see she was winding him up. He grabbed her and, as he pulled her down under the duvet again he said, "A woman with insight!" Thirty minutes later the alarm clock went off.

Grace said, "We'd better get up. I have to go home and change."

"Don't ever change, Grace!" he said mocking her.

"Shut up, Luke." Then, "I don't know about you, but I don't really want to arrive at Harcourt Terrace together, I couldn't take the slagging today."

"Good point. Drop me at the car park so I can pick up my car."

"I thought you said it was in the garage?"

"So I lied!"

A little later Luke stood in Grace's kitchen and listened to her moving around next door. He poured the boiling water over the tea bags in the tea pot and rinsed two dirty cups under the hot tap. Grace came in freshly dressed and picked up the biscuit jar. He went up behind her and slipped his arms round her waist.

"I really did enjoy myself a lot last night, Grace, I hope you did too."

She slid round still encircled by his arms to face him. "What do you want? Marks out of ten or something?" Then seeing his expression change, she added quickly. "Just kidding. You were just what I needed last night. But let's not make too big a deal out of it." She was attracted to Luke, despite her initial assessment of him, though she was very wary of becoming involved with anyone, particularly him. She was still stung that he had assumed the worst about her when they had first met.

His face fell. He stood back and held her at arm's length. "That's supposed to be my line!" he said, but she grinned at him and it broke the tension.

"Let's just play it by ear," she said kissing him on the nose.

"Fine by me," he said and shrugged, but she sensed that she had bruised his ego.

Phoebe passed them on the stairs as they were leaving. She eyed Luke up and down and said, "Where's Xin?" Luke walked on and waited for Grace at the bottom of the stairs.

"I let her do the night shift at Tessa's," Grace said. "Mungo's going to pick her up. I persuaded Tessa that there was no point in any of us going out till early this afternoon. Carl Rose thinks Tessa isn't getting the money until then so he won't call."

"OK." Phoebe said. "Can you remind her to call the signwriter again? We nearly missed a prospective client yesterday because he couldn't find the place."

"I can't. I'm going to Harcourt Terrace. Tessa insisted I sit in on the final briefing for the hand-over of the ransom money seeing as I'll be going with her."

"OK," said Phoebe. "I'll switch the answering machine on and leave Xin a note."

"Why won't you be here?" Grace was going to kick up if she was swanning off with her Italian diplomat again.

"I'm going out to talk to the prospective client from yesterday, of course. I want to make sure he doesn't get lost today. He's an old friend so I'll try and twist his arm a little to give us the work. He has a couple of clubs in the city centre." Adding under her breath, "I see you got a life!"

Grace felt herself blush. She said, "Fine, see you later," and hurried to catch up with Luke. She arrived at Harcourt Terrace just after nine and joined Garda Jim Dougan from Ballyfingal and the rest of her former unit in the CID office. They gathered round the map and Dermot was just about to start the final briefing when Luke hurried in.

"Sorry I'm late, I had to pick up my car from the garage."

Dermot nodded impatiently, anxious to get on with it.

"Right. As you know we think the Ballyfingle area is where Carl Rose is holding Eoin Peace and, although it's small, it's quite heavily built-up. It's dissected here by the main rail line, and here by the canal." He pointed at the map. "The nearest the trace could get to the phone Carl Rose used was this area." He circled an area near the top of the map. "Of course he may not have called from a phone near his base but we have to start somewhere."

"The local Gardaí are having a look around for any likely empty properties," said Jim. "And we're checking with the two local estate agents for recently rented out properties."

"Good, good," said Dermot. "Grace, I want you in the back of Tessa Peace's car to relay her instructions from Carl Rose."

"Have they fitted the tracking transmitter yet, Dermot?" she asked.

"Yes. And as I said last night we're going to place six cars in a circle round Tessa Peace as she heads off, then we can cross wires on the signal and get a better fix on her position at all times. There'll be an officer with local knowledge in each car."

"What about Eoin Peace?" asked Jack Mulloy.

Dermot looked around. "What about him?"

"Are the local lads going to look out for him on their own, or are any of us joining them?"

"I think the Ballyfingal lads know the area better than us, and we don't want too obvious a presence in case Carl Rose gets driven to ground or worse." Jack nodded, he was relieved, he didn't want to miss a car chase and hated leg work.

"How do we know that he'll send her to Ballyfingal, Dermot?"

"We don't, but it's sixty percent probable. The point of the exercise is to grab Carl Rose at the money drop, so we'll rely on you, Grace, to be as precise as possible in relaying Carl Rose's instructions to Tessa." Grace nodded. "You'd better get over to The Oaks and talk Tessa through what will probably happen. Try to make it sound matter-of-fact. Don't give her any ifs or buts. Don't let her dwell on the possibility of anything going wrong." He turned to Kevin. "You and Jane better get over there to relieve the night shift on the phone tracer." They both got up to leave and Grace followed them. Luke gave her a wink as she passed him on the way out. Dermot noticed and raised one eyebrow. "Luke, you come with me to Ballyfingal. We can only wait for Carl Rose's call now as far as the ransom's concerned, but I want to be over there if there's any chance of finding him and Eoin Peace before the event."

* * *

Carl and Eoin were still asleep. They had stayed up until the early hours watching videos and, even after they had both turned in, Carl lay awake mulling over and over the plan in his mind. At one point he found himself wondering *what the hell am I doing here?* as well he might. In less than three weeks he had done the unthinkable, not once but twice, not counting Grant who had claimed he had taken an overdose anyway. He began to wish that he had never seen Georgie Warren. If it hadn't been for Curtis Clough he might have thought that he was mistaken, but there was no mistaking the picture of the two of them together. He felt sorry for Eoin. Georgie had ruined his life too, and his mother was splitting hairs, bargaining for his freedom. That seemed to upset Eoin more than his memory of his father's dominating and humiliating treatment. He wanted to phone his own mother. They must have been to see her by now, asking about him. He knew that they would never get any information out of her. But it hurt him to think she was so near, yet so far away. How ironic it was that Georgie Warren and his partners were still ruining his life even from the grave. He fell asleep with this thought still in his mind.

* * *

Tessa felt as though she were in a film, but standing back and watching the action from a distance. Any moment someone would shout cut and things would be the way they were, with Warren alive and no Carl Rose or Angelo Steffani.

210

No threat to Eoin's life and no danger to her future. She really needed to speak to Curtis but Portia wouldn't hear of it. She hovered like a vulture waiting for Curtis to do her the service of dying peacefully and leaving her a rich widow. What a shame Carl Rose hadn't bashed the back of her skull in and sat her in her shiny red Porsche with a hose through the window.

Tessa's thoughts were interrupted by Grace who was stood directly in front of her chair looking down at her. She had been so far away in her thoughts that she hadn't heard her come in to the room.

"Tessa?"

She looked up at Grace and smiled, "Hello, Grace." She liked this tall self-confident girl and wished that she were more independent. Leaning on someone can become a habit, and she had leaned on Warren all the time.

"We've fitted a tracking device to your car, Tessa, and one in the case with the ransom money, so all we can do now is wait for Carl Rose to call you."

"He said that he wouldn't call until five."

"We have to be ready anyway, that might have been just a bluff. We can't take the chance."

Grace went over the probable sequence of events with Tessa, trying to make it all sound like normal procedure. In fact Grace, and to her knowledge Dermot, had never been involved in a kidnap investigation before. Then they sat and waited for Carl Rose.

Chapter Eighteen

It was just getting dark outside when the call came. Tessa sat rooted to the spot until Grace picked up the receiver and handed it to her after Jane had given her the thumbs up.

"Hello."

"Write this down," said Carl. Grace thrust a pad and pencil at Tessa. "Drive to Dun Laoghaire then take the coast road towards town. Stop at Booterstown at the first phone box past Booterstown Dart Station. I'll call you there with further instructions. You have half an hour to reach the box. If you're late you'll miss my call and Eoin gets it." He slammed the phone down.

Tessa was frozen to her seat so Grace hustled her, "Come on Tessa, time to go." Then to Phoebe, "Call in and tell Dermot I'll call you as soon as Tessa speaks to Carl Rose again."

Tessa got to her feet and had grabbed her bag.

Grace picked up the case of money and, when they reached the car at a run, settled down on the floor in the back. She tested the radio. "Escort One to Minder, testing."

"Hearing you loud and clear Escort One. Proceed to rendezvous." Tessa raced down the drive and turned left at the bottom heading for Dun Laoghaire as Carl had directed. The traffic was fairly heavy and she was worried that Carl Rose might not have taken that into account when he gave her the deadline for the journey. She kept her eye on the dashboard clock, drumming her fingers on the steering wheel whenever they missed the lights or got into a slow-moving lane. She made excellent time, a fact Grace could verify having been bumped black and blue in the back of the car. The car screeched to a halt outside the phone box at five forty-five. From the back Grace said, "Don't turn round in case he can see you. Just take the call and tell him you'll meet his instructions the moment you get back to the car." Tessa checked her watch against the clock, it was two minutes faster. "Do you think we've missed him?" she asked, sounding tense.

"Relax, Tessa, we're early." As soon as the words were out of her mouth, the phone rang and Tessa jumped out to answer it. Grace called in to get the team on standby.

Thirty seconds later Tessa jumped back into the

car and had already kicked it into gear when she said, "I have to follow this road and head for the East Link and then along the East Wall Road to Fairview Park, to the public phone at the post office by Marino College. I've got fifteen minutes." Grace relayed the message back to Dermot.

"That takes him away from Ballyfingal!" said Luke.

"It's early days yet. I still think that's where he'll end up, he doesn't know we traced the last call there." Tessa watched the clock and became worried when she got stuck behind a cattle truck. The minutes were ticking by. Then, round a bend in the road, she saw the post office. The phone was already ringing by the time she skidded to a halt. She left the car door flying open as she rushed towards the box. Grace sucked the fresh air into her lungs. The motion of the car was making her feel nauseous.

Tessa was only away half a minute. "Down to the end of this road to the intersection, and up Malahide Road to Collins Avenue. Then left into Swords Road, and along to a phone in the first service station on the left past the canal on Drumcondra Road. I've got forty minutes to get there."

Grace relayed the instructions to Dermot and the other cars.

"They're still heading away," said Luke.

Dermot was still confident that Carl Rose would bring them back towards Ballyfingal, but he wondered how far around the country he would take them first. By the time they got onto the dual carrageway he felt it safe to catch up with Tessa's car, and shortly afterwards he could see the tail lights of the grey BMW about forty yards ahead. They cruised along at a steady fifty in the stream of traffic, which was much lighter now, and ahead he saw the BMW turn off towards town and Drumcondra Road. Dermot looked at his watch. They were five minutes early. Obviously Carl Rose had allowed for the traffic to be heavier.

Twenty yards short of the petrol station Dermot turned into a side road and stopped. Tessa wound down the window and waited. Grace could see her breath steamy in the cold night air.

"We're early," she said for something to say. Grace didn't bother to answer. A man sauntered over from the cabin between the petrol pumps.

"How much?"

"What?" said Tessa taken aback.

"How much petrol, missus?"

"I don't want . . . I'm waiting." The phone rang and she dived out of the car and picked up the receiver. Grace heard the pump attendant muttering as he stomped away.

Carl Rose continued to send them round in circles for the next two hours. Eventually the route turned back towards Ballyfingal. After the tenth call Grace got on to Dermot again.

"We're to head to Ballyfingal and the iron bridge over the railway by Mulligans pub. She's to put the money in the box he's left by the fourth girder, then drive away. He'll call Tessa at home to say where Eoin can be found. We've six minutes, we should just make it, I think."

"Got you, Grace. We'll wait at this end and all other cars can close in. Get Tessa to drive straight home."

Dermot gave a sigh of relief. Ballyfingal was well sewn up. Rose wouldn't have a chance of escape once he picked up the cash.

The roads were fairly empty by this time, Carl had planned it that way. Tessa drove slowly along the iron bridge looking for the box.

"I can't see it. I can't see it," she was panicking again.

"Stay calm, Tessa, don't lose it now. It'll be there, keep looking."

"I see it. I see it," she shrieked relieved, and slammed on the brakes, smacking Grace against the front seats, momentarily stunning her. Tessa grabbed the case and Grace heard the click of her heels as she hurried across the pavement towards the forth iron girder. Tessa couldn't fit the case into the cardboard box that Carl had left for the purpose, and felt a wave of terror overtaking her.

"Calm down," she said to herself. She took three deep breaths to slow her heart rate, and jammed the case in sideways. She looked around but saw no one and then got back in the car. "It's done," she said. "We'd better go back to the house." She did a U turn, heading back towards Killiney. Grace got on the radio to Dermot.

Dermot parked back from the bridge with the headlamps off and they waited. The other cars were covering all the roads leading from the bridge. The minutes ticked by.

"D'you think he's clocked us?" Luke said.

Dermot shrugged, "I hope not for young Peace's sake. We'll give him a couple more minutes then we'll drive over and take a peek."

Dermot started the engine and cruised along the deserted bridge. As they passed the fourth girder Dermot let out an uncharacteristic stream of expletives. The box had gone. The three Gardaí leapt from the car and rushed over to the side of the iron structure. The box had definitely vanished.

"What?" shouted Dermot.

"Shhhush," said Luke, staying Dermot with his hand. "Listen!" In the dark of the railway cutting they could hear the phut phut buzz of a light motorbike. "Sounds like a scrambler or trail bike," he said. "The bastard!"

Luke shone his flash lamp over the bridge, and

lying on the ground forty feet below, they could just make out the shape of the box. It had obviously been yanked over the edge with string or twine.

Dermot was already on the radio, and the cars ringed around the area homed in on the signal transmitted from the case. The local gardai cross-checked with each other over the air and pin-pointed the moving steady beep of the electronic homing device. Ten minutes later the signal was static. "Barna Road, he's stopped on Barna Road, sir," someone said. Dermot and Luke, driven by Jim, raced to the location, arriving at the same time as two other garda cars with blue lights flashing. They stopped at the end of the road. All was quiet and the signal was strong and loud. Lying in the middle of the road, illuminated by a street lamp, lay the case, wide open and very empty. Dermot and the other officers walked over to it. He prodded it with his foot then in a fit of anger went to kick it down the street, only regaining control at the thought that it was evidence.

He left the road blocks in place and started house-to-house enquiries.

Much later, back in the CID office of Ballyfingal Garda station, after it had become too late to carry on with the house-to-house, Dermot, Luke and Jim stood round a map of the area.

"He can't have got out. Every road was blocked off within five minutes. He's got to be holed up somewhere in this area," Dermot made a circle in the air over the map with his open palm. "He couldn't have made it anywhere else. Did your lads come up with anything?"

"They checked with the estate agents for premises recently let, but Carl Rose could have had a private let," said Jim. "They checked a few over here." He pointed at the top corner which was heavily built up with streets of terraces.

"That's the same general area he made the calls from," said Luke.

What was worrying all three of them more was the fact that Carl Rose hadn't contacted Tessa, and Eoin hadn't shown up anywhere.

Eoin, at that moment, was sitting on the floor drinking lager from a can and helping Carl to count the money.

"I thought it would look, I don't know, more!" They kept losing count and decided eventually to pile it up in ten thousands. They were getting drunk, and very skittish and it took about two hours to complete the ten stacks, each containing two hundred fifty-pound notes. Carl divided the money into two piles by placing his arm in the middle of the mass and pushing one half towards Eoin. Then he stuffed the rest back into the hold-all that he had transferred it into after the drop.

"What's this?" Eoin was puzzled and very drunk by this time.

Carl, who was equally drunk, had difficulty getting his tongue round the words. "S'fer yoo hoo!"

"For me?"

"Fer you." Carl slapped him on the chest and overbalanced sideways, knocking over the pile of empty beer cans. He rolled through the bank notes that he had just given to Eoin. Suddenly Eoin had an attack of hysterics. "'You having your daily roll in money?" he said. When Carl's laughter had subsided a little he replied, "Something like that."

Eoin became serious. "Why are you giving me this? You're going to need as much as you can get."

Carl shrugged. "Put it away somewhere, then you'll never have to take crap from anyone again."

Eoin reached for another can of lager. "You could go through the North to Scotland. You could catch the ferry. No one would know you in Scotland."

* * *

Tessa was beside herself with worry by this time, and Grace and Phoebe had difficulty keeping her calm. Dermot asked them to stay with Tessa until the doctor arrived to give her a sedative, then to leave her with the night shift and go home to get some sleep. Unable to do anything but wait for first light to continue the search, Dermot, Luke and the others also called it a day.

Chapter Nineteen

At the crack of dawn, which at that time of year was around eight, the team once again assembled in the incident room of Ballyfingal police station. Dermot called them all to order.

"Right. We'll systematically search each area house-to-house. Luke Ryan has divided up the area into sections and assigned teams of two to each. Get your assignments from him on your way out. I don't have to stress that we have a hostage situation here, so any sightings or evidence of the whereabouts of either man, get back onto base. We want to avoid a siege situation at all costs."

The team of Gardaí muttered amongst themselves for a few minutes and then each got their assignments from Luke, who had paired himself off with Grace.

It had started to drizzle as they set off from the station and the early morning traffic congested the streets. People were trudging to work under umbrellas and standing at bus stops waiting for buses that always arrived full. Luke parked and took out his map.

"We can take alternate streets if you like, we'll cover more ground that way." Grace shrugged, "Sure, fine by me," and got out of the car.

The streets in the area they were covering were tidy terraces. The rain glistened off the concrete roads, and cars swished past as Grace made her way along from house to house. Where there was no reply she would ask a neighbour about the absent occupant and she made good progress.

At about ten-thirty she got peckish and headed for the corner shop for a bar of chocolate to keep the hunger at bay. The oldfashioned bell pinged as she walked in and an elderly man shuffled from the back room. The smell of the little shop brought back childhood memories for an instant.

"Yes, love?"

Grace picked up a bar of fruit and nut and handed it to the man along with a pound coin.

"You with the guards?" he asked.

"No, I'm a private investigator. I'm looking for two young men," she said, handing him a picture of Eoin and the photofit of Carl Rose. "Have you seen either of these two in the last few days?"

He scrutinised the pictures and pursed his lips. He shook his head. "No love, not that I remember.

What've they done?" Grace told him that the two men were missing persons. "I see," he said. "And the two of them are missing?"

"That's right. Are you sure you haven't seen them?" He looked at the picture and after a while shook his head. "Don't think so." He gave her her change.

On the way out of the shop she took a look at the notice board display of postcard ads. There were two advertising houses to let so she wrote down the addresses. The shop-owner watched her without comment.

"Which one's Davitt Street?" she asked.

"Third one down," he said pointing at the sky. Davitt Street was the third street down that ran parallel to the one in which the shop was situated. She looked out for Luke but couldn't see him. She found number eighteen and pressed the doorbell. There was no sound from inside so she cupped her hands against the glass of the front window and looked in. The net curtains made it difficult to see, but she could just make out a shabby three piece suite and the usual bric-a-brac you would expect to find in a front room. She rang the bell again and heard the sound echo through the house. The front door of number nineteen opened and a young woman peeped out. Grace stopped her before she shut the door again.

"Excuse me. Do you know your neighbours in

number eighteen?" she asked. The woman opened the door fully and stood on the doorstep with her arms folded.

"Students." She mouthed the word, as if it were bad language or a mysterious female complaint. "I think they're students."

"Oh," Grace nodded. "How long have the . . . " and she mouthed the offensive word, " . . . been there?"

"About a year, a little more maybe."

"Is there anyone new in the street, say in the last few weeks?"

The woman put her hand over her mouth and screwed up her eyes as if thought was a great effort. Grace prompted, "How about number twenty-three?"

"Hmmmm," said the woman. "Now you come to mention it, I think three lads took it. I expect they're . . ." Grace finished the sentence for her, "Students?"

The woman nodded, not sure if Grace was talking the mickey or not.

"What do they look like?"

"Two of 'em are blond and the other fella's dark, with a little 'tash." Grace thanked her and the woman watched as she walked down the street. The fact that there were three men made Grace think that this was another dead end. She rang the bell. The sound of music was dimly audible from within.

* * *

Carl woke at about ten with a cracking hangover. He stumbled out of bed and stood under the shower for ten minutes, letting the hot water play on the back of his neck. He felt awful, not just as a result of the hangover but about the situation in which he found himself in general. All this business went totally against the grain, he hadn't wanted any of it. Events had just taken over after the nail gun had accidentally gone off, killing Georgie Warren. If only he hadn't gone to the funeral he'd never have seen Lou Armitage and followed him home, or seen Grant arrive and tailed him home from there. Armitage had been the worst of them, Carl had lost his temper when that sod had started to laugh at him and called him pathetic. He should just have taken the money, but he had enjoyed watching Georgie Warren squirm. That was the only worthwhile bit of the whole affair. Now the only way out seemed to be to go to Scotland and start over. He desperately wanted to speak to his mother but didn't dare in case the guards were with her. He didn't want to have to put her in that position. He climbed out of the shower, towelled himself down and put out his jeans, then he went into the front bedroom to get his sweatshirt. He could hear Eoin moving about downstairs and the sound of the radio tuned into 2FM. As he glanced out of the window he saw the woman coming towards the house. She looked very familiar, and with growing horror he recognised her from Georgie Warren's funeral.

He made dash for the top of the stairs, meaning to call to Eoin to switch off the radio, but he was too late. He could see the shadow of her body reflected through the glass in the front door. The doorbell rang. The shotgun was sitting on the landing so he grabbed it and took the stairs two at a time, leaving the gun behind the door jamb as he opened it.

"Good morning," said Grace. "I'm Grace de Rossa, I'm looking . . . " She didn't recognise him. She had only seen a photofit of him with longish blonde hair.

Just then Carl heard Eoin step in the hall behind him, the racket from the radio must have hidden the noise of the bell. Grace froze in mid-sentence as she recognised Eoin.

Thinking on his feet, Carl yanked her through the door and slammed it after her. She struggled, but he snatched up the shotgun and pressed it to her temple.

"Not a word!" he warned. Eoin was rooted to the spot. Carl hissed at him, "Get into the back." Eoin mutely did as he was told, and Carl pushed

Grace down the narrow hall ahead of him with the two barrels of the gun cold against her cheek. She started to speak but he prodded the gun into the flesh of her neck so she shut up. He was dragging her to the back of the house, his arm round her throat. His grip was too tight and she felt herself slipping away.

When she came to, she was slumped on the floor, her hands tied with a piece of flex to a radiator. Her shoulder was throbbing with pain. She was sure it was dislocated. The room was empty but she could hear the muffled sound of voices from next door. She strained her ears to try and make out what was being said but the door was almost closed and so made the sounds indistinct. She shuffled on her bottom as close as she could, and lay down with her ear as near to the gap as the wire binding her wrists would allow. She winced with the pain that the effort inflicted on her shoulder. She could see Eoin standing near the window but Carl was out of her field of vision.

"What the hell did you do that for?" Eoin said.

"She saw you! She saw you, you prat! What was I supposed to do, let her go and call the bloody cavalry?" There was a silence and the sound of footsteps pacing back and forwards across bare floorboards.

"What are we going to do?" asked Eoin.

"We? I'm the one they're after, remember." Carl snapped.

"Not any more. She's seen me. She isn't as stupid as she looks, she'll have sussed out I'm in it too." Thanks a bunch, thought Grace.

"Then I suppose in for a penny, in for a pound. I'll have to top her." Grace's heart started to thump.

"You can't do that! She's a woman." There was panic in Eoin's voice.

"What's the difference? You know, your old man was an accident, I only meant to frighten him." Carl had forgotten that he had already told Eoin this. "It was brilliant, he nearly wet himself, he was so afraid, so I asked for more money, I'd already had three grand. Anyway, the fucking nail gun went off by accident. I thought he was winding me up when he wouldn't move, then I cracked on to what had happened." He looked into the fireplace, not seeing the flames, just a replay of the events of the night that he killed Eoin's father.

"What did you do?"

Carl didn't answer so Eoin poked him in the back.

"What?"

Eoin stared intently at him. "What did you do when you realised that you'd killed him? What did it feel like?"

"Feel like? Well, I felt sort of powerful. It was so easy. I'd brought a hose to fix to the exhaust to wind him up into thinking I was going to gas him, because that's how my dad topped himself. So I did it anyway as a sort of message, I suppose." He was staring into space again. Suddenly he turned to Eoin and said, "When you've done it once it's easy. Lou Armitage laughed at me when I asked him for more money so I walloped the back of his head with the back of an axe I'd brought with me. It was a bit on the messy side, so I wrapped my tee shirt round his head and stuck his hat on top." He had started to laugh but without any humour. "By the time I got to Grant I was disappointed that he'd done it for me, so I stabbed him anyway to make sure." An uneasy silence hung in the air then she heard Carl say, "How hard would it be killing her, if it meant the difference between getting away with the others and not?"

"We could still get away to Scotland. She couldn't have recognised you." Eoin's voice sounded very anxious now. "We'd have been home free if I hadn't come into the hall."

"Maybe. D'you think she's OK?" Footsteps sounded across the room towards the door. She slithered back to the wall just as the door opened.

"Are you OK?" Carl asked.

Grace shook her head. "No. I think you dislocated my shoulder."

Eoin came into the room behind Carl and stood looking down at her. "He didn't mean for any of this to happen."

Carl cut him off abruptly. "Shut up, Eoin, I'll handle this." Eoin looked hurt but did as he was told. "Who knows that you're here?"

Grace didn't know how to handle the situation. Her gut instinct told her to try and placate Carl, who was obviously at best at the end of his tether, at worst unstable. "No one yet. But they'll start to look for me soon." Carl started to speak but she butted in. "I could negotiate a deal with the Gardaí." Her two captors looked at each other.

"What d'you mean do a deal with the Gardaí. Aren't you a Ban Garda?"

"I'm a private investigator. I'm working for Eoin's mother, she hired me to find him." They thought about this then Carl said, "What kind of deal?"

"You could give yourselves up and return the money. That would knock the abduction charge on the head."

She knew it sounded feeble as she said it.

Carl guffawed. "Some deal. Knock kidnap on the head, that only leaves three counts of murder!" Grace tried to think fast. "I know. But if you give yourselves up, there's less chance of anyone else getting hurt." Carl didn't look very convinced so she stumbled on, "I'm sure you didn't mean to kill

Peace and the others. If you give up now there's a chance that the charge could be reduced to manslaughter." She was really stretching credibility now. Carl took Eoin by the arm and they went back into the other room. Grace could hear them mumbling but couldn't make out what they were saying. After a few minutes they returned.

"We're going to take our chances as soon as it's dark," said Carl.

* * *

Luke and Grace had arranged to meet for lunch at twelve in the pub on the corner of McBride Street. When she hadn't arrived by twelve-thirty Luke began to get a little irritated. But later, after he had phoned Ballyfingal CID and no one had seen or heard from her since ten, he began to get anxious. At the end of the shift at two he reported back to the CID office having finished his house-to-house area. Dermot was talking to Jack Mulloy.

"Anyone seen Grace?" Luke asked as casually as he could under the circumstances. Dermot looked round. "I thought she was with you."

"We split up. I was supposed to meet her for lunch but she didn't show up."

Dermot furrowed his brow. "Did you call her on the radio?"

Luke shook his head. "No."

Dermot took out his radio and called Grace.

After five minutes with no response he looked very worried. "If she was on to anything she should have called in. It's not like her."

Luke went over to the map. "This is the area she was covering. I saw her just before ten here." He pointed to McBride Street. "She was just going into the corner shop."

"We'd better get over there," said Dermot, "and see what we can find out."

Chapter Twenty

Carl watched the group of Gardaí going house-to-house from the upstairs window and, because he was prepared this time, bluffed his way through when Luke rang the doorbell.

"I'm on my own," he said covering his Scouse accent with a fair imitation of Belfast, when Luke asked him who was in the house.

"Who else lives here?"

"No one." Luke flashed the photofit of the blond Carl and the picture of Eoin. Carl shook his head thoughtfully but promised to call if he saw either of the two men.

Luke wasn't quite happy with Carl, but couldn't put his finger on why. The accent wasn't quite right maybe.

"Thank you, sir. By the way, did anyone else call here today?"

"No."

The woman down the street had told Luke that she had seen Grace ring the bell. Luke hesitated then said, "Thank you again, sir." He was trying to look past Carl into the hall, but the younger man blocked the view with his body. Carl stood waiting for Luke to leave. After a moment Luke nodded and walked to the house next door and rang the bell. He heard Carl close the front door again. When he met Dermot at the end of the street he said, "I'm not happy with twenty-three. I think they could be there. A dark-haired man answered the door but I think it could be Rose. He had a queer accent and was very jumpy." Luke was very jittery and Dermot could sense it. "Take a look round the back, I'll get the Rapid Response team down."

"Do you think we'll need them?"

"I'm not taking any chances when Grace may be in danger," Dermot said. Luke was both apprehensive and relieved as he crept round to the rear of the row of houses. It was dusk and lights were shining out of the windows into the back entry. Jack caught up with him and grabbed his arm. "Look up there, Luke." Luke looked and saw Eoin clearly through the window on the first floor, pulling the curtains and talking to someone over his shoulder.

"What the hell's going on?" he hissed to Jack. "He doesn't look like he's there under duress, does he?"

"No, he doesn't. I think we'd better treat them both as potentially hostile. I wonder where they've got Grace?" Luke was wondering the same thing. The residents on either side of twenty-three were being quietly evacuated and listening devices were being eased into the plaster of the adjoining walls. Two uniforms relieved Luke and Jack at their post and they went back to see Dermot.

"We saw Eoin Peace, Dermot, but he didn't seem to be a prisoner. It looks as if he and Rose may be working together."

"Hardly likely." Dermot said, taken aback. "Rose killed his father, remember." Luke looked at his boss and shrugged. "I'm only telling you what I saw. It might be safer to assume that young Peace might be aiding and abetting Carl Rose."

"Point taken," said Dermot. "OK. The Rapid Response firearms squad are on standby. Hopefully they won't be needed. We'll go and knock at the front door and see what happens."

"Have you decided what you're going to do with the woman?" asked Eoin, drawing the curtains against the night. Carl was sitting on the single bed packing the money and his change of clothes in the hold-all. They had moved Grace to the front bedroom, bound and gagged.

"I'm going to make a run for it soon. If you want to stay here, I'll have to kill her, or she'll get

237

you charged with conspiracy, and they can throw away the key on that one. They may even implicate you in the murders if anyone lets on that you and your old man didn't get on."

"I don't want you to kill her!" said Eoin. "I'll take my chances with you."

"OK. I'll check the street. Are you fit?"

Eoin nodded. "As I'll ever be."

Carl walked through to the front bedroom and lifted back the curtain. "Shit!" he exclaimed and let it drop again. "The place is crawling with the law. Eoin, get the sawn-off from downstairs. *Quick.*"

Eoin raced downstairs and grabbed the gun just as Dermot and Luke knocked on the door. In fright he squeezed the trigger and a six-inch hole was blown in the panel. He screamed, terrified by the noise and the strong smell of cordite. He raced back up the stairs two at a time, slamming the bedroom door behind him and slumping to the floor. Dermot and Luke were equally shocked as the hole appeared in the door panel in front of them. Fortunately they were standing to one side but they both flung themselves to the pavement on impulse. A silence hung over the street like the calm after a storm, then the two men heard the sound of running feet.

"Are you OK, Dermot?" shouted Jack. Dermot, who had been temporarily deafened, sat against the wall of the house and examined himself for injury.

"I'm fine. How about you, Luke?" Luke, who was also examining himself for perforations, rolled over and sat up on the other side of the door. He just nodded, too stunned to speak. He had never been shot at before.

They both sat and listened but couldn't hear any sound from within the house. Gingerly Luke got on all fours and scuttled across the doorway to Dermot's side and together they ran down to the end of the street where barriers had been erected.

"This is the last thing I wanted," scowled Dermot. "We don't need a siege situation to develop. We'd better start to negotiate straight away so they haven't too much time to think."

"There's a phone in the house, sir," said Jim and gave him the number.

"Shit! Shit! Shit!" yelled Carl. "What the fuck did you do that for, you stupid little prat." He slapped Eoin round the face and shoulders. Eoin tried to protect himself with his arms.

"It just went off in my hand. Stop hitting me, Carl. It wasn't my fault."

Carl calmed down and sat next to Eoin on the floor, panting with the exertion.

Grace had heard the explosion and didn't like the way the situation was developing. Also she was well aware that she was literally at the mercy of these very strange and unstable young men. She eased herself up a little. Her shoulder was giving her hell, and she looked over at them, sitting on the floor. Carl clasped the sawn-off shotgun between his knees and rocked back and forth, very agitated. Eoin had his head in his hands, nearly doubled up, whimpering. Suddenly the jangling of the phone cut through the charged atmosphere in the little room. Carl jumped up and ripped the plaster off Grace's mouth, then he yanked her off the bed by her arm. "Answer it," he ordered as she screamed with pain. The phone was sitting on the landing outside the bedroom door. He shoved her forward and she screamed again. Excruciating pain shot down from her shoulder and right through her body as she stumbled onto her knees.

"Pick it up," he yelled as he untied her hands. Grace picked up the receiver and Carl held it so he could listen in to the conversation.

"Hello."

Dermot's voice came on the line. "Is that you Grace? Are you OK? Are you hurt?"

"Yes. think I dislocated my shoulder, but I'm OK."

"What's the situation there?"

Grace looked at Carl and when he didn't react said, "I'm a hostage and . . . " Carl snatched the receiver and, breathing heavily, spoke to Dermot. "We want safe passage out of here."

Dermot could hear how agitated he was, and

tried to calm him down. "Take it easy, Carl, let's talk about this."

"I don't want to talk, I want out. I want out now."

"There's a bit of a problem with that, Carl. We need you to let Miss de Rossa and Eoin Peace go first."

"He wants to come with me. We want to take the money and for you to let us go." His voice was rising again and Grace felt his grip tighten on her good arm. He was hurting her. "I've got your private eye and I'll kill her if I have to."

"OK, OK, Carl, calm down. There's no need for any more violence. We'll see what we can arrange. I'll get back to you."

"Do that. And soon." Carl slapped down the receiver and looked over at Eoin who was on his feet near the window. "Can you see them?"

Eoin moved the curtain a fraction. "I think they're at the end of the street. I can see the blue lights."

Carl shoved Grace backwards. "Sit over there," he said, indicating the corner of the room near the fire place.

"Don't *do* that," she snapped. "It fucking hurts!"

Surprised, he backed off. "I'm sorry," he said. "But don't think I won't kill you if I have to."

Grace sat on the floor watching the two men. Carl was looking out from behind the curtains. "I think you're right. There seems to be a sort of barrier. If they let us go we'll have to take her for a hostage. We can't afford to let her go free. She's our insurance."

Suddenly Eoin sat down heavily on the bed. "I don't think we can get out of here, Carl. It's too late. Where could we go? We should give up. They might even shoot us." Carl spun round and slapped Eoin hard on the cheek.

"Don't be such a wimp, Eoin. If you want to give up that's your business, but I'm going to see what that guard comes up with first." Eoin sat rubbing his cheek, and staring at Carl open-mouthed.

Luke was listening to this conversation through the wall in the adjoining house and didn't like the way things were going down.

Then he heard Grace's voice. "The longer you wait, Carl, the worse it gets. Let me call them and tell them you're coming out, unarmed. It doesn't have to be as bad as it looks for you right now."

Carl was sitting tapping his foot against the fireplace. The shotgun was under his arm.

"Just put the gun down and think it through, Carl. You can plead temporary insanity to the murder charge if you pack it in now, and Eoin won't press the kidnap charge, will you, Eoin?" She looked over at the young man who was now terrified. "Will you, Eoin?" she repeated urgently.

"No, no. Of course I won't."

"What about the money? What about the ransom money?"

"Well, I think if you gave it back, Tessa Peace wouldn't bring charges against you."

Carl thought this over. "How can I trust you?"

Grace shrugged. "It'll be an act of faith on both sides. How do I know you won't shoot me in the back as I go out the door?" The phone rang again and the three of them looked at it. "I could talk to them now and arrange it."

The phone was still ringing. Carl was still thinking. Next door Luke and Jack were still listening through the wall. After what seemed like an eternity Carl picked it up.

"Yes?" Dermot didn't expect that Carl would speak first and was thrown for an instant.

"Yes?" repeated Carl.

"Have you thought your situation through, Carl?" Carl looked at the receiver and at Grace and was about to hand it to her, then at the last second he changed his mind.

"I want more time to think. Call back in a while. And don't try anything daft, the sawn-off's pointing right at the woman."

"Don't worry, Carl, we'll stay away. I'll call you again in a while."

Luke crept out of number twenty-two and down to the barrier to join Dermot. Then he saw

Andrew. *Shit,* he thought. Andrew was the last person he wanted to see. Andrew made a point of joining the two Gardaí.

What's going on?" he asked Dermot. "Someone in the office told me that Grace is a hostage. Is it true?"

Dermot nodded. "Yes, Andrew, but she has the situation under control, she has plenty of experience, remember."

"If hours spent at work equate to experience I can't argue with that," he said, looking irritated. The Rapid Response officer joined them. "We've managed to place an marksman directly opposite in an upstairs room. If we can get yer man to the window, he could get a clear shot. He's had him in his sights a couple of times already." Dermot, who hated the use of firearms, was hoping against hope that it wouldn't be necessary. He moved away from Luke and Andrew to talk to Jack on the radio to see what was being said about the last call to number twenty-three.

Luke and Andrew stood together looking up the street.

"What are you doing here?" Luke finally asked.

"I came to make sure that my wife was all right," said Andrew.

"I thought you turned her in for a new model."

Andrew thrust his hands into his pockets to prevent himself from punching Luke.

"I'm not going to get into an argument with you, Ryan. It's none of your business."

Luke opened his mouth to speak but changed his mind. This wasn't the time or place and he wasn't sure what Grace's reaction would be when she saw Andrew, assuming, of course, she got out in one piece. The last thought left a knot in his stomach. Over the other man's head he saw Mungo and Phoebe and Xin at the other side of the barrier arguing with the garda on duty there. He hurried over and let them through.

"It's OK, they're with me," he said.

"What's going on Luke?" Phoebe sounded frantic, uncharacteristically so. "Andrew phoned and said something about Grace being held hostage. Is it true? Is she OK?"

"She's OK. Carl Rose has her hostage in that house up the street," he said.

"I heard a shot," said Mungo. "Is she hurt?"

"No. That was Carl Rose taking a pop at Dermot and me. But now we know he's got a shotgun things are looking a bit iffy."

"Looking a bit iffy!" Xin mimicked "I'd say it's a total fuckin' shambles." Luke's jaw tightened and he glared down at the pint-sized Ninja.

"Give me a break," he growled and stomped off.

A different drama was unfolding inside number twenty-three. "I think she's right, Carl. I think you should give up now," pleaded Eoin, not wanting Carl to become any more of a victim than he already was. Carl was biting his nails. "How long d'you think I'd get?" he said looking at Grace.

"Hard to say," she replied. "It would depend on what the charges are and how you plead. But it could be next to nothing if you're sent to a psychiatric hospital."

"But I'm not a loony."

That's a matter of opinion, she thought but said aloud, "I know, but if you plead temporary insanity, that's where they'll send you."

"What would he get?" he asked, looking over at Eoin, who was looking more like Bambi caught in the headlights than the self-confident young man she had first seen at his father's funeral.

"A rap on the knuckles?" she replied.

Carl paced back and forth again, turning the options over in his brain. Across the street the crossed hairs of a telescopic sight followed him. Eventually he stopped.

"All right, this is what we do," he said sitting down on the bed, still holding the gun. "He goes out first, then you, then me. In that order or not at all. No kidnap charge, and diminished responsibility on the rest."

Jack, who was listening in the next house, cued Dermot who dialled again. Carl snatched up the receiver and told Dermot what he already knew.

Dermot paused before answering as if taking in what he was being told. "All right, Carl. We'll do it your way. Send out Eoin and Miss de Rossa."

After he had put down the phone Grace said, "You did the right thing, Carl, you did the right thing."

He gave a deep sigh. "So long, Eoin. I'm sorry we met again like this."

Eoin shook his hand. "Me too. I'll come and see you and sort out a solicitor. It's the least my mother can do." Carl just nodded in reply. Eoin went down the stairs ahead of Grace and the two of them stepped into the dark street. Grace could see Andrew standing with Luke behind the barrier. As she hurried Eoin ahead of her, the armed officers, with revolvers drawn, were moving up towards the house close to the walls. Suddenly Carl appeared in the doorway with his hands above his head. The officers ran past her and spreadeagled him on the ground. Eoin tried to turn back but she pushed him on towards the barrier with her good arm.

Luke watched her walking down the street towards the cordon. He moved forward to meet her, relieved that she was OK, then Andrew pushed past him and got to her first. He stood and waited to see what would happen and his heart sank as he saw Grace smile up at Andrew and say something. Then Andrew's smile faded from his face and he turned abruptly and stalked off. Still not sure what was going on, Luke reached where she was still standing.

"What did you say to him?"

"Let's just say I wasn't exactly gracious about his sudden concern for my safety," she said. Phoebe, Xin and Mungo rushed over.

"Are you OK? Are you hurt?" Phoebe asked anxiously, hugging Grace who yelped with pain. Phoebe jumped back. "What's the matter? Were you shot?"

"I think I dislocated my shoulder," she said, nursing it with her other arm.

"I'll put it back for you," Xin volunteered, but Grace declined.

Tessa pushed through the cordon calling to Eoin. Grace saw him standing like a zombie, looking back along the street. When Tessa reached him, she embraced him and started to weep but he just stood with his arms at his sides.

"I think she has a lot of explaining to do," said Mungo as if reading Grace's mind.

"I don't think she'll be able to fix the damage," she said. "Warren Peace has succeeded in destroying his son's life too."

Luke walked back to where Carl Rose lay on the ground. Jack Mulloy had handcuffed his hands behind his back and was helping him to his feet. Dermot cautioned him and then told him that he was under arrest for murder and abduction. It must have taken a few moments for his words to register, because Carl was being led away to the garda car before he turned back to Dermot and shouted, "You said you'd knock the abduction on the head and I'd be up for manslaughter."

"Did I?" said Dermot with an air of innocence. They could still hear Carl's screamed insults echoing down the street as he was driven away to Harcourt Terrace.

The four sleuths headed back through the barrier towards Phoebe's car. Luke called to Grace and she dropped back to talk to him. "Will you be OK?" he asked. He looked worried.

"Fine," she said. "I'm going to James's to get this bloody shoulder put back."

"Can you come down to Harcourt Terrace some time to make your statement?"

"Sure," she said and turned to rejoin her friends.

"I'll phone you later," he called after her.

"Do that," she answered, smiling to herself, but without looking back. By the time they had waited in Casualty and Grace's shoulder had been fixed and strapped up, it was nearly dawn. Xin had insisted on staying with her, as had Phoebe and Mungo. That left her feeling quite touched. They dropped Xin off at her flat on the way to Baggot

Street, and Mungo parked opposite their building to save her the walk.

"Oh look," Grace said. "The signwriter's been." Phoebe and Mungo looked up. The first rays of the morning sun glinted off the freshly painted gold lettering above the door. It read,

SLOOTS,
Investigation & Security
Specialists.

THE END

BYRON
OF THE
WAGER

by Peter Shankland
THE PHANTOM FLOTILLA

with Anthony Hunter
MALTA CONVOY
DARDANELLES PATROL

BYRON
OF THE
WAGER

PETER
SHANKLAND

Coward, McCann & Geoghegan, Inc.
New York

Endpaper art depicts Anson's squadron off the north entrance of the harbour of St. Catherine's on the coast of Brazil. From *A Voyage Round the World* by Richard Walter; first edition, 1748.

First American Edition 1975
Copyright © 1975 by Peter Shankland

SBN: 698-10669-5
Library of Congress Catalog Card Number: 74-25237

PRINTED IN THE UNITED STATES OF AMERICA

TO MY DAUGHTER
CATHERINE

ACKNOWLEDGEMENTS

I wish to thank the officials of the Public Record Office for their unfailing courtesy and assistance, particularly Mr Michael Godfrey; and also Mr John Munday of the National Maritime Museum, Greenwich. It is always a pleasure to record that the staff of the British Museum Library and of the London Library have given me their usual helpful and efficient service. I should like to take this opportunity to express my gratitude to Mr Richard Ollard for his valuable advice and constructive criticism as editor of this book for Messrs Collins.

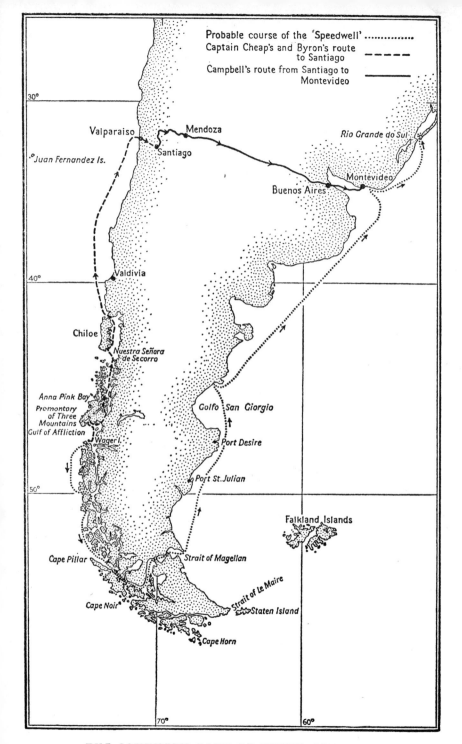

Probable course of the 'Speedwell' ....
Captain Cheap's and Byron's route
      to Santiago − − − − −
Campbell's route from Santiago to
      Montevideo ─────

30°

Valparaiso
Juan Fernandez Is.
Santiago
Mendoza

Rio Grande do Sul

Montevideo
Buenos Aires

40°
Valdivia

Chiloe

Nuestra Señora
de Socorro

Anna Pink Bay
Promontory
of Three
Mountains
Gulf of Affliction
Wager I.

Golfo San Giorgio

Port Desire

Port St. Julian

50°

Falkland Islands

Cape Pillar
Strait of Magellan

Strait of Le Maire

Cape Noir
Staten Island

Cape Horn

70°   60°

THE SOUTHERN PART OF SOUTH AMERICA

Illustrations follow page 160.

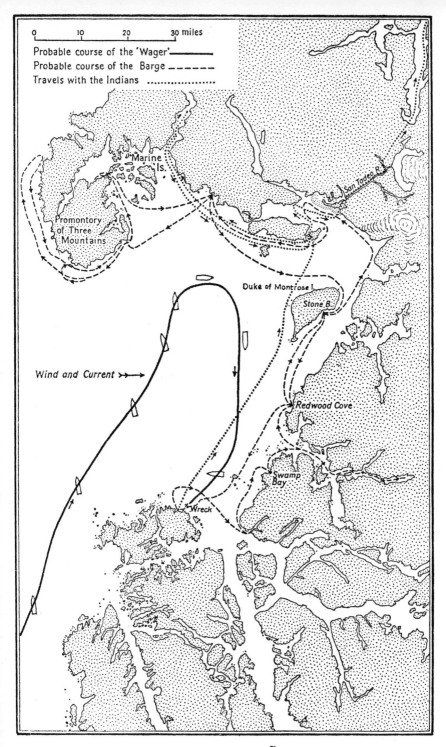

THE GULF OF PEÑAS

CHAPTER

1

⇥⇥⇥⇤⇤⇤

In the spring of the year 1740, in the reign of George II, nearly 200 ships were lying in the great anchorage at Spithead off Portsmouth Harbour, and others were constantly coming and going. First in importance there was a fleet of twenty-one ships of the line under the commander-in-chief, Admiral Sir John Norris, with frigates and store ships: it was Britain's main striking force. He was preparing for a cruise in the Bay of Biscay to intercept any Spanish ships attempting to sail from their bases there, particularly from Ferrol. Next in importance was a fleet of twelve ships of the line under Rear-Admiral Sir Challoner Ogle preparing to escort a large convoy of transports, fire-ships, bomb-ketches, tenders and hospital ships to the Caribbean. There was also a small squadron commanded by Captain George Anson who had the most difficult and the most hazardous assignment of them all – he was to sail down the Atlantic Coast of South America, round Cape Horn, and attack Spanish settlements in the Pacific: this was the most important strategic move contemplated by the British Government: it was not to be merely a piratical raid but a serious attempt to wrest Spain's empire from her, or at least so to threaten it that she would be constrained to sue for peace. After rounding Cape Horn, Anson was to capture a base from which to operate, preferably Valdivia, the most southerly Spanish port in Chile, in the neighbourhood of which the still unconquered Arrauco Indians were still resisting the Spanish forces: once established there he was to form an alliance with the Indians, support their independence, and establish permanent trade relations with them. Spain would have to retake Valdivia, or by a peace treaty give large concessions for it in Europe, to prevent the independence movement from spreading to the rest of her South American dominions.

For a long time tension between Britain and Spain had been gradually building up over the West Indies trade: during the past year relations had become strained because of illegal acts on both sides, and particularly because of attacks on British shipping by Spanish *Guarda Costas*, which were semi-piratical privateers. War had been declared on the 19th October, 1739, precipitated by a protest by Captain Jenkins, master of the barque *Rebecca* of Glasgow: he claimed that his ship had been stopped by a *Guarda Costa* and ransacked, that his crew had been ill-treated and that his ear had been cut off: he brought it with him to the House of Commons, wrapped in cotton wool. The war was known therefore as 'The War of Jenkins's Ear'.

The plans for Anson's voyage should have been kept secret: he should have been able to appear unheralded on the Pacific Coast of America where the ports were not strongly fortified and where there were only a few frigates to oppose him; but ever since the days of Sir Francis Drake and the *Golden Hind* a voyage to the South Seas had been a matter of intense interest and speculation. It had no sooner been determined upon than the secret was out: three weeks later it was known in Madrid and dispatches were being sent by every available craft to warn all the Spanish colonial governors.

The Spanish Government were surprised that Britain was prepared to risk the loss of trade that war would entail but, at the same time, they recognised how vulnerable their own American colonies were: to force the Royal Navy to concentrate in home waters they had planned to threaten

England with a pro-Jacobite invasion, and also to attack the British Naval Base at Port Mahon on the island of Minorca. Both these plans were upset when they learned of Anson's projected voyage to the South Seas. They judged it necessary to send Admiral Pizarro with a stronger force than Anson's to stop him: but apart from their main fleet, which was blockaded in Cadiz, they had only nine ships of the line at Ferrol and three at Cartagena: the invasion of England had to be cancelled for lack of escorts, and also the attack on Port Mahon, although the assault force, by July 1740, had already been concentrated with its artillery in the neighbouring island of Majorca.

The squadron, of which Anson had assumed command in the previous November, consisted of:

The *Centurion*	60 guns
Gloucester	50 guns
Severn	50 guns
Pearl	40 guns
Wager	28 guns
Tryal	8 guns

He was a very popular commander, and he had selected his officers with great care. Among them was a young midshipman, the Hon. John Byron, whose elder brother William was a lieutenant in Vice-Admiral Balchen's flagship, the *Victory*.

It was customary in those days for youths of good family, or with useful connections, to enter the Navy either as 'Gentlemen Volunteers' or as 'Officers' Servants'; but the Honourable John Byron, second son of the fourth Lord Byron, is supposed to have started his career in the 'Merchants' Service'. When Anson sent for him he was sixteen and he had been serving for nearly the past two years as Able Seaman in his Majesty's ship *Romney* on convoy duty between Newfoundland and Lisbon. In the same ship

Rodney, later renowned for his victories of Cape St Vincent and The Saints, was serving as Midshipman.*

Byron obtained his discharge from the *Romney* at Lisbon on the 28th February, 1740, and returned to England. He spent some weeks in London with his sister Isabella, his senior by two years, to whom he was greatly attached: ('She was very agreeable,' Lady Mary Wortley Montague wrote of her, 'but, if I am not mistaken in her inclinations, they are very gay.') Then he received his appointment as Midshipman in his Majesty's ship *Wager*, the store ship of Anson's squadron. With the help of Isabella he got his gear together – white breeches, sword, newly laundered shirts, three-cornered hat, quadrant, compasses, books, and a sporting gun – and made his way to Portsmouth. As a midshipman he ranked as a petty officer, below the boatswain, the gunner and the carpenter, but with additional though undefined authority as a prospective lieutenant: he was expected to assist the boatswain with the discipline and order of the ship's company, to act as Signals Officer, handle the boats, and be ready to lead a boarding-party or take command of a prize; so it looked as if he would have plenty of opportunities to distinguish himself – but he was destined instead to live through one of the strangest and most harrowing adventures in the annals of the sea.

The *Wager* was an old East Indiaman, built like a frigate but more for comfort and carrying capacity than for speed: being broad in the beam and very deeply laded, she would no doubt be difficult to handle in the heavy seas they must expect to encounter in the passage round the Horn. She carried her twenty-eight guns all on one deck, was pierced for thirty, and looked more like a forty-gun cruiser than an

---

* The writer of the article on Byron in the D.N.B. was evidently not aware that he went to the *Wager* from the *Romney* which he had joined when he was fourteen. (P.R.O. Adm. 36 4456.) It has been stated that he went to sea when he was eight, but according to his own account he was fourteen. (Journal of his Circumnavigation, p. 28.)

ex-merchantman. One great advantage she had, with a long voyage in prospect, was her ample accommodation, because she had been designed to carry passengers and a large enough crew to allow for the high percentage of mortality that was usual during the tedious passages to and from the East Indies. She had been bought especially for this service, and named in honour of Sir Charles Wager, First Lord of the Admiralty and principal instigator of the expedition.

After reporting to the captain, Lieutenant Dandy Kidd, and to the first lieutenant, Mr Baynes, Byron found a place for his sea-chest at the bulkhead of the wardroom, and repaired to the midshipman's berth which was on the port, or 'larboard' side of the lower deck, just abaft the mainmast. There were already two inmates, Henry Cozens of Somerset, who was sleeping off a heavy night ashore, and Isaac Morris, a Devon lad from Topsham, near Exeter: he had served in the 'Merchants' Service' and had joined the expedition in the hope of gaining vast riches in the voyage to the South Seas. They went round the ship together to meet the other officers: the boatswain, John King, a powerful, domineering type, was having a hard time trying to discipline the sullen crew: part of them had brought the ship round from Deptford where she had refitted, part were good seamen pressed from incoming merchant ships, and others were from the slums of Portsmouth. The carpenter, Mr Cummins, excitable and volatile, was frantically trying to repair the deficiencies of the dockyard. The gunner, Mr Bulkeley, a solid block of a man, was going quietly about his business and finding time to sit down and read *The Imitation of Christ* by Thomas à Kempis to himself or to anyone who would listen. He always carried the small leather volume in his pocket. These two, the gunner and the carpenter, were friends: they were both Portsmouth men, and their wives were friends also. The cook, Thomas Maclean, was nearly eighty years old: he had spent all his life at sea. The first lieutenant was courteous to Byron, but rather evasive in his manner: Morris thought he was a 'trimmer' – trimming his sails to any favourable wind, and without any serious convictions of his own. The captain was curiously morose, either from worry, from ill-health, or from premonitions of disaster. The *Wager* was evidently not a happy ship. In spite of the lure of the South Seas she was still short of men. The captain ordered a boat ashore to impress some more: six of his press-gang took the opportunity to desert, and the rest came back empty handed.

Anson's squadron should have been given priority in ships, men and equipment, and nothing should have been allowed to delay it. Not only was it necessary for it to reach the Pacific before Spain could send reinforcements there, but the winter season was approaching in southern latitudes and every day's delay increased the hazards of the voyage. But the dockyard and the victualling stores were already working to capacity to get the admiral's fleet ready for sea, and Sir Challoner Ogle's fleet with its hundred transports which contained 6,500 troops commanded by Lord Cathcart: news had reached England in March that Admiral Vernon had captured the important Spanish base of Porto Bello on the Isthmus of Panama, and therefore strong reinforcements were being sent to exploit this success by capturing other places in the Caribbean and by sending a force across the Isthmus to occupy the rich town of Panama on the Pacific Coast which, it was hoped, Anson would use as a base for further operations, should he succeed in getting there via Cape Horn. Unfortunately, as he was a comparatively junior officer, little attention was paid to his demands. Although he had much farther to go than the other two fleets, and would have to face the storms of the southern ocean, he was issued with old rope relaid twice or even three times, and with defective spars: the mainmast supplied to the *Centurion* had a rotten knot in it nine inches deep, and the dockyard officials were unwilling to provide a new one. The victualling yard was equally negligent. The peas and the oatmeal 'were generally decayed and not fit to issue,' and of the seventy-two puncheons of beef supplied to the *Gloucester* forty-two were rotten and stinking. After prolonged wrangles with the dockyard officials and the victualling agents these, and other defects, were remedied, and on the 28th June Anson was at last ready to sail, except that he still required 300 seamen to complete his crews. He applied to the Admiralty and was informed that Admiral Norris would supply the men. When he asked the admiral for them he was met by a curt refusal: he was himself short of men and he was about to sail. Admiral Balchen who succeeded to the command at Spithead was scarcely more helpful: instead of 300 seamen he gave Anson thirty-two from the hospital and sick quarters, thirty-seven from the *Salisbury*, three officers from Colonel Lowther's Regiment, and ninety-eight marines.

It had been intended that Colonel Bland's Regiment, and three independent companies of 100 men each, should also be embarked in the squadron as land forces, but this was changed and 500 Invalids were sent instead who were outpatients of Chelsea Hospital. Anson protested indignantly, and his protest was supported by the First Lord of the Admiralty: they were informed by the Government that those responsible for their selection were better judges of men than either of them. The Invalids were sent to Portsmouth: those who had the use of their limbs immediately deserted, but Anson was forced to embark the pitiful remainder — 260 decrepit wretches who had deserved better of their country. They were hoisted on board — not one of them could climb the ladders — and many, wasted by disease or crippled by old wounds, could not stand without being supported. To make up for the losses by desertion, 210 marines, undisciplined recruits who had not yet even learned how to load or discharge their muskets, were drafted into the squadron.

The marines, or The Maritime Regiment, were under the War Office, not the Admiralty: they were included with the regular soldiers in the land-forces. Those in the *Wager* were commanded by Captain Pemberton who maintained an attitude of haughty reserve towards the naval officers, and considered himself answerable only to the senior army officer in the flagship, Colonel Cracherode. His staff consisted of Lieutenants Hamilton, Ewers and Fielding of the marines, an elderly lieutenant of the Invalids, and Mr Oakley, the surgeon.

On the 10th August all the women were sent ashore and the squadron moved from Spithead to St Helens, a distance of three miles, to wait there for a favourable wind. The crew shook off their lethargy and began dreaming of Spanish treasure ships and of returning to Portsmouth with their pockets heavy with gold. It was now extremely urgent that the squadron should sail, or it would be faced with a passage round the Horn at the most tempestuous season of the year. The authorities, however, thought it proper to order it to put to sea in company with the fleet bound for the West Indies to provide additional escorts for it. They made up in all twenty-one men-o'-war and a hundred and twenty-four sail of merchantmen, victuallers and transports: they would require a fair wind for some considerable time to get out of the Channel with so large a number of ships. The wind came fair for the first time on the 23rd August. The whole fleet got under sail, but a change of wind obliged them to put back to St Helens with considerable hazard and some damage to the transports. They made three more attempts to sail, always having to put back again. On the 6th September the *Centurion* was for some time in danger of driving foul of a 70-gun ship moored under her stern. The constant manœuvring to no purpose soon discouraged the *Wager*'s crew and they turned out more and more unwillingly. Every morning the exasperated boatswain's mates went down the hatches, lantern in one hand and swinging rattan in the other, lashing about among the sleeping forms, shouting, 'Show a leg there!', 'Out or down!' and cutting the hammock lanyards of any who didn't leap out at their summons.

On the 18th September, after forty days at St Helens still within sight of Portsmouth, Anson at last received permission to sail independently of the larger fleet. He at once ordered his ships to weigh, and they drifted eerily down-channel under bare poles on the ebb tide against the wind, anchoring when the tide turned. By the 20th they were off Plymouth with a fair wind: here he had to pick up a convoy consisting of ships bound for Turkey, for the Straits and for North America, with their escorts: it had already put to sea and was awaiting him. In accordance with his instructions he now hoisted his broad pennant, signifying his rank as commodore,* and was saluted by every ship in the squadron with thirteen guns each. They proceeded in company, being in all eleven men-o'-war and about 150 sail of merchantmen. On the 25th they parted company with the American convoy, on the 29th with the Turkey and the Straits convoys, and then they were free to pursue the objects of their voyage without further encumbrance. They took with them two small Admiralty victuallers, the *Industry* and the *Anna* — they were both pinks, a class of small ship having a very narrow stern with a platform above it.

Anson had placed almost all his hopes of success on the chance of making up at sea some of the time he had lost at Spithead and St Helens, but violent and contrary winds persisted, and the passage to the Portuguese island of Madeira, which might have been accomplished in ten or twelve days, took forty.

* A commodore was a senior officer in command of a detached squadron of five or six ships: he ranked above a captain and below a rear-admiral.

At daybreak on the 25th October they made the land, and in the afternoon of the same day they came to an anchor off Funchal, a fair town of white-walled houses and red roofs straggling up a steep hillside among vineyards and orange groves. It was protected by a fortress with a battery of cannon, and also by a castle on a high rock standing in the sea. A British privateer sloop came in, ran under the *Centurion*'s stern, and saluted the commodore with nine guns which he returned with five.

Anson went ashore and paid a courtesy visit to the Portuguese Governor, who informed him that shortly before the arrival of the British squadron seven or eight ships of the line, probably Spanish, had been reported cruising to the westward of the island: this was no doubt Admiral Pizarro's squadron which Anson was already aware was being fitted out to intercept him and which Admiral Norris was supposed to blockade in Ferrol.* He returned at once to the *Centurion* and sent one of his officers in the privateer to investigate: he returned without getting a sight of the enemy ships. For more than a week they stayed at Funchal, watering and taking on board as much wine, brandy and fresh supplies of all kinds as the ships could carry: to avoid getting the longboats damaged in the surf, the captains were ordered to employ Portuguese boats.

When they were about to sail, the captain of the *Gloucester* asked to be allowed to give up his command and return to England for the benefit of his health. The captain of the *Pearl* was given the *Gloucester*, Dandy Kidd went to the *Pearl*, and Lieutenant the Hon. George Murray succeeded him in the *Wager*. The officers were not advanced in their naval rank by these promotions, but they were always addressed as Captain of their respective ships. Captain Murray brought with him a midshipman, aged about

---

* Owing to contrary winds the fleet commanded by Sir John Norris got no farther than Torbay and then returned to winter in Portsmouth.

thirty-five, called Alexander Campbell: to this man Byron took an instant dislike because of his brutality, and he contemptuously christened him the 'Patroon', which meant, in the West Indies, the Slave Driver, and it was by this name that he was always referred to by the seamen. Lieutenant David Cheap took command of the *Tryal*, sloop.

On the 3rd November they weighed from Funchal. They kept a sharp lookout for the Spanish fleet, hoping to avoid it because clearing for action would have entailed throwing overboard so many of the bales and barrels that encumbered their decks that the expedition would have had to be abandoned. They had their usual ill-luck with the weather: even the Trade Wind, nearly always constant, was for a long time to the southward, instead of to the northward of east.

On the 16th November one of the chartered victuallers, the *Industry*, asked to be unloaded and dismissed: three days were spent, therefore, in transferring the brandy from her to the other ships. Because all of them had such quantities of provisions between their decks, and were so deep, it was necessary to retain the other victualler, the *Anna*, pink, although she had fulfilled the terms of her charter-party. The ships were now so deep that they could not open their lower scuttles. The crews, who had been healthy as far as Madeira, began to be very sickly. To increase the circulation of air the commodore ordered six scuttles to be cut in each ship in places where they would least weaken her, and broad pieces of board, shaped at one end into a handle, were used as fans.

It took them seven weeks to cross the South Atlantic. Then, on the 21st December, they reached St Catherine's, a small fortified island with a fine harbour under the mountainous coast of Brazil. Here again they found an accommodating Portuguese governor, Don Silva de Pays: they were able to put the sick men ashore and to give the ships a thorough cleansing, scraping the decks, smoking them between decks, and washing every part with vinegar to get rid of the noisome stench and to destroy the vermin. They took in wood and water, caulked the ships' sides and fixed new standing rigging, setting up a sufficient number of preventer shrouds to each mast to secure it against the tempestuous weather they expected to meet with in their passage round Cape Horn. To enable the ships to carry more sail, and to prevent them straining their upper works, some of the great guns were struck down into the holds. They sailed again on the 18th January, 1741.

The land to the southward of them was hostile, belonging to Spain; and farther south again it was desert, and most of it unexplored. As a rendezvous in case of separation, the commodore appointed the uninhabited Port St Julian which he knew of from the accounts of earlier navigators, particularly from the detailed description by Sir John Narbrough who had been sent on a voyage of exploration by King Charles II.

Two days after leaving St Catherine's the *Wager* was separated from the other ships by fog and heavy weather. The commodore signalled to her, by firing guns, to bring to under the larboard tacks, the wind being due east. When the fog cleared she rejoined the squadron and they saw that the *Pearl* was missing and that the *Tryal*, evidently damaged, was being taken in tow by the *Gloucester*. For a whole month they proceeded in company to the southward, keeping well clear of the Estuary of the River Plate where it was most probable that the Spanish fleet would be encountered, for they did not wish to jettison their deck cargoes and clear for action if it could possibly be avoided: then, keeping in soundings, they sailed down the Coast of Patagonia, the fabled land of giants. The weather was fine, but a slight haze altered the appearance of the land and of the ships in an odd manner, giving at times a pleasing and then a frightening effect: sometimes the land seemed to be of

24

prodigious height, then it would be low and level, then it appeared to close them all around with huge broken mountains: it would not retain the same shape for ten minutes together. The ships underwent similar transformations, sometimes appearing like large ruinous castles, sometimes in their proper shapes and sometimes like logs of timber floating on the water. A strange bird with spurs on its wing tips perched on the *Tryal*'s rigging, and the sea in many places appeared as red as blood. In the midst of all these enchantments a sail materialised to the southward. The commodore immediately made the *Gloucester*'s signal to chase, whereupon she cast off the *Tryal* and made all sail in pursuit. She soon discovered the chase to be the *Pearl* who had been missing for about a month. They rejoined the squadron. The *Pearl* ran under the *Centurion*'s stern and reported to the commodore that her captain, Lieutenant Dandy Kidd, had died on the 21st January. She also reported that on the 10th February she had been chased by five large Spanish ships and had only escaped by standing across a rippling where the enemy did not care to follow her, suspecting it to be a shoal.

Because of the damage sustained by the *Tryal* it was necessary to put in at St Julian instead of making directly for Cape Horn: the head of her mainmast had been carried away by a sudden gust of wind while there were eight men on her main topsail yard: they fell into the sea but were all rescued, though terribly cut and bruised, except one who became entangled in the rigging and was drowned.

The entrance to Port St Julian was difficult to discern, the northern point shutting in upon the southern, so they stood along the coast while the cutters went close inshore and found it. The squadron entered on the 19th February and anchored in twenty-five fathoms. The country was all rolling downs with coarse high grass and bare patches of gravel, and not a tree was to be seen. There was no fresh water, all the streams being brackish. It was here that Sir Francis Drake had landed in 1587 and, on a small island in the bay, the Island of True Justice, beheaded Sir Thomas Doughty for sedition and incitement to mutiny; and in this same mournful and deserted spot Magellan in 1620 had quelled a mutiny, executed one of his captains, marooned another and hanged and quartered the body of a third who had been killed in the fray. Then he had gone on to discover the straits known afterwards by his name, and had made his way through them to the Pacific.

The place afforded nothing for their refreshment. Salt was supposed to be good and plentiful at certain seasons of the year, but they found only a little of poor quality. The sole purpose of their delay there was to refit the *Tryal*: her foremast was found to be so defective that it was impossible to repair it and her mainmast had broken off twelve feet below the cap. The carpenters immediately set to work to convert the *Wager*'s spare main topmast into a new foremast for her and to make the stump of the mainmast serviceable. At the same time the *Wager* was ordered to supply twelve butts and six puncheons of fresh water to the *Pearl* because she had stoved and jettisoned fourteen tons to clear for action against the Spaniards.

The Hon. George Murray became captain of the *Pearl* in place of the melancholy Lieutenant Dandy Kidd who had died prophesying with his last breath that the expedition would end in poverty, vermin, famine, death and destruction; Lieutenant David Cheap was promoted to the *Wager*, and Lieutenant Saunders to the *Tryal*. Lieutenant Cheap, an energetic Scotsman with a commanding presence, was one of Anson's right-hand men: he had started the voyage as First Lieutenant of the *Centurion*.

The enemy ships, after giving over the chase of the *Pearl*, had been observed to direct their course to southward: it seemed probable, therefore, that the Spanish admiral's plan

26

was to get round the Horn and into the Pacific ahead of the British squadron, not only to warn the settlements but to be in a position to operate from secure bases where his enemies had none. But the commodore could not risk being taken at a disadvantage if the two squadrons should chance to meet, and so, instead of discharging the *Anna*, pink, and sending her home as he had intended, he ordered the captains to put all their provisions aboard of her that were in the way of their guns, and to remount those that had been struck down into the holds.

On the 24th February he summoned all his captains and Colonel Cracherode to a council of war on board the *Centurion*. In accordance with the article in his Majesty's instructions, that they should endeavour to secure some port in the South Seas where the ships could be careened and refitted after they had rounded the Horn, it was decided that their first attempt should be made against Valdivia: it was eighteen hundred miles up the Pacific Coast of South America from Cape Horn, but it was the nearest place that would serve their purpose. Until then, the island of Juan Fernandez had been their rendezvous, a pleasant uninhabited island far out in the Pacific where they knew they could obtain water and fresh fruit and rest their crews. New instructions were now issued to the captains by which, in case of separation, they were to make the best of their way to an island, much nearer and lying close to the mainland, called Nuestra Señora de Socorro, Our Lady of Succour. Little was known about it except that it contained fresh water. They were to cruise off that island only for ten days, and then proceed to cruise off Valdivia. If they were still not joined by the squadron they were to go to their original rendezvous of Juan Fernandez. Anson impressed upon them that the separation of the squadron might prove to be of the utmost prejudice to his Majesty's service, and he told them they were to see to it that the officers of the watch kept their ships at no greater distance than two miles from the *Centurion*. This applied particularly to the *Wager* which carried the careening gear and also the mortars, platforms and ammunition they would require for the reduction of Valdivia: the whole of the goods, to the value of £10,000, with which they were to open up trade with the Arrauco Indians, had also been stowed in her ample holds.

On Friday the 27th February, with thick hazy weather, rain and a little wind, the squadron put to sea and stood to the southward. On the 4th March they were within sight of Cape Virgin Mary at the entrance to the Straits of Magellan. That day was remarkably fine, but the wind freshening from the south-west as night came on, and continually increasing, they were forced next morning to bring to and lie to under a reefed mizzen. At midnight, the wind abating, they made sail again and next day sighted the desolate snow-covered mountains of Tierra del Fuego, the Land of Fire: they saw that it had been well named, for under a lowering sky its glaciers burned like cold fire in the slanting rays of the setting sun.*

Because he was aware that the Spaniards had a fortnight's start of him, the commodore determined to pass through the Straits of Le Maire between the mainland and Staten Island instead of keeping to the open sea farther to the westward: they opened the straits on the 7th March and entered them with clear weather and a fair wind. In about two hours the leading ships were hurried through them by the rapidity of the tide — it was a distance of about twenty miles. As these straits were considered to be the boundary between the Atlantic and the Pacific Oceans, it was believed on board the *Wager* that the greatest difficulties of the voyage had been overcome. They rejoiced that the squadron was still

* According to some earlier voyagers Tierra del Fuego derived its name from the supposed practice of the natives when they sighted a ship of lighting huge fires and calling upon the four winds to destroy it. Others ascribed it to the presence of volcanoes or subterranean fires.

intact, in good fighting trim and that the crews were reasonably healthy. Encouraged by the brightness of the weather and the serenity of the sky, they felt themselves a match for any number of Spaniards and they began once more to think of the wealth and glory awaiting them.

But before the *Wager* and the *Anna,* pink, the two stern-most vessels, had quite cleared the straits the sky darkened, the wind shifted suddenly to southward and blew in such violent squalls that they were obliged to hand their topsails and to reef the mainsails. Then the tide turned furiously against them and drove them back towards Staten Island. The men in the other ships gazed in horror as the *Wager,* firing distress signals, was driven closer and closer to a line of savage rocks and gloomy precipices that rose up to tremendous snow-covered heights cleft by deep defiles as though rent by earthquakes. Her crew gave themselves up for lost. Only the example of their new captain, David Cheap, partly reassured them, for he stood unmoved and gave his orders in a voice that rang through the storm like a trumpet. Gradually he manoeuvred the ship clear of the rocks. With little room to spare they weathered the southern end of the island and were swept seven leagues beyond it out into the Atlantic again where the unusual appearance of the short but mountainous seas filled them with terror, and where the quick and violent movement of the ship frequently hurled them on to the deck or against the bulwarks. For five succeeding days they lay under a reefed mizzen, and at last were reduced to lying under bare poles at the mercy of the sea. On the 12th March the rails and timbers of the ship's head carried away on both sides; but after this the weather moderated, so they ventured to make sail with courses double reefed. Then they set their topsails: but without warning the wind rushed down upon them with redoubled force, and in an instant tore their sails from the yards. Snow and sleet swirled over them, casing the rigging with ice and numbing their fingers and toes with frostbite. The labouring ship was swept continually by heavy seas, and as each roaring crest rushed along the deck in a wall of foam sometimes six feet high, the men had to cling desperately to the rigging and stanchions to prevent themselves from going overboard. For two long weeks the storm raged. The scuttles could not be opened. The stench below became appalling. The salt meat could not be cooked. The men, covered with vermin, were falling sick of the scurvy in increasing numbers. When at last the wind moderated, they bent new sails and set a course to rejoin the commodore. In these hard conditions all the officers, including the captain, wore seamen's clothes: long trousers, short canvas jackets, striped shirts, woollen caps and griekos which were short duffle coats, and bare feet.

All the captains reported that their ships, by incessant labouring in heavy seas, were loose in the upper works and leaking in every seam. The *Gloucester*'s main topsail yard was broken in the slings; the *Tryal* reported that she had shipped a great quantity of water and that her pumps were broken: and all the crews were suffering from scurvy. Because the commodore feared that the *Gloucester*'s damaged yard would detain the squadron in these inhospitable latitudes, he ordered the carpenter of the *Wager* to be put aboard her to help with the repairs; and a new pump, ready fitted, was sent on board the *Tryal*.

On the following day, the 1st April, the sky looked dark and gloomy and the wind began to freshen and blow in squalls. They were now due south of Cape Horn and gradually making good their course to westward. On the 3rd a storm broke which seemed to the exhausted men to exceed in violence all they had hitherto encountered. At its first onset a furious sea swept over the *Wager* like a deluge. On the 8th, as she fetched a deep roll, the chain plates to windward, securing the standing rigging to the hull, broke with a loud report and her mizzen-mast went by the board, followed by her main topsail yard. While the men strove in the storm and darkness to cut away the wreckage, guns were fired as signals of distress. The commodore, being on the weather quarter, bore down under their lee and spoke with them: Captain Cheap reported that his chain plates had broken because of defective ironwork, that his rigging was shattered, and most of his people taken ill and down. The whole squadron were ordered to run before the wind till all was made secure on the *Wager*: then they turned into the wind and beat to westward again.

On the 10th April the *Severn* and the *Pearl* were missing. The commodore spread the other ships and beat about for them for many hours, but did not find them.

When the squadron was, according to their reckoning, more than 300 miles to the westward of the westernmost point of Tierra del Fuego, and well out in the Pacific, they altered course to the northward to reach a warmer climate and more tranquil seas. On the night of the 13th April, which was dark and hazy with the wind blowing in squalls from the south-west, the moon unexpectedly shone out and the *Anna* made the signal for sighting land right ahead: it was made out to be Cape Noir, part of Tierra del Fuego. It was less than two miles distant, and had the wind not shifted to west-north-west none of the ships could possibly have avoided running ashore. As it was they were able to get clear. They headed southward again, which increased the despondency of the crews, and the scurvy increased in the same proportion. By noon next day, the 14th, they had gained an offing of about fifty miles: the weather was fair and it was possible to launch a boat, so the carpenter was returned to the *Wager*. He fitted a cap to the stump of the mizzen-mast, got up a lower studding-sail boom, forty feet long, and hoisted a sail on it to keep the ship to. They repaired the rigging, bent on a new mainsail, and reefed it.

They had no sooner done this than the storm wind blew again, and in spite of all their efforts they gradually fell astern of the rest of the squadron. On the night of the 24th, in thick weather and with the wind increasing, the lieutenant of the *Wager*, who had the first watch, lost sight of the commodore's light at nine o'clock. At ten they were obliged to hand the foresail, and in so doing they lost a man overboard. In the morning they could see the *Gloucester* far ahead, with the *Anna* astern of her; but soon they lost sight of them, and they were alone in the empty sea that raged with elemental fury as if the Spirit of God had not yet walked upon the waters.

CHAPTER

2

IT had been generally understood and assumed that as soon as the squadron had rounded the Horn it would make directly for the semi-tropical island of Juan Fernandez, two hundred and twenty miles from the Coast of Chile in latitude 33° 40′ South: the *Wager* was clearly not heading for it. With increasing anxiety the officers saw that the courses given to them by the captain were keeping them close to the coast: every night, for four nights in succession, they had orders to heave to, and they lay under a reefed mainsail, head to windward and making only leeway, wallowing in the mountainous seas that moved in endless succession continually from the westward out of the darkness. Every morning they made sail again and were ordered to steer NNW by the compass. For a fortnight they saw no other ship, no land, no sun, no moon nor stars, because of the unbroken canopy of thick grey cloud. On one side of them stretched the limitless unknown southern ocean; on the other the Coast of Chile, a thousand desolate miles of uncharted rocks, shoals, inlets, channels and islands.

Mr Bulkeley wrote in his journal: 'I ask'd the Lieutenant the Reason of our bearing for the Land on a Lee-Shore, when we had a fair Wind for our Rendezvous, which I had always thought was for the Island of *Juan Ferdinandez* (sic). The Lieutenant told me the Rendezvous was alter'd to an Island in the Latitude of 44: South. Upon this I said to the Lieutenant, This is a very great Misfortune to us; that we can do nothing with the Ship in the Condition she is upon

33

a Lee-Shore; and am surpriz'd, that we should be oblig'd to go there. The Lieutenant told me, he had said every Thing he could to dissuade the Captain from it, but found him determin'd to go there. The fifth Night, and every Night after, made Sail; the Wind to the Westward. I never reliev'd the Lieutenant, but I ask'd him, What he thought of a Lee-Shore with the Ship in this Condition? He always reply'd, He could not tell. We saw Rock-weed in abundance pass by the Ship. The Honourable *J - n B - n*, Midshipman, being on the Quarter-Deck, said, We can't be far off the Land by these Weeds. The Lieutenant and Mate being by, I said, Gentlemen, What can we do with the Ship in the miserable Condition she is in on a Lee-Shore? The Lieutenant answer'd, Whenever I have been with the Captain since our first lying to, I always persuaded him to go for *Juan Ferdinandez*; therefore I would have you go to him, he may be persuaded by you, tho' he will not by me. I said, if that was the Case, my going to him is needless. In a Quarter of an Hour afterward, the Captain sent for me, and said Gunner! What Longitude have you made? I told him 82 : 30. What Distance do you reckon yourself off the Land? I answer'd about 60 leagues,* But if the two Islands we saw are those which are laid down in your Chart to lay off *Brewer's Straights*,† and the same Current continues with the Western Swell, we can't be above a third Part of the Distance off the Land. The Captain made Answer, As for the Currents, there is no Account to be given for 'em; sometimes they set one Way, and sometimes another. I said, Sir, very true; but as the Ship has been always under Reeft Courses,‡ with the Mizen-Mast gone, she must wholly drive to Leeward, and nigher the Land than expected. The

---

* A league is three nautical miles.

   † They had sighted these islands seventeen days ago while they were still with the squadron.

   ‡ A ship is under her courses when she has no sail set but the foresail, mainsail and mizzen – the sails hanging from the lower yards.

34

Captain then told me, I suppose you are not unacquainted of my Rendezvous for the Island of *Nostra Signora Di Socora* (sic), in the Latitude of 44. I reply'd, Sir, the Ship is in a very bad Condition to come in with the Lee-Shore; and if it is possible to bring the Ship to an Anchor, we shall never purchase him again. The Captain answer'd, I don't design to come to an Anchor; for there are no Soundings until you come within seven Leagues of the Land. I purpose to stand off and on twenty-four Hours; and if I don't see the Commodore, or any of the Squadron in that Time, we will go for *Juan Ferdinandez*. To this I said, Sir, the Ship is a perfect Wreck; our Mizzen-Mast gone, with our standing Rigging afore and abaft, and all our People are down; therefore I can't see what we can do in with the Land. The Captain's Answer was, It does not signify, I am oblig'd and determin'd to go for the first Rendezvous.'

Byron says that the captain replied to his officers 'that he thought himself in no case at liberty to deviate from his orders; and that the absence of his ship from the first place of rendezvous, would entirely frustrate the whole squadron in the first object of their attack, and possibly decide upon the fortune of the whole expedition.' He goes on to explain that the island of Socorro is in the neighbourhood of Valdivia, and its capture could not be effected without the *Wager* as she carried the ordnance and military stores. Although Byron wished with his whole heart that they were making for Juan Fernandez, he admired the captain's determination to carry out his orders: Mr Bulkeley and the rest of them seemed to be thinking only of the dangers of the lee shore and of the pitiless western wind.

The weather instead of improving as they sailed to northward grew steadily worse. Squalls laden with sleet and rain frequently cut down visibility to only a few yards. The longboat and the cutter, stowed in the waist of the ship, were stove in, the starboard anchor broke adrift and had to be cut away, but still the captain headed for the island of Socoro.

On the 13th May at nine in the morning, the carpenter going forward to inspect the chain plates shouted to the lieutenant and Byron that he could see the land bearing NNW, distant about eight miles. They hurried to him on the forecastle and saw on the horizon a dark patch between two low-lying clouds. When they looked again, it had gone. 'Shall I call the captain?' Byron asked. The lieutenant hesitated. 'No – it couldn't be land on that bearing. There's nothing to westward but thousands of miles of ocean. Keep a good lookout to starboard.' He turned and left them. 'But it was the land,' the carpenter muttered resentfully to his retreating form.

At two in the afternoon Mr Bulkeley saw the land to westward very plainly from the foreyard – it was a line of hillocks, and there was one remarkable sugar-loaf mountain bearing NW a half N. He came off the yard and ran down to the captain who immediately came on deck and gave orders to wear ship – to bring her about by turning her away from the wind, because in her condition it was impossible to turn her into the wind. All hands were called: the hardships of the voyage, and the scurvy, had taken so great a toll that of the original ship's company of 180, not including the land forces, only twenty were still capable of going aloft. As they worked the weather cleared, and they could see from the quarterdeck that they were within the headlands of a very large bay, though on their chart no large bay was shown. It was surrounded by jagged snow peaks, glaciers and beetling cliffs, with no sign of habitation. They looked round anxiously for a haven in which they might find shelter, and saw none: the line of breakers was continuous.

Suddenly, with a crack like a pistol shot, the strops of the forejeer blocks parted, and the foreyard came down with a run. The captain started forward to lend a hand but, just at that moment, the ship gave a violent lurch and he fell down the after hatch, the grating having been displaced by a heavy sea. He pitched upon his head and shoulder. The men ran to lift him out. They found him much bruised, and his left shoulder had been put out so that the head of the bone came below his armpit. They carried him below and laid him in the surgeon's cabin which they thought would be more convenient than his own for the rendering of his arm.

The crew were so weakened by illness and fatigue, and so dispirited by the sudden accident to the captain in whom they had complete confidence, that it took them three hours to wear ship, and all the while she was losing ground to leeward; and the nearer they drifted to the coast the more forbidding it appeared. At 5 p.m. they got her round and brought her on to the starboard tack so that she was heading back southward across the bay. Everything depended now on whether they could get her round to westward and sail out of it before they hit the southern shore.

The surgeon, Mr Elliot, with great difficulty and perseverance, and with great torture to the captain, succeeded in rendering his shoulder, but he lay ashen-white, helpless and barely conscious, listening to the seas crashing on to the deck above his head, and to the working of the timbers. Every hour Byron came down and reported to him the direction of the ship's head, and the force and direction of the wind. At eight o'clock the ship's head was south by west, which meant that they were now heading slightly away from the land, but they were still making too much leeway. He sent for the lieutenant and the gunner and urged them to make every effort to set more sail and crowd the ship off the land. He rearranged the watches, making two instead of the usual three. Learning that the wind was now northwest by north, he ordered the fore, main and mizzen staysails to be set, and then the topsails. Both officers demurred. The lieutenant said it was impossible to set the topsails because the wind was increasing every hour and the night was so dark that they couldn't see the length of the ship. The gunner said they were too weak to manage it, and that if they loosed the sails from the yards they'd split them, and they hadn't a spare one in the ship that didn't want mending. The captain asked for John Jones, the master's mate, to be called, and he seemed much downcast when they told him he had fallen sick. 'Try to set the topsails,' he said earnestly. 'Do the best you can, for the safety of the ship could depend on it being done; and you should keep all hands on deck all night, or until we are out of danger.' He lay back exhausted in the surgeon's bunk, and his officers left him.

Seeing that the captain was unable to move, the lieutenant considered himself to be in command, though he refrained from saying so. He took the next watch below and gave Mr Bulkeley the watch on deck. The night was dark and the wind increased to hurricane force blowing right in upon the shore, but nevertheless Mr Bulkeley did his utmost to carry out the captain's orders: he managed to get the fore, main and mizzen staysails set. The ship then lay gunwale to the water. At midnight he called all hands on deck and sent the midshipmen aloft to loosen the topsails: the lieutenant called them down again and told Mr Bulkeley that if he set the topsails the masts would go by the board. Byron's opinion was that the topsails could have been set, that the ship would have carried them, and he and Campbell volunteered to go up again and loosen them. They were overruled. The ship drove on through the night, her rotten cordage snapping as it took the strain and streaming away from the yards that it should have held firmly to the wind. Her head was S by W or SSW, but at four in the morning she came up with her head due west, directly for the open sea, and they began to hope again. At 4.30 she struck on a shoal or sunken rock. It was not a violent blow — no more than if a heavy sea had taken her under the main chains, but they felt it with sickening disappointment and foreboding of disaster. They had missed getting out of the bay, perhaps by only a few yards: perhaps with the topsails set her head would have come round sooner. This time it was touch and go. She bumped and came off again, apparently undamaged, and they kept her close hauled to the wind. The carpenter's mate sounded and found she was not making water. The lieutenant was about to loose the topsails from the yards, now that it was too late, but orders came from the captain to let go the anchor. They ran forward to do so, but found the cable was foul and they couldn't clear it. They swung the hand lead and found they were in fourteen fathoms. Suddenly she struck again, more violently than before. A heavy sea flung her on her beam ends. She lost her rudder, and the next sea made a fair breach over her. All the sick who could stir fought their way up to the quarterdeck, and some appeared who had not been seen for many days, animated to feverish life by the threat of present death. A mountainous sea drove the ship on again. It was near dawn, and the sky growing appreciably lighter, they saw breakers all around them, and jagged rocks. They sounded the well and found they had sprung a leak and there was six foot of water in the hold. A seaman shrieking horribly seized a cutlass and ran along the deck striking at his shipmates until one of them knocked him down with a belaying pin: another shouted that they were lost and tried to throw himself overboard: some fell on their knees and prayed.

In the midst of the confusion the master's mate, John Jones, came on deck: he had been in his hammock sick two days. He glanced round, walked aft, and asked whether the ship would steer. Though the tiller head was smashed and the rudder gone, the coxswain tried the wheel once more before answering that she would not. Then he asked the

39

carpenter if he had sounded the well, then ran to the fore-castle where the lieutenant was trying to clear the cable which had got over the cat-head: 'It's too late for that,' he said. 'There isn't room now for the ship to swing. If you let go the anchor, we'll be done for.' He turned to the men and shouted: 'Did you never see a ship in the breakers before? We must try to push her through them. Come, lend a hand. Lay hold there! We'll stick her near enough the land to save our lives!' He set them to the sheets and braces, and many who had seemed half dead aroused themselves and went to work under his direction. He set a group of red-coated soldiers who were crouching under the weather bul-warks to man the pumps, and for another hour they kept her afloat while he steered her for the shore with the main and fore sheets, easing off one and hauling aft the other as she came to or fell off. He instinctively found the channels between the rocks and brought her closer and closer to the land in a great tumbling sea.

Byron, going below to report to the captain what was being done, found him perfectly calm and still being attended by the surgeon. He told Byron they must consider only the lives of the people, that they should drive the ship fast ashore and cut away the fore and mainmasts, and he asked whether all the sick had been got up on deck. When he had delivered the captain's orders, Byron took a lantern and went to explore the men's quarters: it was like being in a tomb. The first rush of water had flooded the 'tween decks when the ship lay on her beam ends, and had left them chill and dripping like something raised from the bottom of the sea. Some of the hammocks were still bowed with the forms of men: he peered into one, then into the others — all the men were dead, drowned when the sea poured in. They had been too weak to climb out of their hammocks. He bethought him then of the two midshipmen whom he had left sick in their berth: he found them fallen from their bunks but still alive, and he helped them to the quarterdeck. He went down again and looked into all the cabins, but there was no one else. In the lazaretto the boatswain, who should have been keeping order, had broken into the lockers and was drinking the brandy stored there for the sick.

At 5.30 a.m. she struck again, so heavily that an anchor weighing forty-eight hundredweight that was secured in the main hatchway broke loose and fell down through the bottom of the ship. She brought up and stuck fast between two great rocks, the one to windward sheltering her somewhat from the violence of the sea. They immediately seized axes and cut the rigging of the mainmast so that it crashed overboard taking the foremast with it, and to ease her further they cut away the sheet anchor from the gunwale, but she was beating on the rocks and it seemed she could hold together only a little while. Some whose strength now failed them fell to the deck and rolled to and fro like logs with the motion of the ship. The land loomed through the mist that hung above the breakers. John Jones had brought them to within a musket shot of the shore.

CHAPTER

3

-»»«‹-

INSTEAD of daylight bringing comfort to the shipwrecked crew, it showed them the full extent of the disaster. All around them boisterous seas churned among grey rocks and shoals, and the land they could discern through low scurrying clouds and squalls of bitter rain was wild and desolate. The ship lay in a small bay formed by two rocky promontories; the one most southerly was fairly low, and that to the north rising up steeply to an unknown height among the clouds. The masts being gone, they couldn't hoist the boats, and it took them some hours to launch the barge, the damaged cutter and the yawl over the gunwale.

The captain ordered John Snow, another of the master's mates, to take the barge ashore, see whether the land was inhabited, and return directly. So many crowded into her that she nearly foundered on the way, and when they reached the shore they stayed there. So the captain sent Lieutenant Baynes in the yawl, the smallest of their boats, to fetch the barge: he stayed ashore also, but he sent the yawl back again. Then Byron took charge of her, and Campbell took the cutter, and they plied back and forth taking the sick ashore, and the soldiers, and as many of the people as they could, landing them through heavy surf on a shingle beach.

Meanwhile, by the captain's orders, the main hatch had been opened so that as much as possible of the provisions could be got out before the ship broke up. In the first sling that came up there was a cask of brandy: the boatswain ran forward brandishing an axe, stove in the head of the cask, and called on all the men to drink, for the ship was now theirs and everything in her. Soon most of them were running about broaching all the wine and brandy they could find, and they arrogantly refused to stow the casks in the boats to be taken ashore: those who had prayed most abjectly on their knees when the ship struck were now the most uproarious in their drunken defiance of the captain's orders.

Seeing that the situation was completely out of hand, and the captain was still lying in the surgeon's bunk unable to move, the midshipmen proposed to carry him ashore. He said that he wanted to be the last to leave, and he consented only when they had assured him that all who wished to go had already left. Assisted by the surgeon and the captain's servant, Peter Plastow, they carried him on deck, thrust their way through the shouting and mutinous crew, and laid him in the bottom of the yawl. They collected his clothes from his cabin, and also his cane, his books and his pistols with powder and shot. Then Byron ran back for his own things, but a rush of water from a breaking sea prevented him from reaching his sea-chest by the wardroom bulkhead: he could get nothing except his shotgun and some charges for it. He returned to the yawl and pushed off. Meanwhile Campbell brought off Captain Pemberton, Commander of the Land Forces, with three of his officers in the cutter.

Byron was as glad to be on dry land as any man who had narrowly escaped perishing in a shipwreck, yet when he looked about him he felt that his prospects were but little mended by the change. At a small distance from the beach there was a solitary wigwam, a large conical hut, constructed of stout poles and covered all over with growing grass. It had a triangular opening to the east, away from the prevailing wind. They entered, and found it contained nothing except some Indian spears and bows and arrows, from which they deduced that it had been recently occupied and that the owners, evidently warlike, might return at any time. Here they laid the captain and the rest of the sick; and as night was coming on and the rain began to fall in torrents, as many as possible of the people crowded into it also: the remainder sheltered as best they could in a clump of trees near by. Although they were in fear of the Indians they were too exhausted to take any measures for their defence. Byron, clasping his shotgun which was all that he possessed, found himself jammed against a pole, which was of charred wood, in the centre of the wigwam. He could neither lie down nor stretch his limbs. It became insufferably hot and he was soon streaming with sweat and gasping for air, the ground seemed to sway beneath him, and he passed into a sleep that was a sort of coma.

At daybreak they all crawled out, and the cold and the rain revived them. Their first task was to bury a lieutenant of the Invalids who had died in the hut during the night, and two others who had died of exposure under the trees. The crew were mustered: they numbered all told 140 men, including the land forces and three boys. Nothing had been brought as yet from the wreck except a large cooking pot and a bag containing two or three pounds of biscuit dust. Most of the men had eaten nothing for the past two days, so it was necessary to search for food. Two parties were sent out, with strict orders not to straggle for fear of surprise by the Indians: one went along the beach, and the other headed for the woods which began about a quarter of a mile inland. A third party remained to guard the hut and tend the sick. They dug a well for fresh water which they found in abundance, and they built a fire with dead branches broken from the trees, and started it with gunpowder.

The foraging parties met with little success. They couldn't enter the woods because of marshy ground and impenetrable undergrowth, but they brought back some wild celery, known to seamen as 'scurvy grass', which they found growing in profusion along the edge of the line of trees. Byron, who led the beach party, shot a seagull, and his men picked up a few shellfish: that was all they could find, although they passed some heaps of empty shells lying in circles on the beach, no doubt left there by the Indians. The seagull, very welcome in spite of its fishy flavour, because it was the first fresh meat they had seen for many weeks, was thrown into the pot with the shellfish and the wild celery and boiled into a kind of soup, together with the biscuit dust. Soon after gulping it down the men were seized with a painful sickness, falling to the ground retching, swooning and showing other symptoms of having been poisoned. They first blamed the celery, then the seagull: then they discovered that the biscuit dust, the sweepings of the bread-room, had been put into a tobacco bag which had not been entirely emptied, and this had acted as a powerful emetic. So they gathered large quantities of the celery which they boiled and ate with no further ill-effects. It proved indeed to be a cure for the scurvy, even the worst cases showing an immediate improvement, but it did little to appease their hunger.

At midday the captain, still very weak, came out of the hut, meticulously dressed in his cocked hat, tail-coat, flowered waistcoat, knee-breeches and stockings. He was leaning heavily on his silver-headed cane. He called the men to him and asked for volunteers to go out to the wreck which contained everything necessary for their survival. Four seamen volunteered to go with Byron in the yawl. The weather had so far moderated that they were able to take her alongside the *Wager* without much difficulty.

When Byron clambered on board he found a scene of extraordinary confusion: some of the mutineers were singing psalms, some were swearing and fighting, and some were lying prone on the deck which was littered with broken casks and bottles and odd articles of clothing. The ship's papers, including the captain's journal, had been crumpled and torn up, and the pieces were scattered about. Some of the drunken men had fallen into the water within the ship and drowned – their bodies were floating about in the waist, none heeding them. The captain had particularly instructed him to bring back any of the mutineers who were willing to go ashore, so he sought out the master's mate, John Jones, for whom he had the greatest admiration, and found him willing to come; and with him Mr Bulkeley and John Cummins, the carpenter. They collected their gear and a number of barrels of provisions – but the boatswain intervened with an unruly crowd at his back and objected to them taking anything with them. As the mutineers were armed with pistols and cutlasses, they were forced to leave with only a chest of tools and a little bread.

Although he had failed to get any provisions, Byron was glad to be bringing back three of the key men in the ship's company who would be needed in the difficult times ahead. Of the worth of John Jones and the skill of the carpenter he already had abundant evidence; of Mr Bulkeley he was less sure: he had served in many famous ships – in the *Nassau*, the *Solebay*, the *Winchelsea*, the *Cornwall*, and the *Royal Oak*, sometimes as midshipman, sometimes as Master's Mate, and finally as gunner in the *Success*. His department in the *Wager* was 100 per cent efficient, and he had proved himself a first-class seaman while in charge of the watch. He was also a bit of a sea-lawyer, knowing all the answers. A fortnight before the disaster he had reported to the captain that there was a mutinous conspiracy in which the boatswain's brother, Seaman Joseph King, was implicated, and he had begged for permission to issue pistols to the officers: they had all thought him absurdly cautious at the time, but now it seemed that he might have been justified. When Byron thanked John Jones for taking over the command and saving them when all were in despair, Mr Bulkeley reproved him, saying: 'We owe our deliverance not to any man, but to the hand of Divine Providence alone which guided us through all perils and fixed our ship immovably between the two great rocks.' Byron protested that he had no wish to deny the workings of Divine Providence, but he would give Mr Jones his due also, who had not lost his faith and had been the instrument in saving them. Mr Jones shook his head sadly: 'I freely confess to you now,' he said, 'that I had not the smallest hope that any of us would be saved from the fury of the sea. My only purpose in keeping the men employed was to keep up their spirits for as long as possible.' Mr Bulkeley commented that the lack of true religion among their masters was the great evil of the times, 'and particularly is this so aboard the *Wager*. When were the forms of worship last observed among us? Not since Captain Cheap came aboard, though the people were regularly docked of fourpence a month for the support of a minister of religion. I was certain that no good would come of it.'

They were received coldly by the captain who was seated on a log outside his hut: he remarked that he was glad to see them returned to their duty. Mr Bulkeley, who believed in the superiority of a humble attitude, quietly rejected the suggestion that they had been in any way associated with the mutineers: 'We have never departed from our duty,' he said, 'and it would have been well if others had known their duty as well as we. We stayed on board, at some peril to ourselves, only to try and restore order, and to provide for the bringing ashore of those necessaries of which we all stand in need. Unhappily we found the people on board the ship so thoughtless of their own danger, so stupid and so insensible of their misery, that upon their principal officers leaving them, they fell into the most violent outrage and disorder.'

The captain refrained from saying that the outrage and disorder were well under way before he and the other officers had left the ship, and that there was no evidence that any attempt had been made to control them – but probably only the captain himself, if he had not been injured, would have been able to restore order. He allowed Mr Bulkeley to continue: 'I think you would be wrong, sir, to treat them as mutineers. They consider that, as their wages ceased from the hour the ship struck, they owe no further obedience to you, to us, or to any of the officers. And I would remind you, sir, that in this view they are technically correct. They are well aware of it because two of them are survivors of the wreck of the *Bideford*.'

'According to the regulations,' the captain sharply reminded him, 'the whole ship's company are on half pay, and therefore still under my orders, until salvage work has been completed.' 'I put it to you, sir,' Mr Bulkeley rejoined, 'that the possibility of anyone receiving half pay is extremely remote. No, sir, I still think,' he calmly maintained, 'that they are not technically in a state of mutiny. It would be illegal for you to punish them, and you would not have the support of your officers.'

It was becoming clear to the captain now that Mr Bulkeley also considered that his authority was technically at an end, and that he and his friends were prepared to continue their obedience only for as long as it suited them. 'Do you still consider me to be your captain?' he asked outright. 'Certainly!' Mr Bulkeley replied warmly, 'and we will obey you to the best of our strength, in all reasonable commands.' Mr Jones and the carpenter murmured their assent. With this qualified assurance of obedience he had to rest content, and he sent them to supervise the building of shelters for the coming night. He was in a difficult position for he knew that he had in fact no longer any legal authority, or soon would have none: and yet it was obvious that unless discipline could be re-established and maintained there would be little hope of survival for any of them.

He was not at all satisfied with the results of Byron's visit to the wreck: he ordered him to go back with a larger party of seamen in the barge and to bring back provisions and a good supply of powder and shot. This time he put Campbell in command of the expedition.

When they boarded the wreck again, the mutineers were collecting armfuls of loot from the officers' cabins, depositing it in a heap on the quarterdeck and wrangling over it. Some of them ran up to Campbell and told him to clear out and touch nothing. Another, James Mitchell, a carpenter's mate, shouted: 'Patroon! You've carried a straight arm all the voyage, and now you'll suffer for it!' He picked up a bayonet and hurled it at Campbell; but missed his mark. The rest of them seized their weapons and advanced threateningly. As the two midshipmen were unarmed, they had to beat a hasty retreat and jump into the boat again.

They went back and reported to the captain that it would be impossible to take anything from the ship without bloodshed. He seemed to consider for a while whether he should lead a boarding-party to overpower the mutineers, but the idea of setting one part of his crew against the other was most distasteful to him, and he already saw that in any violent measures most of his officers would not support him. In a day or two, if the wreck held together, hunger would no doubt constrain all those on shore to return with him and take the provisions by force, and in the meantime the mutineers might come to their senses. 'We can do nothing more at present,' he said. 'We cannot help it; but I should be very glad if all the people were safely ashore.'

The new shelter was rapidly taking shape under the carpenter's direction: the damaged cutter had been turned keel upwards to form a roof and raised upon stout props driven into the ground: boat sails provided the walls. It was finished by nightfall, and it housed all the people to their very great contentment. In the captain's hut there remained only the lieutenant, the midshipmen, the surgeon, the purser, the land officers and the captain's steward. Thus the ship's company was divided into three groups: those in the hut consulting upon measures to restore discipline without which all would be lost, those in the new habitation consulting upon how far they might safely resist the authority of the captain, and those still in the ship openly defying him.

At dawn they were awakened by the boom of a cannon and the whistle of a round shot passing close above the captain's hut. They all ran out and found that the wind had risen again, and the seas were pounding the wreck and throwing up clouds of spray so that it looked as if it soon would part. The cannon, the four-pounder on the quarterdeck, boomed again and another shot passed over their heads and crashed into the trees. The captain, not liking that they should send cannon balls on messages to him, ordered Campbell to man the barge and bring the mutineers ashore. But when the Patroon called for hands to take the barge off to the ship, not a man would go: they all cried out that the ship was lost and that everyone was at liberty to shift for himself. The officers and petty officers, therefore, manned the boat; but the wind was boisterous, and the shattered mainmast lying in the sea and surging against the side of the ship encumbered their efforts so that they found it impossible to get aboard and they were forced to turn back. They shouted that they would make a further attempt as soon as the weather moderated. The mutineers, having looted the officers' cabins, were wearing tail-coats faced with silver, lace cravats, cocked hats and velvet waistcoats. Now in their rage, instead of cutting away the mainmast that had prevented their rescue and letting it float clear, they ran up and down the quarterdeck howling and swearing and hacking with axes and crowbars at everything within their reach.

The wind and sea moderating towards evening, the barge went for them again, and this time it got alongside the wreck. The mutineers came ashore, cursing arrogantly, still in the officers' clothes and carrying muskets, pistols, dirks and cutlasses. The captain, armed with a brace of pistols, stood on the beach to receive them, with Lieutenant Hamilton of the marines beside him: these were the only two who had arms, but the other officers and the marines were drawn up in a line supporting them. The rest of the people stood at a short distance to see what would issue from the conflict.

As soon as the boatswain leapt ashore brandishing a cutlass, the captain ran forward and felled him with a blow of his cane. Then, seconded by Lieutenant Hamilton, he drew his pistols and commanded the mutineers to come ashore and drop all their weapons on the beach. This they sullenly did, seeing their leader prostrate. The midshipmen quickly collected the arms and ammunition and distributed them to the officers and to the marines of the captain's party.

The boatswain, recovering consciousness, staggered to his feet and, seeing the posture of affairs, tore open his velvet coat, bared his chest, and dared the captain to shoot him. The officers stripped him of his finery, and when they had done so he knelt on the stones and cried for mercy. The captain turned contemptuously from him and ordered all the mutineers to be divested of their lace and velvet clothes, and when they appeared in the dirty checked shirts and greasy trousers that they had been wearing underneath, they looked like a gang of jailbirds. As soon as their pockets had been emptied of stolen money and valuables, they were allowed to slink away up the beach followed by the jeers and derision of their comrades. In the barge they had brought a quantity of ball and powder and some kegs of brandy, all of which, with the officers' clothes, were taken and laid within the captain's hut. Among them Byron found his cocked hat, his red velvet waistcoat, and also his watch which the mutineers had kindly brought ashore for him: it was a present from his father who had been a Gentleman of the Bedchamber to Prince George of Denmark. His cocked hat still had a gay but bedraggled feather round it. The waistcoat, which was long with wide pockets on either side, had been richly embroidered with gold by the loving fingers of his sister. He put it on at once and was glad of it because the weather was bitter and he had no clothes except those he had been wearing on the night of the wreck.

CHAPTER

4

-»>«<-

THE captain's authority had been re-established by his
victory over the mutineers: there had been no bloodshed,
and even Mr Bulkeley could find no fault, at the time, with
the way it had been achieved. He had demonstrated, in his
combat with the boatswain, that he had recovered from the
injury that had laid him low when his presence and his skill
as a seaman were most needed. His officers, and the land
forces, now had arms and ammunition whereas the rest of
the ship's company were without them: the captain was
again in command. He made plans to begin discharging
the *Wager*'s stores on the following day as soon as it should
be light enough: he ordered the midshipmen to have the
barge and the yawl manned and ready at daybreak.

It was perhaps too much to expect that the fine weather
or, rather, the lull between the gales that were nearly constant in those latitudes, the 'roaring forties', should continue
for another day. While it was still dark they were awakened
by violent gusts of wind and the ominous thunder and surge
of breakers. All that day and the next they could do nothing
but watch helplessly while the seas crashed over the wreck
and lifted her and pounded her against the rocks: they
marvelled that her timbers still held together. When Byron
saw that the boats could not be used he joined the parties
that were searching along the beach for shellfish: they got
very few because the heavy surf impeded them. The wild
celery was hardly sufficient to sustain them. Hunger was
becoming the greatest of their miseries, containing and

absorbing all the others. The steep mountain barred their way to the north, but they got round the southern promontory to the next bay where they found some timbers driven ashore from the wreck, but no kind of provision. They called the land they stood upon Wager Island – they imagined it to be an island – and the steep mountain they called Mount Misery.

On the third day, the 19th May, the weather moderated. Byron called for hands for the yawl and set out for the wreck, heartily cursing the mutineers who had prevented them from getting at the provisions sooner. Now it was almost too late. The wreck had settled deeper, the hatches were under water, leaving only the quarterdeck and part of the forecastle showing: she had been bilged – a jagged rock had pounded its way through her bottom and into the hold. Sprawled on the quarterdeck lay the body of a seaman: he had not died a natural death. It was a body twisted in agony, its eyes and blackened tongue protruding, its throat marked by the grasping fingers of one who had been a comrade. The utter callousness of the mutineers was shown by this, that they had not even thought of pitching the body over the side and letting the merciful sea hide it from human eyes, together with the evidence of their guilt. Byron told his men not to touch it until he had reported the murder to Captain Cheap. He threw a piece of canvas over it, and they turned to the main object of the expedition.

The mutineers had left the hatches open, but the holds were full of water. Byron's party lashed hooks to long poles and dredged for what they could find. First came more bodies, those of the sick who had died in their hammocks, and those of the mutineers who had got drowned while carousing. Byron would have liked to take the bodies and give them decent burial, but the people ashore wanted food, not corpses. Salvage operations proved so difficult that all they retrieved that day was two barrels of flour and three of wine. They filled up the yawl with an assortment of canvas, spars, boards and rope to enable them to build more huts.

Captain Cheap received Byron's report with no apparent interest: he didn't want a trial for murder on his hands in addition to his other vexations. He took the view that the mutineers had been seized with madness and that the murder was a part of it, and not the most serious part. His main concern was not justice, but survival. He needed a united effort from his people, and the way to get it was not to hang some of them and antagonise the rest.

When Byron returned to the wreck on the following day, the body of the strangled seaman had disappeared and no one seemed to have any recollection of it. In the quietness of the night he couldn't get the picture of that horrible mis-shapen thing out of his youthful mind: all their other afflictions were from without, and a man with fortitude might bear them, but this was from within and it filled him with a kind of terror.

Mr Bulkeley also returned to the wreck, bringing the carpenter and his mates: they spent a whole day breaking through the solid deck above the carpenter's store-room to get nails and other things of value. While they were doing it, Byron and Campbell secured some barrels of beef and pork from the hold, and some more flour. When they brought all these articles ashore the captain ordered them to be placed in a bell tent which he had had erected close to his hut, and he put an armed sentry to guard them.

The salvage operations had brought in so little in comparison with their expectations that it was a sadly dispirited group of officers and petty officers that faced the captain that evening in his wigwam round a table made of deck boards from the wreck. The only light came from a ship's lantern hanging on the charred pole in the centre. Rain lashed the roof and sides of the hut. They were hungry, weary, dishevelled, and soaked to the skin. Only the captain took a hopeful view of their situation. To encourage them he told them the story of another shipwreck, that of the *Speedwell*, Captain Shelvocke,* the last British ship before the present expedition to penetrate into the Pacific. She was cast away on the island of Juan Fernandez, but from her timbers the crew succeeded in building a bark thirty feet long in the keel, her breadth in the beam sixteen feet, and seven feet deep in the hold. In this craft, provisioned only with eels which they had caught and dried in the sun, and manned by forty stout fellows, Captain Shelvocke had put to sea and captured a Spanish ship of 200 tons into which he transferred his crew. With her they captured a larger vessel in which they raided Spanish settlements and made several other prizes; then they took a turn round the world and finally reached home. He thought that what the carpenter and crew of the *Speedwell* had done the carpenter and crew of the *Wager* could do also. He prayed them all to consider, therefore, what each could contribute in his way towards the construction of such a vessel, for they must get themselves afloat again, or die a miserable death.

The men listening to him took new heart from his words, and when they had discussed his proposal for some time among themselves, the captain asked the carpenter for his opinion, for it was clear that all would depend on him. He replied that he didn't see how to build a ship, for there was nothing to build it with. The captain then asked the armourer, John Russell, if he could provide the ironwork for a small ship. He replied that he had not his bellows for a forge, but if they could be brought ashore, and pieces of

* Captain Shelvocke was, according to his epitaph in St Nicolas Church, Deptford, 'bred to the sea service under Admiral Benbow.' He sailed from England in 1719 in company with the *Success*, Captain John Clipperton, who was in command of the expedition. Six days out they were separated in a storm and the two captains only met again two years later. Shelvocke got back to England in 1721.

iron collected from the wreck and from among the drift-wood, and charcoal burned for him, he would make everything that the carpenter might require for such a task. They all pleaded earnestly now with the carpenter to save their lives, promising him the support of all the people if he would undertake to build the ship: the captain asked him if he thought anything could be done with the stove-in longboat which was still in the wreck. He considered this, and told them that if it could be got ashore he could probably lengthen it ten or eleven feet by the keel and so construct a vessel such as the captain desired.

With that, from the depths of despair, the spirits of the company revived to such a pitch that they already felt that their troubles were at an end and saw themselves entering Portsmouth Harbour with flags flying to be acclaimed by the rest of the fleet; the captain had to remind them that it would require the utmost endeavours, and some sacrifices, from them all. It soon became clear what kind of sacrifices he had in mind.

He felt it his duty on the following morning to call all the people to him and tell them his plan for their salvation. They thought they had been sent for to receive their share of the provisions that had been salvaged from the wreck: when they learned that there was to be no share-out, and that all the unbroached barrels of beef and flour were to be kept to provide a sea store for the vessel it was proposed to construct, they broke out into shouts of rage and abuse. The captain, quite unmoved, sent them about their business. They had no mind to continue barely to subsist on shellfish while there was food in the store tent. They held meetings, they debated with noise and clamour what should be done, they sent delegation after delegation to the captain: he refused all their demands. Byron noted again that the men who had been in the greatest fear and crying out for mercy when the ship struck, and who then had mutinied and had been so very much the cause of their common distress, were now the ones who raged most bitterly against the captain for refusing to dissipate the small store without which they couldn't hope to make their escape by sea.

At the first favourable opportunity the carpenter and his crew went out to the wreck and began cutting away the gunwale in the waist of the ship in order to get at the long-boat upon which all their hopes were now centred. They cast the ship's awning overboard and let the seas carry it ashore to strengthen the deck of their new vessel which they determined to christen the *Speedwell* in honour of Captain Shelvocke and his men whose example had pointed the way to their salvation.

They did not yet know for certain that they were upon an island. When the sky was clear, but the sea too boisterous for salvage work, Byron was sent with a party of seamen to scale Mount Misery and survey the land about. They had to cut steps in the steepest places, and the going was hard: the rocky slopes facing to westward were denuded of all vegetation, even of soil, but in the ravines protected from the prevailing wind the trees were thick and close, cutting off the view: they were mostly a kind of evergreen beech with a profusion of particularly bright green shiny leaves. As they scrambled up the slope their feet sank deep into the sodden moss-covered ground which in places had been torn up by small rodents – they heard them squeaking under the ground but couldn't catch them or even see them. There were a few humming birds, equally elusive, spots of throbbing scarlet blown in the wind.

They toiled to the summit which was round and bare. Turning their backs to the open sea from which blew the pitiless cold west wind, they gazed to the eastward across a wild expanse of inlets and broken hills which rose to a majestic snow-covered mountain range that lay right along the horizon. The scene had a terrible beauty, but it was desolate enough to appal their hearts. No ship, no curl of smoke from lonely camp-fire spoke of human habitation. All was as it had been at the creation of the world. Glistening peaks, black rocks, primeval forests, riven valleys with glaciers, blue against the snow, thrusting right down into the sea. To the northward lay the great gulf that had entrapped them, its farther cape some fifty miles distant: to the landward side of it they could make out the tall sugar-loaf mountain that had been their landmark on the day before they were cast away.

A narrow lagoon on one side of them and a broader one on the other seemed to cut them off from the mainland, but they could not absolutely determine this because their view to the southward was obstructed by another high wooded mountain; some of the men thought they were on an island and some thought they weren't: but even if they were on the mainland there seemed to be little hope of reaching civilisation by attempting to journey on foot across that empty and savage country.

On the way down the men scattered to look for food. When they assembled at the foot of the mountain, having found nothing except some wild black currants with hard seeds in them, one of the men was missing – Thomas Lark, Assistant Cook, a simple and inoffensive fellow. Fearing that he had met with an accident, Byron turned back to look for him, stopping now and again to hail but getting no answer. Halfway to the top he saw a circling vulture. He hurried to the spot and found poor Lark lying dead in a small natural clearing in the bushes. He had been stabbed repeatedly and horribly mutilated. Byron smoothed back the grey wispy hair and closed the staring pale blue eyes, then ran falling and stumbling down the slope to get away from the sight that revolted him.

When he reported to the captain he said he suspected that James Mitchell, Carpenter's Mate, was responsible both for this murder and for that of the strangled seaman on the *Wager*'s quarterdeck: Mitchell had been among the most violent of the mutineers, he had made the murderous attack on Campbell, and he had been one of the party of exploration on Mount Misery. He had no proof, but he could not conceive that any other man of their company was capable of this cold-hearted ferocity. The captain told him to observe Mitchell closely and to let him know anything that transpired.

Several more tents had been pitched now, and huts had been built of the timbers that were coming ashore from the wreck: there was great need of them for it had rained almost continually since they landed. Thus the ship's company was divided into small groups, or communities, giving more or less obedience to the captain. In the wigwam there remained only Captain Cheap, the lieutenant, the surgeon, the purser, Lieutenant Hamilton and the captain's servant. The land forces had formed their own encampment of four tents a little apart from the rest with Captain Pemberton who still considered that he had an independent command. His men, though inexperienced as soldiers, were the best disciplined in the camp: they each had a musket and a uniform, with a great-coat: they did duty as sentries. They suffered even more than their companions from hunger, for they had no opportunities to help themselves to anything from the wreck, and they proved less adept than the seamen at scrounging a living from the beaches. One only of their officers, Lieutenant Hamilton, elected to stay in the wigwam with the captain: he and Mr Elliot, the surgeon, tramped many miles a day in search of something to shoot, and occasionally they brought home ducks and geese, all of which went into the common pot. Byron joined them whenever the weather made salvage work impracticable. By far the largest group occupied the hut for which the upturned cutter formed an efficient roof: Mr Bulkeley, supported by his friends, Mr Cummins the carpenter and John Jones the master's mate, was its undisputed leader. Their views were moderate, their opposition to the captain respectful but unrelenting. More huts were appearing: they were made from poles cut from the wood, baulks of timber and pieces of canvas, and they were constantly being enlarged and improved as suitable material was washed ashore from the wreck. The most mutinous and complaining of the men had moved of their own accord into a separate hut, and among these James Mitchell was the leading spirit. The four midshipmen had built a hut of their own because the captain wished that the same organisation should be observed in their living quarters ashore as on board ship: it was not a happy arrangement as they had little in common. Isaac Morris, always ill at ease as a petty officer, would have much preferred to live among the ordinary seamen. Cozens was Byron's only really congenial companion, but he spent most of his time gambling in Mr Bulkeley's hut, where he was always welcome and where he could always be sure of a drink: unfortunately he also imbibed the views of his boon companions who were opposing the captain. Campbell, who went about armed and in constant fear of his life, professed a friendship for Byron which was far from being reciprocated. He disapproved strongly of the attitude Cozens had adopted, and maintained that it was the spirit of dissension that was ruining them: 'It is an evil spirit,' he said, 'that appeared at the hour the ship struck and has been growing ever since. Only the captain stands out against it, and I, who have done my best to support him and uphold discipline, have become the object of the general hatred.'

On the 25th May, eleven days after the ship struck, the first regular issue was made from the store tent: half a pound of flour per man and one piece of pork for three men. They fried the flour with tallow candles and seaweed to make it go further.

During the night of the 28th the west wind died away. For the first time since they landed the thunder of the surf was hushed to a soft whisper in the shingle; there was an uncanny stillness in the air, and an icy chill. At daybreak the wind was light at north and north-east. Snow had fallen; all the land was white with the mist rising in faint grey spirals from the sea. At low water they took the longboat from the wreck and brought her ashore. The captain and the carpenter had already consulted about the best place to rebuild her, so blocks were quickly laid to receive her and she was drawn up out of the sea. The ship's awning, supported on long poles, was spread over the whole length of the vessel to protect the men working on her from the rain.

Late in the night of the 2nd – 3rd June the midshipmen were awakened by the sound of angry voices and cries for help from the captain's servant. They seized their arms and rushed out into the darkness. As they hurried towards the wigwam they saw tossing lanterns and sharp silhouettes against the watch fire of men tumbling out in confusion from the dimly glowing tents. They came upon Captain Cheap standing in a circle of light with pistols drawn and cursing his servant for a blundering fool. Seeing Byron, he shouted, 'Get that powder away before some god-forsaken lubber sparks it off! There, behind my hut!'

Byron ran to the back of the wigwam where he found Lieutenant Hamilton and the surgeon standing guard over half a barrel of gunpowder: they told him that some of the people had mutinied, rifled the store tent and tried to blow up the captain's hut. They had failed only because one of their number, David Buckley, Quarter Gunner, had had a change of heart at the last moment and had argued and tried to dissuade them from the attempt. Lowering his lantern, Hamilton showed him that a train of loose powder had been laid up to the half barrel. The stern voice of the captain was ordering the men back to their quarters, and he continued to abuse Peter Plastow for raising the alarm too soon: he had overheard the conspirators quarrelling among themselves and had hoped to catch them red-handed.

When the half-barrel of gunpowder was safely in the store tent under guard, Byron took a burning branch from the watch fire and ignited the train so that the fizzling flame ran in the opposite direction from what had been intended: it led them to a spot near the edge of the wood. Here their lantern showed them many tracks which they followed until they lost them among the trees and undergrowth. When they returned to the wigwam they found Captain Pemberton reporting that he and his marines had searched the camp and found the tent empty which had been occupied by Mitchell and the most discontented of the people. Mr Bulkeley, who had a way of not being present when anything dramatic was happening, had now come up with the carpenter to discuss the disturbance and the general dissatisfaction. They assured the captain that the men in their hut were generally very well affected to him, and that they never would engage in any mutiny against him or against any other officer who would act for the public good and his Majesty's service. The captain said that he had no reason to suspect him and that they were the only two men in the ship's company in whom he put any trust or confidence.

CHAPTER

5

-»»«-

IT was not to be expected that Mr Bulkeley and his
followers would submit to being the only group unprovided
with arms for their defence. As the captain refused to give
them any they took the boats without his knowledge or
authority, visited the wreck under cover of darkness, weather
and tide being favourable, and helped themselves. They
brought ashore pistols, cutlasses, muskets with bayonets,
and a store of powder and ball, all of which they secreted in
their own hut. They also took the opportunity to provide
themselves with some barrels of provisions and kegs of
brandy. The captain's party was still the strongest, not only
because it was assumed that in any conflict with his ship's
company he would have the support of the land forces, but
because of his personal prestige. No man doubted his
courage, his seamanship, or his power of command. He was
their natural leader. He alone had seen a possible way of
escape from their desperate situation: but his plan depended
for its realisation on the skilled work of the craftsmen who
were to reconstruct the longboat.

It did not appear that the deserters, now that their *coup*
had failed, would be very dangerous: they would be unlikely to attempt an armed raid unless driven by the desperation of hunger, and for the time being, having supplied
themselves liberally from the store tent, they were better off
than those who had remained in the camp. The captain
thought, however, that they might attempt to steal one of
the boats in which to make their way to the mainland, so

he had the oars kept in the store tent when they were not in use; and in order to prevent the marine sentries from being overpowered or seduced from their duty, he ordered continuous watch to be kept by the officers and petty officers, each one standing his watch in turn.

There were some very useful men among the deserters. They were James Mitchell, Carpenter's Mate; John Russell, Armourer; William Oram, Carpenter's Crew; Joseph King and John Redwood, Boatswain's Yeomen; and Dennis O'Leary, John Davis, James Roach, James Stewart and William Thompson, Seamen. The carpenter came to the captain with a long face and told him that without them the longboat could not be constructed. He particularly needed the armourer who had to make all the special fittings and also various tools – hammers, files and gimlets – that they had not succeeded in salvaging from the wreck.

Mr Bulkeley said that as the carpenter had been promised the co-operation of all the people, the deserters would have to be brought back. He offered to go and parley with them upon condition that the captain would pronounce an amnesty and furnish him with a letter promising that neither in the camp nor after their return to England would they be punished for their behaviour. The captain saw no alternative to this proposal, much as he deplored the dangerous precedent of allowing his stores to be plundered with impunity. He wrote the letter. Because Mr Bulkeley was looked upon as the leader of the opposition, he was obviously the best man to carry on the negotiations: an officer more closely associated with the captain might have met with a hostile reception.

The first attempt to persuade the deserters to return was unsuccessful. Mr Bulkeley and Mr Cummins went together to see them and found that they had settled some two miles farther along the coast on the shore of the southern lagoon: they were hard at work building a punt from timbers that had drifted ashore. Asked what they were going to do with it, they said they had concluded that they were on an island and by means of the punt they would reach the mainland which, they calculated, was about sixteen miles distant. Then they would make their way on foot to the nearest Spanish settlement. Their minds were set upon this project, and nothing would turn them from it. On the following day Mr Bulkeley tried again, and this time he found John Russell, the armourer, and William Oram of the carpenter's crew alone: he showed them the captain's letter and succeeded in persuading them to go back with him. He took them before the captain where they expressed their regret at having been led astray by Mitchell and their willingness to return to their duty. They received confirmation of what had already been promised them – that no proceedings would be taken against them either in their present situation or in England, should they be so fortunate as to return there.

Work was now begun in earnest on the longboat: she was sawn in two and all the men the carpenter had asked for were employed in fitting and shaping timbers under his direction, or in setting up the armourer's forge and bellows in a separate hut and in burning charcoal for him.

Meanwhile an improvement in the weather enabled them to make better progress with the salvage: in one day they got eight barrels of flour, which was a record, together with two casks of wine and a quarter cask and three hogsheads of brandy. Every day during the landing of the stores the captain stood with the surgeon and the purser, all three of them with drawn and loaded pistols, and met each boat as it came ashore. They saw to it that all the food, and all the arms they could lay their hands on, were deposited in the store tent. Byron had a first-class crew for the yawl: John Bozman one of the best seamen, John Duck a Mulatto born in London, Joseph Clinch, and David Buckley the quarter gunner who had at first sided with Mitchell and then changed his mind and prevented him from blowing up the captain's hut. They were all good men and they worked willingly together. One day they were surprised to see three Indian canoes in the bay out among the foam-flecked rocks: they stopped paddling when they were still some distance from the wreck. Evidently they had no hostile intentions: had they been planning an attack they would certainly have landed somewhere else and crept upon the camp at night or in the uncertain morning light – an operation that might have perfectly succeeded. The fear of hostile Indians that had been so real on the night of the shipwreck had been forgotten, and recently guards had been posted only before the captain's wigwam and the store tent. No one thought any more about the possibility of the Indians being hostile – they all waved their hats to them, made signs of welcome and reassurance, and shouted to them to come alongside. This they finally did. Their paddles were rudely made of pieces of board lashed to poles, and they rowed with them as if they were oars. The canoes had smoking fires in them on beds of clay: they were crowded with men and dogs, and laden with shellfish, including some mussels as large as a man's fist. Some of the leaders came aboard the wreck and looked around with the greatest astonishment: they were people of short stature but broad and strong, of an olive complexion with long coarse hair, jet-black: they had fine white teeth and they were very civil in their behaviour. For clothes, in spite of the cold, they had nothing but a bit of some beast's skin about their waists and something woven from feathers over their shoulders. They spoke freely but uttered no word that the seamen could understand nor, it seemed, could they understand a word of any language except their own. They were shown some articles of iron, such as tools, nails, and so on, but they could not comprehend their use or value; it was concluded, therefore, that they had never been in contact with Europeans before. Two bales of cloth had been salvaged that day, so the men unrolled them and traded pieces for handfuls of shellfish which they eagerly devoured.

When everyone's hunger had been satisfied, Lieutenant Baynes, who happened to be on board, went with Byron in the yawl to lead the Indians to the shore and conduct them to the captain, hoping that they wouldn't object to their wigwam being appropriated. The effect on them was totally unexpected: when they landed and saw the captain coming out of the wigwam they burst into loud laughter which was immediately quelled by their head man with a stern glance. Then, selecting two attendants, he followed the lieutenant and Byron up the beach, but carefully choosing a circuitous route of his own when approaching the wigwam as if to avoid some dangerous obstacle, or perhaps an imaginary hole in the ground, that was invisible to the white men.

The captain, who had been observing the proceedings through his perspective glass, was ready to receive them: he swept off his hat and bowed politely, and the Indians bowed also. He held out his hand to the head man who at once held out his own hand but made no attempt to take the captain's: he was doing everything that the captain did, even mimicking his words of welcome without in the least understanding what was being said, instead of speaking his own language. The captain gave them hats, which they perched in the most comical way upon their unkempt heads, and soldiers' red coats with which they were highly delighted. Some small mirrors puzzled them extremely – they kept searching behind the mirrors for the men who appeared to be looking at them.

As soon as the interview was over they returned to the canoes, pushed off, paddled along the shore for a short distance then landed again. They carried their canoes up the beach to some circular heaps of shells that had been noticed on the day of the shipwreck: they constructed wigwams with long poles and brushwood within these circles which acted as windbreaks. In a miraculously short time they were completed and fires transported from the canoes were burning before them.

The captain, thinking that their own survival might depend on the help of the Indians who knew how to wrest a livelihood from that inhospitable land, and also that they might prove useful as guides, issued the strictest orders that they were not to be constrained in any way and that nothing should be taken from them except by fair exchange of goods. At nightfall he posted a sentry to prevent the deserters from molesting them. Next morning they had gone, leaving nothing behind them except some pieces of decayed seal meat which were quickly seized upon and eaten.

A few days later the same Indians appeared again in their canoes and, going straight to the captain's wigwam, presented him with three sheep and a large quantity of mussels. This was thought to show a fine sense of gratitude on their part for the great civility with which the captain had received them on their previous visit. The sheep were immediately slaughtered and shared out equally. How the Indians came to be in possession of the sheep in a part of the world far distant from any Spanish settlement remained a mystery. This time they had brought their wives and children, and it seemed they intended to settle with the *Wager*'s people. They numbered about fifty altogether. They chose a site nearer to the camp, hauled up their canoes and built stouter wigwams than before, covered with bark and seal skins. It was remarkable that in spite of the clothes Captain Cheap had given them, and the materials they had got by trucking with the seamen, they still wore nothing but the small piece of fur about their waists and the rough blanket of feathers or of skin about their shoulders which they threw off whenever they were actively occupied.

The captain called the people together and again warned them that the Indians were not to be molested and that no discourtesy should be offered to them, particularly to their women: for if they could remain on friendly terms with them they might never be in want again. He advised every man to observe all that the Indians did, how they went about finding shellfish and how they caught birds and seals, so that they should know how to fend for themselves.

Next morning there were hard gales of wind with lightning and showers of rain and hail, but as soon as it was daylight the women brought fire from before the wigwams into their canoes, for they went nowhere without carrying fire with them, launched them through the surf and paddled out into the bay. There were twelve of them, all naked in the bitter weather, and they had taken the girl children with them. It was low water. When they had reached about a mile from the shore they began diving into the sea, each carrying a small basket which she held in her teeth while swimming: the seamen thought they were diving for things cast from the wreck, but when the canoes reached the shore again they were half filled with sea urchins, known as sea eggs, which, without consulting their husbands, they bartered freely with the seamen.

At every tide the women went diving and always brought back sea eggs, or maggots about three-quarters of an inch long and as large round as a wheat straw, or fine mussels, or clams which they gathered from the beds of kelp which were thick in places among the rocks: they seemed also to be teaching the girl children to dive and swim, for often a young child would be sitting on its mother's shoulders, or even on her head in an effort to keep out of the cold water. And every day, and all day long, the men sat in the smoke of the camp-fires, and the boys played with small spears or practised shooting with bows and arrows. They were very interested in death. When one of the seamen died — a frequent occurrence because those that were sick could not be given the care and nourishment necessary for their recovery – the Indians would sit beside the body, watching over it, carefully covering it, and looking every moment with much gravity on the face of the deceased. At the funeral service their deportment was grave and solemn. They were very attentive and observant, and continued so until the burial was over.

One day a seaman caught a fine fish in a pool, rather like a mullet: it was the first live fish they had seen, for neither by hook nor net had they yet succeeded in catching any. They carried it to the Indians and let them know by signs that they would willingly pay cloth for fish. As soon as the Indians understood this, they took their canoes and paddled along the shore to a tidal creek which ran some way into the land. At low water they built a wall of branches weighted with stones across the entrance. When the tide had risen high enough to cover it they paddled out to sea and threw their dogs overboard. These, with much barking and splashing, swam towards the shore, converging at the mouth of the creek. The Indians threw more stones and branches on to their wall, building it up until it was level with the surface of the water; then they sat down and waited for the tide to fall. The *Wager*'s people also waited and watched curiously. As the tide fell and the water drained away through the wall of branches, they could see that the creek was alive with fish. As soon as it was shallow enough, the women went in with their baskets and picked up so many that both camps were supplied. Captain Cheap rewarded the women, when they brought in their laden baskets, with some lengths of cloth and some hand-mirrors – but whatever was given to them was immediately taken away by their men.

On the following morning when everything seemed peaceful there was a sudden uproar among the wigwams. Soon the Indians, suddenly transformed into savage warriors, began advancing in a compact body with angry cries, brandishing bows and spears. They were naked, and they had painted themselves all over with black and yellow stripes. The alarm was sounded, the people seized their weapons, and Captain Cheap drew them up in a double line to bar the way to the camp: he ordered them to load their muskets but on no account to fire without his orders, for a blood feud was to be avoided at all costs. If it became necessary to open fire, he told them, to save their own lives, they must shoot to kill, for the Indians being ignorant of firearms would not be alarmed merely by the sound and smoke: they had watched Byron and Hamilton with a sort of puzzled expression when they were shooting sea birds, but with no fear.

The Indians came on until they were about fifty paces from Captain Cheap and his men: they halted, poised their spears and fitted arrows to their bowstrings. Then, at a word from their head man, three of their most powerful warriors laid down their arms: each picked up two large smooth stones and, balancing one in each hand, they advanced with threatening gestures. It was evidently a challenge to three of the *Wager*'s people to come out and fight, but the captain ordered that no one was to stir: he thought that his own men, weak from their privations and undernourished, and also unskilled in this primitive form of combat, would quickly have had their brains beaten out. He stood forward and addressed the angry warriors, hoping that through some reaction of theirs he would be able to understand the reason for their sudden and unexpected hostility; but they only redoubled their cries. All at once there was a tremendous shout and some of the Indians ran at top speed towards the woods: they returned dragging three of their women by the hair, and beating them. They evidently thought, and had some reason for thinking, that they had been consorting with the seamen. The captain at once sent three of his officers to search the tents and huts and drive out any Indian women there, but none were found. All day long the warriors kept up their demonstration, and only retreated at nightfall. A strong guard was posted and all the people were warned to have their loaded muskets by their sides and to be prepared to turn out at a moment's notice. During this crisis every man obeyed the captain without question or demur.

An hour before daylight there was a stir among the wigwams, then fires were seen moving down the beach. The Indians were leaving, and there was no way to stop them or to recover their friendship.

CHAPTER

6

-»»)«««-

It almost seemed as if the Indians had left a curse behind them for the outrage to their women. Day after day the rain lashed down in torrents, the wind screamed in from the sea, shaking the miserable huts and tents, and a great roaring surf made it difficult to get shellfish or to cut seaweed from the rocks. Byron on one of his lonely excursions in the woods with his fowling-piece made friends with a half-wild Indian dog that had got left behind: he was white with light brown patches, smooth haired, prick eared, and about the size of an English terrier but heavier in build like a stunted wolf-dog. He was soon answering to the name of Boxer and following his new master wherever he went.

As soon as the weather permitted, great efforts were made to obtain nourishment from the sea as the Indians had done. They sought first for the large mussels, the best of the shellfish, not with much hope of getting them, because they were uncertain where to look: on the one occasion on which a boat had gone with the Indians to mark the beds, none had been found. Then they went after the sea-eggs: here they were more sure of themselves for the captain had taken cross bearings of the place where the women had dived for them. The best swimmers went out in the boats at low water, but when they reached the place and sounded they found nowhere less than six fathoms – an impossible depth for any of them to reach by swimming. Finally they sought for clams which the Indian women had gathered from the kelp beds: they dragged up fathoms and fathoms of the long brown floating weed and found nothing except tiny darting animalculae too small to eat.

Their last hope of profiting from the experience of the Indians was the fish trap. They rowed along the beach on the rising tide until they reached the mouth of the creek, and spread out, just as the Indians had done: then they threw Boxer into the sea and made a great commotion, shouting and beating upon the water with their oars as they closed in. They went one better than the Indians, putting their fishing net right across the mouth of the creek at high water in addition to the wall of branches so that fish once in the trap could not possibly get out again: then they sat down to wait. On the day they had made such a haul there the dogs had entered whole-heartedly into the excitement: this time, although he did his best, Boxer did not show much enthusiasm and consequently Byron concluded that the haul would be poor, but he kept his opinion to himself. He passed the weary time of waiting for the tide to fall in watching the faces of his comrades, their eager expectancy as they gazed at the cold wind-streaked surface of the creek, imagining that every ripple was caused by the fin of sparkling fish that would soon be in the pot, and their growing uneasiness as the level of the water fell and none were seen. When it was shallow enough they waded in, feeling along the bottom with their feet, and then with their hands, till finally some were left kneeling in the mud when all the water had gone, unable to believe that they had caught not the smallest fish. They had learned nothing, and they were back in the same miserable situation from which the Indians had temporarily relieved them. Their resentment took the form of angry abuse of the captain. When they got back to the camp they demanded more rations, and when this was denied to them they held meetings of protest in most of the tents, and the day ended in riot and drunkenness.

On the 15th July the upper works of the wreck parted

from her lower deck. The stump of the mainmast floated in and drove up the lagoon: then a gun-carriage drifted in, and part of the ship's pump; but they secured little of value except a quarter cask that was three parts full of wine. Then the cabin bell came ashore without its being attached to any wood or with any part of the wreck near it, which was considered very odd, then dozens of seamen's checked shirts were picked up, and bales of cloth and shoes, but no provisions except a few pieces of beef and pork. The men suffered much from the inclement weather, particularly with their eyes which were blinded and inflamed by the raindrops incessantly striking against them as they ranged up and down the beach looking for something to eat. The lads, aged from twelve to fourteen, were in pitiable condition: one of them picked up the liver of a drowned man, and he wailed in despair when he was restrained from eating it — the body had been torn to pieces by the force of the seas driving it against the rocks: but they preyed on the vultures that came to feed on the bodies: they were fairly easily killed with sticks because, to launch themselves into the air they required a clear run along the ground for some distance with wings flapping. No one except the officers and the petty officers would work on the longboat: the search for immediate nourishment took precedence over all their hopes for the future. One day the carpenter, seeing a man cut up an anchor stock for firewood, fell down in a fit of madness: he was taken to his tent and held there by force. Twenty-four hours later he recovered, and the work went on.

Byron spent his evenings reading a book of voyages that the captain had lent him: it described in detail the loss of the *Speedwell*, the construction of another vessel out of the wreckage, and the subsequent adventures of her crew of which Captain Cheap had given a brief account in order to persuade his own men to save themselves in the same way. He had told them all that it was good for them to know, and it is surprising that he didn't keep the book safely locked away in his sea-chest. Byron now read that Captain Shelvocke had also had trouble with his crew, a succession of disturbances and mutinies to deal with, a second captain who tried to take the command from him, and even a truculent boatswain who caused much mischief: in the end the whole ship's company had successfully defied his authority – which was surely a bad example for the people of the *Wager*. Their ship was a privateer, so they were not under naval discipline: they were partners in the venture: and they considered that when the ship was lost the old articles were no longer valid. They drew up new articles for the new vessel they had constructed, excluding the London merchants who had financed the expedition from any share in the profits, and they refused to launch it until Captain Shelvocke had signed them. When at length he agreed they put to sea and quickly took a prize, the *Jesu Maria*, which they renamed the *Happy Return*. In her they raided Iquiqui, Payta, Mariata and Sebeco, carrying off much booty. Then they took a larger prize, the *Sacra Familia*: in her they sailed right across the Pacific to China, and then to India where, in spite of Captain Shelvocke's protests, they shared out all the captured treasure and deserted the ship. Of course it was impossible to find them again, or the treasure. When Shelvocke eventually got back to England he was sued for a very large sum by the company of merchant adventurers that had financed him: he was arrested and imprisoned, but he succeeded in escaping and in lying low until the affair had blown over. Although there were many curious similarities between Captain Cheap's predicament and Captain Shelvocke's, their characters were entirely different: Captain Cheap's loyalty to Commodore Anson and his devotion to his duty could not be doubted, whereas Captain Shelvocke got his independent command by not keeping a rendezvous with his commanding officer, Captain Clipperton, when he might

77

easily have done so: he was guilty of at least one act of piracy; and in spite of all his troubles in London after he returned he managed to hold on to his share of the booty, about £7,000, a very large sum for those days, while the owners of the *Speedwell* lost the whole of their investment.

Byron discussed all this with the other midshipmen, and also with Mr Bulkeley who said that the crew of the *Speedwell* in tearing up the old articles were probably justified in the eyes of the law, for it was reasonable to assume that the interest of the gentlemen adventurers had come to an end with the wreck of their ship; and that their behaviour to Captain Shelvocke might be justified also: 'When constituted authority comes to an end,' he said, 'the only possible course is to hold a meeting and let the majority appoint a new authority which from then onwards all must obey.' Isaac Morris agreed with Mr Bulkeley, but Campbell and Byron could see no excuse or justification for the crew of the *Speedwell* to take the law into their own hands and make off with the treasure. All of them were thinking, of course, of their own parallel situation, and they were influenced in their opinions by their feelings towards Captain Cheap.

Midshipman Cozens, so sweet tempered when sober, and so respectful of authority, was still frequenting Mr Bulkeley's hut where there was a good store of brandy taken secretly from the wreck: when he had been drinking for some time and listening to the men's grievances he was always ready to pick a quarrel with one of the captain's supporters. One day when Mr Elliot was leaving the hut, after attending to a man who was sick, Cozens followed him out and struck and abused him. Mr Elliot, being very strong, threw him to the ground, tied his arms behind him, and left him.

Cozens was always quick to repent of his behaviour, but he did not mend it. A few days later Byron came from the wreck in the yawl and landed a cask of peas. The captain came down as usual to make sure that it was deposited in the store tent, but there were no men to handle it. He sent Byron up to the tents to collect some hands, but he could find no one except Cozens who immediately came down with him to the captain and started to roll the barrel of peas up the beach while Byron returned to the yawl. The beach was rather steep and after a while Cozens stopped rolling it, saying that it was too heavy for him: whereupon the captain told him he was drunk and struck him with his cane.

When Byron came ashore again with several chests of candles and bales of cloth he found Cozens under arrest in the store tent: he was busily employed in trying to stave a cask of brandy with a hammer. The purser, trying to prevent him, was roughly hurled aside and he ran out calling for help. Byron then grappled with Cozens, and as they fought together among the chests and barrels the captain came in and again struck Cozens with his cane, whereupon the marine sentry intervened and shouted, 'No one shall strike any prisoner of mine!' The midshipmen scrambled to their feet, and Cozens asked insolently, 'Well? Am I to be kept here all night?' and he went on to abuse the captain, saying that he knew why he was rebuilding the longboat, that he was a villain, and that he had taken money from the company of gentlemen adventurers to turn privateer and capture Spanish prizes to repay them for Captain Shelvocke's debt. 'But you'll never do it,' he shouted, 'Captain Shelvocke was a rogue, he was not a fool – and by God you are both!' The captain made no answer to this accusation: he merely released Cozens and sent him back to his tent. There can be little doubt, however, that he took it as a mortal insult. The implication was that he intended to desert the commodore and seek his own personal gain, and that he had betrayed him even before they left England.

In the next incident, which had the direst results, Cozens behaved reasonably well. He happened to be in Mr

Bulkeley's hut when the boatswain's servant came in with the wine allowance: he was a Portuguese boy from Goa who spoke English indistinctly, and the boatswain and the cook understood from him that one of the men had had his allowance stopped. Cozens said he would go and ask the purser about it. When he entered the store tent he was told to get out, but he insisted on putting his question: whereupon the purser picked up a pistol and fired at him and would have shot him had not the cooper canted his elbow. 'Captain! Captain!' the purser shouted. 'Here is Cozens come to kill us!' and Lieutenant Baynes, whose unhappy fate it was always to do the wrong thing, ran up shouting, 'Cozens has mutinied!' The captain, naturally assuming that it was Cozens who had fired the shot, ran from his hut with a cocked pistol, met him as he was advancing threateningly, and promptly shot him through the head.

Byron, running up at the sound of the firing, found Cozens lying in a pool of blood, still conscious but unable to speak. He knelt beside him and took his hand. Cozens opened his eyes and shook his head sadly as if to tell him that his case was hopeless. It was raining hard. The captain had exchanged his pistol for a firelock, and standing in a line beside him were Lieutenant Baynes, the purser, the surgeon and the three lieutenants of the marines, Hamilton, Ewers and Fielding, all armed. Other men came running up and stood silently watching: Cozens shook hands with several of them as if to say goodbye. The captain looked sternly round and noticed that neither Mr Bulkeley nor any man from his hut were there. He sent the lieutenant for them.

Mr Bulkeley was sitting quietly in his hut awaiting the summons. When the lieutenant came and told him what had happened and delivered the message, he asked, 'Must we go armed?' The lieutenant said, 'Yes,' but he decided it would be unwise. He went unarmed to the captain with all his men, eighteen of the stoutest members of the crew. They looked with the deepest concern at their wounded messmate, but they listened respectfully to the captain while he explained that Cozens had come to mutiny and that he had shot him. 'Sir,' Mr Bulkeley replied, 'you see that we have not come to mutiny. We are unarmed.' The captain laid his firelock on the ground and said that he had only sent for them to let them all know what had happened, and that he was still their captain, and that it was his resolution to maintain his command over them as usual. Then he said that every man should now return to his tent. They silently obeyed. He ordered Cozens to be removed to the sick tent which was little more than an awning thrown over some bushes. They laid him on the ground, and the surgeon's mate examined and dressed the wound: the ball had lodged about three inches below his right eye.

When Byron felt that he could leave his friend he went to Mr Bulkeley's hut to discover what had brought about the tragedy. The men, who greatly loved Cozens, were seething with indignation against the captain, but at the same time they were awed by his attitude and by his readiness to use his firearms. They said that Cozens had not been drinking that day and that he was unarmed: in fact, he had never been seen to carry any kind of weapon since they landed: but all agreed that drink had been his downfall and that on several occasions he had used most unbecoming language. Certainly the captain had every reason to expect that he would mutiny and that others would join him, and to look upon his gross abuse of him and his open defiance as undermining to his authority: no doubt he had made up his mind to deal summarily with him at the first favourable opportunity. Perhaps he was still in ignorance of the fact that it was not Cozens but the purser who had fired the first shot, or perhaps he found it impossible to admit that he had made so tragic a mistake, but he continued to treat him with the greatest severity: he refused to let the midshipmen carry him off to their tent and he refused to allow Mr Elliot to attend him because of the bad feeling between them, but he said that Doctor Oakley of the land forces might do so. In the event it was the surgeon's mate who extracted the ball. A few days later he extracted another bit of steel and a piece of bone which he supposed was part of the upper jaw. After this the patient began to show signs of improvement.

At the time of the accident Cozens had been living in Mr Bulkeley's hut — the upturned cutter had been removed and brought back into service — and the gunner now had a very fine hut constructed of timber with a double roof and with a floor raised off the wet ground. He went with the carpenter to the captain to ask as a favour that Cozens might be brought there instead of having to lie on the ground in the sick tent. When they returned they reported that the captain had refused, saying, 'No. I am so far from it that if he lives I will carry him a prisoner to the commodore and hang him.' This answer aroused great resentment. A fortnight after the wound was inflicted, Cozens died. His shipmates buried him in as decent a manner as their circumstances would allow. The fact that he had rallied after the ball was extracted caused them to believe that his life might have been saved, for he was strong and healthy, if he had not been denied proper assistance. He was, according to Mr Bulkeley, the forty-fifth man to die since the ship struck, and there remained a hundred to be provided for, including the land forces but not including the seven deserters.

Until the death of his friend, Byron had unhesitatingly supported the captain and defended his actions: now he was shocked and angry. 'If Mr Cozens' behaviour to his captain,' he wrote, 'was indecent and provoking, the captain's, on the other hand, was rash and hasty: if the first was wanting in that respect and observance which is due from a petty officer to his commander, the latter was still more unadvised in the method he took for the enforcement of his authority; of which, indeed, he was jealous to the last degree, and which he saw daily declining and ready to be trampled upon. His mistaken apprehension of a mutinous design in Mr Cozens, the sole motive of his rash action, was so far from answering the end he proposed by it that the men, who before were much dissatisfied and uneasy, were by this unfortunate step thrown almost into open sedition and revolt.'

Mr Bulkeley, aware that Byron disliked Campbell and did not find Isaac Morris particularly congenial, offered him quarters in the hut, but he refused: although he was no longer in sympathy with the captain, he did not wish to associate himself with the party whose policy it was to oppose him. He had formed the opinion also that Mr Bulkeley's followers had exploited Cozens' weaknesses and encouraged him to make trouble, that he had been 'kept warm with liquor,' as he put it, 'and set on by some ill-designing persons,' for he had never known a better-natured man when sober or one more inoffensive. He resented, therefore, the way in which both sides had treated Cozens, and he didn't want to belong to either. There may have been grounds for his suspicions for, immediately after the shooting, Mr Bulkeley turned the boatswain out of the hut 'for breeding quarrels.'

Not liking any of the factions therefore, and having no taste for arguments and recriminations, Byron retired to a small hut he had built for himself: while he was away at work on the wreck, Boxer guarded it and bit anyone who went near it.

On the evening of the 16th September the boom of a distant gun was heard. The men looked blankly and questioned each other, wondering what it should mean: it was the first sign that had come to them from their own world for many days: as it was the hour of sunset they thought that it must have been fired by a ship lying in a haven not far away. Some cried out that they should man the barge then and there and go out and seek for her: the captain restrained them, saying that it would soon be dark and they could not tell from which direction the sound came nor whether the ship were friend or enemy. There was no choice but to wait for daylight and even then, he thought, the chances were small that a ship would enter the gulf.

Next day dawned clear and frosty with the wind at north-east. All eyes were fixed upon the horizon. From the slopes of Mount Misery the captain scanned the sea for hours through his perspective glass, but he saw no sign of a ship. Again that evening the gun was heard. The officers had to guard the boats to prevent the men from seizing them and starting out they knew not whither, for at what distance and in what direction the ship might lie none could agree or determine. On three successive nights the sunset gun was heard. Then it was heard no more, and their hopes ended in despondency.

CHAPTER

7

-->>)(<<-

Byron in his solitary hut lit by one guttering candle continued to read the book lent to him by the captain: besides the adventures of Captain Shelvocke and his men it contained the voyages of Hawkins, Drake, Thomas Cavendish and Clipperton. Reading of their trials, their endeavours, hardships and disasters and almost incredible escapes from death, and of the rewards of Spanish gold and plate for the few who survived, he forgot for a while his own desperate situation.

One evening he started on a narrative that touched him more closely than any of the others: that of Sir John Narborough in the *Sweepstakes*, whose course had taken him into the same latitudes as the *Wager*: he thought that his sailing directions, his admirably lucid account and careful notation of every feature he observed, might be of the greatest value to them when they should set forth in the longboat. Instead of entering the South Seas by rounding the Horn, Narborough had taken his ship through the Straits of Magellan, the first English captain to do so, through 120 miles of narrow uncharted channels winding between mountains and glaciers – a passage of the utmost hazard because of the racing tides, the icy squalls and the infrequent anchorages, but perhaps one degree less hazardous for a reconstructed longboat than a passage round the Horn, and certainly far shorter. In a flash he saw that the way back to the South Atlantic and home was through those straits. The entrance should lie, he thought, about 120 miles to the southward of Wager Island; and such was the excellence of Narborough's descriptions that he could visualise the coastline, the leading marks, the positions of the shoals and sunken rocks to be avoided, the strength of the tides, the havens in which one might find shelter if overtaken by a gale, the bays where wood and fresh water were to be found, and above all the four islands called 'The Islands of Direction', marking the entrance to the straits. As he followed Narborough's course in his imagination, England, which had been a fading dream, became real again: he believed that he would live and see his home once more, and Isabel, because this master navigator had charted the way: they only had to follow his directions to win through to salvation.

A rumbling growl from Boxer recalled him to the present. Footsteps were approaching the hut: they stopped outside, and a friendly voice hailed him – it was the voice of the man he most wanted to see, John Jones, the second master, their most skilful navigator: if he agreed that Narborough's directions were sufficient to get them through the straits, his opinion would weigh heavily with the captain. When Boxer had been driven protesting into a corner, John Jones came in, and Mr Bulkeley with him. Neither of them was familiar with Narborough's narrative, and they listened gravely while Byron told them about it, admiring the descriptions which he read out to them and smiling at his enthusiasm. They agreed that going through the Straits of Magellan might indeed be the way to save all their lives, but they begged him to say nothing about it to anyone else until John Jones had studied the book and made up his mind whether, with its help, he could find the straits and navigate the longboat through them. It would be fatal, Mr Bulkeley warned him, to raise the people's hopes only to disappoint them. He asked if he might borrow the book. Byron really saw no objection, but because of the way

Cozens had misused the material of the Shelvocke story to abuse the captain he felt that he could not part with the book without authority – not that he imagined that Mr Bulkeley and John Jones would misuse it, but because the experiences of the earlier voyagers had such a direct bearing on their situation he thought it should be the captain's responsibility to decide who should read it.

His caution did not appear to have been necessary, for on the very next day Mr Bulkeley came again and said he had obtained permission from the captain to borrow the book if Byron had finished with it. He handed it over and for a few days heard no more about it.

On the 1st August the ration was again reduced; every man was to get only a quarter of a pound of flour a day. The announcement was greeted with shouts of rage, and later there were serious disturbances which were sternly suppressed by the captain and his officers. Since the shooting of Cozens none of the men dared to brave him openly: their resentment found another outlet: that night the store tent was again robbed.

On the evening of the 2nd a seaman came to Byron with a message from Mr Bulkeley requesting his attendance. Going across to the large hut, he found an assembly of all Mr Bulkeley's friends. He was greeted with enthusiasm, given the place of honour and shown a chart which John Jones had drawn from Narborough's directions, and which he now explained in detail: he ended by giving it as his considered opinion not only that the route through the Straits of Magellan to the coast of Patagonia was practicable, but that it was the only route they could attempt in the longboat with any prospect of success. It was unanimously agreed that they should go to the captain and beg him to lead them home by the way which Byron had so providentially discovered. Mr Bulkeley proposed that, in order to show the captain that all their dissensions were at an end, they should draw up their request in writing and get every man in the camp to sign it. This seemed to be such a good idea that they immediately set about it. Mr Bulkeley put pen to paper and wrote as follows:

'We whose names are undermentioned do, upon mature consideration, as we have met with so happy a deliverance, think it the best, surest and most safe way for the preservation of the body of the people on the spot to proceed through the Straits of Magellan for England. Dated at a desolate island on the coast of Patagonia in the latitude of 47 degrees 00 minutes south, and west longitude from the meridian of London 81 degrees 40 minutes, in the South-Seas, this 2nd day of August 1741.'

When this had been read aloud and approved it was expected that Mr Bulkeley would sign it first, but he hesitated, saying that he thought they should allow the lieutenant that honour, being next in command to the captain. The principal officers therefore went to the lieutenant, told him their resolution and showed him the paper. After hearing all the details he said that he thoroughly approved of it but that he thought the captain would receive it more favourably from Mr Bulkeley, and he could not be persuaded to put his name to it. So Mr Bulkeley signed it himself, although he was only seventh in the chain of command, followed by the carpenter, the boatswain, the master, and the two assistant masters, all of whom were senior to him. Then the midshipmen signed, and all the other petty officers. The question of whether the land forces should be invited to join in the project was hotly debated, and at last it was decided that Captain Pemberton should be informed of their petition and assured of their peaceable intentions towards the captain.

A delegation waited upon Captain Pemberton. He listened patiently to their arguments and carefully studied the

petition: then he said that it might be considered presump
tuous by the captain if any of the land forces should associate
themselves with the petition, or venture an opinion upon
matters of navigation, but he was willing to promise not to
oppose their project which seemed to offer him and his men
a chance of survival. Mr Bulkeley was aware that the captain
could not go south, while the commodore was expecting
him in the north, without betraying his own high concept of
his duty: it was important, therefore, to convince him that
it was the unanimous desire of the whole ship's company to
abandon the commodore and consider only the best way to
save their own lives. He continued the discussion until he
found a satisfactory formula by which the land forces might
be included, and he added it to the document in the form
of a postscript. It read as follows:

'We whose names are undermentioned have had sufficient
reasons from the above-mentioned people to consent to
go this way.'

Captain Pemberton approved and signed this with two
of the marine officers, Lieutenant Fielding and Lieutenant
Ewers. It was not thought advisable to approach the closest
friends of the captain, Walter Elliot the surgeon, Thomas
Harvey the purser, Lieutenant Hamilton of the marines,
and Peter Plastow the steward.

On the following day, about noon, while the rations were
being issued, Mr Bulkeley went to the captain, taking with
him Byron, Campbell, John Jones, the carpenter, and the
boatswain: he explained their project and presented their
petition, saying that they felt it was a duty incumbent on all
of them to try to preserve life before all other interest. The
captain answered that he required time to consider the
petition and that he would give his decision later: it was not
possible to tell from his attitude what that decision would
be, and he gave no indication of whether he was pleased or

otherwise with Byron and the use which had been made of the book of voyages.

Three days later, at midday on the 6th, Lieutenant Baynes called upon all the officers who had signed the petition, requesting them to wait upon the captain at three o'clock that afternoon. Byron went with high hopes to this conference, feeling that the captain had only to take up his wonderful new plan with the same enthusiasm as Mr Bulkeley and John Jones had done, or merely to signify his approval, and the worst of their difficulties, including the disunity and discord in the camp which threatened to destroy all their hopes, would at once be removed. Mr Bulkeley had spent the intervening time in earnest consultation with Lieutenant Baynes and Captain Pemberton.

They all assembled in the captain's hut and took their places expectantly round the table: the captain looked tired and heavy-eyed, and Byron observing this had misgivings for the first time about what was to follow. Looking round the table he noticed that Mr Bulkeley, though outwardly calm and affable as usual, had his eyes fixed with curious intensity on the captain. The rain had set in again: it drummed against the sides of the hut and came swirling in gusts through the triangular opening that served as an entrance. Outside, the guard struck three sharp double blows on the *Wager*'s bell. 'Gentlemen,' said the captain when the echoes had died away, 'I have maturely considered the contents of your paper so far as it concerns the safety of the people's lives. It has given me great uneasiness so that I have not closed my eyes all last night till eight o'clock this morning.' Then he told them that they had not weighed the matter rightly nor considered the vast distances it would be necessary to run in taking the route they proposed. The entrance to the straits, he said, was 160 leagues to the south-west, the wind would probably be against them all the way: and on the other side of the continent, should they be so fortunate as to reach it, they would be on a lee shore where there was no fresh water to be had. He pointed out also that in running to the southward they would find ever colder and more inclement weather, whereas in running to the northward they would quickly be in a warmer clime with more favourable weather, and they would have the hope of meeting with the commodore there or, in any case, of making a prize to which they might transfer as the men of the *Speedwell* had done. Mr Bulkeley very carefully noted down in his journal everything that was said.

The carpenter, who had with difficulty restrained his impatience, asked how they were to take a vessel when they were without guns, and what good a vessel would be to them if she had no provisions on board of her for their ninety souls. The captain replied that they would take one of the vessels plying between the island of Chiloe and the mainland laden with flour, and what were their small arms for if not for boarding. The carpenter continued to protest, saying that if a shot should take the longboat under water it would not be in his power to stop a leak of that kind, the planking being in some places only three-quarters of an inch thick. Mr Bulkeley begged the captain to consider that they might not meet the commodore, that he might have met with the same fate as themselves, or a worse one. And if he had not, then his appearance on the Pacific Coast would have warned the Spaniards, and all the settlements and the shipping would be on the lookout for them. In his opinion the captain by going north would be putting them at the mercy of a cruel, barbarous and insolent enemy. They had read how Sir John Narborough had sent a boat ashore at Valdivia and the Spaniards had seized and imprisoned the boat's crew; and if that could happen in a time of deepest peace, what would their treatment be now if they fell into their hands! 'Very bad, I fear,' the captain said. Therefore, Mr Bulkeley continued to argue, they should go by the straits, the entrance being, he maintained, not 160 but only 90 leagues to the south-west, where they would be unlikely to meet any enemies more formidable than Indians in canoes.

Although the captain spoke only of the best way to save the lives of the people, his officers did not believe that he was no longer influenced by thoughts of his duty to the commodore and to the rest of the squadron. The carpenter directly challenged him on this point: 'Sir,' he said, 'I always took you for an honourable gentleman, and I believe you to be one. On your honour, sir, I beg you will give the true sentiments of your mind, whether going through the straits is not the surest and safest way to preserve our lives?' and the captain answered, 'I really think going to the northward is the safest.' He said he thought they should go to the northward at least until they had taken a prize and then, with a stout ship under them, they could return home by any route they pleased. Finding no one in agreement with him, he tried to postpone the decision, saying that there would be time enough to decide what to do when the longboat was ready to sail: Mr Bulkeley, however, was prepared for this move: taking the same line as Captain Shelvocke's mutinous crew, he announced that no further work would be done on the longboat until their proposals had been accepted. Faced with this ultimatum the captain unwillingly agreed to go south, 'or any way that would be for the preservation of the people.'

Mr Bulkeley and the carpenter were still not satisfied. They had been saying all along that it was entirely the captain's fault that they were in that miserable situation, that with a sickly crew and a damaged ship he should have exercised his discretion and not attempted to keep the rendezvous with the commodore at the island of Nuestra Señora de Socorro, and that if he had consulted his officers and been guided by them they would not have been shipwrecked. They now stipulated that when they sailed in the longboat he would not come to an anchor, weigh, or alter course without consulting them. The captain indignantly rejected this demand and the conference broke up. It was renewed on the following day, on the day after that and on the next day, but no conclusion was reached; Mr Bulkeley continually protesting that they would obey the captain in the strictest manner and support him with their lives so long as he was ruled by reason, and the captain insisting upon the full exercise of his authority.

The people assembled outside the hut to lend their support to Mr Bulkeley and his friends, so the captain came out and addressed them, giving them his reasons for wanting to go north and saying that he wished to consult every man individually – but they all cried aloud for the straits and seemed overjoyed at the prospect of going that way as if it would take them to England directly without any further affliction or trouble: Byron could hardly blame them for this when he thought of his own optimism and excitement when he first hit upon the idea. Things looked very different now. The door was closed as far as he was concerned. It was obvious to him that the captain would not go south, and therefore Midshipman the Honourable John Byron would not be going south either. It would have been better if he had spoken to him first about the Straits of Magellan instead of to his opponents, and no doubt he would have done so if he had not been avoiding him as much as possible because of the death of Cozens. It had never been his intention that the captain's authority should be restricted in any way: this was part of the plan that Messrs Bulkeley and Cummins had not confided to him.

On the night of the 10th–11th August, when Byron had the watch, he caught a marine corporal, Rowland Crusset, robbing the store tent: he had on him upwards of a day's flour for ninety souls, and a piece of beef, under his coat, while three more pieces were found concealed in the bushes near by. The captain ordered the arrest of the sentry also, Marine Thomas Smith, who must obviously have been an accomplice, and sent both men under guard to their own commanding officer, Captain Pemberton.

When it was noised abroad next day that two marines had been caught robbing the store tent, the people's fury knew no bounds. Enthusiasm for the Magellan plan had spread through the camp and they understood at last that they could not sail without a sea store and therefore the theft of their provisions might cause their deaths. The store tent had been robbed frequently, and many had had a hand in it, but until that day they had felt that they were merely helping themselves to their own property that was being wrongfully withheld from them by the captain. Now they came in arms to Captain Pemberton's tent and cried out for the summary execution of the thieves.

Within the tent, Captain Pemberton was consulting with his officers to decide what should be done. He called in Mr Bulkeley and Mr Cummins to advise him. Studying the Articles of War they found that there was no death penalty for robbery, they could only sentence the marines to corporal punishment. While the carpenter protested that any lenity would have evil consequences, Mr Bulkeley proposed a punishment that would be next to death: he proposed that, if it were judged proper by Captain Pemberton and Captain Cheap, they should be put on a rocky island in the bay and left there until the longboat was ready to sail; 'to strike terror in all for the future, that if any man should be guilty of a like offence, without any respect of person, he should share the same fate.' This idea was approved. A court-martial was held and the men sentenced accordingly, and to receive in addition six hundred lashes each. Before the sentence could be carried out, Corporal Crusset succeeded in making his escape: he joined the camp of the deserters.

On the 15th April Marine Smith received two hundred lashes, and on the following day two hundred more. On the 20th August Mr Bulkeley waited on Captain Cheap and protested that Marine Thomas Smith had received only four hundred of the six hundred lashes and that the people were very uneasy about this mitigation of the punishment. It was agreed that he should have no sort of provision in future out of the store tent, and Byron was ordered to take him out in the yawl to the rock upon which the *Wager* struck and leave him there.

As the wretched man was scarcely able to move, Byron and two of his crew landed on the rock and collected a heap of shellfish for him: then they laid him by a sheltered pool of rain water, built a hut for him from the abundance of timber strewn about from the wreck, made a fire of driftwood and left him, promising to return as soon as they could obtain permission to do so from the captain. When they returned two or three days later, bringing with them a little store of food that they had saved from their own miserable rations, they found him dead and stiff.

CHAPTER

8

->>)<<-

AFTER the breakdown of the negotiations the captain came
but seldom from his hut, and this, according to Mr Bulkeley,
caused a great deal of uneasiness and disturbance. Although
the people had shouted for returning to England by the
Straits of Magellan not all of them had lost their respect for
their commander: Mr Bulkeley soon found that his popularity was waning and that the people were splitting up into
factions, in 'a Sort of Party-Rage,' as he described it. When
Richard Noble, one of the quartermasters, threatened to
shoot him for setting up an opposition plan he made capital
out of it by telling the seamen that he was standing up for
their interests at the risk of his life; but he was alarmed all
the same, for the party in favour of going north with the
captain was gaining ground from day to day. There had been
a complete revolution in his mind: he looked upon himself
and his friends as constituted authority and anyone opposing
them as rebellious, and he accused the captain and the
purser of bribing the men with liquor to favour their cause.

The carpenter had a habit of sending his case flask to the
captain whenever he wanted it filled with wine, and the
captain had always complied. One morning he sent a quarter
keg for wine: it came back empty. The people were in-
dignant at this insult to the man everyone was trying to
cajole and flatter into completing the longboat: they took
their arms, ran to the store tent and shouted that they would
take the wine by force: the captain thereupon ordered the
quarter keg to be filled. They bore it back in triumph to
the carpenter who gave it to them to mix with their brandy

ration: they held a celebration in the hold of the longboat – the grating deck and its covering were already in place, giving good shelter – and they quickly got roaring drunk. By midday the camp was in an uproar, but still the captain remained in his hut as if he wanted to show his officers that they couldn't keep order without him. Captain Pemberton paraded his marines: the people resented this so much that they rushed for the tents of the land forces and began to throw them down. Pemberton had no choice but to dismiss his marines or fire on the people, so he dismissed his marines. The people celebrated this victory with a *feu de joie*, loosing off their muskets and pistols into the air. Then some looked apprehensively towards the captain's hut, for the expenditure of ball and cartridge had been strictly controlled until that day – but still he didn't appear, so they ran for more ammunition from their tents and marched about shouting and singing and firing at anything that took their fancy: the only casualty was the carpenter who was shot, but not seriously, in the thigh.

Mr Bulkeley and his friends, finding that no man heeded them, went to Lieutenant Baynes and begged him, as second-in-command, to restore order. The lieutenant, who usually trusted his judgement so little that he would agree with anyone he happened to be talking to, came out with a suggestion: he said that it would be impossible to end the dissensions until they had a paper signed by the captain saying that he agreed to go south, and that the officers should keep copies to show on their return to England to justify them for not attempting to join the commodore. Mr Bulkeley agreed: he said that the captain was playing for time while secretly building up a party to go north, and that this treachery, as he called it, must be stopped immediately. He wrote as follows:

'Whereas upon a General Consultation it has been agreed

97

to go from this Place through the Straits of Magellan for the Coast of Brazil in our Way to England: We do, notwithstanding, find the People separating into Parties, which must consequently end in the Destruction of the whole Body; and as also there have been great Robberies committed on the Stores, and every Thing is now at a Stand; therefore, to prevent all future Frauds and Animosities, we are unanimously agreed to proceed as above mention'd.'

This paper was given to Lieutenant Baynes: he said that he was sure the captain would sign it, and that if he did not he should be confined for shooting Mr Cozens, and he would take the command himself.

On the following morning, the 28th August, they went to the captain's hut attended by their armed followers. The lieutenant entered with the master, the boatswain, Mr Bulkeley, the carpenter, Mr Jones and Midshipman Campbell, who all waited for him to speak and produce the paper: but in the presence of the captain he was speechless. Mr Bulkeley, therefore, brought out his copy, read it aloud, and requested the captain to sign it. Naturally he refused, 'and seemed very much enraged that it should be proposed to him.' Mr Bulkeley then demanded that the sea store, ten weeks' provisions for all hands, should be given to him immediately so that he could keep it secure from theft in his own hut, and also that the liquor should be buried so that none beyond the agreed ration could be issued before they sailed – this was because he suspected the purser of using it to bribe men to join the captain's party. Both these demands were refused. The officers withdrew.

When they came away from the hut they saw that a flag was hoisted on Captain Pemberton's tent and that Pemberton himself was seated in a chair in front of it with his officers and some of the people round him. They went over and joined him. There, in open assembly, it was agreed between them that should the captain persist in refusing to sign the paper, the command should be taken from him and given to Lieutenant Baynes. Captain Pemberton stood up and addressed the people, saying that he would stand by them with his life in going through the Straits of Magellan, the way proposed in the paper. The people gave three cheers, crying aloud for the straits and England.

The captain, hearing the noise, came to his hut door and called the people, asking them what they wanted, and he called his officers also. Mr Bulkeley came to him and explained that the reason of the noise was that since he refused to sign the paper, and had no regard for the safety of the provisions, the people had unanimously agreed to take the command from him. Hearing this, the captain said in an exalted voice, 'Who is he that will take the command from me?' No one answered. He turned and addressed the lieutenant: 'Is it you, sir?' The lieutenant, looking like a ghost, replied, 'No, sir.'

So they left him with the captain and returned to Captain Pemberton to acquaint him with the lieutenant's refusal to take the command. While they were debating what should be done, the captain sent for Mr Bulkeley. There was an ominous silence. Mr Bulkeley slowly drew his pistol, and cocked it. Requesting Mr Jones and four men with muskets to accompany him, he walked up to the captain's hut and stepped inside alone: the captain was seated on his sea-chest, also with a cocked pistol in his hand: it was resting on his right thigh. Mr Bulkeley immediately withdrew.

When safely outside again he said, 'Mr Jones, kindly enter the hut and tell the captain that I do not think it proper to come before a cocked pistol.' Mr Jones went in and delivered the message; whereupon the captain threw his pistol aside, came out of the hut and told Mr Bulkeley and the people there that he would go with them to the southward. He desired also to know their grievances, and he said he would redress them. They all called out for their sea store of provisions to be secured in Mr Bulkeley's hut, and for the rest to be equally divided between them on the spot.

To accede to this demand would have been fatal both to the captain's and to Mr Bulkeley's plans, for the shared provisions would have been immediately consumed and they could not have lived without their regular issue of rations to supplement their diet of seaweed and shellfish until the longboat was ready: but all came running now, armed, shouting and jostling, from all over the camp to seize the provisions. This was not the sort of situation that Mr Bulkeley liked. He left the captain to deal with it and watched from a distance.

The captain stood alone in front of the store tent facing the excited crowd and ordered them to stand back in a voice they had heard ringing through many a storm – but this time they ignored him and began pulling down the store tent and dragging out the provisions. He ran among them, seizing and shaking one and then another, and shouting, 'Scoundrels! Will ye feast today and starve tomorrow?' and 'You'll never see England, none of ye!' and 'How will ye live till the boat is ready?' At last some of them desisted. The captain formed them into a fighting group to check the others, and as the battle swayed back and forth he suddenly shouted in a great voice: 'Put all the provisions back, and I'll share the brandy! Is it a bargain, men?' Some paused, others cried, 'How much?' 'A pint a day for three weeks, and then we sail! Is it a bargain, men? What do ye say?' They answered lustily, 'Yes! It's a bargain!' and began to cheer. 'Back with the stores then!' They set to it with a will, and he called to the purser to issue a pint of brandy to each man then and there. Then he invited his officers to step into his hut for a glass of wine.

The captain's resolute bearing in the face of the mob so

impressed Byron that his resentment was lost in admiration: he had never seemed so much himself since he stood on the quarterdeck of the *Wager* before her shipwreck. Mr Bulkeley shared his admiration: he noted in his journal that the captain showed all the conduct and courage imaginable, a single man against a multitude, all of them dissatisfied and all of them armed.

When they were comfortably seated in the hut and drinking their wine, Mr Bulkeley states, he remarked to the captain, 'Sir, I think it my duty to inform you that I am not, as you appear to imagine, the principal in this affair.' The captain looked at him sternly: 'How can I think otherwise?' 'The paper I read to you,' Mr Bulkeley said, 'was your lieutenant's projection. There sits the gentleman. Let him disown it if he can.' They both looked at Lieutenant Baynes, who turned away. 'Mr Bulkeley has honestly cleared himself,' the captain announced to his officers.

'I have my character at stake,' Mr Bulkeley went on, 'for drawing back from your cocked pistol, but had I advanced one of us must have dropped. I had no desire, sir, of falling by your hand, and I should have been greatly disturbed to have been compelled, for my own preservation, to discharge a pistol at you, sir, against whom I never had any spleen.'

'The pistol,' the captain assured him, 'was not designed for you but for another, for I knew all before.' They filled up their glasses again and the rest of the evening was spent 'in a very affable manner.'

There was some reason for Lieutenant Baynes to play an equivocal role because it seemed, from what the captain had said, that he was prepared to kill any man who tried to take the command from him, and neither the lieutenant nor anyone else was prepared to shoot it out with him. 'A man who does not value his own life,' Mr Bulkeley said, 'has another man in his power.' And there was the uncomfortable thought that if they got back to England, as they all hoped, a court-martial would probably uphold the captain's action if he had shot one of his mutinous officers, whereas an officer who had shot his captain would have some awkward explaining to do. Also, unlike the rest of the ship's company, his pay had not ceased with the loss of the ship: he was on half-pay and therefore, presumably, still under naval discipline.

The wreck yielded little now, the wild celery near the camp had all been used, shellfish along the beach were becoming scarce, but whenever they were able to launch the boats through the surf and explore the many rocks and islands in the bay they found an abundance of clams and limpets: this they could do only on rare occasions, for in the sixteen weeks they had spent on the island there had only been ten fine days. The men who could find no place in the boats went out on improvised rafts and punts: one of the most adventurous was Richard Phipps, a boatswain's mate, who made a crazy sort of craft out of a water puncheon with a log lashed on either side: he would go out in almost any weather and frequently managed to steal up on sea birds and capture them. Once, when his craft had capsized, one of the boats happened to pass that way and found him sitting on a small rock two miles from the shore. Two days later he was out again, this time in a canoe he had made of barrel hoops and an ox's hide, used on board for sifting gunpowder and called a gunner's hide.

Byron usually went shooting with the surgeon or Hamilton, finding little in the woods but an occasional woodcock; but when they went out in the yawl among the islands and in the southern lagoon they got painted geese, cormorants and loggerhead ducks which they called racehorses because they didn't fly but raced along the surface of the water at a tremendous rate, flapping with their stumpy wings. They were as large as turkeys, and much prized. But all this amounted to very little when shared among a hundred famished men. One day a deputation came to his hut and told him that their necessities were such that they must either eat his dog or starve. Byron refused to give him up, so they held him by force while they dragged Boxer out and killed him. To Byron's distress at the loss of his faithful companion was added resentment when he found his friends eating a succulent stew while he was starving. He sat down and joined them, saying that he was as hungry as the rest of them and it was his dog so he thought he had at least as good a right to a share as they had. 'It was exceedingly good eating,' Mr Bulkeley noted in his journal. 'We thought no English mutton preferable to it.'

In spite of the apparent reconciliation between the captain and Mr Bulkeley, neither had given way an inch. It was not long before another riot broke out among the seamen, which happened the more easily because of the doubling of the brandy ration which both relieved and added to their misery: it was noised abroad by the boatswain that the store tent had again been robbed, and he accused two marines, Smith and Butler. There was a meeting of protest, then the seamen took up their arms and ran to the tents of the land forces to search them: the marines paraded with their muskets and formed themselves into a line of defence. Captain Pemberton, summoned in haste, sent word that he was too sick to leave his bed, and it was left to his officers to deal with the situation: they spoke calmly to the seamen and, on obtaining assurances that the search would be carried out in an orderly manner, and by only two men, and that no personal property would be touched, they ordered their men to ground their muskets. They stood aside and made their way for the seamen's representatives who entered the tents accompanied by Lieutenant Hamilton. In the first they found nothing; in the second also nothing; in the third – triumphant shouts announced that they had found what they were looking for. They came out displaying four bottles of brandy and four small parcels of flour. The people surged forward demanding the punishment of the offenders but, before Lieutenant Hamilton could order the occupants of the tent to be arrested, five of them made a dash for freedom. There was a hot pursuit and a few shots were fired, but they had had a good start and they reached the shelter of the woods where none cared to follow them, for they had snatched up their muskets and taken them with them. The remaining four were placed under guard.

The seamen's anger was soon appeased. On the following day they began to realise that the provisions found in the marines' tent were no more than might reasonably have been laid aside from their rations; and that a search of their own tents would have yielded more: consequently when Captain Pemberton proposed that the four men in custody should merely be conducted to the camp of the deserters, this was unanimously agreed. And so it was done. The other five were already there.

On the 5th October the longboat was completed. They heeled her, caulked her sides, and paid her bottom with wax, tallow and soap from the wreck. On the 8th Mr Bulkeley checked the powder and found there were twenty-three half barrels in the store: he told Lieutenant Baynes that they could carry only six half barrels in the longboat, and therefore he intended to start the rest, pour the powder into the sea and use the empty half barrels as water-casks. He requested him to inform the captain. The lieutenant wouldn't go to the captain, neither would the carpenter, neither would Mr Bulkeley himself. Finally they sent Thomas Clarke, the master: the captain told him, 'I desire you will not destroy any one thing without my orders.'

The climax of the struggle for power came so suddenly and so unexpectedly that it took Byron unawares: no doubt his solitary habits and his anxiety not to be involved with any of the parties made him less observant than he should have been. On the morning of the 9th October, while it was still dark and there was only a faint gleam of dawning in the sky, he was awakened by shouts and the violent ringing of the *Wager*'s bell. When he ran to the captain's hut in response to the alarm it seemed that everyone in the camp was there before him. Looking over the heads of the crowd he saw the captain being led out by a guard of seamen: he was wearing only a shirt and his cocked hat, and his arms were tightly bound behind him: he stopped and asked the seamen guarding him what they were about: they didn't answer, so he turned to the crowd and asked, 'Where are my officers?' The master, Mr Bulkeley, the carpenter and the boatswain stepped forward, and Mr Bulkeley told him that their assistance had been demanded by Captain Pemberton to secure him as a prisoner for the death of Mr Cozens, and as they were subjects of Great Britain they were under obligation to carry him to England. The captain seemed genuinely puzzled. 'What has Captain Pemberton to do with me?' he asked. 'I am your commander! One of you call Mr Baynes.' There was a stir in the crowd, and the lieutenant came forward. The captain looked him up and down: 'What is all this for, sir?' From long habit of deference and submission the lieutenant looked away then, recollecting that he had nothing more to fear, he repeated, 'It is Captain Pemberton's order, sir.' Then they told him that they had arrested him because he opposed them on the question of their going from thence. The captain smiled ruefully: 'Very well, gentlemen, you have caught me napping: it is what I feared. But there is not one of you who would dare to meet me on the beach.' Then he turned to the seamen who had arrested him and said, 'You are a parcel of brave fellows. I don't blame you, my lads, but my officers shall answer for their villainy.' On that, the boatswain went up to him and struck him repeatedly in the face, shouting, 'You struck me once! Then it was your turn but now, God damn ye, it is mine!' and he struck him again. The captain replied, 'You are a scoundrel for using a gentleman ill when he is a prisoner.' As he was being led away with the blood streaming down his face, he turned and said with the greatest civility, 'I'm sorry I can't take my hat off to you, gentlemen, but my arms are bound'; and then, as if he had caught Byron's eye at the back of the crowd, he added, 'If I do not live to see England, I hope some of my friends will.'

Mr Bulkeley justified himself by saying that Lieutenant Baynes, the carpenter, Mr Jones and himself were convinced that the captain had no intention of going to the southward, therefore they resolved to make him prisoner for the shooting of Mr Cozens: it was reckoned dangerous to suffer him any longer to enjoy liberty. 'But . . .' he wrote, 'let us do so much Justice to his Character, to declare, that he was a Gentleman possess'd of many Virtues; he was an excellent Seaman himself, and lov'd a Seaman; as for personal Bravery, no Man had a larger Share of it; even when a Prisoner he preserved the Dignity of a Commander; no Misfortunes could dispirit or deject him, and Fear was a Weakness he was entirely a Stranger to; the Loss of the Ship, was the loss of him; he knew how to govern while he was a Commander on Board; but when Things were brought to Confusion and Disorder, he thought to establish his Command ashore by his Courage, and to suppress the least Insult on his Authority on the first Occasion; and Instance of this was seen on the Boatswain's first appearing ashore; shooting Mr Cozens and treating him in the Manner he did after his Confinement, was highly resented by the People, who soon got the Power in their own Hands, the Officers only had the Name, and they were often compell'd, for the Preservation of their Lives, to comply sometimes with their most unreasonable Demands; and it is a Miracle, amidst the Wildness and Distraction of the People, that there was no more Bloodshed.'

CHAPTER

9

➤➤➤✕◄◄◄

BYRON must have been one of the very few men in the camp who hadn't known that the captain was going to be arrested. It was generally understood that as a professional officer and a member of the aristocracy he was naturally bound to support the captain although, so far as his duty permitted, he had withdrawn from him since the death of Cozens: no doubt it was partly out of sympathy for his dilemma, as well as on account of his youth and his popularity with the men, that the conspirators had excluded him from their councils without, however, treating him as an enemy. Lieutenant Hamilton, the captain's most courageous supporter, had also been arrested and confined – on the trumped-up charge of 'breaking his confinement.' It is difficult to see how Captain Pemberton reconciled this with his sense of duty which, he claimed, made it incumbent upon him to arrest Captain Cheap, for Hamilton had nothing to do with the death of Cozens: the only reason for his arrest was that the conspirators were afraid to leave him at liberty in case he should form a party sympathetic to the captain. The surgeon, the purser and Midshipman Campbell, being closely watched, avoided each other and kept silent.

Mr Bulkeley and his associates, to replace the rules of the navy by which Captain Cheap had attempted to govern them, drew up articles 'for the Good of the Community': any man refusing to sign them was to be left behind. Naturally no one refused to sign: all believed that being left behind meant being left to perish. These articles covered discipline, and provided for the equal sharing of whatever food was available; they stipulated that the crews of the barge, the cutter and the yawl should have one week's provisions served out to them: they were always to keep within musket-shot of the longboat 'and on no Pretence or Excuse whatsoever go beyond that Reach.' They stipulated also that Lieutenant Baynes should have no power to release the captain. The lieutenant, when he had agreed to the articles and signed them, was given a limited command.

The idea of taking the captain back to England with them, and keeping him in confinement during the hazardous passage, seemed rather unrealistic: even Mr Bulkeley admitted that he was the best seaman among them, and that he had the greatest power of command; consequently, as soon as the longboat found itself in difficulties and the people felt that their lives were in danger, they would be bound to remember how he had saved them from the lee shore at Staten Island and insist upon him being reinstated.

All opposition to Mr Bulkeley's plans having been swept aside by these rough measures, the people set to work to prepare the longboat for launching. The purpose of the expedition, to attack the enemy in the Pacific, was now so far from their thoughts that they cheerfully rolled most of the gunpowder barrels down to the beach and staved them: the gunpowder, which the captain had so jealously guarded, was poured into the sea and the empty barrels handed over to the carpenter. The *Wager*'s bell sounded no more: it was the heaviest piece of metal they possessed so it was taken to serve as an anchor for the barge. The captain and Lieutenant Hamilton, in adjoining tents, were guarded by sentries of the land forces with one of their officers always on duty.

Because Cheap's Bay, as they now called the scene of the wreck, was too exposed to serve as an anchorage except in unusually favourable weather, Byron was given command of the barge, with a crew of ten men, and ordered by Lieutenant Baynes to take Mr Bulkeley, John Jones and Mr Harvey the purser, who was a good draughtsman, on a reconnaissance to the southward with the object of finding a secure harbour for the longboat. About ten miles down the coast, which appeared to be very dangerous, they found a place where she might conveniently shelter; they went on, in spite of the usual heavy seas with wind and rain, and found another harbour, which was rather larger, and then a third.

When they got back the longboat looked ready to be launched: the masts had been stepped, and the awning, laid in several thicknesses on the grating-deck, had been painted: it was sufficiently strong to withstand the breaking of the seas upon it.

On the 12th October, at daybreak, they launched her. Mr Bulkeley in honour of the occasion was wearing a small sword and some fine clothes that the captain had given him. He named her the *Speedwell*, which had been his intention from the beginning, after Captain Shelvocke's ship which had been their inspiration, and prayed God to preserve her to deliver them. They rushed her through the breakers and brought her clear into the bay. For a full hour those left on the shore, proud of their handiwork, stood gazing at her as she rode easily to an anchor, the fulfilment of their dreams, a ship to carry them to England. At last they bestirred themselves. Some filled the water breakers and carried them down to the beach, others stripped the broadcloth from the outside and the inside walls of the fine house that Mr Bulkeley had had built for himself and sewed it into trousers and watchcoats. Because there was small convenience for cooking on board the *Speedwell* twelve days' provisions were served out to every man and boy for them to prepare and dress before sailing. The barge and the cutter were manned, and they plied back and forth between the ship and the shore with fresh water, stones for ballast, provisions, stores, the remaining six half-barrels of gunpowder, and all that would be necessary for their preservation. The little yawl was not available for these duties: during Byron's absence she had been stove against a rock.

The officers responsible for the navigation of the *Speedwell* had intended to try her out with a crew of fifteen, but the people crowded aboard with all their gear and could by no means be persuaded to go ashore again. Only the marines remained under discipline and command, being sensible that they had a most important prisoner to be ceremoniously handed over when all was ready. There were separate cabins only for the lieutenant, the boatswain, who was second in order of command, and Captain Pemberton. When Byron came aboard with his small shotgun which was almost his only possession, Mr Bulkeley remarked, 'I'm afraid the accommodation will be little to your honour's liking. You'll have to lie forward with the men, as I will also, and the carpenter.' Byron answered that he supposed that he could put up with hardships as well as another. When the *Speedwell* was fully loaded she had a freeboard of five feet, and there was so little deck space that it was difficult to see how the helmsman was going to steer her without falling overboard.

On the morning of the 13th October Captain Pemberton drew up his men on the beach for the ceremony of delivering up his prisoners to the lieutenant for passage to England: he was justly proud of the appearance of his men, each with a well-oiled musket, and red coat in fairly presentable condition in spite of the hardships they had had to endure. He formed them into a hollow square with Captain Cheap in the centre and Lieutenant Hamilton beside him, and waited. But the lieutenant remained obstinately in the *Speedwell*: he was convinced that the captain wanted to murder him, so the very last thing he wanted or intended was to receive him on board. At last Mr Bulkeley came ashore and told Captain Bombast (as Captain Cheap called him) that unfortunately there was no suitable accommodation on board for the prisoners. Pemberton replied that he had been persuaded by the sea officers to arrest Captain Cheap for the death of Mr Cozens and therefore he designed, and must, carry him to England. With this intention Mr Bulkeley throroughly agreed, and suggested that he should remain on Wager Island with the captain until a more favourable opportunity presented itself. Faced with this alternative, Pemberton said he would consider himself released from all obligation once he had delivered his prisoner to Lieutenant Baynes. Thereupon Mr Bulkeley sent for the lieutenant who came ashore, accepted the prisoner on the beach and immediately released him. Captain Pemberton then embarked with all his men. Lieutenant Hamilton and Mr Elliot the surgeon both elected to stay with the captain.

It thus became apparent that poor Captain Pemberton had been shamelessly exploited and made a fool of. Unknown to him, Mr Bulkeley had made a deal with the captain who would rather have stayed alone on Wager Island than be dragged back ignominiously a prisoner to England, and if he had three men with him, or even one, he told Mr Bulkeley, and a few boards to lash together in the form of a boat, he would still try to join the commodore, having too much honour to turn his back upon their enemies. This suited Mr Bulkeley admirably: he agreed to leave the captain, Lieutenant Hamilton and the surgeon with their share of the rations, and he gave them the yawl that was lying on the beach with her broadside out. The captain bargained for rations for the deserters also, whom he intended to bring in and take with him to northward, and it was agreed that they should be allowed half rations. All this was arranged, and the rations handed over – six pieces of beef, six pieces of pork, and ninety pounds of flour for the captain and his friends, and eight pieces of beef, eight pieces of pork, and a hundredweight of flour for the deserters – without Captain Pemberton knowing anything about it. The captain also got back his arms with a limited supply of ammunition, some tools, a quadrant, a compass and a bible. 'I'm sorry,' he said at their last meeting, 'that so many brave fellows should be led to go by a route with which they are unacquainted by those who are not acquainted with it either. No farther than ninety leagues to the north of us lies the populous island of Chiloe where there is a Spanish settlement. We need not fear of taking prizes there and at one blow provide ourselves not only with provisions but with a ship; and we may have a chance to see the commodore.' Once they were out of the gulf in which the *Wager* was trapped, the open Pacific would lie before them.

Mr Bulkeley forcibly reiterated his objections: that if the captain still had the command he would lead them from their unhappy situation to a worse – to the inside of a Spanish prison or to labour in the salt mines; that they could not take a prize with the Spaniards everywhere expecting them, and Pizarro's fleet searching the coast for them, and watching for their coming. 'You have said, sir, that we shall be called to account in England for your arrest: I must tell you that, for my part, I should make it my choice to go there by the straits rather than to sail with you to the northward, even if I had committed a crime and was sure of being hanged for it when I arrived.' 'Then I wish you well and safe to England,' said the captain, shaking his hand, 'with all my heart.' And so they took leave of each other.

Byron had not in the least suspected that the captain would not be coming with them: when he discovered what Mr Bulkeley and the lieutenant had done he determined, he wrote, to leave them at the first opportunity. It was not possible to do so then because they were lying some distance offshore at anchor. As soon as Captain Pemberton and his men were on board they got under sail with the wind at north-west by west. There were fifty-nine men in the *Speedwell*, twelve in the cutter, and ten in the barge. The captain, Lieutenant Hamilton and the surgeon were standing on the shore to watch them go: the men gave them three hearty cheers, which they returned. Going out of the bay a sudden squall split the *Speedwell*'s foresail so that she nearly ran upon the rocks, but the boats towed her clear.

On that day they made good only about five leagues, to the first secure harbour discovered by the barge at the southern entrance of the lagoon, and anchored there at four in the afternoon in ten fathoms to complete their preparations. The bottom was fine sand. They named this harbour Speedwell Bay. There being so little room on board, most of the people were sent ashore and a camp was established. Meanwhile the principal officers felt the necessity of drawing up some kind of document to explain and justify themselves to the Lords of the Admiralty for abandoning the captain. They had widely different reasons for having done so: Mr Bulkeley said it was on account of the shortage of accommodation and provisions, and because in so long and tedious a passage the captain would have had opportunities to influence the people and regain his authority: the lieutenant said it was to prevent the captain from murdering him: Captain Pemberton, still smarting from the trick that had been played upon him, wished it placed on record that he had insisted on delivering his prisoners to the charge of the lieutenant. It was impossible to reconcile their views, so they tried to incorporate all of them, and wrote as follows:

'These are to certify the Right Honourable the Lords Commissioners for Executing. the Office of Lord High

Admiral of *Great Britain*, That we, whose Names are under-mention'd, do beg Leave to acquaint your Lordships, that Captain *David Cheap*, our late Commander in his Majesty's Ship *Wager*, having publickly declar'd, that he will never go off this Spot, at his own Request desires to be left behind; but Captain *Pemberton*, of his Majesty's Land Forces, having confined him a Prisoner for the Death of Mr *Henry Cozens* Midshipman, with Lieutenant *Hamilton* for breaking his Confinement, did insist on delivering them up on the Beach to the Charge of Lieutenant *Beans*; but he, with his Officers and People, consulting the ill Consequences that might attend carrying two Prisoners off in so small a Vessel, and for so long and tedious a Passage as we are likely to have, and that they might have Opportunities of acting such Things in Secret as may prove destructive to the whole Body; and also in Regard to the chief Article of Life, as the greatest Part of the People must be oblig'd, at every Place we stop, to go on Shore in Search of Provisions, and there being now no less than eighty-one Souls in this small Vessel, which we hope to be deliver'd in; we therefore, to prevent any Difficulties to be added to the unforeseen we have to encounter with, think proper to agree, and in order to prevent Murther, to comply with Captain *David Cheap*'s Request: The Surgeon also begs Leave to be left with him. Dated on Board the *Speedwell* Schooner in *Cheap*'s Bay, this 14th Day of *October*, 1741.'

The principal officers put their names to this document: only the midshipmen, who had been kept in the dark both about the captain's arrest and about his release, did not sign it.

On the following day they took the *Speedwell* out and cruised three or four times up and down the sheltered lagoon to try the vessel. They were well pleased with her performance. At daybreak on the 16th they made a signal by firing muskets for the boats to come off, and as soon as all were on board they sailed with the wind at west by north: there was a great swell and it was blowing hard. They passed the next harbour, which they called Harvey's Bay after the purser who had surveyed it, and anchored in the third, inside a very large ledge of rocks which broke the sea off: it was a small bay with very good shelter. The people were sent ashore to seek their sustenance, and they found such an abundance of clams that they called the place Clam Bay. The ship had not worked so well in heavy weather, so they began taking in more ballast and making adjustments to the rigging.

Mr Bulkeley said he already regretted not having brought more canvas and that he would like an officer to go back in the barge and collect some; the large sail that had served as a tent for Captain Pemberton he thought would be particularly useful. Byron, seeing an opportunity to rejoin the captain, volunteered to go. He quickly mustered a crew from among those whom he thought would favour his design. When they were ready, Campbell came up and said he would go also. They pushed off hastily, fearing that Mr Bulkeley would object to two officers going, particularly two whom he might suspect of sympathising with the captain, but he raised no objections: perhaps it didn't occur to him that they would deliberately choose to share his fate instead of sailing to England.

As soon as they were clear of the bay Byron told his men that he had embarked in the *Speedwell* under the impression that the captain would be taken along with them; he thought it was not right that he should be left behind, so he was going to join him: if anyone was not of the same opinion he would put him ashore and let him go back on foot. Campbell said he had also seen in the return of the barge an opportunity to serve the captain, and all the others declared that they had the same intention. The crew consisted of Richard Noble the quartermaster who once had struck Mr Bulkeley and harboured thoughts of shooting him; William Rose, another quartermaster; two quarter gunners, William Harvey and David Buckley; Peter Plastow, the captain's steward; John Bozman, seaman; and Corporal Crosslet and Joseph Clinch, marines. They landed again, out of sight of the *Speedwell*, collected a good supply of clams, then put to sea and, running before a fresh gale at west-north-west, made a swift passage to Wager Island which they reached the same evening.

The captain had seen them coming – he was standing on the beach waving his hat and shouting welcome as they approached. He was beside himself with joy, dancing about and shaking every man in turn by the hand, and embracing Byron and Campbell. The surgeon and Hamilton ran down to welcome them also. The men were lodged in the house Mr Bulkeley had had built for himself and his associates – it was still the best although it had been stripped – and their necessities were, as far as possible, provided for. All the officers were invited to dine with the captain – he had been cooking his dinner when the barge was sighted – and they discussed the problems and the possibilities before them, and wondered how long Mr Bulkeley would wait before realising that the barge was not coming back, and what steps he would take to recover it: they decided that he would do nothing about it because it wasn't his way to come looking for trouble and as long as he had the cutter he didn't really need it.

The captain had been left a fair supply of arms and ammunition – swords, pistols, muskets with spare flints, five half-barrels of gunpowder, two kegs of musket balls and six hand-grenades. Five of the deserters had come in with their muskets and some ammunition: they reported that the other three, including James Mitchell, had hollowed out and shaped a section of the *Wager*'s mainmast to form a canoe, and in it they had set out to northward to find a Spanish settlement. Byron was relieved that the unruly James Mitchell who had hurled a bayonet at Campbell and whom he suspected of the blackest crimes, had taken himself off: the captain, however, only regretted that he wouldn't be there to repair the yawl, for he was a good craftsman. He now had four officers and fifteen men with him, all devoted to his service. The crucial problem was how to feed them with only three full rations and eight half rations, and at the same time to lay in a sea store. Byron suggested that they should go back to the *Speedwell* and ask for their share of the provisions which, he thought, could not with justice be withheld. The captain objected that Mr Bulkeley would certainly take the barge from them by force if they gave him an opportunity, but he agreed that they might be landed by the barge at some distance from Clam Bay and make their way there on foot. So, on the following morning, they crossed to the far side of the lagoon and found a small cove in which the barge could lie sheltered and hidden from view: leaving three men in her, Byron and Campbell with the other three started on an exhausting tramp over broken rocky country interspersed with thick woods and swamps.

Towards evening they came to the *Speedwell*'s camp: they saw that most of the people were scattered along the beach picking up what they could find, so they walked among them until they came upon Mr Bulkeley and Lieutenant Baynes who seemed very surprised to see them, and asked where the barge was. Byron told them that they were going to stay with the captain and that they had come back for their share of the provisions. Mr Bulkeley protested that they had all signed a paper agreeing to go south, to which they replied that they had understood that the captain was being taken along with them, and now that they found he was left behind they considered it their duty to stay with him. Mr Bulkeley went on stooping down and picking up clams and stuffing them into his pockets: 'You'll get no provisions,' he said over his shoulder, 'until you bring back the barge.' 'Then what are we to live on?' Byron asked. Getting no reply he turned to the lieutenant and asked if he could be taken out to the *Speedwell* in the cutter. 'No, you can't,' he said: 'The people are all out fishing. We're not serving provisions today.' Campbell protested that they had nothing to eat and no change of clothes and that the few things he possessed were in the *Speedwell* and what were they to do. 'You must bring back the barge,' the lieutenant repeated. 'We can't do without her. If anything happens to the cutter we'll have no boat to take the people ashore.'

So Byron and Campbell went along the beach too, collecting clams for their supper. They spent the night in the camp. In the morning, seeing the cutter going off to the *Speedwell*, Byron went in her and again tackled Mr Bulkeley who angrily accused him of deserting them after having been the first to propose attempting to return to England by the Straits of Magellan. He would give him nothing. 'I'm astonished,' he said, 'that you have allowed yourself to be influenced by Campbell, the Patroon, whom you have always held in contempt.' None of his friends would listen to him or give him the smallest morsel of food, and Mr Bulkeley threatened that if he didn't bring back the barge he would come and take it by force. Seeing that it was hopeless to continue the argument, he climbed down into the cutter that was waiting to take him ashore. The weather was misty with rain and hail: a sudden gust blew his hat away. One of the boat's crew pulled off his woollen cap and thrust it on to his head. 'I can't accept it, John,' Byron said, putting it back on the seaman's head. 'It's as cold for you as it is for me.' The man's name was John Duck, a Mulatto born in Stepney.

When he rejoined Campbell and their three seamen, they

agreed that nothing further could be done. They hung about the beach for a while picking up clams and then started on their long walk back to the barge. They saw a great flock of very large seabirds flying southwards, and from a hill they looked back enviously at the *Speedwell* which they imagined weighed down by the food that rightfully belonged to them. The share for the barge should have been thirty pieces of beef or pork and 300 pounds of flour, a great part of which they had themselves salvaged from the wreck in long miserable hours of patient work, nearly always drenched with spray and freezing in the bitter wind. The cutter was coming off again. They watched idly and saw Mr Bulkeley and eight men jump ashore and head straight up the hill. Realising that they were being followed, Byron got his men out of sight as quickly as possible: they ran down the farther slope, crossed a ravine, and hid in a thick wood. Here they waited, wondering what had decided Mr Bulkeley to come after them. There must have been a conference as soon as Byron had left — of course he had made it clear that he wasn't coming back, saying goodbye to his friends, wishing them well in their hazardous passage by the straits, and so on: a more skilful diplomat would have pretended to submit to their terms, and that he was going to fetch the barge, and got away without any trouble. In a few minutes the pursuers appeared on the hill: they stopped and looked across the apparently deserted landscape, evidently hoping to catch sight of Byron's party. Being disappointed in this, one of them produced a map — it must have been the purser who had surveyed the coastline: they consulted it, and then went on again more or less in the direction in which the barge was lying. Byron and Campbell set off on a parallel course, trying to keep out of sight which made the going harder, wading through swamps, scrambling over rocks and struggling in the undergrowth, encouraging the men to go faster and faster, wondering how they would ever be able to face the captain again if the barge were lost; he would think they had deserted him, and they wouldn't even be able to get back across the lagoon unless he managed to repair the yawl and come looking for them, but even if he did so she was too small to take them all to the northward except in relays. Occasionally they caught a glimpse of their pursuers who were making surprisingly good progress, and they hurried on hoping that the men they had left in the barge would have the sense to push off and get help from the captain if the wrong party got there first. Now they lay panting on a hill, and they could see Mr Bulkeley's party on another hill moving doggedly forward: they were about equally distant from their goal with a marshy wooded valley between them. Byron thought they would probably reach it at about the same time and that, being unarmed, they would be at a disadvantage, so he decided on a stratagem: it was reasonable to suppose that Mr Bulkeley didn't know that they had seen him, so he told his men to light a fire to give him the impression that they had stopped to roast their clams: leaving it smoking they crawled through the bushes until they were hidden by the shoulder of a hill, and then they ran full speed to the barge while Mr Bulkeley led his men across the valley to surprise them at their camp-fire. They rowed until they were out of the lee of the land, then hoisted foresail and mainsail to a steady breeze, and were bowling away up the lagoon when their pursuers reached the place where the barge had been lying.

CHAPTER

10

M R B U L K E L E Y waited in Clam Bay for five days after Byron had left him; until Monday, 26th October. Then, the weather being fair and the sea calm, he went ashore in the cutter, brought off all the men, weighed the *Speedwell*, and took her in tow over the bar where there was ten foot of water but a great swell.

As soon as they got clear of the bay a breeze sprung up at north-west and he had the satisfaction of setting his course towards the southernmost point of land they could discern, a bluff headland, distant about twenty-eight miles: he was really on his way at last. He had with him eighty-one men all told: eleven of them were in the cutter. They made good progress. The land receded from them in a wide bay. Towards evening the wind increased and blew from the west, and the mist came down: Mr Bulkeley went ahead in the cutter to find a harbour. At eight o'clock they anchored in eight fathoms of water in a fine sandy land-locked bay. Here they remained stormbound for the next three days. The people were sent ashore to dress their provisions: each man was allowed a quarter of a pound of flour a day without any other subsistence but what providence brought in their way. Every morning flocks of large seabirds flew towards the north, and they flew back again to southward in the evenings.

Early on the 29th they got under weigh: it was calm again, with thick weather and light rain, but by 5 a.m. it had cleared and they had a fine fresh south-westerly breeze. They saw a small island about eight miles out to sea which they called the Rock of Dundee because it was similar in shape, though smaller, to the island of that name in the West Indies. Again they had a fair day's run, but again the wind freshened and blew hard in the evening. They had to take the cutter in tow. By next morning it was blowing a gale and there was a great sea, so they ran for an opening that appeared between two headlands: there were sunken rocks on both sides with the sea breaking over them, but by steering due east they got past them and into a safe harbour that nature had formed like a dock: they had no occasion to let go an anchor, they ran alongside the land and made fast ahead and astern. Here they found plenty of wood and water, and fine large mussels in great quantities, but in spite of this, because the weekly ration was due, they served out to each man half a piece of beef. The entrance to this harbour, Mr Bulkeley noted in his journal, was so dangerous that no mortal would attempt it unless his case was desperate, as theirs was. There were a few huts in the vicinity, but no Indians. Next morning they cast off and rowed towards the mouth of the harbour, intending to put to sea, but the wind blew so hard when they left the shelter of the land that they decided to anchor: in the afternoon, in attempting to weigh the grapnel, which they could not afford to lose, they found that it was foul among some rocks: all hands hauled, took a turn round the mainmast and went aft: this weighed the grapnel but straightened one of the flukes. The land was very high and steep, and there were great waterfalls all along the coast.

They again set a course to the southward. On the 2nd November Mr Bulkeley's observation at noon showed them to be in latitude 50° south, which meant that they were already 140 miles south of Wager Island. After establishing their position they bore away and ran into a broad smooth passage between a large island and what they supposed to be the mainland.

Because the men in the open cutter suffered greatly from exposure, it had been determined that her crew should be relieved every seven days. She was now manned by a new crew commanded by Mr Harvey, the purser, who had already shown his ability in surveying the coast in the vicinity of Clam Bay: their duties were to find harbours in which the *Speedwell* might shelter when necessary, to take the people ashore to find their sustenance, and to refill the water-casks. During the day, while they were on passage, they had been warned repeatedly that they were to keep as close to the *Speedwell* as possible: they considered, however, that the course Mr Bulkeley was steering – keeping well out to sea to avoid the navigational hazards, and taking the most direct route from headland to headland – was not right for them: they wanted to be closer to the shore where, if the weather should grow worse, they could beach the cutter and wait for it to improve. Therefore, on the morning of the 3rd November, they steered away into a deep bay.

Mr Bulkeley made the signal for the cutter to return by hoisting an ensign at the topping-lift. As she ignored the signal he followed her into the bay, but lost sight of her in the mist: hauling down mainsail and foresail, he waited for her. At eleven o'clock she returned: her mainsail was split. She came alongside and he called to the crew to take hold of a tow rope: they refused, saying that she wouldn't bear towing because of the swell of the sea; and they asked for a course nearer the shore where they would have smooth water: he assured them that the water was smoother farther out and the sea nothing like as high as that which was running close to the shore; and that the *Speedwell* could not go farther in without the risk of being embayed: therefore he desired them to come aboard and he would take the cutter in tow. They paid not the least regard to what he said. For above a quarter of an hour both vessels lay in the trough of the sea: the crew of the cutter would neither come aboard, nor row, nor make sail. The purser could do nothing with them. Finding them so obstinate, Mr Bulkeley hoisted the skirt of the mainsail and edged away south by west: when they saw that he would not go farther into the bay, they made sail and took station ahead of him. At one o'clock they again bore away, steering south by east which brought them closer inshore, and for some time the two vessels ran on parallel courses with about four miles between them. Then the mist came down and Mr Bulkeley, fearing to lose the cutter, bore away after her. She disappeared in a very heavy squall of wind and rain. When it cleared there was no sign of her, and the *Speedwell* was within two miles of the shore in a great swell with the tide running rampant; and on all sides there were shoals and breakers: the oldest seaman among them had never seen a more dismal prospect. They saw an opening and ran for it before the wind, expecting at every rise and fall of the sea to strike upon a rock: at last they got into a sheltered cove. They lay there for three days depressed and hungry, for they now had no boat with them to go ashore and look for food. They served out half a piece of beef and some flour per man for a week's subsistence. The boatswain made a raft of oars and water-casks upon which three men attempted to go ashore: as soon as it put off from the ship's side it canted over and they had to swim for their lives. He set off again by himself, reached the shore and returned in the evening.

On the 5th November they went out under sail but could make no hand of it and were obliged to put back. On the 6th they tried again and failed to get out because of the heavy sea but, as they turned back, they caught sight of the cutter: she followed them to their anchorage and came alongside. The people at once went ashore in her to get shellfish of which they were in great need.

According to the standing orders the cutter was to be taken ashore every night, whenever it was possible, to be hauled up clear of the breakers and safe from all hazards: the crew were supposed to camp on the beach. On this night the crew refused to take her ashore: they made her fast astern of the *Speedwell,* leaving only two men in her although she was supposed never to be left with less than four. At eleven o'clock one of these two came out of her into the *Speedwell*: it was blowing hard at NNE with such heavy rain that they could not see a boat's length. At two in the morning the cutter broke loose: they called to the seaman in her, James Stewart of Aberdeen, to take a line, but he could not hear them, and in a short while she drifted out of sight.

When day dawned and there was no sign of the cutter, the people completely lost heart and refused to exert themselves on any kind of duties about the ship: they seemed not to care whether the voyage was continued or not, or whether they lived or died. In vain Mr Bulkeley entreated them to come on deck to assist in their own preservation, 'they were ripe for Mutiny and Destruction.' Neither he nor Lieutenant Baynes nor the carpenter knew what to do to bring them under command, for they all looked upon themselves as equal partners in their enterprise. 'They have troubled us to that Degree, that we are weary of our Lives;' Mr Bulkeley wrote, 'therefore this Day we have told the People, that, unless they alter their Conduct, and subject themselves to Command, that we will leave them to themselves, and take our Chance in this desolate Part of the Globe, rather than give ourselves any farther Concern about so many thoughtless Wretches.' It was very uncomfortable in their quarters: 'the stench of the Men's wet Clothes makes the Air we breathe nauseous to that Degree that one would think it impossible for a Man to live below:' but they preferred it to lying in the open. They now had ten extra men to accommodate from the cutter. After long argument the people allowed themselves to be divided into four watches to make more room; and they promised to be under government in the future. But the next morning they demanded that provisions should be served though it was four days before the usual time. Mr Bulkeley reasoned with them, told them that considering the badness of the weather and the length of the passage, they must all inevitably starve if they were not exceedingly provident – but they would not listen and he was obliged to comply with their demands and serve out the provisions. Thus was the voyage delayed, the cutter lost, and all of them brought into the greatest hazard because everyone thought himself entitled to do as he pleased.

The officers' threat to go ashore and leave the crew of the *Speedwell* to their fate – a threat which they hadn't the remotest intention of carrying out – had the surprising result that eleven of the crew asked to be given their share of the rations and to be put ashore. The country, whenever it could be discerned through the mist and cloud, was as inhospitable as any that could be imagined. On being asked what could have induced them to make such a request they answered that they would either find the cutter or build a canoe and return to northward, and that they didn't fear of doing well. The bare precipitous mountains and the clefts and valleys filled with matted forest and deep bog below the glaciers, were practically impassable: therefore their sole hope of salvation would depend upon finding the cutter in the near vicinity, which seemed extremely unlikely, or boat-building material which seemed still more unlikely. They were now 180 miles south of Wager Island. There was no one with any authority, or indeed with any desire, to forbid this suicidal project. The question was put to 'the Body of the People' who approved it. Whereupon Mr Bulkeley drew up a paper for the men to sign so that no one but themselves could be held responsible for their action. It read as follows:

'These are to certify the Right Honourable the Lords Commissioners for Executing the Office of Lord High Admiral of *Great Britain*, &c. That we, whose Names are under-mention'd, since the Misfortune of losing the Cutter, have consider'd the ill Conveniences and Difficulties to be attended, where so great a Number of People are to be carried off; therefore we have requested, and desired the Officers and Company remaining of the same Vessel to put us on Shore, with such Necessaries of Life as can be conveniently spar'd out of the Vessel. We, of our own free Will and Choice, do indemnify all Persons from ever being call'd to an Account for putting us on Shore, or leaving us behind, contrary to our Inclinations. Witness our Hands, on Board the *Speedwell*, Schooner, in the Latitude 50.40.S. this eighth Day of November, 1741.'

This was signed by the eleven men and they were put ashore 'with proper necessaries.' Among them were John Russell the armourer who had made all the iron fittings for the *Speedwell* and the tools required for building her, and Richard Phipps, the indomitable hunter of seabirds. They had actually landed on an island though they were unaware of it.

On the following day in the evening the *Speedwell* weighed and was rowed out of the anchorage: there was a large western swell rolling in and the wind was blowing right on shore. Sunken rocks, breakers and small islands continued for many miles along the coast, and the vessel was constantly being swept into danger by the strong tides: there was evidently a great shelf of rock extending under the sea and showing frequently on the surface. They had to steer west by north, then south by west and then west before they at last reached open water and could get a clear run to southward. According to Mr Bulkeley's observation they were in latitude 50° 50′ south.

At four o'clock in the morning of the 10th November, because they were nearing the latitude in which they believed the Straits of Magellan to lie, they closed the land again. At 8 a.m. they sighted a headland bearing south-east, distance twelve leagues, which they assumed was Cape Victory because there was no more land visible to the south. When they drew abreast of it they saw four islands which Mr Bulkeley decided were the Islands of Direction described by Sir John Narborough as marking the entrance to the straits. They had no leisure to rejoice, for a south-westerly gale swept down upon them and put them in such peril that Mr Bulkeley gave himself up for lost and was for ever afterwards convinced that it was not by their conduct and ability that their lives were saved that day. He wrote in his journal: 'I never in my Life, in any Part of the World, have seen such a Sea as runs here; we expected every Wave to swallow us and the Boat to founder. This Shore is full of small Islands, Rocks and Breakers; so that we can't haul further to the Southward, for fear of endangering the Boat; we are oblig'd to keep her right before the Sea. At Five broach'd to, at which we all believ'd she would never rise again. We were surrounded with Rocks, and so near that a Man might toss a Biscuit on 'em: We had nothing but Death before our Eyes, and every Moment expected our Fate. It blew a Hurricane of Wind, with thick rainy weather, that we could not see twice the Boat's Length; we pray'd earnestly for its clearing up, for nothing else could save us from perishing; we no sooner ask'd for Light, but it was granted us from above. At the Weather's clearing up, we saw Land on the North-Shore . . . After sailing amidst Islands, Rocks, and Breakers, for above a League, we got safe into a good Harbour, surrounded with small Islands, which kept the Sea off; here the water was as smooth as in a Millpond. We call this Harbour the Port of God's Mercy, esteeming our Preservation this Day to be a Miracle. The most abandon'd among us no longer doubt of an Almighty Being, and have promis'd to reform their Lives.'

On the following morning, the 11th November, in heavy rain but with the wind much abated, they ran farther in towards the straits, passing great sounds and broken islands. They risked approaching the steep rocks on the northern shore – the southern shore being not yet visible – in order to find a place where they could land. Towards evening they saw two Indians lying on their bellies on the top of a cliff just above the vessel, peeping with their heads just over the edge. A little farther on they found a sheltered cove and anchored. Next morning Mr Bulkeley went ashore with four men and succeeded in getting in touch with the Indians: in exchange for a pair of trousers they got from them a mangy dog which they immediately killed, dressed and devoured. They also found plenty of mussels, and Lieutenant Ewers of the marines shot a very large seal, or 'sea-dog'.

On the 14th, with the mist and rain continuing and with a little wind at WNW, they cast loose and went out between the islands. When the weather cleared they saw the south shore: it first appeared like a large island stretching away to the westward and ending in a high cape from which two peaks arose, the western one being in the form of a tower: Mr Bulkeley took this for Cape Pillar, the southern head-land of the entrance, and felt assured that they were in the straits. A furious north-westerly gale forced them to put back into their cove and shelter there for two days, the people crying aloud for provisions: some of them drove a trade with their allowance, selling flour for silver buckles, or at twelve shillings a pound. On the 15th they ran up the straits which closed in rapidly with spectacular mountains and glaciers on either hand: they were borne on by a favourable wind and tide, and there was a heavy swell still following them from the Pacific. Again they found a secure anchorage. Getting under way at 3 a.m. on the next morning, the 16th, they were perplexed to see several alternative openings which might have been channels, or perhaps lagoons. By eight o'clock they were off Cape Monday where the land on both shores was as Narborough had described it: 'high rocky hills and barren, very little wood or grass growing on them.' At noon the passage they were in divided into two, one lying SE by S and the other ESE, and they couldn't agree upon which was the right one. Mr Bulkeley took the ESE passage because it lay on the course that Sir John Narborough had directed them to take: the other officers said that Sir John had told them to follow the southern shore and therefore they should have taken the other one. Mr Bulkeley insisted that he was right and that he would stake his life upon it, so they grudgingly let him have his way.

They expected to sight Cape Quod next, on the north shore, a few leagues farther on; but it didn't appear: Narborough had described it as an outstanding landmark, 'a steep cape of a rocky greyish face, of a good height before one comes at it: it shews like a great building of a castle.' How could they have missed such a landmark? After running another league or two there was still no sign of it. Lieutenant Baynes said they were in the wrong passage and that they must return to where the ways had divided and take the right one: Mr Bulkeley said they must continue on their course and he was positive that in an hour or two they would sight Cape Quod: but the majority sided with the lieutenant and he was overruled: he had little expected, when he gave Lieutenant Baynes a limited command, that control of the enterprise would be wrested from him at this crucial moment. In vain he exhausted all his arguments in favour of continuing on their course: not one league farther would they go. The farther they went in the wrong passage, they said, the longer they would take to get back again.

Having the wind astern and blowing hard at WNW they could not turn, so they put into a cove on the north shore where they found good anchoring in four-fathom water; but it was a barren rocky place, producing nothing for the preservation of life. The people were now in great want, and greatly depressed in their spirits and despondent. 'This Afternoon died *George Bateman*, a Boy, aged sixteen Years:' Mr Bulkeley recorded in his journal. 'This poor Creature starv'd, perish'd, and died a Skeleton, for want of Food. There are several more in the same miserable Condition, and who, without speedy Relief, must undergo the same Fate.'

For three days they tried to work their way back against the wind, making fast to the rocks at night and living on limpets and clams. By the 19th they had only made one mile. Instead of the shellfish being brought on board and equally shared, those who were most active and fortunate in the search ate what they found and sold their flour ration to those who were too sickly or too weak to forage for themselves: those who had no money or valuables to dispose of were left to die. 'This Night departed this Life *Mr Thomas Caple*, Son of the late Lieutenant Caple, aged twelve Years, who perish'd for want of Food,' the journal continues. 'There was a Person on Board who had some of the Youth's Money, upwards of twenty Guineas, with a Watch and Silver Cup. Those last the Boy was willing to sell for Flower; but his Guardian told him, he would buy Cloathes for him in the Brasil. This miserable Youth cry'd, Sir, I shall never live to see the Brasil; I am starving now, almost starv'd to Death; therefore, for G - d's Sake, give me my Silver Cup to get me some Victuals, or buy some for me yourself. All his Prayers and Intreaties to him were vain; but Heaven sent Death to his Relief, and put a Period to his Miseries in an Instant. Persons who have not experienc'd the Hardships we have met with, will wonder how People can be so inhuman to see their Fellow-Creatures starving before their Faces, and afford 'em no Relief: But Hunger is void of all Compassion; every Person was so intent on the Preservation of his own Life, that he was regardless of another's, and the Bowels of Commiseration were shut up. We slip no Opportunity, Day or Night, to enter into the suppos'd right *Streights*, but can get no Ground. This Day we serv'd Flower and a Piece of Beef between two men for a Week. Capt. *P - n*, of His Majesty's Land Forces, gave two Guineas for two Pounds of Flower; this Flower was sold him by the Seamen, who live on Muscles. Many of the People eat their Flower raw as soon as they are serv'd with it.'

It was not until Tuesday the 24th that they got back to the place where the channel had divided: they sailed into the supposed right passage, which was two miles wide: it gradually narrowed and, six miles from the entrance, came to an end, so they had to work their way out again. Still Lieutenant Baynes would not admit that Mr Bulkeley had been right: he decided that they were not in the Straits of Magellan at all but in a deep lagoon to the north of them: therefore they must return, he said, to the headland that Mr Bulkeley had mistakenly believed to be Cape Pillar, and look for what he called 'the right straits' farther south. Again the majority supported him, and Mr Bulkeley was powerless. He wrote in his journal that day, 'if ever there was such a Place in the World as the *Streights of Magellan*, we are now in them, and above thirty Leagues up. If he, (the lieutenant), or any of the Officers, had given themselves the Trouble of coming upon Deck, to have made proper Remarks, we had been free from all this Perplexity, and by this Time out of the Streights to the Northward. There is not an Officer aboard, except the Carpenter and myself, will keep the Deck a Moment longer than his Watch, or has any Regard to a Reckoning, or any Thing else.'

They continued their laborious attempts to go back the way they had come: the *Speedwell* was difficult to handle, being long in proportion to her beam, and she swam so buoyant upon the water that when close hauled the wind constantly threw her to leeward. '*Sunday* the 29th, Hard Gales from N.W. to S.W. with heavy Rains. Great Uneasiness among the People, many of them despairing of a Deliverance, and crying aloud to serve Provisions four Days before the Time. Finding no Way to pacify them, we were oblig'd to serve them. We endeavour'd to encourage and comfort them as much as lay in our Power, and at length they seemed tolerably easy. *Monday* the 30th, Fresh Gales at W. with continual Rain. This day died three of our People, *viz. Peter Delroy* Barber, *Thomas Thorpe* and *Thomas Woodhead*, Marines; they all perish'd for want of Food: several more are in the same Way, being not able to go ashore for Provisions; and those who are well can't get sufficient for themselves; therefore the Sick are left destitute of all Relief. There is one Thing to be taken Notice of in the Death of those People, that some Hours before they die, they are taken light-headed, and fall a joking and laughing; and in this Humour they expire.'

It was not until the 5th December at four in the morning that they sighted Cape Pillar again, bearing west by north, distant eight leagues. At three in the afternoon they also sighted Cape Deseado, 'the cape that all men desire to see,' two miles south-west of it, a very high cape and unmistakable because it had a black island in front of it. There was no longer any doubt that they had been in the right passage all along, so they wore ship and again steered ESE. The people's lack of confidence in Mr Bulkeley, and his lack of authority over them, had delayed them fifteen heartbreaking days, and cost five lives.

CHAPTER

11

⇥⟫⟪⇤

T H E captain and the men who had elected to stay with him were still on Wager Island: there were too many of them for the barge to carry so they had to repair the yawl before they could make a move to the northward. They were faced with the problem of how to live while they did so, for the food that Mr Bulkeley had left them, reckoning only half rations for the deserters and none at all for the crew of the barge, was barely sufficient to provide a sea stock. The crew of the barge were given a few things from the captain's store, and a little food, but soon they had to forage for themselves which meant that they had little time or energy left to work on the yawl. Byron, who was now eighteen, became seriously ill – the result, he says, of famine and of a diet of seaweed fried in tallow candles: he became so weak that one day, while searching for shellfish, he fell from a rock into the breakers and with difficulty saved himself by swimming. Once their hopes were raised by the appearance of some Indians: they were not the same ones, neither were they so friendly; and when they saw that the strangers had practically nothing to barter they refused to part with even a morsel of food, and went away.

When their distress was at its greatest a rare fine day made it possible for them to visit the wreck again – of which nothing was visible now except the dark outline of her keel and shadowy ribs on the ocean floor: before the gales set in again, which they did that evening, they had hooked up three casks of beef and brought them safe to shore. This providential find quickly restored their health and spirits. All hands set to work to repair the yawl and the barge, which had also suffered damage, though they had only a few worn-out tools and little skill except what some of them had acquired by working on the longboat with the carpenter. All of them were solidly behind the captain in his bold plan to sail to the northward and take a Spanish prize: so great was their confidence that even the thought that Admiral Pizarro's flagship, the *Asia*, with her sixty-six heavy guns and her crew of above seven hundred, might be on the lookout for them held no terrors.

It took them nearly two months to shape the new planks and complete the repairs. Both boats had a small foresail and a mainsail, but neither could sail close to the wind: for a great part of the time they would have to row, with the masts unshipped and laid along the thwarts. Though the seasons seemed to make little difference to the severity of the weather, the days were now nearly at their longest, and all were impatient to start. Every morning, if it were clear, the captain would climb up Mount Misery and gaze out across the gulf, well named by the Spaniards, 'The Gulf of Affliction', towards the far headland, the Cape of Three Mountains, which barred his way like a fortress to the northward.

On the morning of the 15th December the wind was fair and the day was tolerably fine. Officers and men went in a body to the captain and told him that they thought it was a good opportunity to run across the bay. He, being doubtful if the weather would hold, took them up to his lookout place and showed them, through his perspective glass, that there was a great sea without. However, this had no effect on the people, who were impatient to be gone while their food lasted. They launched both boats, got everything on board as quickly as possible, and started on their great adventure. Captain Cheap, the surgeon and Byron were in the barge with nine men, and Lieutenant Hamilton and Campbell in the yawl with six. Byron steered the barge, and Campbell the yawl. They headed for the Cape of Three Mountains which they could dimly discern at a distance, they supposed, of about fifty or sixty miles.

They had not been two hours at sea when the wind shifted more to the westward and began to blow very hard, so that they were obliged to bear right away before it. Although the yawl was not far off, Byron could see nothing of her except now and then upon the top of a mountainous sea, and then he lost sight of her altogether. The captain and the surgeon huddled close to him in the stern sheets to receive the breaking seas upon their backs and prevent them from filling the boat and sending her to the bottom which they every moment expected. The men bailed frantically with the water gaining on them, and when she was wallowing half-full they threw overboard in desperation nearly everything they possessed, even the *Wager*'s bell that served them for an anchor, even the compass, even the meat that they had salvaged from the wreck. With night coming on they were running on to a lee shore where the sea broke in a frightful manner against high cliffs, and not one of them imagined that it was possible for a boat to live in such a sea. While they were being driven closer and closer, expecting to be beaten to pieces by the first breaker, they descried through the smoke of the spray an opening in the face of the rock. They ran into it, and found themselves in a narrow passage with a precipice on either side, where the air was suddenly still and they were protected from the fury of the sea. It was as if God had smitten the rock and opened a way for them. Byron relaxed his fierce grip upon the tiller and became aware that it was raining. They got out the oars, rowed along the narrow passage and came to a harbour as calm and smooth as a millpond, and there, to their great joy, they found the yawl that had got in before them. They went on together up the harbour, which seemed to extend a great way into the mountains, looking for a suitable place to land and build a fire, but they found none: the rocks on both sides remained high and precipitous, and there was no fire-wood. When darkness fell they secured the boats and climbed up to a hollow where they lay all night on the bare rock with no shelter from the incessant rain and thought longingly of their huts on Wager Island. A hard frost came on, making it impossible for them to sleep.

Early in the morning the captain, seeing that the weather appeared to be somewhat more favourable, and that there was no prospect of finding anything to eat where they were, ordered every man back into the boats. They were now bare of provisions, for nearly all their stores had gone overboard: they had only the iron cooking pots and nothing to cook in them, but the captain had saved his arms and ammunition, the officers' sporting guns and cartridges, and his silver-mounted cane. They pulled out of the haven and found that the storm had much abated, but there was still a heavy sea running and the wind was contrary. All that day they plied with the oars. Their chart showed them that once past the Cape of Three Mountains they would be able to proceed by more sheltered ways for the coast was broken up into a maze of channels and islands. The captain hoped indeed to find a channel leading northward from within the gulf which, if they could find it, would enable them to reach Chiloe without going out into the open sea. They passed several more inlets but decided not to venture into them because they seemed to lead in the general direction of the high mountains and glaciers to the east, and because the sides of all of them were precipitous: the sun, had it appeared, would not have been visible for them to steer by, and the channels wound so deep under the mountains in perpetual shadow that they feared to lose their way there, being now without a compass.

Towards evening they came to a group of small islands lying very low and covered with trees and undergrowth. Finding a sheltered bay in the largest one they ran the boats on to the beach and landed: it was a mere swamp, but the other islands looked no better. The captain ordered the barge's mainsail on shore to shelter them from the rain which had not ceased all day. The marines collected brushwood and made a large fire under a tree, starting it with gunpowder; then they constructed wigwams while the seamen put off again in the yawl and cut sea-tangle from sunken rocks. While it was cooking they tried to dry themselves, but to little purpose: as they dried one side the rain drove against them and wet the other. They called this place Swamp Bay.

Next morning it was still raining and the wind had risen. The people were sent to look for food all over the island: two marines still lay in their wigwam half dead from the wet and cold. The captain sent Campbell to beat them out with a rope's end, which he did with a will, and they joined the others. Hamilton and Campbell dragged branches from the far side of the island, Byron cut them into logs and made up the fire, the surgeon shot a wild goose and the captain cooked it. They stayed for three days at Swamp Bay, the weather being all the while so bad that they could not put to sea.

On the fourth day they went on again, following the coast of the mainland, pulling against an unfavourable wind. They rounded a high headland which had a long line of breakers extending from it. Between this and the next point, which was low with outlying rocks, they perceived a large opening which they hoped was the entrance of the channel to the north. They entered it and found themselves in a waterway which soon narrowed to a passage between mountain ranges. They followed it all day long: and it abruptly came to an end, so they had to turn back. In its whole length they saw neither bird nor fish nor any sign of life, and they found no shelter nor any place where they could land. They rowed all night, and when they got back to the gulf they followed the coast again, which was low and wooded now. For the next night they found shelter in a little cove, very convenient for the boats, but not for the men: they found nothing to relieve their hunger, not even edible seaweed. Their only comfort was a fine fire, for the redwoods grew there in abundance, and the branches burnt very well, though green. They called the place Redwood Cove.

Next morning they had the wind southerly, blowing fresh, and they made much way to the northward under sail. They sighted very high land ahead which soon resolved itself into a fairly large island with a channel about four miles broad between it and the mainland. Captain Cheap, being a good Scotsman, christened it The Duke of Montrose's Island: it was about twelve miles long, low-lying at the southern end, then rising steeply with imposing cliffs. With a fine southwesterly gale they skirted its southern shores, which were lashed by furious surf, and had almost reached the northern end before they found a sheltered bay where they could bring the boats to land. Clams and limpets were here in abundance, and many large pieces of driftwood with which they built a brisk fire and dressed their dinner. They were on a narrow beach at the foot of high steep cliffs of slippery clay, impossible to scale: above the cliffs the land went steeply up and was covered with large trees that towered above them, the finest they had ever seen, each rising to a great height without knot or branch, as straight as cedars: some of them had dimensions equal to the mainmast of a first-rate man-o'-war. Because they had to sleep upon the stones they christened the place Stone Bay, but they slept soundly by their warm crackling fire. They had now completed the first stage of their journey and had reached the upper part of the gulf. The next stage would be to search the mainland shore for the hoped-for opening that would lead them by sheltered ways towards their objective, the Island of Chiloe, where they expected to find a Spanish ship that they could cut out.

As if to make up for its previous harshness the weather was kind on the following day; the men awoke from their almost drunken sleep of exhaustion blinking in the serene sunlight of a perfect day. They got up stiffly from their bed of stones and found themselves covered with splinters of charred wood from their crackling fire and their clothes burnt full of holes. The wind had fallen right away and the sea was glassy calm. The nearer slopes of the hills on the mainland were clothed with forests that swept high up the valleys and darkened the ravines of the lofty-peaked snow-covered mountains above them. Farther up the coast a dazzling white glacier of huge dimensions flowed down to the sea; then the mountains lay farther back, and the coast of the north-east corner of the gulf was a crescent of low beach marked by a line of breakers curving away to the north-west towards the sugar-loaf mountain which they had seen from the *Wager* on the day before she was wrecked: just to the northward of it there was a higher mountain, a large rounded mass, which Byron christened The Dome of St Paul's both because of its form and as a sign that home and safety lay that way. Far beyond lay the dim shapes of still more mountains and the captain said that some of them were on the island of Nuestra Señora de Socorro where, according to his instructions, he was to meet the commodore. For the hundredth time he took the almost illegible document from his pocket and showed them that the rendezvous was in latitude 45° south: they had come perhaps fifty miles northward from Wager Island, so they must now be within a hundred miles of it.

The formation of the land seemed to indicate that there

might indeed be a channel leading out of the gulf, or a navigable river flowing into it, so they started out that day with high hopes. It took them two hours to pass the end of the glacier, and then they had a clear view of the low-lying country which continued far inland before rising slowly to some rounded hills. They were much encouraged by the appearance in the water of muddy discoloured streaks which made them think that they were near the estuary of a river, though they might also have been caused by streams of fresh water pouring from the glacier. Soon after leaving the shelter of the island they had found a heavy swell coming in from the west, and long before they reached the crescent beach they could hear the thunder of the surf upon it. They went as close in as possible and rowed along it, keeping just outside the breakers, looking for an opening that would indicate the entrance to a channel; but nothing interrupted the even line of the beach except two groups of sand-dunes close together, and the stumps of some dead trees farther inland. After four hours the land began to rise again and they had found not the smallest gap in the wall of roaring surf. Their only alternative was to head for the open sea and try to get round the formidable Cape of Three Mountains.

A northerly wind sprang up so they thankfully shipped their oars and went on under sail, keeping close to the steep wooded northern shore of the gulf to be in smooth water. After a few hours, with the wind still rising, they came to a large bay, still within the gulf, and saw ahead of them the menacing outline of the cape from the landward side. They were feeling the full force of the wind now, and it was growing dark, so they put back and entered a small cove just big enough to shelter the boats. In the usual quest for food the crew of the barge, after long searching, came back empty handed and found that the crew of the yawl had shot and dressed a cormorant and eaten it themselves. The captain was so incensed that he set off in the barge at daybreak without waiting for them, but the yawl, being lighter and easier to row, quickly caught up with him. It was Christmas Day, 1741, according to their reckoning. The wind at west was dead against them so it took them the whole day to row across the bay, a distance of about twenty miles. When they were approaching the steep to mountainous coast on the farther side, the captain sent Campbell on ahead to seek out a haven for them, for the wind and the rain were now violent. He returned and led the way to a fine sandy bay he had discovered: as they entered it, a breaker picked up the yawl and hurled her on to the beach, and the next sea filled her. The captain, determined to save at least one of the boats, immediately took the barge out and sheltered in another bay more to northward where it was smoother lying: here they rested miserably on their oars, for it was impossible to land. An hour later the yawl appeared, the men all safe in her but trembling with cold. They asked for a little fresh water and dry clothes, but the captain answered that he had none.

In the morning the weather appeared to be so bad and the men so dispirited after a night spent lying on their oars that he decided to give up for that day the attempt to round the promontory. Campbell records that he ate for his Christmas dinner a pair of raw sealskin shoes he had obtained in truck with the Indians at Wager Island. Both boats weighed anchor and rowed along the shore, looking for something to allay their hunger; but not finding anything they returned to the same bay: by this time the surf had abated so they managed to land, find a few shellfish, and go to sleep.

Next day there was a sudden alarm when a sealion with large and shaggy mane came charging towards them down the beach: Hamilton ran towards it and shot it twice with his pistols, whereupon it turned, bellowing with fury, and came upon him open mouthed. He seized a musket, fixed the bayonet, and thrust it down the animal's throat, but it bit through the barrel as easily as if it had been a twig and got clear away into the sea. They hunted up and down the beach for more of these animals but found none.

They weighed at daybreak to go round the triple promontory: it was the most westerly land that they could see, and distant about twelve miles. They sailed along the shore with a favourable wind, but long before they reached it the wind changed and there ran such a sea that they heartily wished themselves back again: they put about and made for the bay they had left in the morning. It grew dark before they found it, and they spent another miserable night lying upon their oars. As soon as it was light they found the bay, landed at low water and cut sea tangle which grows only upon sunken rocks: it was all the food they had.

The captain did not appear to be discouraged by the failure of their first attempt to get round the cape which he looked upon as the only obstacle now between him and the realisation of his plans. The weather was still too bad for them to make a second attempt so he decided to spend the next few days hunting for food and laying in, if possible, a sea store. They weighed and rowed along the coast, which trended eastward and then north, and came to some fine sheltered lagoons in which they found a good supply of mussels and killed some seals. Greatly refreshed by this abundance of food they began their second attempt on the cape which they found to consist of three great headlands of equal height towering out of the sea. With a fair wind they passed the first; but then the wind was dead against them so they unshipped their masts and rowed until they had passed the second. They toiled on, making no headway, until approaching night warned them they must find a haven, but there was none to be seen. They had again to give up, hoist sails and run back before the wind. They returned to the familiar bay oppressed by the difficulty of rounding the cape: yet it remained their only hope.

Next day the weather had not improved. All hands went ashore to seek provisions, leaving two men in each boat to take care of them. Byron, with one of the marines, was left in the barge riding at a grapnel well outside the breakers, and being very tired he went to sleep. He was awakened by the unusual motion of the boat and the roaring of breakers everywhere about him, and he heard shrieking like that of people in distress. He got up and saw the yawl being canted bottom upwards by a sea, and a moment later she disappeared. The wind that had been north had changed suddenly to south and in an instant filled their bay with tumbling seas. He quickly hove up the grapnel and with the help of the marine who was with him got the barge's head to the seas, and they began to row laboriously away from the shore. Using their utmost efforts they managed to get some distance outside of the breaking seas, then shipped their oars and let go their grapnel again. For the rest of that day and all night the storm raged unabated until Byron and the marine began to fear that they would die there of cold and hunger. By the following morning the wind had changed again and somewhat moderated: they could see their companions ashore cooking and eating, so they ventured in with the barge as near as they dared. Hamilton threw them some seal's liver of which they ate ravenously and were violently sick. Another whole day passed before they were able to land. The seal's liver affected them so much that their skins peeled off from head to foot. They learned that William Rose, one of the *Wager*'s quartermasters, had been lost in the yawl, but the marine who was with him had been saved by Campbell from drowning in the surf.

CHAPTER

12

THE destruction of the yawl was a great misfortune, apart from the clothes and the ammunition that were lost in her, for there was not room in the barge for all her crew. Four men had to be left behind. Because he needed men who could row, the captain decided to keep the seamen and to leave four of the marines to make their way, if possible, to some Spanish settlement on foot: their names were Corporal Crosslet, and Privates Hereford, Hales and Smith: they were already so disheartened and worn out by the distresses and dangers they had undergone that they made no great objection to this decision. The captain gave them arms, ammunition, a frying pan and some other necessaries, and then prepared to embark the rest of the people for a third attempt to round the cape in which all were determined to succeed or perish. As the barge rowed out of the bay, the four marines stood on the beach, gave their comrades three cheers, and called out, 'God bless the king!' For some time afterwards they could be seen making their way along the beach and helping each other to cross a hideous stretch of rocks.

With the wind against them at west and north, the boat's crew had to row along the coast towards the Cape of Three Mountains. When they got abreast of the first of its three headlands there ran such a sea that Byron says he expected every instant that the boat would go down, but none thought of turning back: in this final desperate attempt the men completely disregarded their own safety. The captain urged them to greater and greater efforts. They passed the second headland and at last drew abreast of the third, opening a wide bay to northward. In all their lives they had never seen so dreadful a sea as drove in here, but the captain, with his eyes on the coastline ahead of them which he had so long dreamed of seeing, seemed oblivious to their danger. They toiled for another hour, and Byron steering with one eye on the shore could see that they had made no further headway. After another hour the men too were beginning to realise that all was in vain: their pace slackened, and they looked at Byron in dismay. At last they stopped rowing and lay upon their oars. Byron turned to the captain and reported, 'We've made no headway, sir, for the past two hours,' but he gave no sign that he had heard. He sat rigid in the stern-sheets leaning slightly forward, both hands clasped on his silver-headed cane, his head raised, his eyes fixed with exultation upon the goal before them, the goal they would never reach but which he would not surrender. Along that misty coastline were the Spanish ships that he would capture, the Spanish towns that he would hold in tribute, and there he would meet the commodore at Valdivia or Juan Fernandez. Byron dared not recall him to reality, fearing that at another word from him the captain's dream, the mainspring of his life and of his endeavour, the dream which supported the whole crew also, would be broken in an instant. There was in fact nothing left now for the captain, and for all of them, but the choice between instant death among the breakers at the foot of the promontory and a painful return to the life of misery they had so long endured, but this time without the hope of alleviation or with any prospect of being able to deliver themselves. It was for the captain to choose for them, but he made no sign. At last the vision gradually faded from his eyes while the crew as if mesmerised let the boat drive closer and closer to the breakers: it was as if the weariness and the despair that they had fought off for so many months had descended upon them like a cloud, dulling their minds and robbing them of all capacity to speak or move. 'This is the end,' Byron decided. 'The men are determined to put an end to their lives and to their miseries at once,' and he was as powerless as the rest of them to break the spell that approaching death had cast upon them. When they were only half a mile from the shore, and the mountainous rollers were rising more steeply around them to gather momentum before dashing themselves against the cliffs, the captain suddenly spoke in a voice of mingled agony and despair. 'You must either perish immediately,' he said, 'or pull stoutly for it to get off the shore – but for my part you may do as you please,' and he took no further notice of them; but they dipped their oars and began to exert themselves again. With great difficulty they cleared the headlands and returned the way they had come. Night overtook them long before they reached their haven. The idea that they might fail to get round the cape had not occurred to any of them, and as they pulled, and lay upon their oars, and pulled again in the rain and darkness, they began to wonder why they had abandoned the four marines: if even the possibility of failure had crossed their minds they would have told them to stay where they were, at least for a few days, instead of starting at once along the shore to find a Spanish settlement to the northward – a hopeless quest because of the jagged formation of the rocks, and there was no travelling inland because of the swampy ground and the woods choked with old rotten trees and undergrowth. To find them again became the most important object of their endeavours. It had seemed inevitable at the time that they should be left behind, and indeed the barge would certainly have foundered that day with the extra burden had they been aboard; but now that there was not the least prospect of life for anyone it seemed to them a shameful thing that they had been abandoned: they recalled their courageous bearing and their entire lack of any feeling of resentment at their treatment, and they thought they were the finest fellows they had ever met, and they prayed that they would be found alive. They imagined their joy at seeing their shipmates returning for them, and they half persuaded themselves that they would be lined up on the beach to welcome them.

At daybreak they were able to land at the familiar bay: there was no one there. They fired four musket shots to announce their return and waited anxiously for an answering shot, but there was none. 'Perhaps their powder is damp,' Byron suggested, though it seemed an unlikely explanation. Breaking off dead branches from the trees they made a fire, piled green leaves upon it and sent up a column of thick smoke. When they had collected shellfish and satisfied their hunger they set off in all directions to look for the marines; they were determined to find them and crowd them into the barge even if it should founder as soon as they put to sea: they felt that they would rather drown all together than separate again. The whole of that day was spent in feverish search, but all they found was one musket on the beach and some ammunition. How it came to be there with no other trace or clue they were unable to determine. On the following day they put to sea again, convinced that the search was hopeless. They called that haven Marine Bay, and the first four islands that they passed they named individually after them – Crosslet Island, Hereford Island, Hales Island, and Smith Island.

Even now the captain could not reconcile himself to the thought that there was in fact no escape for them from the Gulf of Affliction: it was bitter to reflect that what they had so nearly accomplished in an open boat would not have presented any serious difficulties for the *Speedwell*: being decked, she could keep the sea, and she could have gone far enough out to escape the dangers which all lay close inshore in the waters to which the barge was restricted. By forcibly depriving him of the longboat, the mutineers had not only betrayed the commodore and their comrades in the other ships of the squadron; they had also made it impossible for him to do his duty either, and this in his eyes was unforgivable. His men were now so dispirited, and so exhausted, that it was useless to expect them to try again: all they asked now was to be led back to Wager Island, which in their memories had become a sort of home to them, and to be allowed to die there.

Before they could start they had to find food, so they went back along the coast to the lagoons where they had previously shot some seal. They kept as close to the shore as possible, still hoping to find the marines, but seeing no sign of them. When they reached the lagoons they landed and ranged along the beach in detached parties. The surgeon and Byron, foraging together, came upon a curious cave with an artificial passage leading back from it into the hillside: hoping that it might be some kind of a food store, they entered and crawled along the passage for some distance: they came to a spacious chamber with a hole at the top for light and air. In the centre there was a bier on which ten or a dozen bodies were lying in two tiers: they were without covering, the flesh hard and dry, and they were all in the same posture in which an infant lies in the womb. It was not a welcome sight for the two earthly visitors who were so nearly in the same condition themselves: the main difference between them was that their own sunken-cheeked and hollow-eyed features lacked the calmness and nobility of death. Finding nothing to eat there, they crawled back to the open air. They could not guess from whence the bodies had been brought for burial or how long they had been lying there. Nowhere since leaving Wager Island had they seen any traces of Indian settlements, no places where there had been fires, no deserted wigwams or heaps of shells:

it seemed that owing to the violence of the seas continually beating upon it and to the very swampy soil that everywhere bordered upon the coast, the country was uninhabited except by the dead.

Meanwhile their companions had been more successful, and they were able to start on their return journey with a good supply of boiled seal. They put in to the cove they had left on Christmas morning and lay there weather-bound for two days; but as long as they had food and could live from day to day the delays no longer mattered: unsupported now by any prospect of seeing their homes again they faced the same hardships with calm despondency. After further delays due to contrary winds they reached The Duke of Montrose's Island with its straight and lofty trees, the pleasantest place they had yet found though it provided nothing to eat except some berries which tasted like gooseberries but were black and had large seeds. They rested there for some time living on these berries and on the remains of the seal meat, now quite rotten. When it was all consumed they decided to move on. One of the seamen, thinking it as good a place as Wager Island in which to end his days, said he would stay there: the others seized him and forced him to embark, so determined were they to return to Wager Island and live and die there all together; but now the wind had risen and changed direction so that their first two or three attempts to put off from the island were unsuccessful. They finally got away on the following day when the wind was fair and moderate with a little rain: as soon as they had cleared the end of the island the wind rose again screaming and tearing at the surface of the sea until the air became thick with phantoms of swirling mist. They lost sight of the land and couldn't tell which way to steer. All at once they heard breakers ahead: they hauled the sheet aft and barely weathered them by a boat's length. At the same time they shipped a sea that nearly swamped them: it struck them with such force that Byron was thrown down into the bottom of the boat where he was half drowned before he could get up again. During a lull in the storm they ran into Redwood Cove, and they sheltered there that night.

In the morning the weather was very little mended, but the only alternatives were to go on or to stay there and starve, so they put to sea again. Soon the weather cleared, and about noon they saw a long line of grey jagged mountains continuing into the distance with black rocky islands in the foreground, and then the familiar outline of Wager Island which they had hoped never to see again. They sheltered that night in a cove in a small island where they could gather shellfish and seaweed: because the wind blew the smoke of their fire into the wigwam they had constructed, they called the place Smoke Cove. Here they found an Indian canoe which had been washed up by the sea: it was twelve feet long and consisted of one plank for the bottom and two planks for each side bound together by split strands of the supple-jack creeper, and caulked so well with some fibrous material of pounded bark that not the least drop of water leaked through. The labour of cutting out and shaping the planks with no tools but flints and shells, though aided by fire, must have been enormous. Thinking it would be useful at Wager Island, they put two men in it and towed it astern of the barge.

On the following day towards evening, the weather being fair with little wind, they got back to Cheap's Bay. This was the moment that Byron had dreaded as marking the end of their final journey but, he writes, instead of being in the depths of despair as he had expected, he was aware for the first time of the presence of a supreme power supporting him and guiding his destiny. Looking from one to another of his comrades, he found no signs of despair in them either, but only a calm acceptance of their fate.

When they had hauled up the canoe and moored the

barge with her grapnel to the sea and her stern fast to the land, they went up to the huts which they found still in good repair – but the door of one of them had been nailed up. They broke it open and found within it some pieces of iron which must have been picked out with much pains from those pieces of the wreck which had been driven ashore. The Indians with whom they were already acquainted had set no value on iron, nor had they understood its uses, so they concluded that those who had evidently visited the huts while they were away must have been from a different tribe, and one that had learned to trade with the Spaniards. Upon further search they found, thrown aside in the bushes at the back of one of the huts, some pieces of seal meat in a state of putrid decomposition: only men in their condition could have borne the smell of it, but they divided it equally between them and ate it all up and thanked God for it.

Only a few hours after their arrival a violent storm arose making it impossible for them to gather nourishment from the beach. Day after day it raged, and they had nothing to eat but celery. Two men died of starvation: the rest began to look at each other with madness in their eyes: Byron caught whispers that convinced him they would descend to the final horror before they too died – the sacrifice of one of their number to prolong the lives of the others. In desperation one evening he sought out the place where Boxer had been done to death, searched round, found his paws and a rotting piece of his skin which he gnawed feverishly and had a vision of Mr Bulkeley contentedly smacking his lips over the succulent dog stew.

That night he could not sleep. The memory of the four marines came back to haunt him as he tried for the hundredth time to account for their disappearance. As he lay tossing on his couch he imagined them being swept from the rocks while trying to round some promontory that barred their way, or drowning in some foetid swamp inland. He fell into restless sleep and dreamed of great seas rushing through the woods and sweeping away his flimsy hut; and then there was a steady vision of the crescent beach fringed with foam, low and desolate with dead trees and with two clumps of sand-dunes close together upon it: suddenly a fearful shriek shattered the silence of the night. He bolted out of his hut and stood shivering in the misty moonlight. From other huts the men all came tumbling out and then stood and gazed at each other in consternation: the full moon had sailed into a clear patch of sky, and their faces were ghastly white. They waited expecting, and yet fearing to hear it again; and then it came, starting with a low cavernous moan which rose and swelled unbearably into a wild shriek of agony which was, at the same time, a cry for help and pity. It had come from the sea. As one man they ran down to the beach and there, half a mile out, they saw a man swimming, but in a curious way: he was upright in the water which covered only the lower half of his body, and he was rowing himself rapidly towards them with his arms. He shrieked a third time, even more horribly, and even more piteously, and then vanished. They strained their eyes but could distinguish nothing on the sea but tumbling light and shadow. They listened intently to hear again what they most dreaded to hear, for the sound was like nothing human or animal that they could recognise – but there was nothing but the rush and surge of breakers on the pebbled beach and the sobbing of the wind. They stood petrified, for they didn't know how long, while the moon slid behind a cloud and the night again grew dim. The captain was the first to find his voice: he called the roll and found everybody present. Then he left them, telling them to return to their huts, but they would not. They shivered, and paced up and down, and prayed silently for the sun to rise and let it be day again. Cut off from their kind, they were beset by ancient fears, and the únwelcome thought of the murdered Thomas Lark, whose bones even then lay unburied on the dark mountainside above them, came into their minds. His spirit had found no rest, they said, and in consequence theirs had found no rest either, and ill-luck had attended them.

In the morning, led by Captain Cheap, they took such implements as they could find and wound solemnly up the steep slope of Mount Misery. They looked wonderingly at the white bones and the hollow skull, remembering their kindly inoffensive shipmate whose spirit, they believed, had summoned them so strangely. They dug a grave – it took them the whole day because of the hard ground and their weakness. When it was finished the captain read the prayers for the dead, they laid the bones reverently to rest, raised a mound over them and fashioned a rude cross which they set above it. Descending the mountain, they felt their spirits once more at peace.

CHAPTER

13

MEANWHILE Mr Bulkeley and the people of the *Speedwell*
had been making the best of their way homewards without
wasting any more time looking for the entrance to the straits
that they were in already. The men who had been sunk in
despondency and resigned to die of hunger while they
believed they were lost found new strength to go on living,
so great was their joy at finding they were on the right way.
In less than twenty-four hours, driven by the prevailing
westerly gales, they again reached the place where they had
faltered and turned back. An hour or two later they were
abreast of Cape Quod, a vast imposing mass of rock on the
northern shore with trees growing on its high ledges
wherever they could find a foothold. Opposite to it, on the
southern shore, they saw a column of smoke: they crossed
towards it and found a little group of Indians on a point of
land at the entrance to a cove: they traded with them and
obtained two dogs, three brant geese and some seal. That
night they supped on the dogs which was the meat that they
preferred. They also got a canoe made of the bark of trees,
but they soon towed her under the water and were obliged
to cut her adrift.

Abrupt mountains of slate or granite with snow peaks
and spectacular glaciers now towered above them on all
sides with openings between them so that without Narborough's directions they would have been at a loss which
to take. On the 7th December they passed Cape Froward:
beyond it the mountains appeared less savage and began to

slope more gently to the eastward. Two of the marines, John Turner and Robert Vicars, died for want of food.

They also followed Narborough's directions to find water: when the supply on board was exhausted they put in at a cove which he had called Freshwater Bay and succeeded in refilling one of the casks before they had to cast off again. Next they identified Elizabeth Island, so called by Sir Francis Drake, where they expected to find more water and plenty of firewood. They rowed up to it in a flat calm, landed, and searched all over it without finding any, but there were great numbers of shagg and seagulls; because it was breeding time, 'We got a vast Quantity of their Eggs, most of them having young ones in the Shell: However, we beat them up all together, with a little Flower, and made a very rich pudding.'

The shortage of water was now acute: having no small boat with them they needed an unusually calm day and a sheltered cove where the shore was steep to before they could risk taking the *Speedwell* close enough to get their barrels ashore and fill them. They had seen several rivulets and waterfalls but never in places accessible to them. On Friday the 11th December, when they had passed through a very narrow part of the straits, the land suddenly trended to the northward and a strong set of the tide carried them into a deep bay where they had smooth water with little wind. They anchored while the tide was ebbing and went ashore to look for water, which they soon found. Meanwhile the *Speedwell* had been left high and dry. They got out all the water-casks, carried them ashore and filled them. At eight in the evening, with four feet flood, they ran the ship close inshore and took off all the water, the whole quantity being four tons. The wind changed and blew hard; the seas came tumbling into the bay: if she had stayed where she was she must have been stove to pieces, the ground being very foul: they were obliged to leave two puncheons and a quarter cask on the shore, and they had great difficulty in re-embarking all the men. Now that they were approaching the eastern end of the straits the hills were lower and covered with pasture, but right inland from the bay where they had refilled their water-casks there were several sharp rocky peaks which Narborough called the Asses' Ears. At midnight they rounded a white cape with a long spit of shingle extending from it; and then they were out in the South Atlantic: it was Cape Virgin Mary which they had last seen when outward bound in company with the whole squadron nine months ago. They had only taken a week, on their second attempt, to get through the straits, a distance of more than 300 miles. Mr Bulkeley noted, 'Sir John Narborough's Account is so just and exact that we think it impossible that any Man should mend his Works.' There was nothing now between them and England but the open sea, but the distance was great for so small a craft so overcrowded with human freight and so ill-provided with all the necessities of life.

Instead of steering for St Julian's, the nearest harbour, 180 miles to the northward where they had discovered on the way out that the water was brackish, Mr Bulkeley determined to make for Port Desire, 120 miles farther on, where Narborough had found fresh water and also seals and penguins in large numbers. On the 12th December they passed along an even line of cliffs extending from Cape Virgin Mary where a range of hills came to an end: after that the country was all one wide grassy plain. At noon, the wind being at north-east, they sighted some horsemen riding towards them, waving their hats as though they wanted to speak with them and making signs for them to go into a bay which lay about a league to the northward. They had a large herd of cattle with them, and by their actions, their clothes and their whole behaviour they seemed to be Christians. The swell tumbling in from the sea wouldn't

157

permit the *Speedwell* to enter the bay or to get closer than about a mile from the shore where the horsemen were racing backwards and forwards waving white handkerchiefs: all day she waited for conditions to improve, but the wind veering to westward and blowing hard she was obliged to bear away for Port Desire.

For three days they were out of sight of land. On the 15th, at 8 a.m., they sighted ledges of rock and a point of land that made like an old castle. At noon on the 16th they were abreast of Penguin Island which was, in fact, covered with penguins. At 5 p.m. they reached Port Desire: the entrance was marked on the south side by a high-peaked rock like a tower which looked as if it had been placed there as a mark for their guidance: strong tides swept through the narrow reef-strewn channel. The north-east point of the rocky entrance was a dark imposing bluff with a small island before it coloured white with guano from myriads of seabirds: here they landed and killed more seals in half an hour than they could carry away. Meanwhile the carpenter and six men had gone in search of water: a mile from the harbour entrance they found Peckett's Well, described by Narborough: its source was a spring that gave only about thirty gallons a day, but it supplied their needs. While they were dressing their victuals the grass caught fire: the flames spread so rapidly that soon the whole country was in a blaze. It burned all that night, and in the morning they could still see a column of smoke in the distance.

For ten days they rested at Port Desire which, like St Julian's, was uninhabited. While their condition was desperate the crew had been fairly quiet, but now that they had surmounted so many dangers, and the way to salvation lay open before them, they were becoming unmanageable. The question of their subsistence was a constant source of irritation and dissension: the most turbulent faction demanded that the marine officers and such people as could not assist in the working of the vessel should have but half the allowance of the rest: they named about twenty who, in their opinion, should be served with only half a pound of flour to each man while they insisted upon a full pound each for themselves. The half-pounders complained bitterly of this distinction, saying that according to the articles that all had signed whatever food was available was to be equally shared; so the full-pounders and the half-pounders were constantly in dispute: everyone said what he pleased and expected to be given what he wanted. Although they had abundance of food at Port Desire they all insisted upon their regular allowance, with the consequence that when they sailed again, on the 26th December, there was only one barrel of flour left. Instead of jealously guarding it as sea stock they demanded that it should immediately be shared out among them. Mr Bulkeley pointed out to his improvident crew that the flour would keep whereas the seal meat wouldn't, and therefore they ought to husband it: they refused to listen. The barrel was shared out; each man received three and a half pounds of flour. A few days later they were again famished, but now they were far out at sea, crossing the great Gulf of San Giorgio, and there was no immediate prospect of renewing their supplies. The seal meat was stinking very much, but they were obliged to eat it, having nothing else: 'A most nauseous Diet,' the cooper wrote in his narrative, 'which only extreme Hunger prevailed with us to feed on. And truly it was suitable enough both to the Disposition and State of those who were forced to eat it, for as in respective Temper they were vile enough to deserve even worse, so were their external Circumstances as filthy and loathsome as the putrefied Fish. Nay, of the two I think we stunk the most besides being overspread with Vermin.' Mr Bulkeley wrote in his journal, '*Friday, January* the 1st, 1741–2. Fresh Gales, and fair Weather, with a great Sea. At Ten last Night shifting the Man at the

Helm brought her by the Lee, broke the Boom, and lost a Seaman overboard . . . We are now miserable beyond Description, having nothing to feed on ourselves, and at the same Time almost eaten up with Vermin. *Wednesday* the 6th, Departed this Life Mr *Thomas Harvey*, the Purser; he died a Skeleton for want of Food: This Gentleman probably was the first Purser, belonging to his Majesty's Service, that ever perish'd with Hunger. We see daily a great Number of Whales. *Sunday* the 10th, This Day at Noon, in working the Bearings, and Distance to Cape *St Andrew*, do find myself not above thirteen Leagues distant from the Land; therefore haul'd in NW to make it before Night. We saw To-day Abundance of Insects, particularly Butter-flies and Horse-stingers. We have nothing to eat but some stinking Seal, and not above twenty out of the forty-three which are now alive have even that; and such hath been our Condition for this Week past; nor are we better off in Regard to Water, there not being above eighty Gallons aboard: Never were beheld a Parcel of more miserable Objects; there are not above fifteen of us healthy, (if People may be call'd healthy that are scarce able to crawl.) I am reckon'd at present one of the strongest Men in the Boat, yet can hardly stand on my Legs ten Minutes together, nor even that short Space of Time without holding: every Man of us hath a new Coat of Skin from Head to Foot: we that are in the best State of Health do all we can to encourage the rest. At Four this Afternoon we were almost transported with Joy at the Sight of Land, (having seen no Land for fourteen Days before) the Extremes of which bore NW about seven Leagues; we ran in with it, and at Eight anchor'd in eight Fathom, fine Sand, about a League from the Shore . . . This day perish'd for want of Food Serjeant *Ringall*.'

On the following morning they steered north-east into a sandy bay and anchored in three fathoms. There was a

Vice Admiral Byron.

The fleet lying in the great anchorage at Spithead off Portsmouth Harbour in the spring of 1740.

*rom REGULATIONS AND INSTRUC-
*IONS RELATING TO HIS MAJESTY'S
ERVICE AT SEA; third edition, 1740.

The fleet under way in August, 1740.

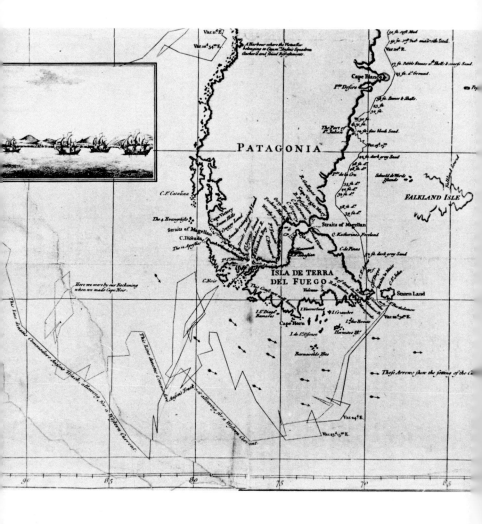

The track sheet of Anson's squadron, showing passage around Cape Horn.

Merchantman and yacht off Dover.

The Patagonian coastline a little to the northward of Port St. Julian. The squadron anchored here on the 19th February, 1741, to refit a vessel before rounding Cape Horn.

The *Wager* shipwrecked. "...Byron was ¿ glad to be on dry land as any other man wh had narrowly escaped perishing in a shi| wreck, yet when he looked about him he fe that his prospects were but little mended b the change."

Commodore Byron conversing with a Patagonian woman.

great swell and shoal water, so they named that place Shoalwater Bay. On board there was nothing left to eat, and but one cask of water to drink: on the shore they could see horses and large dogs: the surf looked very dangerous, but to go from thence without meat or drink would be certain death. The boatswain, the carpenter and Lieutenant Ewers were the first to leap into the water, and eleven of the people followed: they all got safely to the land except Seaman James Greenham who was drowned within three fathoms of the beach, being quite spent and none of the others near enough to assist him. Four quarter-casks with firelocks and ammunition lashed to them were tossed overboard to be filled with fresh water: these drifted in, and the men on shore dragged them out of the surf. They filled them from a good spring of fresh water, and they killed some seal which they cut up into quarters ready to bring on board. One of the casks leaked, so they broke it up to make a fire, and they added dry horse dung as fuel as there were no trees or bushes in sight.

Those left on board could see their friends feasting, and abundance of seal cut up in pieces and cooked ready for them: only two of them could swim, so they cast lots which of them should attempt to carry a line ashore. The lot fell on the weakest, a lad of fifteen: when he got up he was scarcely able to stand, so they would not let him go. On the hatch there was a sealskin serving as a tarpaulin: they burnt the hair off it, cut it up and chewed it to allay their hunger.

Next day, January 13th, the weather was fine and the sea was calm, so they veered the *Speedwell* in, made a raft by lashing oars to the hatch covers, piled the meat on to it and hauled it aboard: it consisted of a horse that the boatswain had shot (it was branded on the left buttock with the initials AR), a wild dog, four armadillos and a large quantity of seal. Meanwhile the people still on shore swam off three casks of water and took another quarter-cask and two breakers up to the spring: while these were being filled a sea breeze came in and blew so hard that the *Speedwell* weighed and moved farther out, leaving eight men behind. During the night a sea broke off the rudder-head, and it seemed at every moment that she would be driven ashore or founder at her anchor. On the following day, the 14th, the wind was still at ESE which was unusual, the prevailing winds on this coast being from the west or north. They got up an empty cask, put into it four small-arms, a few necessaries, and a letter telling their comrades that it was still too dangerous for the *Speedwell* to go in for them. They watched it drift ashore. They saw the men receive it and wave their acknowledgements.

The crew, now that their needs had been supplied, were chafing at the delay and agitating for the voyage to be continued: 'Every Man's Opinion was that they must put to Sea or perish, the Wind coming out of the Sea and there not being a Stick of Firewood in the Vessel to dress their Victuals,' so they decided to sail away and abandon their companions. Mr Bulkeley wrote one of his usual letters for the officers to sign to justify their conduct, 'These are to certify the Right Honourable Lords Commissioners, etc.' describing the perilous situation of the ship. It was dated the 14th January. They weighed, but could not clear the land, so they anchored again in five fathoms.

On the next day, the 15th, the wind was no longer coming out of the sea; there was an offshore wind at NNW and the *Speedwell* was no longer in a perilous situation. In spite of this, the crew would not risk going inshore again. At 4 p.m. they weighed and stood out to sea. The men they were abandoning knelt down on the beach and implored their comrades to come back for them, but they would not. 'We leave 'em,' Mr Bulkeley remarked, 'to the Care of Providence and the wide World.' Again, as at every crisis during the voyage, the lack of a commander was apparent: there was no one to accept the overall human responsibility and make himself obeyed. Of the eighty-one men who had started out so optimistically to return to England, only thirty-four remained.

The weather continuing fair they ran up the coast to the northward. Four days later, on the morning of Tuesday the 19th, there was a cry of 'Breakers right ahead!' though the only land they could see was twenty miles away in the form of an island. Mr Bulkeley decided that the breakers were on English Bank which lies in the entrance to the River Plate – an area they were anxious to avoid because of the possibility of meeting a Spanish man-o'-war. By now there was not one drop of water on board, so they closed the land to the northward of the estuary and anchored that evening in a fine sandy bay. Two men approached them on horseback. The boatswain swam ashore to speak with them: from the *Speedwell* they saw him get up behind one of them, and they rode away. Several of the people swam ashore with a cask for water which they filled and brought on board: on the return journey one of the men was too weak to reach the vessel and was drowned.

On the 20th Mr Bulkeley and Mr Cummins also went ashore, and four men came down to them: Mr Bulkeley, who could understand Portuguese, learned from them that the English were still at war with the Spaniards who had two fifty-gun ships up the River Plate and one sixty-gun ship cruising off the entrance. He thought that land belonged to the King of Portugal, and he assumed, therefore, that the men were Portuguese: but they told him they lived at Mount de Vidia, two days' journey from thence, which was under the government of Buenos Aires, that they were in fact Spanish fishermen from Castile and that there were many Spanish settlements in those parts. They went with the fishermen to their huts about a mile inland, where they found the boatswain already being entertained: they were given 'good Jurk-Beef, roasted and boil'd, with good white Bread.' When they tried to buy provisions to take back on board, they found the fishermen had none left except twenty-six loaves, about as big as twopenny loaves in England which they would not part with under four guineas. They gave them their price. The leading fisherman told them that they daren't get them any more food because they might be hanged for supplying them: he offered, however, to get them as many wild fowl and ducks in an hour or two as would serve all the people on board, if they would give him a fire-lock. They fetched him one accordingly and gave it to him with some powder and slugs. Several hours passed and he did not return: they began to reflect that they were on Spanish territory and that these hospitable people were in fact their enemies: they noticed that one of the fishermen had gone, and also one of the horses: suddenly the conviction was borne upon them that they were being betrayed: they returned to the *Speedwell*, immediately weighed and put to sea, all ill-provided as they were.

They sailed at four o'clock in the morning of the 21st and set a course for the Rio Grande, the southernmost port in Brazil, which was distant about 350 miles. Long before they reached it their food was again exhausted and they had only a little water left: they were supported and kept going only by the knowledge that they were on the last stage of their long journey. The weather was misty, the sea calm: they kept within soundings and anchored every night. On the 23rd, off Cape St Mary's, the master, Thomas Clark, died, and his son whom he had brought with him as his servant to learn his trade died on the following day. On the 24th they came to three islands, the northmost appeared like a church with a lofty tower; then there were three more islands, all steep to: they could see great numbers of seal on them, but it was impossible to get ashore. At night they cast anchor in thirteen-fathom water and a clean ground: here with as much decency as they could, they committed the bodies of the master and his son to the sea. On the 25th the cook died, Thomas Maclean, the oldest man among them: he was eighty-two years of age.

By the 27th there was no food on board of any kind, nothing but a few sips of water. At noon Mr Bulkeley had a good observation and reckoned they were only eighteen leagues from the Rio Grande. With a moderate gale at west they sailed all day within a cable's length of a long beach of fine sand with undulating grassland behind it and hills in the distance. John Young's narrative tells us: 'On Thursday the 28th about seven in the Morning, through the Mercy of God, we discovered the Mouth of the River Grand. The Opening of the spacious Stream appeared to our weary, hungry and thirsty Souls the very Gate of Heaven. There was a dangerous Bar at the Entrance and several Shoals to be carefully passed over or evaded in going up to it. Mr Bulkeley undertook to carry us in and pilot us to the Town: this he did very judiciously and safely in a few Hours. We dropped Anchor abreast of it on the east Shore in less than two Fathoms Water. Never did any Creatures come there with more joyful Hearts or more miserable meagre countenances.'

The end of the voyage is recorded thus in Mr Bulkeley's journal: '*Thursday* the 28th, kept the Shore close a-board, and sounded every half Hour, not caring to go within three Fathom, nor keep without five, sailing along by the Lead all Night. At six in the Morning saw the Opening of the River *Grand*; kept within the Breakers of the Bar, having at sometimes not above seven Feet Water at half Flood; steer'd NE by E until the River's Mouth was fairly open; then steer'd N and NNW until a-breast of the Town; anchor'd on the East-shore in Two Fathom Water.'

'There presently came a Boat from the Shore,' Mr

Bulkeley continues, 'with a Serjeant of the Army, and one Soldier. The Lieutenant, myself, and Mr *Cummins*, with Captain *P - - - - - n* of the Land Forces, went on Shore with them. The Commandant, the Officers, and People of the Place, receiv'd us in a most tender and friendly Manner. They instantly sent on Board to the People four Quarters of Beef, and two Bags of *Farine* Bread. We were conducted to the Surgeon's House, the handsomest Habitation in the Place; where we were most hospitably entertain'd. At Four in the Afternoon the Governor came to Town; after a strict Enquiry into our Misfortunes, and the Reasons of our coming into this Port, being somewhat doubtful that we might be Inspectors of their Coast, he began to examine me, the Lieutenant having reported me to him as Pilot. He ask'd me if there was a Chart of the Coast on Board; and, if not, how it was possible we could hit the Bar, and venture into so hazardous Place as this is? I told him, as for a Chart, we had none of any kind; but I had a good Observation the Day before, that our Vessel drew but a small Draught of Water; that we kept the Lead always going, and in the Necessity we were in, we were oblig'd, at all Events, to venture; and if we had not seen the Opening of the River before Night, we must have been compell'd to run the Vessel ashore. He examin'd me also concerning the Places we stopt at, from Cape *Virgin Mary* to this Port, and more particularly relating to the River *Plate*. He was very nice in his Enquiry of our putting in at Cape *St Mary's*, and of the Bearings and Distance along the Shore from thence to this Port. When he thoroughly satisfy'd himself, he embraced us, and blest himself to think of our Deliverance, which he term'd a Miracle. He offer'd every Thing the Country could afford to our Relief; the Sick were ordered to be taken Care of in the Hospital: He took the Lieutenant and the Land Officers home with him; and desir'd the Commandant to see that the rest of the Officers and People wanted for nothing . . . He also told us, that we should be dispatch'd in the first Vessel which arriv'd in this Port; for he did not think we could with Safety go any farther on our own; and that there could not be found twelve Seamen in the *Brazils* that would venture over the Bar in her to sail to *Rio Janeiro*; therefore he order'd our little *Speedwell* ashore; this Wonder the People are continually flocking to see; and it is now about nine Months since we were cast away in the *Wager*; in which Time, I believe, no Mortals have experienc'd more Difficulties and Miseries than we have. This Day may be justly stiled the Day of our Deliverance, and ought to be remember'd accordingly.'

CHAPTER

14

THE fate of some of the men left on the Coast of Patagonia is known through a narrative written by one of them, Isaac Morris. He confirms that on the 14th January they received a few articles of clothing, flints, ammunition, etc. in a cask, together with a letter from their comrades in the *Speedwell* saying that they were obliged to stand off till the weather should be more favourable; and he continues: 'Next Morning we had the Wind at NNW with fair Weather. We expected that they would have stretched in for the Land, but to our very great Surprise we saw the Schooner with her Ensign hoisted at the Topping Lift and under Sail from us. The moderate Weather with the Wind off Shore gave them a fair Opportunity of standing in for us if they had thought fit. Why they did not is best known to themselves. The most probable Reason we could give for such inhuman Treatment was that by lessening the Number of the Crew they might be better accomodated with Room and Provisions.'

The men thus abandoned by the crew for whom they had risked their lives by swimming ashore through the surf to get food and water for them were Midshipman Isaac Morris, Guy Broadwater the stalwart Coxswain of the *Wager* who had all but succeeded in steering her clear of the Gulf of Affliction on the night of the disaster, John Duck, Samuel Cooper, Benjamin Smith, Joseph Clinch and John Allen who were all seamen, and John Andrews a marine. They could not at first take in what had happened or believe in the treachery of their shipmates: they stood gazing after the *Speedwell* as her sail grew smaller and smaller and then disappeared over the horizon, half expecting even then that she would return. When it grew dark they lay down in the gully where the freshwater spring flowed out of the sand and slept: the weather being very fair they required no covering over them.

When the sun rose again they were still unable to formulate any plan: they tried to encourage each other by saying that another ship would pass that way and rescue them; but that was clearly out of the question: they were right at the head of a large shallow bay and any normal sea-going ship would be of too deep a draught to enter it. If ever they meant to see England again they must rely upon their own efforts. The nearest inhabited place they knew of was Buenos Aires, seat of the Spanish Government, which they estimated to be about 300 miles to the north-west; but at present they were too weak and exhausted by their hardships, and too close to despair, to do anything at all: they decided to stay where they were until they should be strong enough to undertake the journey. They came to only one firm resolution, that come what might they would never separate: their comrades had betrayed them, but they would be true to each other.

For a whole month they rested, slowly preparing for their journey and living on seals which they knocked down with stones: they made jackets and knapsacks from their skins, and water-bottles from their bladders. They set off about the middle of February, carrying as much seal meat as they could besides their muskets and ammunition: they dared not go inland for fear of losing their way in the vast featureless interior of the country, so they headed up the coast towards the mouth of the River Plate. They soon discovered what extraordinary good luck they had had in finding a spring where they landed from the *Speedwell*: all the rest of the country was scorched with drought. They travelled about sixty miles in two days without finding any water, so they returned to their old quarters to wait for the rainy season. They cut poles from a little wood they had discovered seven miles inland, and they built a hut under the shelter of a cliff near their water spring.

Three months later they had some wet weather: when it had cleared, they made another attempt to reach Buenos Aires, following the same route along the shore. In the valleys of the sandhills there was water in plenty that had ponded up after the rain, but this time they found nothing to eat: there were no seals and no game, only flocks of small parakeets fluttering in the grass. When they had travelled more than seventy miles in three days, and were crossing an open plain where there was no shelter, they were overtaken by a violent rainstorm with thunder and lightning: they cowered all night under their home-made sealskin jackets wet through and shivering with cold. In the morning they felt profoundly discouraged: some of them were for pushing forward, be the event what it might, others thought it was too rash to go on when they had just enough food to carry them back again. Although they had sworn never to separate from each other, this time they nearly did so: but when it came to the final act of parting they could not face it: they all turned and retraced their steps. They thought, on reflection, that this was probably the right decision, considering the great distance they had yet to go, and the impossibility of finding fresh supplies.

When they got back to the hut, and had rested for a while, they decided to divide themselves into two groups to lessen the labour of hunting, four men to scour the country for food one day, and four the next: they had to find new sources of supply because seals were no longer very plentiful; they had killed so many and the rest were grown shy; and the horses at the sound of a musket shot would all gallop away and not be seen again for days. Once they came upon three ostrich eggs half buried in the sand, but they never saw any of the birds nor found any more of their eggs. There were plenty of wild dogs about but they could rarely get a shot at them, they wouldn't come close enough: one day on their rambles they saw three puppies disappearing down a hole, so they realised that they were whelped in burrows in the sandhills, like rabbit burrows, only larger. Next day they all went out searching and found four litters, sixteen puppies in all, which they brought home. They fed them on seal broth and bits of the meat cut up small, and they brought them up to be so tame that they answered to their names and would not associate with the wild ones. Soon each man had his brace of dogs which were as much under command as an English spaniel. These dogs were very serviceable: sometimes they killed a deer, they rounded up wild hogs and they frequently caught armadillos: two of the young hogs, a boar and a sow, were taken alive and kept as breeding stock. They too became so tame that they followed the dogs when they went out hunting. At night both the dogs and the pigs took up their lodging with the men. At this period their lives were fairly tranquil except for an encounter with a ferocious-looking jaguar that came upon them when they were without arms cutting poles; and another with a panther which they managed to wound with a musket shot and then beat to death with the bones of a dead horse. They dressed its heart and part of the ribs, and found it 'but indifferent eating.'

One morning Isaac Morris with Sam Cooper, John Andrews and John Duck started out early, without their muskets, to get some seal. They had killed three and were returning to the hut at dusk when they saw the dogs 'very busy at a small Distance, wagging their Tails in a fondling Manner.' Morris, ahead of his companions, went on without taking much notice of them, thinking that they had found a dead colt, but when he came to the hut he was utterly confounded: it had been rifled, and everything of value taken away. In the greatest consternation he ran back to his comrades and told them what he had seen. 'Aye, and that's not the worst,' one of them said, 'for yonder lie poor Guy Broadwater and Ben Smith murdered.' It was a most shocking sight: one had had his throat cut and the other had been stabbed in the breast. They were hardly cold, so the murderers could not be far off.

They went to the hut to inspect it more thoroughly: there was nothing left — powder, ball, muskets, utensils, all gone: they searched and found not the least thing of use. Their fire had been put out and they now had no means of lighting one. There was no indication of what had happened to John Allen and Joseph Clinch, but the ground had been ploughed up by horses' hooves so they concluded that they had been carried off by Indians and therefore there was some hope that they were still alive. That a fatal quarrel had arisen among the people themselves was out of the question, not only because they had all lived in harmony together, but because the dead men had been stabbed with knives and none of them had possessed one. Where to go and what to do they knew not. They dared not trust themselves another night on that fatal spot, and yet they were afraid to venture from it. At last they came to the resolution of going to the next sandy bay, about a mile off, to take up their quarters there for that night. When they got there the wind was blowing strongly from the sea and they could find no shelter, not even a cliff to lie under, so they were obliged to return to the hut and pass a miserable night there expecting every moment that the Indians would come back and slaughter them.

Next morning the dogs that had belonged to their comrades stood on top of the cliff barking at them, and they would not come down though they called them by their names. They buried the two bodies by scraping away the light sand with their hands, and raising a heap of sand over them. They did not stay to mourn their friends. They tore up the seal flesh, raw as it was, and stuffed it into their knapsacks, filled the bladders with water and again started for Buenos Aires with their two pigs and sixteen dogs, praying the Almighty to be their guide. They kept close to the sea coast as they had done before, so that they could not miss the mouth of the River Plate, for they designed to travel up that river until they should reach some inhabited place. There were still ponds of water lying among the sandhills, and they frequently came across dead fish newly thrown up by the sea, and sometimes, also, a few cockles. They passed a very large dead whale, too far gone for them to eat, but it was a feast for their dogs and pigs.

At the end of ten days, having travelled hard and met with tolerable weather, they made what they took to be the cape of the River Plate: when they got close to it they found a multitude of small rivers and muddy swamps which they had to wade across or to swim over with their knapsacks across their shoulders. When night came on they covered themselves with rushes to keep warm and were almost devoured by mosquitoes. Next day they pressed on again, but the farther they went the greater were the difficulties, till they sunk in the marshes up to their shoulders and could hardly extricate themselves and each other. After many fruitless attempts to find a way through they were forced to give up and take the melancholy road back to their camp. They had gained nothing except the knowledge that there were insurmountable obstacles to the realisation of their plan. To reach civilisation they would have to strike inland where, it seemed to them, they would inevitably perish through lack of food or water, or under the knives of the Indians.

And then one day they saw a wonderful thing – a tree-trunk, washed up by the sea. Hope was reborn. They looked at it, and imagined it hewn into the shape of a boat that would enable them to pass the rivulets and quagmires that had stopped them. In the country where they were, they had not seen a tree of anything like this size and, if they had, they wouldn't have been able to transport it to the beach: this one could be floated off again when they were ready by merely digging a trench to bring the water up to it from the sea. They had poles and sealskins to provide masts and sails – but no fire to hollow it out, and no tools to shape it. Then John Duck remembered that he had thrown away a defective musket when they turned back from their second attempt to reach Buenos Aires, eleven months ago: at once they loaded themselves up with food and water and set off in search of it. They found the place – it was sixty miles away – picked up the musket and brought it back. They beat half the length of the barrel flat with stones and whetted an edge to it against a rock: the other half served for a handle. When it was finished they agreed that they had made a tolerable hatchet.

They had not even begun to work on their boat when Fate again intervened. They always left one of their number at the hut to look after it, and one day when the other three were out hunting and Morris was alone there he heard, coming from a distance, the thudding of hooves. He looked out and saw a dozen horses galloping towards him; as they came nearer he could distinguish that there were men on them and that they were Indians. It was in vain to fly. He imagined nothing but instant death approaching, and he prepared to meet it with all the resolution he could muster. He ran towards them and fell on his knees, and was begging for his life with all the signs of humility that occurred to him when he heard an English voice saying, 'Don't be afraid, Isaac, we're all here.' He looked up and saw his three companions mounted behind three of the Indians, some of whom slid from their horses and went to examine the hut while others with knives drawn guarded the seamen, ready to dispatch them if they showed the least sign of resistance. Morris learned now that he had had a narrow escape from being left all alone: when the Indians swooped down on them his companions had persuaded them with much difficulty through signs and gesticulations to come up to the hut to collect him. Now that they were happily reunited they were reconciled to their fate, and they waited patiently to see what their captors would do with them. Soon they remounted, signed to the seamen to mount behind them, gave three confused shouts or whoops and carried them a few miles inland to the south-west where they joined a dozen or more Indians who had about 400 horses with them. They immediately camped. Seeing that their prisoners were in wretched condition and apparently half starved, they treated them with much humanity: they gave them blankets, and they killed a horse for them, roasted a part of it and let them eat their fill.

Early next morning they moved on, and for nineteen successive days they drove the horses to the south-west, being joined from time to time by other groups of Indians, all with captured horses, till they came to a valley of fine pasture between two very high mountains: here, beside a small river, were some huts made of poles and the skins of horses where the women and children had been left. The seamen's work was chiefly to fetch wood and water, and to skin all the horses that were killed. Though they continued to be well treated they were frequently bought and sold for a pair of spurs, a brass pan, ostrich feathers and similar trifles, and sometimes they were played away at dice and changed masters several times a day. Always hoping to find their missing friends, John Allen and Joseph Clinch, they looked anxiously for them when any new group appeared, but they never saw them; neither were they in the village: the children stared as if they had never seen a white man before. During all this time they were learning to speak Spanish, which the Indians understood, and their health greatly improved.

The horses as they were brought in had been added to the common stock and they now numbered 1,500 or more: they were carefully examined and graded by an old Indian who seemed to be a captain over the rest. At last there was a grand feast that lasted many hours: several times on the way they had passed herds of black cattle which the Indians completely ignored, greatly preferring horse flesh which some of them broiled and some ate raw. On the following day the huts were dismantled, and they all moved on together. They wandered for another four months, from one spring or water-hole to another until, more than a thousand miles from where they had started, they reached a more permanent settlement consisting of about thirty huts of low irregular shape built close together and surrounded by a palisade. Here their 'king' resided.

The seamen had most recently been purchased by Indians who lived farther away. They had already been carried some distance beyond the settlement when they were overtaken by a party of galloping horsemen and brought back: the king had claimed them as his property.

He received them in his hut, seated on the ground with a javelin on one side of him and a bow and arrows on the other, a coloured blanket round his waist and a sort of turret of ostrich feathers on his head. He was smoking a long reed pipe. He began by asking what people they were and how they came to that country. They gave him a brief account of their adventures, described how their camp had been raided, and asked what had become of their missing companions. He called two of his chief men and talked to them very earnestly for some time in their own language: then he said that nothing was known of the raid on their camp, but that strict enquiries would be made. He had never heard of people called Englishmen, but when they told him that they were at war with his enemies the Spaniards, he expressed great joy: he sent out and ordered a horse to be killed immediately, and dressed, and he said they would be lodged in his own hut for that night while one was being built for them.

When their hut was ready next day he sent them some blankets, a cooking-pot and four Spanish women to be their wives: they had been taken in a skirmish near Buenos Aires. In spite of this favoured treatment the seamen remained the absolute and undisputed property of the king, to be disposed of as he saw fit.

CHAPTER

15

FOR the men who had remained on Wager Island one day followed another with no alleviation of their miseries. The Captain never mentioned their failure to get round the Promontory of Three Mountains, and no longer spoke of their duty to the commodore or brought out the creased and tattered piece of paper containing his instructions. He brooded, silent and listless, with occasional outbursts of irritation. He had always paid meticulous attention to his appearance, but ever since they had been forced to jettison almost all their possessions to prevent the barge from sinking he had been unable to shave or to dress his wig, but he still wore it as a symbol of authority, stuck on top of his shaggy hair like a hawk drowned in seaweed: he went barefoot like all his men, but his clothes still gave some indications that he had once been dressed like a gentleman.

Once Mr Hamilton came into the camp in triumph carrying some rotten pieces of beef which he had found washing about in the sea several miles from the camp. He immediately shared them out in equal portions. Byron and Campbell hurried to the place where he had found them and took up several more pieces which they also shared. They borrowed the captain's frying-pan to melt down the fat in order to preserve it, and they found that he was highly incensed that Hamilton had apportioned and distributed the beef without consulting him: he still looked upon himself as the sole guardian of whatever provisions might be found. When they brought back the frying-pan and offered him half the fat he was offended and would not accept it.

On the fifteenth day after their return, when the bay was lit unevenly by sunrays slanting through the clouds, they sighted two canoes, far out. They watched them, the captain leaning wearily on his cane: then they hurried to the beach, for the canoes had turned inshore and were coming directly towards them. A party of Indians landed. While they were drawing up their canoes, carrying fire from them and constructing their wigwams, they ignored the white men: then one of them, tall and well formed – evidently from a different tribe – came forward to meet them: he wore a sealskin cloak and little else, except a long bow and a quiver full of arrows slung across his shoulders, and in one hand he proudly flourished a silver mounted cane as if he expected all who saw it to bow down and worship him. At a distance of ten paces he stopped, took up an arrogant pose, and waited. The captain went forward alone and bowed courteously: the Indian, seeing that he had a cane similar to his own, condescended to bow also, almost as to an equal. His first words were in Spanish. The captain, recognising the language in spite of the savage accent, beckoned the surgeon to come forward to act as interpreter. When some polite formalities had been exchanged the captain asked the surgeon to assure the Indian that he would find the store of iron in the hut intact, for they assumed it was his property, and that they laid no claim to it. This appeared to please him. He said his name was Martin, a cacique, or chieftain, of the Chonos tribe who live in Chiloe and its neighbourhood – he insisted that he was an important cacique with authority confirmed by the Spaniards: and as he spoke he looked with pride at the silver head of his cane and crossed himself several times to show that he was a Christian. He asked whether the strangers were English, French or Dutch.

It seemed most probable that news of the shipwreck had been passed from one tribe to another until it had reached the Spanish authorities, and that they had sent Martin to investigate; so the captain, unwilling to admit that they were of a nation which was at war with Spain, instructed the surgeon to answer that they were from Grande Bretagne: this puzzled the cacique who had evidently never heard of such a country. They showed him the barge and said it would be his, and everything in it, if he would conduct them to the island of Chiloe by the route that would be most likely to afford them subsistence on the way, for they were unacquainted with the country. After much persuasion he at length agreed. They questioned him about the other ships of the squadron, but he seemed to know nothing about them or about any naval enterprise.

The sudden prospect of getting to Chiloe after all wrought a profound change in the captain: he inspected their few firearms and jealously measured the small quantity of gunpowder that remained as if he still intended to cut out a Spanish ship before handing over the barge and its contents to Martin. He sent for Hamilton and again bitterly upbraided him for having presumed to distribute the beef he had found instead of saving a proportion for a sea store, so that now they would have to rely for provisions upon the doubtful charity of the Indians. He demanded an apology, which Hamilton indignantly refused to make. An angry scene ensued, the captain threatening to leave Hamilton behind, and the surgeon refusing to stir without him: Byron and Campbell joined in, protesting that it would be shameful to abandon a friend who had generously distributed what he had found instead of keeping it for himself as many another would have done. The people, hearing the quarrel, ran up and roundly declared that they would all go or all stay together, so the captain was forced to give way. He ordered the officers to keep watch in case Martin should attempt to leave during the night, and it was agreed that they should start at daybreak if the weather served.

Byron, taking the morning watch, paced up and down watching the Indian camp-fires and wondering if he was really to leave the island that had been fatal to so many of his comrades. The wigwams showed black against the soft gleam of the sea, and in one of them lay the fantastic, arrogant, crafty and no doubt unreliable messenger of Providence, the *Deus ex Machina*, who had brought them promise of life when all seemed lost. When the outline of Mount Misery detached itself from the night, and the sky grew pale above the more distant hills, the air was bitterly cold but the wind and sea were moderate: it seemed that all would be well. He turned from contemplating the view to arouse his fellows, and caught sight of a figure in a long coat slinking away into the woods – could it be Martin deserting them? But that was impossible: no one had left the wigwams. It looked more like one of the marines. He ran to their hut, and finding only one in it instead of two he shook him roughly awake. 'Where's Crusset?' he asked. The man looked round, missed his companion, and also his coat. He let out a yell and rushed from the hut.

It seemed hardly credible that a man should steal a coat and desert on the very day that they were leaving the island, but so it was. The people ran furiously into the woods to find him – but not to bring him back for punishment: he had lost everything in the yawl and they understood that a man can desire a coat so desperately that he will sacrifice his only chance of safety for the joy of feeling its warm folds about him for the last few hours of his existence. They wanted to bring him back because they had an almost superstitious horror of leaving another of their dwindling company to die: but he eluded all pursuit. The Indians would not wait, so they were forced to set off without him, filled with gloomy foreboding.

To make sure of Martin they took him with them in the barge, and also his servant, an Indian boy of about fourteen whom he called Emmanuel; and Martin brought along his precious store of pieces of old iron. They towed the spare canoe that they had found at Smoke Cove, and the rest of the Indians followed in the other two canoes. Instead of going up the eastern side of The Duke of Montrose's Island, the route they had followed on their previous expedition, they were taken up the western side where there were continuous reefs upon which the sea was breaking high, so they found no shelter. On the third day, after an exhausting passage, they reached a bay in the northern shore of the Gulf where Martin had left his wife and three-year-old son. Here the rest of the Indians, being independent of the Spaniards, left them.

After resting for two days they took Martin's family aboard and continued their journey. They had always imagined that the inland passage to the north, which Martin confirmed that the Indians used, must lead out of the Gulf at its low-lying north-east corner: to their surprise he led them in the opposite direction, to the westward, but still within the Gulf, and into a bay strewn with dangerous rocks through which he guided them to the mouth of a river. As he seemed to know what he was about, they cheerfully entered it, and for a while everything went well; but the stream became more rapid and they found it increasingly difficult to make headway against it. Byron, studying the formation of the hills and seeing that the steep-sided valley they were in was growing narrower and more winding, decided that they were not in fact on a possible route out of the Gulf, and he suspected that Martin was betraying them – perhaps making them deliver the barge and the old iron to his own village or to some place where he could conveniently dispose of them: or else that he had only used that route in a light canoe and didn't understand that the barge could not be rowed up a swift-flowing river. One of the strongest of the seamen, John Bozman, stopped rowing and said he could do no more. He fell from his seat and lay under the thwarts. Byron, who was steering, passed the tiller to Campbell and took the oar. They continued rowing but made little progress. Martin had given the captain a piece of boiled seal which, instead of sharing, he had brought with him as sea stock. Bozman complained that his strength was used up and exhausted by hunger; he pleaded with the captain to allow him some of it for he felt that he was dying and that nothing but a bit of food could save him; but he pleaded in vain. Byron had five or six dried shellfish in his waistcoat pocket, and as he rowed he dropped them one by one into Bozman's mouth: when he had eaten them he lay quite still for a while, then he began to laugh and sing, and suddenly collapsed and died.

Soon another seaman fell down into the bottom of the boat, and he too died: it became obvious, even to Martin, that they could go no farther. They turned and went back to the place that they had left that morning. There was a sandy beach, so they quickly dug a grave and buried the two seamen. Bozman had been with Byron on innumerable salvage expeditions in the yawl; they had always respected each other, and he felt his loss deeply. He deplored the captain's conduct, and his indignation was shared by the surviving seamen when they saw him sit down and eat the piece of boiled seal himself, allowing no one else to have any except Mr Elliot the surgeon who was the only one of them in favour with him at the time.

During the night Campbell woke the captain and Byron told them he had overheard the men plotting to take the barge; and he added that Hamilton, who had been with him, would confirm what he said. The captain wouldn't believe him. He sent for Hamilton and angrily accused him of plotting to take over the command: Hamilton as angrily denied that he had any such intention. This was the first time that the two men had spoken to each other since their quarrel on Wager Island on the evening before they sailed.

In the morning Martin said that he would go and kill some seal and return in three or four days, but that he would leave Emmanuel both as hostage and to show the *Wager*'s people where to find shellfish during his absence. He got into the canoe with his wife and child, and left them. The coast here was particularly rugged and desolate with the surf continually beating upon it, and inland there was one large swamp in which the trees appeared to float rather than to grow: the first day's search for food, even with Emmanuel as a guide, met with little success. When they were returning towards the wigwams the men hurried on ahead and, taking Emmanuel with them, they got into the barge, cast off and made sail to westward. The captain, after running after them in vain and shaking his fists at them like a madman, sat down on the beach unable to speak, astounded at their treachery. Gone in the barge were their few remaining clothes and all their firearms and ammunition except the small shotgun which Byron always carried with him and a few charges for it.

To those who were left behind, the desertion of the barge seemed to be the crowning disaster because they thought they could never reach civilisation without it; and even if Martin did return, as he had promised, he would certainly hold them responsible for the disappearance of Emmanuel, and he could have little inducement to guide them further when they could no longer give him the promised reward.

During the night there was a severe gale, and in the morning the surgeon was found to be seriously ill. Hamilton and Campbell were unwilling to leave him, the captain remained sunk in despondency, so Byron went out by himself to look for something to eat. With a strong westerly wind the surf was still breaking with great fury all along the coast. As he scrambled among the rocks, occasionally stopping to pick up a clam, he kept glancing out to sea, and he imagined he saw at a great distance a small black object. He climbed a rock and gazing intently gradually made out that it was a canoe. He ran as quickly as he could to his companions and told them what he had seen. Knowing that the Indians did not usually venture out in so mountainous a sea, they were unwilling to believe him; but when they went out and saw it for themselves they tore off their shirts and waistcoats, fastened them to long sticks that they found among the driftwood, and waved them frantically as signals. The canoe came in closer but could not land there: it made for a sheltered cove some two miles away. The captain and Byron hurried along the shore and met it as it came in: there were only three people in the canoe, Martin, his wife and their little boy who was not at all frightened by the fury of the sea.

While they were conducting Martin back to the wigwam where the surgeon lay he asked them many questions, and although they couldn't understand his words it was obvious that he was wondering where the barge had gone to, and that he was surprised and alarmed not to see Emmanuel there. In this awkward situation everything depended on the surgeon who was so ill that he could not raise himself from the ground without support.

When the situation was explained to Martin he at once assumed that Emmanuel had been murdered and he prepared to beat a hasty retreat; but observing that Byron was standing with his gun in the doorway of the wigwam, he stopped and listened to the surgeon who gradually calmed his fears, assuring him that Emmanuel would return safely within a day or two. He asked what his reward would be if he still consented to guide them to Chiloe: he pointed to the captain's waistcoat pocket and said that he would like a gold watch. The captain was unpleasantly surprised to find that Martin knew he had a watch; he had carefully concealed it from him and wound it always in secret. He hastily told the surgeon to offer him Byron's gun instead, and to say that they would use their influence with the Spaniards to get him some pecuniary reward as well. With this offer he seemed to be satisfied.

Because they had only the canoe that was too small to carry them all, they next discussed how they should proceed: Martin suggested that he should take Captain Cheap in it to the nearest Indian settlement to get help, leaving his wife and child as hostages for their return: to this the captain agreed, stipulating only that they should take Byron with them as well. Martin hesitated, understanding that the captain wanted Byron to keep an eye on him, but at length he agreed, probably because he didn't want to lose sight of the gun that had been promised him. When he returned to his wife and child, the captain sent Byron with him to stand sentinel all night over their wigwam, with orders to use force if necessary to prevent them from leaving.

Next morning Emmanuel returned. Although it improved their relations with Martin, Byron was sorry to see him for he couldn't imagine what the six deserters would do with no one to guide them. He had hoped that Emmanuel was taking them to Chiloe. Now he could only pray that they would give up and return, which they could safely have done and the captain would have welcomed them. There was little to be learned from Emmanuel except that the barge had put in to a bay to the westward for shelter and he had contrived to escape, returning by ways that would have been impassable for anyone but an Indian.

They decided to move their camp to a site near the sheltered cove because Martin's was already there, and he had instructed his wife to supply the strangers with food. They built a comfortable wigwam for the surgeon, making it tight against the weather, and they brought him to it supported by Hamilton and Campbell, one on each side. They helped Martin to carry the canoe across a narrow isthmus of rocky ground studded with small trees to the other side of the land they were on – they hadn't known before that they were on a peninsula. Then Captain Cheap and Byron started off with Martin, and after paddling for two days in more sheltered waters they came to an Indian encampment of five or six wigwams where they landed about two hours after nightfall.

All this time Byron had been given nothing to eat except one very small scrap of seal meat: he felt exhausted by hunger and fatigue, and asked for food, but got no reply. Martin at once conducted the captain to the largest wigwam and he was left to shift for himself. He waited a long time. It was dark. The rain came down in torrents. At last, feeling that he could not live another day without a little food, he staggered up to the nearest wigwam and crawled in through the narrow entrance. There was a fire burning in the centre, and in the shadows he could distinguish two bronze figures of Indian women wearing nothing but some necklaces of polished shells and gazing at him in astonishment. One of them appeared to be young and was very handsome for an Indian; the other old, and as frightful as it is possible to conceive anything in human shape to be. Having gazed at him without moving for some little time, they both went out; and he, without further ceremony, sat down by the fire and tried to warm himself and dry his clothes. He thought they had gone to fetch some of the men to throw him out, or perhaps to murder him, but they soon came in again, chattering and laughing in great good humour, so probably they had only questioned Martin about him. Seeing that he was soaked through and shivering violently, the old woman went out again, brought wood and made up the fire. He smiled and tried to thank them, and made signs that he was hungry. The younger woman rummaged under some pieces of bark and produced a fine large fish which she put upon the fire to broil; and when it was just warm through they made signs for him to eat it. He fell to, and dispatched it in so short a time that he was in hopes they would understand that he was ready for another; but it was no use, there was nothing else to eat in the wigwam. They strewed dry branches upon the ground for him; he lay down on them and soon fell fast asleep.

Awakening three or four hours later, he found himself covered with a bit of blanket made from the down of birds such as the women wear about their waists. The young woman, who had carefully covered him while he slept, was lying close by him with the old woman on the other side of her. The fire was low and almost burnt out; but as soon as they found he was awake they renewed it by putting on more fuel. What he had eaten had served only to sharpen his appetite, so he made signs that he was still hungry. They consulted together, and then went out. He heard dogs barking, and then he slept again. In about an hour they came back trembling with cold, their hair streaming with water, and carrying two fish which they set to broil while they rubbed and dried themselves before the fire. They gave him the largest share, and then they all lay down, as before, to rest.

When he awoke again he was alone. Light was streaming in through the doorway and through many chinks in the bark that covered the wigwam. He went out and sat on a log in the sun. The atmosphere was so clear that he could see at a very great distance the majestic Cordilleras pure white against the light blue sky. They were perfectly calm and still, but a deep rumbling sound came from them as of thunder or of mighty avalanches. The encampment lay beside a small stream between a dark forest and the glittering sea. The smoke from the wigwams curled up into the quiet air. He sought out Captain Cheap and found him comfortably esconced in the largest wigwam. From Martin he understood that most of the men were away on some warlike expedition, but their return was looked for about this time – news that was by no means pleasant to Byron. He went to the stream and bathed, and washed his shirt which was alive with vermin. While he was hanging it out on a bush to dry he heard a bustle among the wigwams and saw that the women were stripping off the bark and carrying it to the canoes. He put on his wet shirt and ran to join them. They all embarked in four large canoes, leaving the poles of the wigwams standing, but carrying fire with them. He was put into a canoe with the two women who had befriended him and several others, besides dogs and children, and they pushed off.

They paddled out to sea, and when the water was about fifty or sixty feet deep the young woman laid aside her necklaces, took a basket in her mouth and jumped overboard. She dived, and continued under the water for an amazing time. When she came to the boat again she had filled her basket with sea-eggs. The other women emptied the basket and returned it to her: she dived again to the depths and continued doing so for the space of half an hour or so. Byron, watching her with growing admiration, considered that although she was different in build from European women, being short, thick-set, with small hands and feet, she had something of the flashing lines of the dolphins and was admirably formed for the amphibious life she led. Meanwhile women were diving from the other canoes, and when they had a sufficient supply they paddled on until evening when they landed on a low point, hauled up the canoes, carried their bark and their fires ashore and built their wigwams. The two women entertained Byron as before.

The time passed pleasantly in fishing and feasting – but two days later they sighted the canoes of the returning warriors. The young woman came to Byron with a sad face and tried earnestly to explain something, but he couldn't understand her. About thirty Indians, entirely naked but each carrying a lance and a shield or bows and arrows, leapt ashore. They paid remarkable deference to their chief, an elderly but powerful man with a surly and stern countenance. The two women approached him, the younger with a sort of pride, the elder in abject terror. Martin conveyed to Byron that they were both his wives and that the young one was his daughter also: then he went to the chief to explain the presence and the necessities of the strangers. After a long conference, and many glances towards Captain Cheap and Byron, the chief began to question his wives, evidently suspecting some misconduct. Not being satisfied with their answers, he seized the youngest one in his arms with a cry of savage fury and hurled her down violently against the stones. Then he picked up a leather thong and beat her cruelly. Byron watched this barbarous treatment of his benefactress with the greatest concern, particularly as he saw that it was on his account that she suffered: he could scarcely contain his rage and resentment; but it was only too clear that he was not only powerless to protect her but that any move on his part would only serve to make matters worse for her, and perhaps cost both of them their lives. Martin came up to him and gave him to understand that he and the captain must embark directly in the same canoe that had brought them and return to their companions, and that he would accompany them.

CHAPTER

16

-»>«<-

D URING Byron and the captain's absence Mr Elliot had grown weaker for lack of proper nourishment. There were not many shellfish on the sandy beach, and Martin's wife had brought in very few sea-eggs: being without a canoe, she had had to swim out a long way at every low water to dive for them, for they were to be found only in the quiet depths undisturbed by the movement of the surf, and then turn round and swim back again with every basketful: it was not surprising that she had given the strangers only a very small daily allowance from the proceeds of her laborious work. She behaved very sullenly towards them, evidently considering them to be quite unimportant: taking her cue from Martin she respected only the captain and looked upon the rest as little better than slaves: instead of endeavouring to correct this by treating his officers with more respect, he seemed pleased with the distinction made between them.

Now that they had their interpreter again they questioned Martin about the result of their visit to the Indians, and he said that they would come for them in a few days and they would all go north together.

On the day after their return Martin, having found no food in the camp, took his wife out in the canoe and she dived for sea-eggs with such little success that she was able to fill only one basket. Their little boy, watching for his parents' return, ran into the surf to meet them: his father handed him the basket, but it was too heavy for him and he dropped it into the sea: whereupon Martin jumped out of the canoe and catching the boy up in his arms dashed him with the greatest violence against the stones where he lay motionless and bleeding. His mother picked him up and crooned over him, but very soon he died. She was inconsolable, but Martin showed little concern.

Two days later a dozen canoes were sighted. The Indian chief came in with his two wives and his warriors and his whole establishment of women, dogs and children: Byron dared not look at the younger wife to express his concern and his sympathy except from a distance and when he was sure they were not being observed. The chief ordered a sealhunt to provide for all his people before starting on their journey: the Englishmen had rarely seen any seals, but the Indians launched their canoes and went straight to a place where they were lying thick upon the rocks. Some landed a few hundred yards away, scaled a cliff and began clubbing them from behind: when the animals realised their peril the whole mass of them made for the water: as soon as they reached it, other Indians came up in their canoes and killed them with lances and arrows while they were swimming and coming up to breathe, usually striking them through both eyes with unerring aim: others were caught alive in nets extended on hoops as they hurled themselves from the rocks. In a few minutes all the canoes were laden with dead seals to the gunwales.

Not content with this, the chief ordered all the warriors to go out that same night for cormorants. As soon as it was dark they brought their canoes silently under the cliffs where the birds were roosting, then lit torches of birch bark which they waved to and fro, dazzling and confusing them so that they fluttered about and fell into the canoes where they were instantly dispatched. Meanwhile some of the Indians, excellent climbers, got among those that were roosting higher up and silently wrung their necks one after another without disturbing their neighbours. There was a scene of great activity when they returned to the camp, and soon, before a dozen fires, seal meat was broiling and cormorants roasting on spits. For once the strangers were able to eat their fill. There was such abundance that Captain Cheap fetched Martin and asked him, the surgeon interpreting, if some of the food might be set aside for their journey: he replied that these Indians were only poor ignorant savages and it was not their way to start a journey while there was any food left. Even the seals that had been caught alive in the nets and might have been taken with them to furnish fresh meat had been slaughtered like the rest. He himself, of course, being a Christian and the trusted man of the Spaniards, knew better how to manage things, but he was not among his own people and he could not change the customs of other tribes.

When they had feasted for some hours a sort of melancholy settled upon the Indians. Then the elder men began swaying backwards and forwards, emitting deep and dismal groans which rose gradually to a hideous kind of singing in which the younger men joined, slowly working themselves up into a frenzy; they seized bags of coloured powder and smeared each other's limbs and faces with it; they picked up brands from the fires, put them in their mouths, and rushed about burning each other; they wounded each other with sharp mussel shells until they were streaming with blood: after a while they began foaming at the mouth, grew faint, staggered and collapsed one by one, glistening with blood and sweat. Then the women began moaning and swaying and re-enacting the same hideous scenes with even greater frenzy and more bloodcurdling shrieks and more desperate wounding until they too collapsed upon the exhausted heap of humanity – all of which Martin treated with great disdain: he would rather have died, he said, than take part in it. He crossed himself repeatedly and confided that the Devil, *Il Diabolo*, was present in these horrid orgies and that while they were going on he never failed to hear strange and uncommon noises in the surrounding woods, and to see frightful visions. These extraordinary scenes continued for a week together, and then the madness left the Indians as suddenly as it had taken hold of them.

It was about the middle of March when they finally embarked. The Indians were careful not to put more than one of the strangers into each canoe, except that the surgeon, more dead than alive, was laid on the bottom of the one in which Campbell was travelling. A paddle was thrust into Hamilton's hands, but he dropped it, saying that he didn't know how to row. Nothing they could do could change his attitude, but Byron and Campbell had to work their passage. Soon the weather became too bad for them to keep the sea, so they put back into the same bay, having made little progress. Here Mr Elliot the surgeon died. His death cast a shadow over their spirits. Once he had promised the fairest for holding out, being strong and active, but he had endured infinite fatigue tramping many miles over rough country and through swampy forests in search of game: he and Hamilton, being the best shots, had never spared themselves while their ammunition lasted and they had in a great measure provided for the rest. Before he died he thanked them all for caring for him in his weakness. He was particularly grateful to Campbell: he gave him his silver watch and said he wished he could leave him all he possessed, but he had neither pen, ink nor paper to make a last will and testament. They scraped a hole for him in the sand and buried him as best they could on the beach near the thundering surf. They named that place Elliot Bay in memory of him.

A day or two later they put to sea again and made towards the great sandy crescent beach in the north-east corner of the Gulf where three months earlier they had tried to find a way through to the north but had found no opening in the wall of breakers. They had abandoned the attempt too readily, it seemed. As soon as he caught sight of the two groups of sand-dunes again, Byron realised how blind and foolish they had been: could Nature have given them a clearer landmark than a long, low, featureless beach with nothing on it but two groups of sand-dunes? Of course a river flowed between them, and there was no gap in the breakers because it had a bar of sand across its mouth. The consequences of their lack of insight had been the futile attempts to get round the Cape of Three Mountains, the four marines abandoned to their fate, the heartbreaking struggle against the swift-flowing river when Bozman had fallen from his oar and died, the death of their friend the surgeon and the loss by desertion of all but four of their number, and those four no longer a fighting unit buoyed up by prospects of high adventure but sadly changed for the worse, grown careless of each other's needs and even of their own: the captain a broken man soured by many disappointments, resentful, grasping and morose; Hamilton even more cold and proud, Byron with growing bitterness in his heart; but Campbell, once the Patroon, was the exception: he had miraculously changed for the better and had tenderly and patiently nursed the surgeon in his last illness. Now they didn't want the Indians: they wanted twenty good men in the barge and the yawl, but it was too late for that: the four who remained were powerless and would have to put up with the humiliations and cruelties of their guides in exchange for a doubtful chance of life. They were sure they could have got the barge through the surf if they had waited for one of the infrequent days of moderate weather, which was perhaps what the Indians had been doing though they appeared only to have been wasting time.

There was a heavy rolling sea, but nothing like so heavy

as on the day they had failed to find the entrance. The Indians headed directly for the sand-dunes. As soon as they got among the breakers they drove the canoes swiftly forward, and when they could find their feet they leapt out, some thrusting the canoes onward by the gunwales while others snatched up their burdens to lighten them. They got safely across the bar and found themselves in a quiet lagoon about a quarter of a mile wide and flanked on either side by the sand-dunes. This, Martin informed them, was the Santa Deo River — he called it San Tadeo — so they had escaped at last from the iron jaws of the Gulf of Affliction. As they went up the lagoon the familiar roar of the breakers died away, leaving no sound but the merry splash and rustle of swift canoes. At first the lagoon broadened, then after about three miles it narrowed into a sluggish river with dull flat marshy country on both sides covered with the black stumps of dead trees. Beyond them and to the left were sombre wooded hills, and to the right the dazzling white wall of the great glacier with a sloping plateau above it.

At dusk they landed on the riverbank which was a mere swamp. It rained very hard and there was no wood to build wigwams. The Indians brought ashore the pieces of bark which they always carried and propped them up on their paddles to form a kind of shelter. They had some seal meat with them but gave none to the strangers. Seeing his distress, the young woman who had previously befriended Byron threw in his way whatever scraps of food she could secrete from her husband.

Four or five leagues up the river they took a branch of it which ran first to the eastward and then to the northward. It became narrower and more rapid with a tortuous course among low hills, and they were greatly impeded by floating dead trees and masses of decaying vegetation. On the third day they reached the *desecho*, or portage, where the boats had to be carried. They had always looked upon the barge as their only means of salvation, but now they had to change their views for it was obvious they could never have got it across the *desecho* which was a mere track across wooded and marshy country; and they would have been unlikely even to find it without a guide: they could understand also why Martin tried to take it by another route. The Indians dismantled their canoes and started off through the forest, each man and woman carrying a plank or a bundle: everyone had something to carry except Captain Cheap who had to be assisted. Byron had a piece of stinking seal to carry belonging to the captain, wrapped in a piece of wet heavy canvas: it would have been heavy enough for a man in good condition on a fair road, but their way was through a thick wood growing in a quagmire in which he sank knee-deep at every step: there were fallen tree trunks to scramble over, and stumps hidden under the mud and water which he could not avoid stepping on, and he frequently tore his bare feet and legs on them. He was left far behind, and trying to catch up again he slipped and fell from a tree trunk into a deep swamp and was nearly drowned. It was long before he could extricate himself, and when he did he was so exhausted that he couldn't carry his load any farther. He dragged it to a great tree, which he marked, and then set out to join the others. He found them after walking for some hours: they were sitting under a tree beside a lake. He sat down beside them without speaking a word, nor, for some time, did they speak to him: then Captain Cheap broke the silence to ask about the seal and the piece of canvas: he had expected some compassion for his suffering, but he was vastly mistaken: when he explained what had happened, all three turned on him and grumbled about the irreparable loss they had sustained through him of the whole of their food supply for they had had nothing to eat that day except a kind of root which they had seen the Indians use and which tasted bitter in their mouths. He didn't answer, but after resting for a little while he got up, struck into the wood and walked back at least five miles to the tree he had marked; he returned just in time to deliver the seal to his companions who were embarking with the Indians. He wanted to embark with them, but he was told to wait for some other Indians who were to follow them. They pushed off, and he was left alone on the beach with night coming on, and he didn't know where these other Indians were to come from, nor when. They hadn't even left him a morsel of the stinking seal for which he had suffered so much, and they had taken his shotgun which was to be Martin's reward. Worst of all, his protectress had also gone in the canoes: he kept his eyes on them for as long as he could distinguish them, then watched the lake which seemed to stretch right away to the foot of the high Cordilleras. At last he got up and returned to the wood to look for some of the root that the Indians used, but not finding any he chewed the stem of a plant that looked like an artichoke: it had an acid taste so he spat it out. He sat down on the root of a tree and soon fell asleep.

It was almost dark when he was awakened by the sound of voices. Exploring farther into the wood, he came upon a solitary wigwam. He stooped to enter it: there were shouts of anger, and he immediately received three or four violent kicks in the face from a hard and bony foot. He prudently retired. Sometime after daybreak an old woman peered out and made signs for him to enter. He did so and found three men and two women in the wigwam: one of the men, the youngest, had great respect shown to him by the rest, although he was a miserable object, a perfect skeleton and covered with sores from head to foot. The old woman took out a piece of seal, held one end of it with her feet and the other between her teeth, and cut off some thin slices with a sharp shell. She distributed these to the Indians while Byron looked on hungrily. Then she put a slice on the fire, took some of the fat in her mouth and kept on chewing it, and every now and again spirting some of it through her teeth on to the piece that was warming. When it was ready she gave Byron a little bit which he swallowed whole. Then all of them except the sick Indian went out, carried the planks of a canoe to the beach and assembled it. When all was ready they embarked and rowed across the lake to the outfall of a very rapid river where they put ashore and built a wigwam, which Byron was not allowed to enter: neither did they give him anything more to eat.

Next morning they went down the river at an amazing rate, and it required the greatest skill to avoid running foul of the stumps and roots of trees. They landed at the mouth of the river on a stony beach in a violent rain storm. The Indians all disappeared. Byron lay down on the beach, fell asleep in spite of the rain, and awoke several hours later suffering agonies from cramp. He saw that a great fire had been lighted: he managed to crawl to it, but the Indians immediately got up and kicked and beat him until they had driven him away. Some time later he contrived to edge himself close enough to get some warmth from it, and this relieved his cramp. Next day they ran out of the river into another lake – but this time it was an arm of the sea. With relief and joy Byron saw the rich brown seaweed, the line of wrack and driftwood thrown up by the tide, and heard the discordant cries of seabirds: it meant that they had passed behind the Cape of Three Mountains and the way was clear and open to the north. He looked forward now to better fare, for he knew more about finding shellfish than about roots and plants.

At low water they landed for supplies and found plenty of limpets on the rocks. In spite of his hunger, Byron did not dare to stop and eat one lest he should lose a moment in gathering them, not knowing when the Indians might be going again: he believed that they would have no conscience about leaving him behind. He had almost filled his hat when he saw them returning to the canoe, and he ran to join them. He sat down at his paddle, placing his hat close to him. They pushed off, and every now and again he ate a limpet, throwing the shells over the side. Suddenly the Indian next to him spoke to the rest in a violent passion and, getting up, seized Byron by the old ragged handkerchief he had about his neck and almost strangled him: at the same time another took him by the legs, and they were going to throw him overboard into the sea when the old woman intervened and prevented them. He was quite ignorant of how he had given offence till he observed that the Indians, after eating the limpets, carefully put the shells in a heap at the bottom of the canoe, and when they landed they brought all their shells ashore and laid them above the high water mark. That evening as he rambled along the shore he gathered a large bunch of berries from a tree and was about to eat them when the same Indian who had wanted to throw him overboard ran up and dashed them out of his hand, making him understand that they were poisonous.

In two more days they caught up with the other Indians and Byron found his three companions again: not the least pleasure was shown on either side at their reunion. At this place there was a large and cumbersome canoe belonging to Martin to which he transferred his store of iron, his wife and Captain Cheap. The captain told Byron, Hamilton and Campbell to join them also, but Hamilton refused to leave the Indians with whom he had travelled until then: he said he found Martin's insolence insupportable, and that of his wife more so. His resentment was certainly justified, for Martin never touched a paddle, but sat all the time very much at his ease beside his wife, who steered. All the work was done by Byron, Campbell and Emmanuel. Day after day they travelled laboriously northward. The Indians remained insensible to their necessities, and only the solicitude of the chief's two wives made it possible for them to survive: frequently they found a fish lying in their path, or a few scraps of seal, or some sea-eggs, and on these beside what they could pick up themselves they contrived to live. Once they came upon an encampment of about forty Indians, curiously painted, from whom they gleaned the interesting information through Martin, whom Byron had learned to understand fairly well by this time, that a ship with a red flag had lain for some weeks upon the coast not far from where they now were: this, they supposed, was the ship, probably of their own squadron, whose sunset gun they had heard from Wager Island. Apart from this chance encounter they saw no trace of inhabitants.

When they had been travelling in this fashion for about two months the chief decided to turn back with all his Indians: Byron had to watch his two friends embark and paddle away without daring to give them the slightest sign of recognition for their services, knowing that retribution would have been severe if their husband had suspected them of taking an interest in the strangers. Hamilton was left without any form of transport except Martin's canoe, but he still refused to embark, saying that he would prefer to stay where he was. Remonstrances were in vain. At last his three companions went on without him.

CHAPTER

17

SOME three months after entering the San Tadeo River they reached a place on the coast about thirty leagues south of the island of Chiloe: there was nothing now between them and their goal except a wide bay or channel which was open to the Pacific on the western side; but it looked as if Captain Cheap would not live to reach it. He no longer recollected their names, or even his own; his body was like a skeleton, but his legs, puffed out from the bone, were of monstrous size: he was covered with insects like an anthill and he had given up trying to rid himself of them: his beard was as long as a hermit's and thick with dirt and oil, for he was accustomed to use as a pillow the bag in which he kept pieces of seal meat to prevent his companions from getting at it while he slept.

Martin had a particular dread of this bay: the very thought of having to cross it frightened him out of his senses; but after waiting for two days, hoping for better weather, he summoned up the resolution to attempt it. He made a kind of lug-sail out of two Indians' ponchos by sewing them together with split supple-jack creeper; then he spent a whole hour crossing himself, and at length they put to sea with the wind southerly. It soon changed. They ran into a dangerous cross-sea and shipped so much water that they had to bail continuously to keep the canoe afloat: the bottom plank was split and it opened to the sea at every roll. During the following night they made the south-westerly point of the island: Martin was so terrified by then, and so eager to land, that he nearly got them among the breakers where the sea was driving in with such violence upon the rocks that they could not possibly have survived: they made him keep off until they were in smoother water and could land in safety. It was bitterly cold, the whole countryside was under deep snow, and there was no sign of a habitation. They stayed where they were all the next day, in spite of their anxiety for Captain Cheap, because they were too exhausted to go farther. They were in the district of which Martin was cacique, or head man, so he spent the time digging a hole and burying the iron he had brought from the *Wager* to conceal it from the Spaniards who would have taken it from him and not left him even a rusty nail.

Towards evening they set off again in the canoe, and paddling along the coast they saw, about nine o'clock, a rectangular one-storied structure that had the appearance of a house. Martin said that friends of his lived in it. He had taken possession of the fowling-piece, according to their bargain, and he now asked to be shown how to fire it. There was only one charge left: Byron loaded it for him and showed him how to hold it. He pointed it at the house and, keeping his head as far away as possible from the gun, he pulled the trigger and fell back into the bottom of the canoe. The occupants of the house ran out and hid in the woods. After a while one of them appeared on a hillock and shouted to them, asking if they were Christians. When Martin made himself known to them they ran down to the boat, and seeing the three famished strangers they hurried back and brought them some fish and potatoes. They watched them eat and then escorted them to a little village, two miles away, where Martin shouted to arouse the inhabitants and made one of them open his door and light a fire. The rest of the villagers came out to see what the disturbance was: they were strong and well featured, with melodious voices. They were moved by the pitiable condition of the strangers and they vied with each other to tend and care for them. They laid Captain Cheap upon a bed of sheep skins close to the fire, and although it was nearly midnight, they baked a large cake of barley meal, and they went out and killed a sheep of which they made broth.

In the morning the women came from far and near, almost every one with a pipkin in her hand containing chicken or eggs or potatoes or mutton broth or fish, and the whole day was spent in eating, as most of the night had been. In the evening the men crowded into the house bringing jars of a liquor they called *chicha*, and all made merry. The Indians were neatly and cleanly dressed, the men in gaily-striped ponchos, with wide knee-breeches and buskins; the women's dress was a petticoat, also with stripes of various colours, and a shift with a piece of square cloth about the shoulders fastened by a silver pin. Both men and women had bare feet, and their hair was combed very smooth and tightly bound with a ribbon about the forehead: they were as pleasant and friendly as the Indians farther south had been surly and inhuman. When they learned that their guests were English and at war with Spain, they seemed fonder of them than ever, for there was nothing they feared and detested more than the Spaniards.

Martin had sent a messenger to the nearest Spanish garrison to report their arrival, and all too soon orders came back that the Englishmen were to be escorted to the town of Castro, which was fifty miles farther north, on the eastern side of the island. Accordingly they re-embarked, and a large number of Indians went with them in their canoes, more to express their sympathy than to act as escort. The appearance of the island, which was about a hundred miles long by thirty or forty broad, was softer in outline and altogether different to the rugged and savage country to which they were accustomed. The hills sloped gently upward and were entirely covered with dense forest. Along the shore there were sand beaches alternating with cliffs; it was not unlike parts of the South of England. The mainland, on the contrary, which they could see across a wide channel, consisted of towering volcanic mountains.

At nightfall they landed, having completed about half the distance, and were met by a Spanish guard consisting of three or four officers and a troop of soldiers, all with swords drawn: they had ponchos like the Indians, and buskins with no shoes; but in spite of this they all wore monstrous great spurs, some of copper and some of silver, which made a rattling sound when they walked, like chains: they surrounded the prisoners as if they had a most formidable enemy to take charge of instead of three helpless wretches who, in spite of the good fare of the past few days, could hardly support themselves. They were marched to the top of a hill where they were put under a thatched roof which was quite open with no sides to it, and here they lay upon the ground, closely guarded. It was the middle of the Chiloen winter, the month of June, and very cold, but they had no covering except their own miserable rags, for the hospitable Indians who lived well enough on the produce of their fertile land were in fact quite poor, and none of them had had a spare article of clothing to give them.

Many people came to stare at them, but the women never came empty handed, so their wants were provided for. One day a Jesuit priest came and sat with them: he addressed them in Latin which Captain Cheap made shift to understand. He lugged out a bottle of brandy and when each had taken a dram he hinted that he knew from Martin that they had articles of great value about them. The captain declared that he had nothing, but knowing that the Jesuits had great power and authority and might be of service to them, he told Campbell to make a present to the priest of the silver watch that the surgeon had given him when he lay dying.

This Campbell most unwillingly did: he had intended to treasure it all his life in memory of his friend. On the following day a messenger arrived with a present for Campbell from the priest: a piece of coarse cloth enough to make two shirts, two pairs of thread stockings without feet, one pair of shoes that proved too small for him, and a poncho with a hole in the middle to put his head through.

Soon after this the Officer of the Guard informed them that he had been ordered to take them to Castro. They were marched to the waterside again and put into a large canoe called a *periago*, and there were several other similar canoes crowded with soldiers to escort them. The weather was fine and they had an easy passage. They approached the town through a long winding inlet, less than a mile broad in places, with wooded hills on either side rising by level steps to about 400 or 500 feet. At eight o'clock in the evening when it was already dark they were challenged by a sentry, and the boats all lay upon their oars while the commanding officer was acquainted with their arrival. They couldn't see much of the town, but there was a great deal of ceremony in hailing back and forth and asking for the keys to open the gates of the fortifications. When at last they were permitted to land they were conducted up a steep hill lined on both sides by soldiers, and brought before the mayor, who was called the corregidor. He was an old man, very tall, wearing a long cloak and a tye wig without any curl, and there was a sword of immense length by his side. He received them in great state and form, but as they understood little of what he said, they were unable to answer his questions. He ordered a table to be spread for them with cold chicken and ham: the three of them sat down to it and in a short time dispatched more than ten men with ordinary appetites would have done. Then he took them to the Jesuits' College attended by a guard of soldiers and all the rabble of the town: he told the Father Provincial to find out if they had any religion and, if so, what it was. The gates were shut. They were conducted to a cell where beds were spread for them on the floor; they were allowed to shave and make themselves more presentable, and they were given an old shirt apiece, ragged but clean: even the feast of cold chicken and ham did not give Byron half the satisfaction that the old shirt did, for his own had rotted off by bits and there was nothing left of it.

When they looked out in the morning they saw that the town had no walls, gates or any kind of fortification – the ceremonial of their entry was all play-acting to impress them, and most of the soldiers' muskets were merely pieces of wood. Grouped round a central square there were a few fairly large buildings – they had very interesting eaves, reaching up like a bird's wing instead of the usual straight downward edge – but the rest of the town seemed to be little more than a collection of wooden huts with little form or order. Within the college silence reigned as if it had been uninhabited. They remained in their cell until a bell rang and they were conducted to a hall for dinner; there was one table for the fathers – there were only four of them although the college was very large – and one for them. After a very long Latin prayer they sat down and ate what was put before them without a single word passing at either table. When they had finished there was another long prayer which, however, did not appear so tedious as the first, and then they retired to their cell again.

With good cheer and rest Captain Cheap was recovering. He was sent for by the Father Provincial, and on his return to the cell he told his companions that the good fathers, one of whom already had Campbell's watch, were still harping on what things of value they might have saved and concealed about them, and saying that if they had anything of that sort they couldn't do better than to let them have it.

Two days later he was sent for again. This time the

corregidor was present also. The question of their religion was discussed in Latin, perhaps not of the best, with the result that the Father Provincial decided that they were heretics. He told the corregidor that it would be useless to try to make them change their religion while they were in Chiloe and they had no inducement to do so; it would be better to leave it until they were in Chile, for in that delightful country where there would be nothing but diversions and amusements they would be converted quickly enough. The programme of diversions and amusements seemed to Byron, now that he was eighteen, to have possibilities: at least no one had yet suggested that they should be sent to the salt mines, the fate that Mr Bulkeley had so much dreaded.

The Corregidor of Castro had reported their arrival to the Governor of Chiloe whose headquarters were in Chacao at the extreme northern end of the island. A little after dark on their eighth evening at the Jesuits' College they heard a violent knocking at the gate, and a young officer entered, booted and spurred, who acquainted the fathers that he had been sent to conduct the prisoners to Chacao. The young officer was the governor's son whom Byron described as a vain empty coxcomb who ought to have been kept at school. They set out on horseback escorted by thirty mounted soldiers, and rode about eight miles to an estancia, or farmhouse, belonging to an old lady who had two handsome daughters, where they were very well entertained. The good old lady was so distressed by the condition Byron was in that she asked the governor's son if he might be allowed to return and stay at the estancia for a month to recuperate. They left again early in the morning and rode to the small port of Quenchi where there were stacks of fine timber awaiting export, and where several boats were being repaired on the beach where the *periagos* were waiting for them. From Quenchi, because of the swift-running tides, it took them three days to reach Chacao although the distance was only twenty-five miles. Again they were brought in at night with the same ceremony as at Castro, sentries hailing, asking for the keys to the gates; but here there really was a little earthen fort with some old guns and with a ditch and palisade around it, quite useless though and inadequate for defending the harbour. There seemed to be nothing in the whole of Chiloe that could possibly have resisted even a small British raiding force. They were marched up to the governor's house which was called *El Palacio del Rey*, the Palace of the King, but was nothing better than a large thatched barn partitioned off into several rooms. The governor, an elderly Spaniard from Santiago, made them sit down with him and his principal officers at a great table covered with red baize: there was even an interpreter, a stupid old fellow: he said he was an English seaman, born in Falmouth. He had turned buccaneer and been taken by the Spaniards near Panama nigh on forty years ago.

When Captain Cheap had told his story the governor commiserated with them on their misfortunes and said he hoped they would find no reason to complain of their treatment now that they had reached a civilised country. Then he informed them that two of Admiral Pizarro's ships had been lost in the gale that wrecked the *Wager* and that the rest of his fleet, unable to weather the Horn, had put back to the River Plate: it was seen therefore that Mr Bulkeley's main argument for turning south had been fallacious; Pizarro's fleet would not have been waiting to intercept the *Speedwell* if they had obeyed the captain and taken her north. They listened with deep interest and learned how Anson had sailed unopposed along the coasts of Chile and Peru, looting and burning the town of Payta and capturing many prizes. He had taken many prisoners and treated them all with kindness and respect, and therefore, the governor said, he intended to be equally generous with them. The captain thanked him for his courtesy and begged as a special favour that a search-party should be sent out for Lieutenant Hamilton and for the six men in the barge. The governor said he would give the necessary orders immediately.

When they had supped with the governor they were conducted across a courtyard to an apartment that had served to keep firewood in for the kitchen: as it was dry and warm they thought themselves extremely well lodged. Soldiers were always at hand with drawn swords to prevent them from stirring out. One of these soldiers took a great fancy to Byron's embroidered red waistcoat, or what was left of it, that the mutineers had brought ashore for him from the wreck and which he had worn ever since. In its ample pockets he had treasured his gold watch safely concealed from the captain and even from Martin's acquisitive eye, together with charges of gunpowder and other things which Isabella had never suspected they would contain when she made it for him, such as bits of stinking seal meat and the shellfish he had dropped into Bozman's dying mouth: it cost him a pang to let it go, but because of the vermin in the seams and the smell of the seal oil he couldn't go on wearing it. He got in exchange a pair of breeches, and for his old grieko an Indian poncho.

At the end of the first week the sentries were removed and they were allowed to go about the palace: during the following week they were placed on parole and they could walk about the town and go where they pleased. Rain was so heavy and so frequent that the ladies used to go with bare feet, through the mud and wet, to the church opposite the governor's house, pull on their shoes and stockings at the church door, and pull them off again as they came out. Once they were awakened by the eruption of a volcano on the mainland: it burnt very fiercely and sounded like great guns in the night. Next morning the governor mounted his horse and rode up and down between his house and his earthen fort saying it was the English coming in but he would give them a warm reception.

The Creoles, the Spaniards born in that country and who owned most of the estancias, were particularly friendly. One belonged to an old priest who was esteemed one of the richest persons on the island. He had a niece, of whom he was extremely fond, and who was to inherit all he possessed: he had taken great pains with her education and she was reckoned one of the most accomplished young ladies of Chiloe. She did Byron the honour, he says, to take more notice of him than he deserved. She proposed to her uncle to convert him, and afterwards begged his consent to marry him. As the old man doted on her, he readily agreed. He took Byron into a room where there were several chests and boxes which he unlocked, and he showed him what fine clothes his niece had, and then he showed his own wardrobe which, he said, would be his at his death. Amongst other things he produced a piece of linen and offered to have it immediately made up into shirts for him: this was a great temptation but he had the resolution to withstand it. By this time he had learnt enough Spanish to excuse himself for not accepting the honour they intended for him.

One morning there was a great bustle in the town: a ship had come in! People crowded in to Chacao from all the outlying estancias. It was the first since Anson's fleet had interrupted all sea communications. Her captain was appalled when he learnt that three English seamen were there and free to walk about: he came to the governor and besought him to lock them up securely. The governor laughed at his fears, and all the people laughed at him also. He was an old man, well known upon the island: they called him, because he had an unusually large head, *Cabuco de Toro*, Bull's Head. He disposed of his cargo in record time: wheat, linen, hats, ribbons, sugar, brandy, maté tea from Paraguay, wine for the churches, baize cloth and tobacco;

bartering them (for there was no money current in the island) for carpets, quilts, ponchos, cedar planks, hams, hog's lard, and the little carved boxes that ladies of fashion put their work in: never were there such bargains in the history of Chiloe. Then he hurriedly put to sea. Captain Cheap watched the ship sail with tears in his eyes: he had so often captured just such a vessel in his imagination and sailed in her to join the commodore.

When the time came for the governor to make his annual tour of the island he took the three Englishmen with him. At each place he held a kind of court, all the Indian caciques meeting him and informing him of what had passed since his last visit. Among them was a young cacique who had been put in irons for some offence or other, possibly only so that the governor could demonstrate his power over the Indians. Byron recognised him as one of those who had treated them kindly on their first landing on the island, so he asked Captain Cheap to intercede for him. He did so, and obtained his release. This made the English more popular than ever. While they were at Castro the old lady at whose estancia they had lain on the first night after leaving the Jesuits' College sent to the governor and begged that Byron might be allowed to come to her for a few weeks. This was granted and he spent three weeks with her very happily. She treated him as if he had been her own son.

When they returned to Chacao the governor told them that when the annual ship from Lima came in they would be sent in her to Chile. While they were awaiting her arrival one of the search-parties returned bringing in Lieutenant Hamilton: he was in the same miserable condition that they had been in three months ago. Nothing in his dress remained to indicate that he was an officer, but although he walked slowly and with difficulty he held himself upright and he looked as if he were conscious that his boots were highly polished though in fact his feet were bare and bleeding. He greeted his friends with a nod as if he had just come off parade. The missing seamen were not found. Campbell got hold of a story that the barge with two seamen in her still alive had been brought to Chiloe but that the Governor of Castro had kept silent about it because he wanted her for his own use: they could get no confirmation of this story nor any further information.

The Lima ship duly arrived, the prisoners were embarked in her, and they sailed from Chacao on the 2nd January, 1743: she was a fine ship of about 250 tons, built of local timber. They looked at her critically and decided that she would have been an easy prey for the *Speedwell*, or even for the barge had she managed to come so far north, for she had neither guns nor muskets. Even now it was only their parole and not the strength of the vessel in defence that prevented them from making an attempt to capture her. They soon decided that the captain, who was a Spaniard, knew not the least of sea affairs, but that the master, the boatswain and the boatswain's mate, all Frenchmen, were very good seamen; the pilot was a Mulatto; all the rest of the crew were Indians or Negro slaves: the latter were never allowed to go aloft lest they should fall overboard and the owners lose money by it. There was one other passenger, a Jesuit priest: he and Captain Cheap were admitted into the great cabin and messed with the captain and his chaplain while the others had to lie on the open quarterdeck, which they didn't mind in the least, being accustomed to fare so much worse. They lived well, eating with the master and the boatswain who both drank brandy as if it were small beer and smoked cigars all day long.

On the fifth day they sighted land four or five leagues to the southward of Valparaiso. The wind fell so that they no longer had steerage way, and a great western swell drove them very fast towards the shore. They dropped the lead several times, but the coast was steep to, and they found so great a depth of water that they could not anchor. The priest, being informed of the danger, brought out the image of a saint which he desired might be hung up in the mizzen shrouds: when this had been done he addressed it in the most threatening language and told it that if they didn't have a breeze of wind immediately he would certainly throw it overboard. Soon a little wind arose which enabled them to stand off the land, and the priest carried the image back to his cabin with an air of triumph.

CHAPTER

18

--->>><<<---

Next morning they entered the Port of Valparaiso, the Vale of Paradise, a semi-circular bay open to the north and surrounded by steep hills covered with dry grass and stunted trees. There were several other ships there, lying close under the cliffs with hawsers ashore. The town was only a line of warehouses between the sea and the cliffs with a hundred or so mean-looking houses wedged among them: above them stood a large white fort or, rather, a fortified hill-top with high white walls following the uneven contours of the ground.

In the afternoon the prisoners were ordered ashore. They were met on the beach by soldiers with fixed bayonets who surrounded them and marched them up to the fort followed by a motley crowd of excited townspeople including many Creole, Mulatto and Indian women and swarms of children. As they walked the wind blew strongly from the parched hills driving little spouts of choking dust over them. They were taken past a battery of nine eighteen-pounder guns constructed on the beach, and then up a steep slope culminating in a flight of steps. As they entered the imposing gateway of the fort they observed that the walls, about twenty-five feet high, were of brick and only about two feet thick. A couple of rounds from the *Wager* would have brought them down in a heap of rubble.

They were ushered into a long room with dark heavily gilded panelling and high narrow grated windows: it was crowded with Spanish officers wearing swords and embroidered cloaks. At one end there was a raised platform and on it a solitary high-backed chair, the seat covered with purple velvet. A door in the panelling opened and the governor, Don Andres de Arabal, entered, leaning on the arm of his secretary who guided him to the chair because he was blind. The officers all bowed. On being informed that the English prisoners were before him, Don Andres abused them in a high-pitched arrogant voice and asked what they had to say. Captain Cheap took a step forward and replied that he was Captain of His Majesty's Ship *Wager*, driven ashore on Tierra del Fuego: he presented his companions, all officers, he said, and he demanded that they should be treated according to their rank. The governor asked for documents, and to Byron's surprise both Captain Cheap and Lieutenant Hamilton produced their commissions which they must have kept all these months secreted in their rags. He and Campbell had nothing to prove their identity. It made no difference, however. After a short speech in which he boasted of the number of soldiers he commanded, and asked if they had observed that the guns in his lower battery were all of brass, the governor ordered all four of them to be thrown into prison. They were taken out and thrust into the condemned cell, the lowest dungeon in the fort. It consisted of four bare walls; a heap of lime crawling with fleas covered one-third of it. Sentries were posted outside the iron-barred door.

The curiosity of the townspeople was not yet satisfied: the sentry on duty, for a small charge, allowed them to come and gape at the prisoners who felt like wild beasts in a cage. They were tormented by the fleas, and the noise made by seventy felons in the next cell, chained together for work on the fortifications, prevented them from sleeping.

After a few days of this purgatory, orders came for Captain Cheap and Lieutenant Hamilton to be sent to Santiago, the capital of Chile. The captain expressed great concern when he was taken away: he had dreaded all along, he said, that they would be separated, and he promised that if he were allowed to speak to the president he would never leave off soliciting him until Byron and Campbell were brought to Santiago also.

As soon as the captain had gone the prisoners' rations were cut down to a few potatoes in hot water once a day. They sent the soldier who was responsible for feeding them to the governor to protest against this treatment and he returned with some fruit and wine: they thought their rations had been increased, but it transpired that Don Arabal's answer had been that the English might starve for all he cared, they should get no more from him: it was the soldier himself who had brought the fruit and wine for them, ashamed of the governor's inhumanity. He continued to provide for them. All the weeks they were in prison he laid aside half of his meagre pay to feed them, although he had a wife and children to look after as well. Sympathy for the prisoners grew when the governor's answer became known to the townspeople, and they began to bring small presents or a little food; even the mule drivers would open their tobacco-pouches, in which they kept their money, and bring out half a real. All they got they offered to the soldier in repayment, but he refused it, saying that they might have need of it. Some of their guards had been in Admiral Pizarro's ships that had failed to get round the Horn: he had sent them overland across the Argentine and over the Andes to strengthen the Pacific garrisons.

One night there was a terrible earthquake; the roof and the walls of the dungeon seemed about to fall in upon them, and the horror was increased by the shrieks and imprecations, and the clashing chains, of the felons in the adjoining cell; but it passed, and the day of their deliverance was at hand. There were several ships from Lima in the harbour discharging their cargoes, the greater part of which had to

be transported by pack mules to Santiago: large droves of
them were leaving every day. The master carrier of one of
these droves came to the prison with an order from the
governor to take the two Englishmen with him. They took
leave of the friendly soldier, who gave them some fruit and
a flask of wine for the journey, as no provision had been
made for them, and they set out towards the end of January,
overjoyed to be out of the dungeon and dazzled by the white
glare of the sunshine to which they were unaccustomed.
Walking behind a drove of more than a hundred mules,
each of which carried two heavy packs, one on each side,
they toiled up a rough track through the hills that surrounded the harbour like an amphitheatre. Soon they came
to an open plain where everything was withered and the
ground was hard and cracked. When they had gone about
fourteen miles they reached a sparkling stream that splashed
merrily from rock to rock and from pool to pool: on both
sides of it there was a wide strip of fertile green – of lush
grass, masses of flowers and tall shady trees. They stopped
there for the night: it was what the carrier called an *alojami-
ento*, though their only lodging was the open meadow. The
mules were relieved of their packs which were placed on
the ground in a wide circle, and after they had been allowed
to drink from the stream each mule was tethered to its own
two packs. When the work was done, the carrier and his
two drovers willingly shared their provisions which consisted of white bread and butter, black figs and a pot of
maté tea. The mules were given no food; they cropped
the grass and were as fat and sleek as high-fed horses in
England.

They started again early next morning, passed over a high
mountain called Zapata, and crossed another wide plain
and a ridge of mountains by difficult and winding tracks.
The carrier was very civil: Byron and Campbell in return
did their best to help him by driving in those mules that

strayed from the rest and by loading and unloading them at the *alojamientos*. Very occasionally they passed a lumbering waggon drawn by six or eight oxen, the ungreased wheels screeching horribly, and there were a few low two-roomed cottages built of large sun-baked bricks and thatched with palm leaves whose jutting ends made wide eaves giving grateful shade. On the evening of the fourth day, from the summit of the lowest pass, they could see Santiago in the middle of a fertile plain, a city of low white houses with many churches rising above them; and beyond it the majestic rampart of the Andes Mountains which were, in fact, their prison wall, barring them from any possibility of escape to the West Coast of America and so to Europe. On the fifth day they drove the mules down to the rich farmlands and orchards and across the Maipocho River, fed by the snows of the Andes. When they reached the outskirts of Santiago, the carrier advised Byron very seriously not to think of remaining there, but to ask permission to return and work with him as a mule-driver, for he would soon become proficient: he would lead an innocent and happy life, far preferable to any enjoyment he might find in the great city where there was nothing but extravagance, vice and folly. Byron thanked him and said he would try the city first and then, if he didn't like it, he would endeavour to rejoin him.

It was dark when they reached their destination. All the houses looked like prisons, turning blank walls to the street with only a few heavily barred windows. They drove the mules into an enclosure in front of a large warehouse, then the carrier brought Byron and Campbell to the gates of the palace in the main square where he took leave of them and handed them over to the Captain of the Guard. They waited for a long while in the guard-room somewhat apprehensively, the interview with the arrogant blind governor of Valparaiso very present in their minds. A secretary came and informed them that the president, Don Joseph Manso, who was still working in his study, would soon be at liberty, and in the meantime they were invited to partake of a glass of wine. This both cheered and reassured them.

From the moment they were received by the president their troubles were at an end. He allowed them the freedom of the city, on parole, provided for their maintenance, and arranged for them to live with a hospitable countryman of theirs, Don Patricio Gedd, one of the leading physicians in Santiago, who was already entertaining Captain Cheap and Lieutenant Hamilton. They were welcomed with great kindness by the Spanish aristocracy. None of them resented the capture of their ships, or even the burning of Payta — they were used to having their towns burnt in the Indian wars — and the humane treatment of the prisoners made so deep an impression on them that the net result of Anson's warlike incursion was to add greatly to their feelings of friendship for England.

Shortly after their arrival the British officers were invited to dine with the president to meet Admiral Pizarro and his officers: this put them in an awkward situation as they had no suitable clothes, and yet they dared not refuse the invitation. Their difficulty was happily resolved when an officer belonging to Admiral Pizarro's squadron, whose name was Don Manuel de Guiror, called and offered them a loan of two thousand dollars without any conditions about how or when it was to be repaid. Don Manuel was a Spanish Grandee, a nobleman from Navarre and a Knight of Malta; he was also First Lieutenant of the *Asia* and therefore held the same position relative to Pizarro as Captain Cheap had to Anson at the beginning of the voyage. They accepted 600 dollars only, upon his acceptance of their draft for that amount on the Lords Commissioners of the Admiralty, payable by the British Consul in Lisbon. Captain Cheap put aside seventy dollars for emergency, gave himself, Byron and

Hamilton a hundred and fifty each, but Campbell only eighty: he considered that both Byron and Hamilton were gentlemen, and he himself too, of course, besides being senior officer, but he didn't see why the patroon should have as much money as themselves and get himself up like a lord. Campbell protested indignantly that they had all signed the draft and that his necessities were as great as theirs, but the captain stubbornly refused to pay him any more.

The most brilliant figure at the president's dinner table was naturally Admiral Don Pizarro. This distinguished nobleman, born in Zamora, was a descendant of Pizarro the Conquistador who had destroyed the kingdom of the Incas and enslaved the Indians of Peru. After the disaster to his fleet he had left his flagship in the River Plate and travelled overland to Chile to organise the coastal defences and take command of the fifty-gun ship *Esperanza*, the only unit of his fleet that had succeeded in doubling Cape Horn, some six months after the failure of the first attempt: he must have been an embarrassing guest for President Manso who had recently made a truce with the warlike Arraucos on his southern frontier and was attempting by peaceful means to weld Indians and Spaniards into a single nation: the name Pizarro, even after three generations, still stood as a symbol to all South American Indians for the hated oppressors of their country, the destroyers of their liberties. If Anson had succeeded in landing at Valdivia he would have found powerful allies.

The president entreated his guests to lay aside all ceremony and to consider themselves as much at home as if they were dining in England with intimate acquaintances; whereupon Captain Cheap asked Pizarro if Anson was still on the coast, and if so could he arrange for them to be exchanged or ransomed. Pizarro replied, after consulting with the president, that he would gladly deliver them to Anson as some small return for the civilities their own prisoners had received, but that no British ships had been reported on the coast for the past twelve months. The captain then asked if anything had been heard of his people in the longboat who had tried to return by the Straits of Magellan. Pizarro informed them that a small schooner with survivors from the *Wager* had arrived in the Brazils some months ago, a remarkable circumstance that had caused a sensation at the time: he promised that Captain Cheap would be supplied with all the information available about it.

A few days later, Don Manuel de Guiror called upon them again, bringing with him a report from the Spanish authorities upon the arrival of the *Speedwell*. Under Don Patricio's blossoming trees they read that she had sailed into the Rio Grande on the 28th January of the previous year after passing without charts through the Straits of Magellan and up the east coast of South America. It was stated that there were thirty men in her, but only the leaders of the expedition were named – Lieutenant Baynes, Mr Bulkeley and John Jones. For a long time after reading the report, Captain Cheap remained silent and distressed: he knew that eighty men had sailed with Mr Bulkeley in the longboat and the cutter, and he grieved that fifty of them had perished in a hazardous voyage undertaken only to avoid having to meet the enemy.

De Guiror was able to add a curious piece of information: he had heard in Buenos Aires that eight British seamen, said to be from the *Wager*, had been landed by the *Speedwell* on the Coast of Patagonia for food and water and, when they had sent supplies on board, she had sailed away without them and not returned. Four of them, it was said, had had their throats cut by the Indians: the other four had been carried off into captivity. When the time came to ransom them, the Indians refused to give up one of the men who was a Mulatto; because of his colour they considered him as one of themselves and imagined that he would have been ill-treated by the white men. Thus the identity of another possible survivor was established, for their only Mulatto was the Stepney-born John Duck who had offered Byron his woollen cap on the day they parted company. Captain Cheap at once wrote to a British merchant in Buenos Aires, a friend of Don Patricio's called Mr Lindsey, asking him to find out the names of the other men.

They also learned from De Guiror, what they could readily imagine, that the suffering of the Spanish seamen had been as great as their own. He said that they were at Maldonado in the River Plate when the Portuguese Governor of St Catherine's had sent them word that the British squadron had arrived there and would sail again for Cape Horn on the 3rd January. Admiral Pizarro, although he had only one month's stores on board, had immediately sailed in pursuit: on the 4th March, the day the British ships passed through the Straits of Le Maire and were driven back again, the Spaniards were in the same area and had been driven back even farther to the east. Threatened with famine in addition to their other trials they had returned to the River Plate; but the *Hermiona*, fifty-four guns, foundered in the gale, and the *Guipuscoa*, seventy-four guns, dismasted and under jury rig, was deliberately run ashore near St Catherine's by her crew who had mutinied. The loss of the *Wager*, therefore, was compensated by the loss of two larger enemy ships. The *Asia* had made two further unsuccessful attempts to get round Cape Horn, and was now lying dismasted off Montevideo.

Anson, after appearing off the island of Nuestra Señora de Socorro and finding none of his ships there, had proceeded to their more distant rendezvous, the island of Juan Fernandez, where he had been joined by the *Gloucester* and the *Tryal*. The little victualler, the *Anna*, pink, had been driven by the tempest into a bay to the north of the Cape of

Three Mountains and had lain there for two months to allow her sick and exhausted crew to recover before proceeding to Juan Fernandez: it was tempting to believe that Providence had sent her there, giving the men of the *Wager* a chance to reach her and save themselves, if they had all been united and had done their duty, and had taken the bold course that the captain had urged upon them.

CHAPTER

19

→»×«←

THE situation of Byron's shipmates who had reached the Brazils was radically different because they were free men, in theory at least, living in a country that was at peace with England. In this outpost of civilisation naval rank again took precedence, irrespective of ability: Lieutenant Baynes was naturally accepted as commander of the expedition by the governor. Mr Bulkeley was presented to him as the pilot: he had indeed completed his task when he brought the *Speedwell* to an anchor in the Rio Grande: all he had to do now was to get himself safely to England and justify himself to the authorities.

Three days after their arrival the governor came aboard the *Speedwell* with his staff to inspect her: he expressed his surprise that thirty souls could have been stowed in so small a vessel: when he was told that they had numbered seventy-one at the beginning of the voyage, it seemed to him amazing and beyond belief. Mr Bulkeley gave a demonstration of how they had secured themselves while steering, sitting down and clapping their feet against a four-inch rise. When the governor had viewed the vessel all over he told her crew that they were more welcome to him in the miserable condition in which they had arrived than if they had brought with them all the wealth of the world. He said that whenever they stood in need of anything they were to acquaint the commandant and their wants would be immediately supplied. He wished them all well and took his leave of them: to express their gratitude they manned the vessel and gave him three hearty cheers. The local inhabitants, men, women and children, flocked to see the little *Speedwell* in which, they had been told, so many souls had been wonderfully saved from the devouring waters, and they looked at the crew with a mixture of compassion and of horror at their condition.

Mr Bulkeley, taking advantage of the governor's good intentions towards them, applied to the commandant for a house, 'the Vessel in rainy Weather not being fit to lie in.' The commandant allocated one next to his own, and gave him the key: he took ashore with him Mr Cummins, John Jones, John Snow, Mr Oakley, and John Young the cooper. They removed their gear to their new habitation where, although there was no bedding and they had none of their own, they lodged very comfortably and heartily wished, Mr Bulkeley wrote, 'that all the Persons who survived the loss of the Ship were in so good a Situation as ourselves.' The cooper had become Mr Bulkeley's fast friend and admirer as a result of their experiences in the Straits of Magellan although he had been highly critical of him in the past, particularly on account of his share in the captain's arrest which he judged indefensible and 'undeniably an illegal and mutinous Proceedure.'

On the day following the governor's visit they became aware for the first time that all was not well in Rio Grande do Sul, as the little town of single-storey houses was called. It transpired that nearly all the men they had taken for officers because of their resplendent uniforms were in fact mutineers from the ranks who had turned out the commissioned officers and usurped their places — only the major and the commissary in charge of the stores were what they appeared to be. They discovered this because a brigadier arrived from St Catherine's, and the garrison who numbered about 1,000 ran out to meet him, assuming that he had come to redress their grievances: when they learned that he had only come for information about the *Speedwell* they detained him, and would not let him go back until he had agreed to send them their pay, which was twenty months in arrears, and a proper supply of food and clothing. The governor himself, it seems, had been threatened by the mutineers, but with great address he had maintained his position by convincing the soldiers that he was the champion of their rights and that the surest way to have their grievances redressed was to support his authority.

It came as a shock to the people of the *Speedwell*, who had imagined themselves to be in a land of plenty, to learn that those who had been so generous to them were themselves short of bread. Mr Bulkeley and his friends, seeing that their subsistence was threatened, and fearing that the governor's liberality would bring upon them the resentment of the garrison, went to him to discuss the situation. He told them there was sufficient meat and fish but that there was very little bread, and he sent them to the storekeeper to see for themselves how little there was: however, he gave them ten days' supply and promised that their allowance would be increased as soon as more flour came in. They agreed that this was reasonable and as much as they could expect. The men were equally pleased with the civility of the governor and with Mr Bulkeley's handling of the negotiations: John Young tells us he pleaded so earnestly 'and represented our Distress in so moving a Strain not only to the Governor but to the upstart Officers of the Garrison and the Commissary as well, that at last he prevailed upon them for as much Bread out of the Magazine as would suffice us near a Fortnight at an equal Quantity for each Man per Day as the Soldiers had on Duty: this was an Effect of his Eloquence for which we returned him a Thousand Blessings.'

The governor had told them that his Majesty's ships *Severn* and *Pearl* were at Rio de Janeiro in great distress:

these were the two ships of Anson's squadron that had failed to get round the Horn. Their crews had been so depleted by death that they had sent to England for more men and could not sail without them. Here was a way for the *Speedwell*'s crew to get to England and at the same time to be of service. They all went with Mr Bulkeley to see Lieutenant Baynes, and they urged him to arrange with the governor for them to be sent to St Catherine's, for they did not doubt that they would get a passage from there to Rio de Janeiro where their assistance was required on board the two distressed ships. The lieutenant said he had already spoken about this and that nothing could be done until a vessel came in.

A fortnight later Mr Bulkeley learned that a Portuguese pilot and two seamen were being sent to St Catherine's, so he entrusted to them the following letter which he addressed to the captain of the *Pearl*, who had been, for a short time, captain of the *Wager*:

To the Honourable Capt. *Murray*,
Commander of his Majesty's Ship the *Pearl*, at *Rio Janeiro*.
Honourable Sir,
I take it as a Duty incumbent on me to acquaint you, that his Majesty's Ship the *Wager* was wreck'd on a desolate Island on the Coast of *Patagonia*, in the Latitude of 47.00 S. and W Longitude from the Meridian of *London* 81:30, on the 14th of *May*, 1741. After lengthening the Long-Boat, and fitting her in the best Manner we could, launch'd her on the 13th of *October*, and embark'd and sailed on the 14th, with the Barge and Cutter, to the Number of eighty-one souls in all. Capt. *Cheep* – , at his own Request, tarried behind, with Lieutenant *Hamilton*, and Mr *Elliot* the Surgeon. After a long and fatiguing Passage, coming through the *Streights of Magellan*, we

arrived here the 28th *January*, 1741–2; bringing into this Port alive to the Number of thirty, *viz.*

    Robert Beans, Lieutenant
    John Bulkeley, Gunner
    John Cummins, Carpenter
    Robert Elliot, Surgeon's Mate
    John Jones, Master's Mate
    John Snow, ditto
    John Mooring, Boatswain's Mate
    John Young, Cooper
   William Oram, Carpenter's Crew
    John King, Boatswain
    Nicholas Griselham, Seaman
    Samuel Stook, ditto
    James Mac Cawle, ditto
    William Lane, ditto
    John Montgomery, ditto
    John George, ditto
    Richard East, ditto
    James Butler, ditto
    John Pitman, Seaman
    Job Barnes, ditto
    John Shoreham, ditto
    Thomas Edmunds, ditto
    Richard Powall, ditto
    Diego Findall, (the Portugueze Boy)

Capt. *Robert Pemberton*, of his Majesty's Land Forces
Lieutenant *Ewers* and *Fielding*, ditto
Vincent Oakley, Surgeon of ditto
And Two Marines.

All which are living at present, and waiting an Opportunity of a Passage in a *Portugueze* Vessel, our own not

* William Oram died in the hospital at Rio Grande on February 18th.

being in a Condition to proceed any farther, having no sails, and being so bad in all other respects, that the Governor will not suffer us to hazard our Lives in her; but hath promis'd to dispatch us in the very first Vessel that arrives in this Port; where we, with Impatience, are oblig'd to tarry. We humbly pay our Duty to Captain *Leg*, praying the Representation of this to him.

From,

Most Honourable Sir,

Yours, &c

Mr Bulkeley's next idea was to go himself to St Catherine's overland with Mr Cummins and John Young: the governor tried to dissuade them 'on Account of the Hazards of the Journey,' but finding them determined to go he at last gave them his permission and promised them a guide. Three days later, when Mr Bulkeley was trying to sell his watch to defray their expenses, the governor sent him word that four ships were on passage from St Catherine's to the Rio Grande and that he ought to wait for them. Ten days later they arrived. In one of them was the brigadier: he had faithfully kept his agreement and brought money and provisions for the soldiers of the garrison, and also a pardon which he persuaded them to accept. The temporary officers shouldered their firelocks and returned to the ranks, the regular officers took over their commands again, and peace and tranquillity were restored. These ships also brought the news that the *Severn* and the *Pearl* were no longer at Rio de Janeiro: they had sailed about five weeks ago for the island of Barbados in the West Indies.

Because Mr Bulkeley was anxious to get to England before Lieutenant Baynes who, he felt, would prejudice his case with the authorities, and the lieutenant was equally anxious to tell his version of their story first, they both applied to go in the first vessel that should be freighted and ready to sail. Mr Bulkeley's contention was that the lieutenant who, unlike the rest of them, had been sure of his half pay since the *Wager* struck, should not go off first and leave most of the people behind for whom he was responsible, but he saw no reason why he himself should not endeavour to get to England as soon as he could: he rushed off to put his case before the governor, and the lieutenant followed protesting that only half of them could go at a time. The governor ruled that all those who had applied to go to St Catherine's by land were to sail first, and that they might go on board when they pleased; but as the vessel did not belong to the King of Portugal but was privately owned, they would have to buy their own provisions and pay for their passage. This put an entirely new complexion on the affair, and the disputants had to consult together not to decide who should go first but how they could contrive to go at all. They thought of selling the *Speedwell* but found she wouldn't bring in enough, as the captain of the vessel was demanding forty shillings a head.

Next morning they learned that the brigadier had made all the arrangements for their passage: Mr Bulkeley and nine others were to go in the first vessel with their fares paid and everything provided, while Lieutenant Baynes was to wait with the rest of the people until another vessel should be ready.

On Sunday, the 28th March, Mr Bulkeley went on board the *St Catherine's*, brigantine, with the carpenter, the boatswain, the two mates, the surgeon of the marines, the cooper and six of the people. They sailed on the 31st with the wind at west, a fine gale and clear weather. On Monday the 12th April at 8 a.m. they entered the harbour of Rio de Janeiro, the jewel but not yet the capital of Brazil.

Here at last they were really back in civilisation. Their outward circumstances could hardly have been better, but because they were no longer forced to work together for their own salvation, their inner tensions and conflicts became more apparent, particularly between Mr Bulkeley and the boatswain. On the morning after their arrival they were all taken before the governor, whose palace stood on an oblong plaza open to the sea near the landing-place. After a sympathetic enquiry into their misfortunes he sent for a Dutch surgeon who spoke very good English, and appointed him to be their interpreter and to look after their affairs as if he were their consul. He said they should have a convenient house with an allotment of fire and candle and a daily allowance for their maintenance. He had evidently noticed that the boatswain and Mr Bulkeley were not on good terms, for before dismissing them he solemnly charged them to preserve harmony between themselves and to avoid causing any disturbance among the townspeople. They promised to observe his wishes; but the very next day there was a violent quarrel and they began fighting. Mr Bulkeley and Seaman East were arrested by the Town Guard. The governor, after enquiring into the causes of the disturbance, released the gunner and kept the seaman in prison.

The people of the *Wager* had split up into two parties, reflecting the antagonism between their leaders. The boatswain, since his humiliation at the hands of the captain, had been thought of as a person of little consequence, but he was now the senior officer of their little group and, as such, he was entitled to take command, always supposing that they were still under naval discipline which Mr Bulkeley, since the loss of the *Wager*, had always denied. Most of the seamen supported the boatswain, and their ranks were swelled by English and Irish deserters picked up on the waterfront. Fearing that the continual brawling would lead to bloodshed, Mr Bulkeley and his friends left the accommodation provided by the governor and took a house for themselves two miles from the city. Here, they thought, they would be able to live in peace until they found an opportunity to embark for Europe, but they soon realised that they were in a worse position than before, for the boatswain sent his ruffians after them with orders to get hold of the journal. Mr Bulkeley put them off with fair words and rum punch, but they returned during the night, hammered on the door, and threatened to bring the rest of the gang to force an entry. The house was in an isolated position, surrounded by fields. As soon as the coast was clear, Mr Bulkeley and his friends, thoroughly alarmed now, not only for the journal but for their lives, left it and took lodgings in the middle of a fishing village where they thought the inhabitants would prevent any open violence. They also appealed to the 'consul' for help, and he arranged a passage for Mr Bulkeley, the carpenter and the cooper in a ship that was due to sail for Bahia and Lisbon. She was called the *Saint Tubas*, a Brazil ship carrying twenty-eight guns, Captain Orego. They sailed on the 21st May, and they anchored on the 7th June before the City of Bahia, capital of Brazil. This should have been a good move for Mr Bulkeley: not only was he safe from the boatswain but he had gained about 700 miles over his rivals in the race to get to England first. He found, however, that the *Saint Tubas* was expected to stay at Bahia for several months and that there was no other ship there ready to sail for Europe.

They were so accustomed to the courtesy of the Portuguese officials that they were taken aback to find that here everything was different and that no one cared what became of them. The viceroy refused to provide lodging or maintenance, and he would do nothing to help them. In order to live, Mr Bulkeley was obliged to sell his watch. When they were at their wit's end, Captain Orego came to their rescue and lent them a substantial sum of money against bills drawn on the British Consul at Lisbon. They had not been long in Bahia when they had the mortification of learning that one of his Majesty's ships, the *Active*, with three store ships intended for the relief of the *Severn* and the *Pearl*, had called in at Rio de Janeiro and taken all the rest of the *Wager*'s people on board. They had sailed for England via the West Indies.

CHAPTER

20

-->>><<<-

AFTER three miserable months in Bahia without any relief from the viceroy or from the inhabitants, Mr Bulkeley, the carpenter and the cooper embarked once more in the *Saint Tubas* on the 11th September and sailed for Lisbon. The journal of their passage across the Atlantic, which lasted two and a half months, contains little of interest until they were in sight of the Rock of Lisbon, or Cabo da Roca, a high beetling cliff, the most westerly point of Portugal and of Europe: at four o'clock that day, the 23rd November, it was blowing a very hard gale and the ship was standing to under a foresail with her head to southward. At six it blew a storm, the foresail split, so they were obliged to keep before the wind, which was running her right on shore. The ship had sprung a leak, and the people gave her over for lost; they all left off pumping and fell to prayers, crying out to their saints for deliverance, offering all they had in the world for their lives and neglecting all means to save themselves. Mr Bulkeley says he and the carpenter 'could by no Means relish this Behaviour, we begged the People for God's sake to go to the Pumps, telling them we had a Chance to save our Lives while we kept the Ship above Water, that we ought not to suffer the Ship to sink while we could keep her free. The Captain and Officers, hearing us pressing them so earnestly, left off Prayers, and intreated the Men to keep the Pumps going, accordingly we went to pumping, and preserved ourselves and the Ship: In half an Hour afterwards the Wind shifted to the WNW., then the Ship lay South which would clear the Course along the Shore. Had the Wind not shifted we must in half an Hour's time have run the Ship ashore.' And John Young writes: 'We English under God by our Labour and Skill preserved the Vessel and the Lives of all on board again and again, but our Deliverances were by the Captain, and the whole Crew mostly, devoutly ascribed to a She-saint whose Name I have forgotten.'

On Saturday the 28th November they entered the Tagus and anchored off the City of Lisbon. On the following morning the captain, the officers, the Spanish Don and all the people of the *Saint Tubas*, men and boys, walked barefoot in procession, carrying the split foresail, to the church of *Nuestra Senhora Boa Mortua*, Our Lady Deliverer from Death, which was a good mile distant from the landing-place: they made a considerable offering at her shrine: they also presented the foresail and redeemed it from Our Lady for eighteen moydores, nearly ninety pounds sterling. The Englishmen went immediately to the *Change*. Mr Bulkeley tells us that he was pretty well known to some of the gentlemen of the English factory in Lisbon; but they were received coolly enough. 'When we informed them that we were three of the unfortunate People that were cast away in the *Wager*, and that we came here in one of the Brazil Ships, and wanted to embrace the first Opportunity for England; they told us that the Lieutenant had been before us, that he was gone Home in the Packet-Boat, and left us a very indifferent Character.' This was exactly what Mr Bulkeley had feared: he had covered himself pretty well against a possible charge of mutiny by always appearing as a subordinate, or as the voice of the people, and by getting Lieutenant Baynes to take the, strictly limited, command, but he couldn't prevent him from claiming that he couldn't have acted otherwise than he did because the gunner and his friends had the real power. He answered the merchants, who were advising him not to return to England lest he should suffer death for mutiny, that the very person who accused him was the ringleader and chief mutineer, and that the lieutenant would find it much harder to vindicate his own actions than to fasten any just imputation upon others: and that he would be able to give but a very poor account of what had happened as he had kept no journal nor troubled to take any observations since the wreck of their vessel: but he, Mr Bulkeley, had kept a journal which was an impartial account of all their proceedings. He asked the gentlemen of the Factory to read it: several of them did so, and professed themselves very well pleased with it, commending his care and exactness. During his stay in Lisbon they treated him and his friends 'with exceeding kindness and benevolence.'

Greatly encouraged by the favourable impression the journal had made upon people already prejudiced against them, they embarked for England in his Majesty's ship, the *Stirling Castle*, on the 20th December, 1742: they reached Spithead on the 1st January. They thought of nothing now but of going to their homes in Portsmouth to be reunited to their wives and families; but they were told by the captain of the ship that they must remain on board until he knew the pleasure of the Lords of the Admiralty concerning them. Their wives, however, were permitted to come on board: they were overjoyed to see their husbands whom they had long given up for lost, miraculously restored to them: at the same time they were dismayed to find that, in effect, they were prisoners. Mr Bulkeley endeavoured to console them, saying that they had done nothing to offend their lordships and that, if things were not carried on, after the *Wager* was cast away, with that order and regularity which is strictly observed in the navy, necessity had driven them out of the common road. 'Our case was singular,' he explains in his journal. 'Since the loss of the Ship, our chiefest Concern was for the Preservation of our Lives and Liberties;

to accomplish which, we acted according to the Dictates of Nature, and the best of our Understanding.'

They were transferred to his Majesty's ship *Duke*, which also lay at Spithead, and then, a fortnight later, orders came that they were to be allowed their liberty. They immediately landed and went to their homes, having been absent two years and six months.

After he had spent a few days with his family, Mr Bulkeley went to London with Mr Cummins: his object was first of all to clear his name with the Admiralty, and secondly he was anxious to obtain further employment as he had earned nothing since the *Wager* was cast away. He left his journal at the Admiralty Office, together with a request that the authors of it should be tried and either acquitted or condemned, which was their right as British subjects – he had associated his friend Mr Cummins with it as co-author and as another witness to its authenticity. They heard nothing for some days. Then they were informed that the journal was too large ever to be perused, and time would hardly permit the looking of it over, therefore they should draw up a narrative from it, giving an account of the loss of the ship, the murder of the midshipman, the confining of the captain and the leaving of him behind. They did so, and sent it in with a letter saying that they had 'strictly complied with the Desire of the unfortunate Captain Cheap whose last Injunction was to give a faithful Narrative to your Lordships; we have writ it without Favour or Prejudice, and wherever it is deficient, do refer to the Journal. After the unfortunate loss of the *Wager*, we knew, if ever Providence should bring us to our Country again that we should be called to Account. Therefore we have omitted nothing material, at least in our Journal.'

Again they waited, and again they requested trial before the men whom they wished to call as witnesses should be dispersed in various ships sailing to distant parts. Their lordships were at first disposed to comply with this reasonable request, but they were unwilling for judgement to be based only on the information contained in Mr Bulkeley's journal: the narrative presented by Lieutenant Baynes was neither very full nor very illuminating, nor did it agree in all respects with the journal: he suppressed, for instance, the fact that the captain had done everything in his power to lead his men north to join the commodore – the main subject of dispute between him and Mr Bulkeley – and substituted, 'The Captain was for staying (at Wager Island) to see if Commodore Anson might not call there and take us in, but the Majority being for going away in the Longboat, Dissensions arose, and the Captain shot one of the most mutinous dead on the Spot. Having afterwards lengthened the Longboat by Pieces of the Wreck, and stow'd some Provisions in her, the greatest Part went aboard, leaving the Capt. and some others behind.' Their lordships finally decided that it would be inadvisable to hold any enquiry until the arrival of Commodore Anson or of Captain Cheap. They also decided that none of the officers should receive wages or be employed in his Majesty's service until everything concerning the loss of the *Wager* had been cleared up. Nothing had been heard of Captain Cheap, but some account of the commodore's activities in the Pacific and in the far east had filtered through from Spanish sources: they knew now that he had successfully rounded Cape Horn, taken a number of prizes, and raided and burnt Payta. 'We hope,' Mr Bulkeley concludes his journal, 'when the Commodore shall arrive that the Characters he will give us will be of service to us: He was very well acquainted with the Behaviour of every Officer in his Squadron, and will certainly give an Account of them accordingly.'

In order to enlist public sympathy, and also to earn some money to support his wife and children, he wanted his journal to be read as widely as possible. He applied to the Lords of the Admiralty for permission to publish it, and was told that it was his own property and he could do what he liked with it. Jacob Robinson, publisher at the Golden Lion in Ludgate Street, offered them what they considered to be a substantial sum of money for the rights, and it came out later in the same year, 1743. It was dedicated, without permission, to Vice-Admiral Vernon, the greatest naval hero of the day: this idea had been suggested to them by the admiration expressed by a Spanish Don, passenger in the *Saint Tubas*, for the justice and humanity the admiral had shown at the capture of Porto Bello. On the title page there was a quotation from the Caroline poet Edmund Waller which reflected the author's anxiety about the forthcoming enquiry:

'Bold were the Men who on the Ocean first
Spread the new Sails, when Shipwreck was the worst:
More Dangers Now from Men alone we find,
Than from the Rocks, the Billows, and the Wind.'

The book was well received and achieved its purpose: the readers' sympathies were with the authors, and Captain Cheap's harshness and his unreasonableness in desiring to join the commodore were generally censured.

On the 15th June of the following year, 1744, Lieutenant Denis of the *Centurion* arrived in London with dispatches announcing that Anson had reached Spithead with his holds full of Spanish treasure: he had captured the fabulously wealthy galleon *Nuestra Señora de Covadonga*, sold her at Macao in the Canton River, and returned to England via the Cape of Good Hope, having circumnavigated the world. After rounding the Horn he had waited in vain for the rest of his squadron off the island of Nuestra Señora de Socorro and then off Valdivia; and all the time his men were dying of scurvy at the rate of eight or ten a day. By the time he had reached the pleasant green island of Juan Fernandez far out in the Pacific and landed his sick, only 213 men remained alive out of the original 500. He was joined there later by the *Gloucester*, the *Tryal* and the *Anna*, pink. Of the *Gloucester*'s men only ninety had survived, and these were almost too weak to handle her. Altogether in the three men-o'-war there were now only 335 men out of the original 961: at this date a larger proportion of the shipwrecked *Wager*'s crew were alive than in any other ship in the squadron because they had got ashore and eaten wild celery which immediately cured their scurvy. As soon as his men were sufficiently recovered, Anson took the *Centurion* out and captured a Spanish merchant ship, the *Nuestra Señora del Monte Carmelo*: from papers captured in her he learned that the great British expedition to the Caribbean had miscarried: it had failed to take Panama, and nine-tenths of the soldiers, including their commander Major-General Lord Cathcart, had died of fever. Anson therefore was left alone and without a base in the Pacific from which to operate, for it was out of the question to capture Valdivia or any other port with his depleted crews and without the military stores that were missing in the *Wager*: he had no choice but to turn the expedition into a piratical raid in the style of the Old Elizabethans. He had to destroy his prizes as he had no crews for them, and for the same reason, and also because he had no repair facilities, he had eventually to destroy the *Gloucester* and the *Tryal* and the *Anna*, pink, and take their crews on board the *Centurion*. Even then, when he came upon the galleon and engaged her he had insufficient men to fire a broadside.

On the 4th July, 1744, the captured treasure was carried through the streets of London to the Tower in thirty-two waggons with music playing and colours flying, including those taken in the prizes. The officers of the *Centurion* led the way with swords drawn; the crew followed, guarding the waggons: there were 298 chests of silver, eighteen of gold, and twenty barrels of gold dust, and the whole was valued at £1,600,000. The citizens flocked to see the procession. Commodore Anson with the King and the Prince and Princess of Wales watched it pass from a house in Pall Mall. Each member of the original crew received £171 prize money. All this caused a great sensation. There had been no victories to celebrate since the capture of Porto Bello, and Anson's exploit did much to restore public confidence in the navy. Anson himself was tired, and oppressed by the terrible mortality among his crews. 'The service of the expedition being at an end,' he wrote to the Duke of Newcastle, Secretary of State, 'I desire your Grace's leave to return to London for the recovery of my health, which is greatly impaired by the fatigues and hardships of this long voyage, in which I have buried 462 men in the *Centurion*.'

Perhaps the greatest good that came out of the tragedy was that Anson was promoted Admiral of the White and appointed to the Board of the Admiralty where he set to work to reform the maladministration that had delayed the sailing of his expedition and ruined its fairest prospects.

The men who returned in the *Centurion* were naturally critical of the *Wager*'s crew for going home through the Straits of Magellan instead of attempting to join them when the commodore was so desperately short of men, and public sympathy veered round in favour of Captain Cheap. Still no enquiry was held. Mr Bulkeley, and the rest of the officers, remained out of employment.

About two years after the publication of his journal, Mr Bulkeley was asked to go down to Plymouth in order to bring up to London the old forty-gun ship *Saphire* which was to be fitted out as a privateer. He applied to the Board of the Admiralty for permission to accept the offer. 'My Lords,' he wrote, 'I humbly beg Leave to acquaint your

Lordships that I have an offer made me by some Gentlemen of this City which I think it my Duty to accept, and at the same Time would not accept or attempt to go abroad without acquainting your Lordships, lest your Lordships should imagine I had flown from Justice. I am willing and desirous of abiding by the strictest Trial of my Conduct in regard to Captain Cheap and hope to live to see him Face to Face, but in the meantime do hope that I am not to be left on the Earth to perish when I can be of service to my King, my Country, and my Family. Your Lordships' most dutiful and obedient etc. John Bulkeley.' In reply he received a document, dated the 11th June, 1745, giving protection from impressment for forty men to bring the *Saphire*, Commander John Bulkeley, from Plymouth to the Thames. It was signed by four members of the Board of Admiralty, including Anson.

He proceeded to Plymouth, signed on forty men, rigged the *Saphire* with jury masts, and sailed in the middle of July in company with three merchantmen. Next morning they saw two French privateers in chase of some more merchantmen to the southward: they gave over the chase and approached the *Saphire*, whereupon the three merchantmen with her hauled their wind in order to run their vessels ashore – but Mr Bulkeley bore down to the privateers, hoisted the King's colours, ran out ten guns – all that he had – on the starboard side, and fired a shot. Then he ordered his men to haul up all the lower deck ports at once as if he were about to fire a broadside. The privateers, evidently thinking that the *Saphire* was a man-o'-war in commission that had been dismasted, instantly made off. By this subterfuge he not only saved all the merchantmen but brought his own ship safely into the Thames.

CHAPTER

21

->>><<<-

W HEN Captain Cheap had been in Santiago for about two years, President Manso sent for him and informed him that he had at last been able to arrange for an exchange of prisoners: there was a French ship, he said, lying in Valparaiso bound for Europe, and he suggested that the captain should negotiate for a passage in her for himself and his officers. This was the *Lys*, a frigate belonging to St Malo: she was a converted merchantman with sixteen guns and a crew of sixty.

The captain and Hamilton were overjoyed that their term of exile was drawing to a close: they immediately started on their round of farewell visits. Campbell, however, declared that he would on no account go home in the same ship as Captain Cheap: he still resented the unequal division of the money that had been provided for their common needs. To make matters worse, the captain had received a further sum of money, this time from Mr Lindsey in Buenos Aires, and he had shared it only with Byron and Hamilton. Campbell had asked for his share, and when it was refused he had made an angry scene, left Don Patricio's hospitable roof and gone to live with a Spanish family where he had been kindly entertained. His shipmates had seen little of him since that day, but they heard that he had changed his religion and married a Spanish girl. Admiral Pizarro, who was intending to return overland to Buenos Aires to put the *Asia* into commission again, offered him a passage in her to Spain: when he gratefully accepted, Captain Cheap immediately assumed that he had deserted to the enemy.

Byron had changed out of all recognition from the emaciated, half-starved youth of eighteen who had come to Santiago: he was now a full-grown man, six feet tall, broad, strong and self-confident. He had made many friends during the past two years, but he had no sooner heard that he was to be sent home than he became conscious of a painful longing to see England again, and Isabel and smoky London. He was in a fever to be gone, but he parted with great regret from Don Patricio whom he called 'the man of the most extensive humanity I have ever met.' When all the farewells had been said, and all the formalities complied with, he set out with Captain Cheap and Lieutenant Hamilton on his long journey home: this time there were mules to ride, and none to drive.

They sailed from Valparaiso about the 20th December, 1744, four years and three months after leaving England: they were still prisoners on parole because France had now come in to the war and was Spain's ally. As the parched escarpments and the white fort of Valparaiso receded and became blurred in the sunshine, Byron began pacing the deck impatiently as if the cliffs of Dover were just below the horizon: but the current and the winds proved contrary: two months later they were back in Valparaiso, the *Lys* having sprung a dangerous leak, and part of the cargo had to be discharged before the carpenter could reach it.

Meanwhile Admiral Pizarro, taking Campbell with him and four of his own officers, had already left Santiago: they had set out on mules, on the 20th January, 1745, accompanied by a train of 200 pack mules. On the first day they rode forty miles, crossing a plain to the foot of a bare mountain: for the next five days they made their way slowly up a steep zig-zag path, and hardly the least green thing appeared to relieve the grey harshness of the rock. In some places the path was merely a ledge scarcely seven inches across cut into the cliff face at a dizzy height above a river cañon: a mule in front of Campbell slipped and plunged over the precipice: it was dashed to pieces many hundred feet below, and its load scattered. Altogether twenty mules were lost, and two drivers died of exposure in the intense cold and bitter wind. When they reached the top of the pass, Campbell suffered severely from mountain sickness, which was like sea sickness: they were more than ten thousand feet high, and there were snow summits as high again towering above them. The descent was no less difficult: it took them another five days to reach the plain and the little town of Mendoza in the Argentine where a river makes the land fertile. Here they rested three days. Then, with a strong escort to protect them from the Indians, they started for Buenos Aires, Pizarro in an ox wagon and the rest on mules. The distance was 400 leagues. For the first 200 leagues there was only desert and scrub, with no trees, and only in one place was any fresh water to be had. When they approached the River Plate the country was transformed: there was grass with herds of cattle, and trees, and then corn and vineyards. Seven weeks after leaving Mendoza they were in Buenos Aires.

The *Lys* sailed again from Valparaiso on the 1st March, 1745. The season was already far advanced for passing Cape Horn, and in order to reach it they had to stand a hundred and twenty leagues to westward out into the Pacific because the prevailing winds along the coast were against them. They had passed the island of Juan Fernandez before they got a wind they could make any southing with. When they had reached the latitude of 46° south they met with a violent gale at west which obliged them to lie to under a reefed foresail for several days: after spending so long in the delightful climate of Santiago the cold was almost insupportable. Before they got round Cape Horn they had a succession of hard gales with a prodigious sea and constant snow and mist, but this time they had the westerly winds astern and they were driven the way they wanted to go.

When they had doubled the Cape and reached the South Atlantic they won their way only slowly to the northward, for the ship was a heavy-going thing and never went above six knots. On the 27th May they crossed the Equator; then, finding that they were running short of water and that it would be impossible for them to reach Europe without a further supply, they shaped a course for the West Indies. They expected to sight Martinique on the 1st July, but there was no sign of it, and they couldn't tell whether they were too far to the east or to the west. They stood to the northward until they sighted Porto Rico, and found that they had narrowly escaped shipwreck by driving through the Grenadines without sighting them on the night of the 30th June, a long stretch of shoalwater with small islands and rocks lying between the larger islands of Grenada and St Vincent. They now resolved to reach Cape François by passing between Porto Rico and San Domingo. On the 5th July when Byron was walking the quarterdeck, Captain Cheap came out of the cabin and told him that he had just seen a beef barrel go by the ship: he was sure that it had lately been thrown overboard and he would venture any wager that they would see an English cruiser before long. About half an hour later they saw two sail in chase of them. The French and the Spaniards began to look alarmed, and the Englishmen's hopes rose of being at last delivered from their enemies. Soon the wind fell, and all the ships were becalmed, but not before their pursuers had come so close that it could be plainly discerned that they were British men-o'-war; the one a two-decker, and the other a twenty-gun ship. The French now had thoughts that when a breeze should spring up they would run themselves ashore on Porto Rico, but when they came to consider what a set of bandits inhabited that island, and that they had nearly two million dollars on board beside a rich cargo, they feared that they would have their throats cut for the sake of the plunder and they decided to hold their original course. In the evening a breeze sprung up and the two ships approached amazingly fast. The French officers went to their cabins and filled their pockets with what was most valuable: the men put on their best clothes, and many of them brought Byron little lumps of gold, saying that they would rather he should benefit by them than their pursuers. He told them there was time enough to think of that: but he thought they were as surely taken as if the British were already on board. Night fell, but there was a fine bright moon, and they expected every moment to see the ships alongside; but they saw nothing of them during the night. When the sky grew light again there were no other ships in sight, even from the masthead.

In the afternoon of the 8th July they came to an anchor in the harbour of Cape François in San Domingo. Here, in this beautiful and well-cultivated island, famous for having the finest trees in the West Indies, and for its plantations of sugar, coffee and tobacco, they waited for two months while a convoy assembled. On the 6th September the whole fleet put to sea to the number of fifty-three sail, five of them French men-o'-war. They were shadowed all the way across the Atlantic by two British privateers, waiting to pick up stragglers, but the convoy kept in such close formation that none was lost. On the 27th they sighted Cape Ortegal, on the north coast of Spain. On the 31st they were off Brest, the greatest French naval base and arsenal except Toulon. In the approaches to it there were black menacing rocks with the tide swirling round and over them; but by keeping close to the southern shore the narrow entrance that lay between high cliffs was safely negotiated, and they came to an anchor in the fine harbour at three in the afternoon; it was crowded with ships being fitted out for the invasion of England.

The three returning exiles looked round eagerly for a neutral vessel that might take them across the Channel, but they were ordered to remain on board while permission was sought from Paris to allow them to land. They were left alone in the ship with only a few guards. No lights or fires were permitted because of the proximity of powder hulks. In the general haste and preparation no arrangements had been made to supply the prisoners, but some of the *Lys's* officers returning to the ship discovered their plight and brought them food and wine. A week later they were taken ashore and lodged in Landernau, a small town with tree-lined quays and an old bridge, eight miles from Brest. Here they learned that Anson had returned safely to England in June of the previous year. The weeks slipped by. To their repeated requests to the Intendant at Brest that they should be allowed to return to England they got always the same answer, that they were prisoners of the King of Spain and could not be released without authority from Madrid.

*   *   *

Campbell had been living in Buenos Aires on parole for about six months when he received orders to join the *Asia* off Montevideo, about thirty leagues down the River Plate. He boarded her on the 13th October, 1745, and found his shipmates Isaac Morris, Samuel Cooper and John Andrews already there: they had been held prisoners in her for the past year after being ransomed from the Indians by the Governor of Buenos Aires, Don Domingo Rosses, for thirty dollars a head, a decorated waistcoat and a few other trifles. They told Campbell the story of their adventures, and confirmed that the Indians had refused to give up John Duck: the tribe he was with had wandered far into the interior, so they thought he had no chance at all of ever seeing England again. They said they had been treated with greater humanity by the Indians than by their fellow Christians, except that they had not been allowed to bring

249

their Spanish wives and children with them. On board the *Asia*, they said, they were more like slaves than prisoners of war: they were forced to do all the dirty work, swab and clean the decks fore and aft every morning; and after the work was done they were confined between decks with a sentinel over them as though they were criminals. There were sixteen other English prisoners on board, survivors of a merchant ship, the *Philip*, Captain Penkethman, that had been arrested by the Spaniards for trading in their waters. Their usage was so bad that they had made an attempt to escape, but only Morris and one other had succeeded in eluding the guards and lowering themselves into the river. Before they had swum halfway to the shore, a gun was fired from the ship and they knew that they had been discovered. They scrambled ashore and walked till two in the morning, hoping to find a Portuguese settlement, and then they lay down to rest among the rushes: Morris was entirely naked, but the other man had a shirt. Their feet were so swollen by now, and full of thorns, that they could go no farther. Soon after daylight they met with some men on horseback belonging to the plantations, to whom they surrendered themselves. Next day they were handed over to some soldiers who had been sent in pursuit of them, and brought back to the ship. They were put in the stocks, neck and heels, for four hours every day for a fortnight.

The *Asia* put to sea soon after Campbell had joined her. Admiral Pizarro had thirty-two commissioned officers with him, most of them from ships of his squadron that had been lost, and a crew of 444 including twelve Indians who were being taken to Spain to serve as galley slaves: their chief, Gallidana, was cruelly flogged because he would not, or could not, go aloft. One of them secretly visited the English prisoners and invited them to join in an attack on the Spaniards, but they would not: they were being carried towards their homes whereas the Indians were being carried away from theirs, which made a difference, and they thought that such an attempt would have no chance of success.

During their third night at sea Campbell heard thudding on the deck, and he left his cabin to see what was amiss: going up the after ladder he was knocked off it, and he saw dead and wounded men lying around him. The cry of 'A mutiny!' was raised: the Indians had suddenly risen against their persecutors. They had made boleros from the double-headed shot of the small quarterdeck guns secured with thongs secretly cut from the rawhides which formed part of the cargo, and with these deadly weapons they had cleared the quarterdeck. Pizarro and his officers barricaded themselves in the wardroom where there were arms but no ammunition: most of his crew hid among the cattle that were carried for fresh meat in the waist, or climbed into the rigging. For two hours the Indians were in complete control of the ship. Then the Spaniards, finding that the English had not joined the mutiny, began to recover from their panic: some ammunition was lowered in a bucket to one of the wardroom portholes, so the officers were able to load their pistols; Campbell and some other Scottish and Irish officers formed up on the forecastle, and a combined attack was made on the Indians. They resisted bravely with blood-curdling war-whoops until Gallidana was killed by a pistol shot, and then they all jumped into the sea. Eleven Spaniards lay dead, including the master and two of his mates; a Jesuit priest and thirty-eight of the crew were wounded, five of whom afterwards died.*

On the 20th January, 1746, the *Asia* arrived at Corcubion, about five leagues to the south of Cape Finisterre, and then went round to Ferrol. Campbell was ordered to Madrid for an interview with the Minister of the Marine: Isaac Morris

* Walter, in his account of Anson's voyage, calls this chief Orellana, but it seems most unlikely that he would have taken the name of a well-known Spanish conquistador who was one of Pizarro's lieutenants in the conquest of Peru. Campbell calls him Gallidana, which is likely to be nearer the original.

and his friends were taken ashore and lodged in a prison where they remained for fifteen days chained together and living on bread and water. Then they were transferred to the Castle of San Anton, a prison for thieves and felons on a rocky island at the entrance to the Port of Corunna.

Byron and his companions were still at Landernau, apparently forgotten. Some British non-combatant prisoners who were being exchanged had passed through the town on their way to the cartel ship, and one of them had offered to take a letter to England for Captain Cheap. He took advantage of this opportunity to write to Anson. He began by congratulating him on his safe arrival in England, and then went on to give a brief account of the mutiny of the *Wager*'s crew. 'You are no doubt already informed,' he wrote, 'of some of our misfortunes, because I have been told that some of the officers and men are got home, but they know only a few of them and probably have not told the truth, for what can be expected of such poltroons who, rather than do their duty by endeavouring to join you (which might easily have been done) and look the enemy in the face; chose to expose themselves to the fatigue of so long a navigation, and perishing of hunger: after most inhumanly abandoning us and destroying at their departure everything they thought could be of any use to us that they could not carry with them.

'However, sir, I will say no more upon that head until I have the happiness of seeing you. Only give me leave to add that if the rest of the Marine Officers had done their duty as well as Mr Hamilton who is here with me, I have very good grounds to believe I should have brought the mutineers to reason; and although we miscarried in that and some other subsequent projects, yet I hope you will be persuaded it was not from lack of inclination.' He asked Anson to use his influence to effect their release, and ended, 'Messrs Biron and Hamilton (my faithful companions and fellow sufferers) beg leave to kiss your hands. Your most humble and most obedient servant, David Cheap. This was dated the 12th December, 1745.

Six weeks later an order came from the Court of Spain to allow them to return home by the first ship that offered. They made enquiries and learned that there was a Dutch ship ready to sail at Morlaix on the north coast of Brittany, so they travelled to that town: it was a twenty-five-mile ride through pleasantly wooded country – but they had been misinformed. Another six weeks went by before they managed to arrange a passage with the captain of a Dutch dogger, a very common type of trading vessel of about 150 tons, similar to a ketch with a main and a mizzen mast. The captain, who insisted on being paid in advance, agreed to land them at Dover. They went aboard, and when they had dropped down the river into Morlaix Roads, a French privateer that was almost ready to sail hailed them and told them to come to an anchor, and that if they offered to sail before her, she would sink them: she feared that the dogger might inform some British patrolling man-o'-war that a privateer was about to put to sea.

They lay three days in Morlaix Roads cursing the Frenchman, but at last she sailed, and they were at liberty to do the same. They had a long uncomfortable passage but at last, about the ninth day just before sunset, they saw Dover. They reminded the Dutchman of his agreement to land them there, and he said he would: but at daybreak they found that they were again off the coast of France. They complained loudly of this piece of villainy and were insisting on his returning to Dover when an English man-o'-war appeared to windward and presently bore down to them. She sent her boat on board with an officer who informed them that the man-o'-war was the *Squirrel*, Captain Masterton. They went on board of her, and Captain Masterton, when he had learned their identity, immediately sent one of the cutters he had with him to land them at Dover, which she did that afternoon.

When the cutter, having threaded its way through the harbour crowded with schooners, brigantines, smacks, local hoys and bluff-bowed billy boys, which were north-country traders, came alongside the quay, the three travel-stained officers became uncomfortably aware of their strange appearance. Still wearing their Spanish finery, now sadly tarnished, and enormous boots and hats they had acquired in France, they looked more like pirates than like English gentlemen. The seamen, fish-wives and hangers-on who inhabited the quay, obviously expected the crew of the cutter to march them up the long dusty way to the grim castle, or straight to the town gallows, and they seemed disappointed when they were allowed to land and go freely about their business. Followed by a swarm of children whooping and shouting, 'Monseer! Monseer! Pigs! Frenchies!' they made their way to the old town, whose clustered chimneys smoked under the white cliffs: they selected one of the inns whose creaking signs stretched right across the road, and enjoyed their first English meal for upwards of five years. Captain Cheap and Hamilton would have put up there for the night, but Byron could not rest a mere seventy-five miles from the goal they had been endeavouring for so many months to reach, and he persuaded them to start at once for London.

So they took post horses and rode up the pleasant valley of the Dour. At Lydden, where the road went steeply down into a chalky bottom, they passed an eastward-running lane which led to the Church of Knowlton where Sir John Narborough had been laid to rest whose book of voyages, lent to Byron by Captain Cheap, gave the mutineers the idea of attempting the passage of the Straits of Magellan. The captain had never reproached him for the use that had been made of the book, and Byron thought no more about it; but as they slowly ascended the steep road leading to Bramham Down and night closed behind them over churches and villages, and the bitter March wind moaned through the gorse and dead bracken, he remembered that he would soon be meeting Mr Bulkeley again, and John Jones, and he wondered which of the rest of his shipmates had survived.

When they reached Canterbury they went up the High Street where the houses were small and neat, some with bow windows and all with large knockers on the doors, and doorbells. They sought out a comfortable inn with good fare and a friendly and hospitable landlord. Captain Cheap felt quite at home: he declared that he was tired and could go no farther.

Next morning he was still so fatigued that they decided to hire a postchaise for him and Mr Hamilton: this left them, when they had paid the reckoning at the inn and set aside what they would need for sustenance and gratuities, only just enough for Byron's post horses with not a farthing over for him to have a bite to eat on the way, or even to pay the turnpikes: but he was in no mood to be deterred by little things like that: as he clattered out of the West Gate of Canterbury he felt only relief and exaltation at being free of his companions. He let his horse take its time on the long slope up to Herbal Down, but then he shook it into a merry pace more in tune with his thoughts. The distance to London was about fifty-six miles, but only three miles out of Canterbury was the Herbal Down Turnpike. He rode up to it in leisurely fashion then suddenly clapped spurs to his horse and galloped through it, scattering the bystanders to right and left and ignoring the shouts and imprecations that followed him. Soon he was peacefully cantering through silver birches whose purple branches were already full of the sap of spring: then a great forest lay before him with solemn oaks and clearings starred with primroses.

He served every turnpike as he had served the one on

Herbal Down, though it was harder near the towns to elude pursuit, and he dared not linger at the stages when exchanging his tired horse for a fresh one. He stopped at Chatham only long enough to glance at the Royal Dockyard to see what vessels were being built or fitted out, then on through Rochester; and from the village of Chalk above Gravesend he had a wide view over ploughed fields to the Thames as gay with shipping as he had imagined it. From the top of Shooters' Hill he saw the Dome of St Paul's whose name he had given nostalgically to the mountain in Tierra del Fuego.

At the Borough he took a coach and gave the driver the address in Marlborough Street where he and Isabel had been staying until he joined the *Wager*. After the swiftness and exhilaration of his ride he felt suffocated in the slow rumbling coach that was immersed in the clatter and congestion of the traffic, and the shouts and whip-cracking. Soon through it all he could hear the steady roar of the incoming tide forcing its way up from the sea through the narrow arches of Old London Bridge: then he was on the bridge, and looking out through the gaps between the houses on what was, to him, the fairest stretch of water in the world, where St Paul's stood high above the red brick houses, the wharves, the warehouses with hanging chains, the masts of ships and the deep-laden brown-sailed barges.

When they drew up in Marlborough Street he found the house closed and shuttered. With panic in his heart, having been absent so many years and in all that time never having heard a word from home and not knowing who was dead and who was living or where to go next or even how to pay the coachman, he recollected a linen-draper's shop much favoured by Isabel which his family had frequented: he therefore went there and, making himself known, the good people paid the coachman and told him that his sister had married Lord Carlisle and was living in Soho Square. He hastened there on foot, found the address and hammered on the door: it was opened by a lackey who immediately summoned help and tried to throw him down the steps. As he resisted and grappled with the servants he shouted 'Isabel! Isabel!' There was an answering cry, a patter of running feet, a flutter of silk, and she was in his arms.

CHAPTER

22

->>><<<-

MR BULKELEY was in London, having delivered the *Saphire* to her new owners, when he learned that Captain Cheap had arrived in England: and he read in a newspaper an order for all the officers and people of the *Wager* that were in England to repair on board Admiral Stewart's ship, the *Prince George*, at Spithead to give their depositions for a court-martial. He wrote to the Admiralty to say that he was in London but that he was repairing to Portsmouth to comply with the order. The next day, he tells us, 'being on the Royal Exchange' he met one of the Proctors of Doctor's Commons where the High Court of Admiralty was situated that tried cases of piracy and indictable offences on the high seas. The Proctor asked him, 'What news, now our Captain has come Home?' and also informed him that four messengers had been dispatched by the Marshal of the Admiralty with orders to take up the lieutenant, the boatswain, Mr Bulkeley himself, and the carpenter, and on no account to let them escape. Upon hearing this Mr Bulkeley said that he would go and deliver himself up to the Marshal; but the Proctor suggested that, as he knew the Deputy Marshal was to dine that day at the Paul's Head Tavern in St Paul's Churchyard, he might have an opportunity to speak with him there.

'Accordingly I went,' Mr Bulkeley says, 'and after Dinner applied to him, desiring to know his Opinion in regard to the Officers of the *Wager* as their Captain was come Home, for that I had a near Relation which was an Officer that came in that Longboat to the Brazils, and it would give me Concern if he should suffer. His Answer was that he believed that we should be hanged. To which I replied, "For God's sake! For what? For not being drowned? And is a Murderer at last come Home to be their Accuser? I have carefully perused the Journal and cannot conceive that they have been guilty of Piracy, Mutiny or anything else to deserve it. It looks to me, if so, that their Adversaries have taken up Arms against the Power of the Almighty for delivering them." He said, "Sir. They have been guilty of such Things to Captain Cheap whilst a Prisoner, that I believe the Gunner and the Carpenter will be hanged if nobody else." ' Mr Bulkeley then confessed that he was the unfortunate Gunner of the *Wager*, and was taken into custody.

It probably hadn't occurred to him on Wager Island that to seize the longboat from Captain Cheap, its lawful commander, and make off with it might be considered an act of piracy, and that from this charge he would not be protected by the plea that his pay had stopped and he was not under naval discipline. His defence, prepared for him by 'a great good Man' whom he consulted, was that the longboat had been brought ashore and sawn in half on the captain's orders, which made it no longer serviceable: therefore the rebuilt longboat was no longer the property of his Majesty and could be lawfully taken by the crew to save their lives, as if it had been any other part of the wreck that had floated ashore. It didn't sound a very convincing argument, as ships are usually unserviceable during repair or alteration and the ownership is not thereby affected.

The justification for the mutiny, if so it was to be judged, which he had insisted upon in his journal — that they had refused to continue the war against the Spaniards because the odds against them were likely to be too great — was not likely to appeal to the British public in their present mood, so he prepared to justify it on the grounds that Captain Cheap was a murderer, and therefore they were justified in arresting him. This plea was weakened by the fact that he had not been arrested after the death of Cozens but four and a half months later when the *Speedwell* was nearly ready to sail: all the evidence, including Mr Bulkeley's journal, makes it quite clear that it was a mere pretext, and that the real reason was that he was opposing their plan to take the longboat and go home through the Straits of Magellan. Nevertheless, Mr Bulkeley was ready to offer as a precedent the case of the crew of his Majesty's ship *Ruby*, some of whom seized their captain, Samuel Goodyer, for the murder of his brother. This was a callous and premeditated crime: the captain hated his brother, Sir John Dindley Goodyer, to whose Warwickshire estates he was heir presumptive, so, on the 18th January, 1741, he invited him to a tavern in Bristol to discuss their differences: as he was passing through the streets on his way to the rendezvous he had him abducted by a gang of ruffians composed of his own crew with the help of a few men from a privateer. Sir John was hustled aboard the *Ruby* and there strangled. Before she could put to sea, the cooper, supported by one or two of the crew who were not in the conspiracy, arrested the captain and delivered him to the authorities. Three weeks later he was hanged. The people who had arrested him, Mr Bulkeley wrote, had not been considered mutineers although they were in the pay of the government, 'and whether the Officers and Seamen of the *Wager* on that desolate Island, out of pay of the Government, had not as much Reason to confine Captain Cheap for the Death of Mr Cozens and deliver him up to Captain Pemberton of his Majesty's Land Forces, this I leave to the candid to judge, which were the greatest Mutineers of the two?' This again was not a very convincing argument: the candid could only reply that the shooting by Captain Cheap of Mr Cozens under the misapprehension that he was dealing with an armed aggressor could not reasonably be compared to the murder of Sir John Dindley Goodyer, and that the cooper of the *Ruby* was justified in a way that the gunner of the *Wager* was not.

Mr Bulkeley was confined with Lieutenant Baynes, the boatswain and the carpenter on board the *Prince George* at Spithead. He says that in every letter from their friends they were told they would be hanged; and that when some of them waited on Captain Cheap desiring to know what he had to allege against them, his answer was: 'Gentlemen, I have nothing to say for nor against the Villains till the Day of Trial, and then it is not in my Power to be off from hanging them.' On the following Sunday they were had up to prayers where there was a great congregation: in the latter part of the sermon the chaplain used the following words: 'Men should not feed themselves up in vain notions or expectations of a reprieve or pardon, for how often are men deceived, even in their last moments? And men that have seen so many providences of the Divine Being, 'tis not to be doubted that they are prepared, etc.' This sermon, Mr Bulkeley comments, gave them reason to think that they were to fall by the violence of power, contrary to the laws of their country. 'In the Evening of the same Day,' he continues, 'we were informed by the Master and the Gunner of the said Ship that a certain Gentleman had sent Word that we might have Privilege of Pen, Ink and Paper until the Day of Trial, which was to be on the Tuesday following, and that he had made a Resolution that no Man after Sentence of Death should be indulged with it on any Account. All this was done, we imagined, on Purpose to intimidate us to retract from the Truth which was published to the World, but our great, good and just God supported and strengthened our Faith to bear with these insults from Men.'

'The next Day in the Morning,' he continues, 'came on board the Judge Advocate in order to take our Depositions for Trial. When I was sent for I was asked for a Deposition concerning the loss of his Majesty's Ship, the *Wager*. And I answered, "Sir, I am surprised you should offer to ask me for a Deposition whilst a Prisoner, sir. This is not the first but the second time to your Knowledge that I have been confined upon this very Occasion. I always thought, or at least the Laws of my Country tell me that when a Man is a Prisoner he must be accused, and I take my Accuser to be Captain Cheap, expecting he was come here on purpose to give me his Charge to prepare myself for Trial against him." '

He was answered that the purpose of this court-martial was only to know how the ship was lost: any offence or offences committed after she was lost would have to be the subject of a separate court-martial, Mr Bulkeley therefore offered his journal as his deposition, to the truth of which, he said, he was prepared to swear: this was refused because most of it was not appropriate to the occasion, and he was persuaded to make an extract from it and submit it as his Deposition. Lieutenant Baynes and the boatswain wrote only a few lines each describing in general terms what had happened: the carpenter wrote a fuller account mentioning how he thought he had seen the land twenty-four hours before anyone else, and that he had reported it to the lieutenant. These depositions were taken on the 13th April, 1746.

On the 15th April the court-martial to enquire into the loss of the *Wager* was held on board the *Prince George* at Spithead, pursuant to an order from the Honourable Lords Commissioners of the Admiralty. The President was C.-in-C. Spithead, Admiral James Stewart. All the surviving officers were present except Campbell and Morris, but only one seaman obeyed the summons to attend: all the rest had drifted away.

The captain in his narrative said he had no charge to lay

against any of the officers except Lieutenant Baynes, who had failed to carry out his orders on the night of the disaster: he had been ordered to keep all hands on deck all night and to set the topsails, and he had not done so; and after the ship struck for the first time he had been ordered to let go the anchor, and he had not done so.

Opinions differed among the witnesses about whether the topsails could have been set or not: John Jones, in a very modest deposition, considering that he had taken charge of the deck during the emergency, gave it as his opinion that they could not have carried any more sail: he accepted the responsibility for having told the lieutenant, who was preparing to let go the anchor after the ship had struck for the second time and she had lost her rudder, that there was no room to bring her up, and that if they had swung clear of the rocks they must have sunk as they had sprung a leak and the water increased so much upon them.

Byron said that on the evening before the disaster when the captain gave the order, the topsails could have been set, or at least, he thought, it should have been tried because although the ship's head was gradually coming round to seaward she was making only leeway. No doubt Campbell, had he been present, would have agreed with him, as he had volunteered with Byron to set them; but all the rest, including Able-Seaman John George, who was on his first voyage, believed that it would have been impossible, or that the ship having lost her mizzen-mast could not have carried them.

When the court had considered all the evidence and cross-examined the witnesses, Captain Cheap and all the officers and ship's company, except Lieutenant Baynes, were acquitted of the loss of his Majesty's ship *Wager*. The record continues: 'The court, having maturely considered the case of Lieutenant Baynes, are unanimously of the opinion that he was to blame in not acquainting the captain when the carpenter told him he thought he saw the land, in never heaving the lead, nor letting go the anchor.' For these omissions he was ordered to be reprimanded, but because of the weakly condition of the ship, the cable being foul and there being only thirteen sickly hands to clue it, and because of the little reason he had to believe that it was the land that the carpenter fancied he saw, either from its appearance or from the distance his own and the general reckonings made them from the land, he too was acquitted of the loss of the ship.

After this court-martial, when everyone expected the trial of the mutineers to begin, the prisoners were released. There had evidently been some disagreement among the Lords of the Admiralty about whether to proceed against them or not. Fortunately for the prisoners, Anson had by this time become an influential member of the Board; and, as the alleged mutiny had taken place in the squadron he commanded, it was particularly his own affair. A court-martial to consider the behaviour of the ship's company after the *Wager* struck would almost certainly have found itself obliged to pronounce the prisoners guilty upon charges for which there was no alternative to the death penalty except by royal pardon. The only way to save them from the blind working of the law was not to hold a court-martial, and it lay entirely within the power of the Admiralty either to hold one or not. Anson was a sick man when he returned from the South Seas: having lost three-quarters of his crews, he was sick also of seeing his men die. He wanted no recriminations, and no victims. He saw very clearly that it was the system that was at fault, rather than the men; and because his thoughts were always constructive he set about reforming it, and let the men go free.

Mr Bulkeley did not consider himself to be quite out of danger: about a week after the court-martial to enquire into the loss of the ship he went to London and applied to their lordships for his wages: a Member of the Board, he reports, asked him if he were not one of the men that published the book, to which he made answer that he was. Then his lordship replied, 'How dare you presume to touch a Gentleman's Character in so public a Manner as you have done? Do you think that Captain Cheap has nothing to say in vindication of his Character? He will no doubt call you to Account for it. We have not heard yet what he has to charge you with. Therefore, no Wages, nor anything else can be done for you unless on hearing from him.' Mr Bulkeley answered, 'My Lord, I was honourably acquitted with him, and the Book that was published has put it out of the power of Captain Cheap to allege anything against us.' His lordship answered, 'I wish you may clear your Point in it.'

Shortly after this interview he was paid his wages up to the time the *Wager* was lost, and on the 11th July of the same year he was appointed to the command of the *Royal George*, cutter: she was about seventy tons, had a crew of sixty, ten gun carriages, sixteen swivel guns, and rowed with eighteen oars. On mature consideration he declined the command on the ground that she was 'too small to bear the Sea.' On her next voyage she foundered in the Bay of Biscay and every man in her was drowned.

About a fortnight after the court-martial, Campbell landed in England. He went to the Admiralty and explained that his necessities had forced him to take his very peculiar course of action – one that was only possible, he said, because no one could suspect him of being anything but a true and loyal subject of the king: he had accepted an offer from Admiral Pizarro to return with him to Spain with a view to receiving a commission in the Spanish Navy – but this, he maintained, was only a ruse: he had always intended to escape as soon as he had reached Europe, and return home. The fact that he had indeed returned to England lent plausibility to his story. When questioned about his change of religion, however, he did not deny it, and so he was not employed again. For this rejection he blamed the ingratitude of Captain Cheap. He wrote his own account of what had happened, to show that he had always faithfully done his duty and been unwaveringly loyal to the captain, convinced that it would clear him of all suspicion in the eyes of the public and of the authorities: in it he neither affirmed nor denied his change of religion and it failed, therefore, to influence the Lords of the Admiralty to change their decision. It was published in November 1746 and dedicated to Admiral Byng under whom he had served in the Mediterranean as a midshipman in the *Augusta*. Finding that his career in the Royal Navy was at an end, he went to Lisbon and obtained a commission in the Portuguese Navy. In 1753 he published a dissertation on the ideas of Lord Bolingbroke, and in 1754 *A Chain of Philosophical Reasoning* to demonstrate the necessary existence of a Supreme Being.

John Young, the cooper, brought out *An Affecting Narrative of the unfortunate Voyage and Catastrophy of his Majesty's Ship* Wager in 1751. It follows Bulkeley and Cummins closely in its narrative, but it is more sympathetic towards the captain: Mr Bulkeley in this version is not as plausible as in his own; the carpenter, though described as excellent in his craft, is more contentious and quarrelsome, Lieutenant Baynes more shifty, the boatswain more of a scoundrel, and the general mass of the people more brutish and unreasonable than in the other versions. He notes that discipline was lost after the captain had antagonised the people by shooting Cozens, and he laments his own intervention in that affair, for if he had allowed the purser to shoot Cozens, instead of preventing him by canting his elbow, the captain, he thinks, would have been able to maintain his authority and much evil would have been prevented.

Midshipman Morris and the two friends who had shared

his trials, Samuel Cooper and John Andrews, after spending fourteen weeks in the Castle of San Anton, were given half a real each and allowed to make their own way to Portugal. They reached Oporto, where they embarked on the 28th April, 1746, arriving in London on the 8th July. Morris, finding himself in financial straits when he returned, took the first opportunity to retrieve his fortunes by going back into the Merchants' Service. These, as far as can be ascertained, were the last of the survivors to reach England. Nothing more was heard of James Mitchell, the supposed murderer of Thomas Lark, who set off with two companions in a canoe fashioned from a section of the *Wager*'s mainmast, nor of John Duck, nor of his two friends who were missing after the Indians raided their camp, nor of the eleven men who landed of their own free will from the *Speedwell* in Tierra del Fuego with the intention of rejoining the captain, nor of the four marines left behind when the yawl was lost, nor of the six men who made off with the barge after it had been promised to Martin, the Indian from Chiloe.

Mr Bulkeley's contention that a return by the Straits of Magellan offered the ship's company the best chance of survival was not borne out by subsequent events: therefore, as it brought about the deaths of two-thirds of his companions, it must be considered a tragic mistake, although during the voyage he showed great determination and skill in navigation. The disasters that overtook the captain's party must also be laid at his door, for by depriving them of the longboat he foredoomed to failure all their efforts to get out of the Gulf of Affliction. It can hardly be doubted that the captain's plan, besides being the more honourable and the more courageous, was also the more practical. Byron always thought that if they had gone north in the *Speedwell* they would have had as good a chance as Captain Shelvocke's crew to take a Spanish prize and turn their disaster into a triumph.

On one of the crew lists Lieutenant Baynes has noted the fate of each man as far as he knew, or could recall it. Opposite a very few names he has written, 'Come home,' or 'Coming home.' On the pay sheet the bereaved dependents, or their lawyers, or creditors, have signed for the few pounds that the dead had so bitterly earned: 'William Clarke, £14. 11. 1. signed for by William Reynolds for ye man's daughter Ann: Guy Broadwater, Coxn. £17. 14. 10. to ye sister Sarah for ye mother Sarah: John Duck, Prest man, £7. 9. 10. to Mr Dowey, guardian to ye sister Mary: John Halliday for ye widow Isabella . . .' and so it goes on, 'for ye mother Penelope . . . for ye father, for ye brother . . .' It is not known how many boys were in the ship nor how many, if any, survived: not being in receipt of wages from the Admiralty their names are not recorded.

Their disastrous voyage is also recalled by a little group of names on the Admiralty charts. Wager Island is there, with Byron Island beside it: the approximate position of the wreck is marked, but Mount Misery has become Mount Anson. The channel between the mainland and what Captain Cheap christened The Duke of Montrose's Island is now called Cheape Channel. On the north side of the Golfo de Peñas, or Gulf of Affliction, are the Marine Islands, with separate islands of the group named after the four marines who were abandoned, Crosslet, Hereford, Smith and Hales Island. On the mainland is Cirujana (or Surgeon's) Peninsula where Surgeon Elliot died. Farther north are the Sugar Loaf Mountain and the mountain that Byron named The Dome of St Paul's. Beyond the Cape of Three Mountains is Anna Pink Bay where the *Anna*, pink, lay for two months, from the middle of May till the middle of July 1741, after rounding Cape Horn, to rest her crew and restore their health, and where, for the first three days of her stay there, she had fired the usual sunset gun that had caused so much excitement among the shipwrecked crew of the *Wager*. She had discontinued it for fear of attracting hostile Indians. From Mr Bulkeley's voyage, Speedwell Bay has kept its place in the charts, and the Rock of Dundee, and Harvey's Bay, named after the purser who surveyed it and subsequently died of starvation.

Because it was evident that much of the distress suffered by the people of the *Wager* was the direct result of the breakdown of the captain's authority, Anson introduced an Act of Parliament for extending the discipline of the navy to the crews of his Majesty's ships wrecked, lost or taken; and for continuing to them their wages under certain conditions. This new regulation was further explained and confirmed in 1748 when the laws relating to the government of his Majesty's ships, vessels and forces by sea were amended and reduced into a single Act of Parliament which became the basis of the Fighting Instructions and remained in force, substantially unchanged, for nearly a hundred years. The case of the *Wager* had also shown the inconvenience of having a body of troops on board not under the command of the captain: Anson had the Maritime Regiment, ordinarily raised by the War Office on the outbreak of hostilities, made a permanent force and transferred to the control of the Admiralty: this measure, first suggested by the Earl of Sandwich, resulted in the formation of the Marines, now the Royal Marines, in 1755. Thus Anson made sure, as far as it lay in his power, that none of his crews would ever again have to go through the same agonising experiences as the people of the *Wager*.

When he had been cleared by the court-martial, Captain Cheap was given command of his Majesty's ship *Lark* – a curious coincidence, but the spirit of poor murdered Thomas Lark never troubled him: perhaps it was laid to rest by his Christian burial on Mount Misery. The captain suffered no misfortune; on the contrary, in company with Captain Saunders with whom he had served in the *Centurion* under

Anson, he captured a valuable Spanish ship off Madeira. His health had been impaired by his privations, and now the prize-money enabled him to marry the Widow Brown of York and retire from active service. John Jones sailed as Master of the *Aldeburgh*: in her he was again shipwrecked: she was cast away on the coast of Barbary, but again he survived.

Byron had been promoted to lieutenant during his absence in South America: on his return he was made a commander, and after the court-martial he was posted captain of the frigate *Syren*. In 1747 Anson, who had left his armchair at the Admiralty to take command of the Channel Fleet, defeated and captured a French fleet off Cape Finisterre. This, and a similar victory won by Vice-Admiral Hawke six months later, brought the war to a close with Britain's ascendancy at sea well established. During the peace, Byron commanded the *St Albans*, cruising off the coast of Guinea, then the *Augusta* of sixty guns, guardship at Plymouth, and finally the *Vanguard*. When the Seven Years' War broke out in 1756 he commanded the *America*, sixty guns, and then the *Fame*, seventy-four guns: in her, with two other ships of the line, he destroyed a French convoy of twenty schooners and sloops and three frigates carrying troops and stores intended for the relief of Quebec.

When peace had been established once more, with Britain everywhere victorious, Byron was sent on a voyage of discovery with two ships, the *Dolphin*, twenty guns, and the *Tamar*, sloop of war. Because it was considered essential for Britain to have a base in the far south for further exploration and to open up new areas for trade and enterprise, he was instructed first of all to establish the exact locations of Pepys Island and the Falkland Islands; next he was to search the South Atlantic between the latitudes of 33° and 53° South for land or islands: then he was to pass through the Straits of Magellan, proceed up the Pacific coast of

South and North America and search for a passage back to the North Atlantic through Hudson's Bay. He was also instructed to make enquiries about the people who were shipwrecked in the *Wager* and left on the coast, but only if he found it necessary to go there to obtain refreshment for his men, or from any unforeseen accident.

He sailed from Plymouth on the 3rd July, 1764, put in at the Cape Verde Islands for fresh water, and reached Rio de Janeiro on the 12th September. He sailed again on the 21st October. He was passing down the coast of Patagonia, following the track on the chart published in Anson's Voyage, and consequently the one followed by the *Wager* when he was serving as a midshipman, when on the 12th November at 4 p.m. he heard a cry of 'Land right ahead!' where there should not have been any. It made first like an island with two craggy hummocks on it. Looking under the foresail and to leeward, he saw land running a long way to the south-east: it was very blue, as is usual in dark rainy weather at some little distance. He sent officers to the mast-head, and they immediately called out that there was land to windward also, so he feared they were embayed. He brought the ship to, and sounded, getting fifty-two fathoms. He made sail and steered east-south-east to get out again, hoping to be clear by nightfall, for the hills all around seemed very wild, and many of his people told him they could see the sea breaking upon sandy beaches. When they had sailed out to seaward for about an hour, during which time the land did not alter its appearance in the least, it suddenly vanished and there was nothing there at all. 'It was as plain as I ever saw Land in my Life,' Byron recorded in his journal. 'There is not a Man on board but would have freely made Oath of the certainty of its being Land.'

Next day, Tuesday the 13th, the weather was very fine, when all at once, again at 4 p.m., the wind shifted to the south-west and the sky to windward became pitch black.

271

Byron at once ordered the topsails to be handed. The people on deck were alarmed by a very unusual noise, like breakers on a lee shore, then vast seas covered with foam were seen rolling towards the ship while flocks of birds, screaming and flying as if they were being pursued by something terrible, flew over their heads. He called to the men to haul the foresail up and to let go the main sheet, but before this could be done the wind seized the vessel and laid her on her beam ends: 'We cut the Main Tack,' Byron says, 'for it was then impossible to cast it off; the Main Sheet struck the first Lieutenant down, bruised him terribly and broke three of his Teeth. The Main Topsail was not quite handed so was split to pieces. I never remember to have seen anything more dreadful than this Squall, nor anything come on with so little warning.' The *Tamar*, being to leeward, had more time to prepare for it, but she split her mainsail. They continued southward, and while attempting to enter Port Desire the *Dolphin* was again assailed by a sudden wind, coming in very hard flaws from off the land, and driven ashore. She was hauled off again without serious damage.

After a fortnight spent in taking ballast, which was necessary because the ships were now light, having used much of their stores, they sailed for Pepys Island: they searched for it in vain and came to the conclusion that it didn't exist. On the 19th December they approached the Straits of Magellan for fresh water and firewood, neither of which were to be found at Port Desire. Near the entrance they saw a number of horsemen riding backwards and forwards, beckoning them to come ashore, exactly as Mr Bulkeley had described them twenty years ago, and in the same place. Byron ordered out his twelve-oared boat, landed and communicated with them by signs: they were some of the people Magellan had called *Patagones*, big feet, and they had been seen and described by other early explorers, de Weert, Spelbergen and Shelvocke, and the whole country had come to be known as Patagonia. Sir Thomas Cavendish had measured the imprint of one of their feet and found it to be eighteen inches long. Byron on tip-toes could just reach the top of the head of one of the Patagonians: 'Their middle stature seemed to be about eight feet; their extreme nine and upwards,' one of his officers wrote. More horsemen kept galloping up until there were about five hundred of them with innumerable dogs. Four or five of the chief men invited Byron to mount and go inland with them, but he politely refused: he felt no desire for any further acquaintance with the personal lives and habitations of Indians, even of these extraordinary specimens. He gave them some tobacco, ribbon and beads, with which they seemed greatly pleased, and went back on board.

On the 7th January he sailed for the Falkland Islands which were sighted on the 12th. He took bearings and soundings and sent the boats in to look for a harbour: they found a splendid one on the 15th which Byron named Port Egmont after the Earl of Egmont, First Lord of the Admiralty. The islands had been discovered in 1592 by Captain John Davis, and in the following year Hawkins had taken formal possession of them in the name of her Majesty Queen Elizabeth, but nothing had been done since then: Byron again took formal possession of them, in the name of his Majesty King George III. He returned to Port Desire where he met the store ship *Florida* which he brought to the Straits of Magellan in order to find shelter from the incessant gales and transfer her cargo to the *Dolphin* and the *Tamar*.

He should now have searched the South Atlantic in the direction of the Cape of Good Hope, but instead he passed through the Straits to the Pacific, meeting with such fierce westerly gales that it took him two months: off Cape Monday, he says, the wind blew 'so terrible a Gale that it was almost past all description, the Water was tore up all about us and carried much higher than our Mastheads.' There was just a shadow of a trace that some of the men missing from the *Wager* might have passed that way: one of Byron's officers reported that in the neighbourhood of Cape Quod an Indian family approached them and seemed to be offering them a girl who had 'tolerable features, and an English face.' Nothing more is known about her. There was also a suggestion that an old rusted musket barrel with the king's broad arrow upon it that they found at Port Desire might have been left there by the men of the *Wager*.

On reaching Cape Pillar, Byron should have turned north to carry out the second part of his task, but instead he sailed out into the Pacific: seafarers at that time were much preoccupied with the legend of the Solomon Islands, supposed, according to Inca tradition, to be rich in gold and silver and copper: they were also supposed to be the outposts of Terra Australis, the great southern continent. They had been visited in 1568 by the Spaniard Mendaña, and lost sight of again, though many had sought for them. Explorers before Captain Cook were inclined to follow their own instincts rather than their instructions, and Byron was no exception: he evidently felt that fame and fortune awaited him in the Pacific: he steered west, hoping to find the Solomon Islands or to make some other important discovery. His route brought him close to Tahiti and the whole archipelago of the Society Islands, but at the crucial moment he altered course and missed them because so great a swell came up from southward that he was afraid the ships would roll their masts over the side. When he had discovered only a few not very important islands the increasing sickness of his crews caused him to abandon the search and make for Juan Fernandez where he knew he could get them ashore and cure them. He wrote in his journal, 'Some of my best Men (to my great sorrow) begin to complain of the Scurvy . . .' and later, 'My People fall down daily in the Scurvy, &

some of my best Men already so bad in it, that they are confined to their Hammocks.' And finally, 'Bore away and made sail to the Westward greatly grieved I could procure no Refreshment for our Sick here, who are most of them in a very desponding way.' When his crews had recovered he could still have gone north to search for the North West Passage which, if it existed and was found to be practicable, would have opened up a new trade route to the East, but he chose to return to England by Batavia and the Cape of Good Hope. He was unlucky in not discovering more than he did, but he was not a dedicated explorer. It was his constant solicitude for the welfare of his men that made him turn back when he might have gone on and won for himself an important place in the annals of the Pacific: his greatest success was to prove that a long voyage was possible without the loss of half the crew from scurvy: only six men died in each ship during the two years they were away. The Royal Society criticised him severely for 'his dearth of scientific results.' He commented that they would no doubt have accepted the deaths of a few more seamen if a few more islands had been discovered. The Admiralty, however, found the information he brought home of great interest and the acquisition of the Falkland Islands of great importance: their policy of exploration was continued, and Byron's effort became the first of a series leading to the great voyages of Captain Cook. After acting as adviser in the preparation of a new expedition, he was appointed Governor of Newfoundland and the *Dolphin* was sent out again, commanded this time by Captain Wallis.

John Hawkesworth, who edited, and romanticised, the journal of voyage, changed the large Patagonians into giants and Byron became the butt of the wits and satirists of the day. In 1768 he published *The Narrative of the Honourable John Byron (Commodore in a Late Expedition round the World), containing an Account of the great Distresses suffered by Himself and his Companions on the Coast of Patagonia.* It was by far the most successful of the narratives published by the people of the *Wager*: it has been reprinted frequently and there have been a number of foreign editions.

Mr Bulkeley brought out a second edition of his journal in 1757. It was published in Philadelphia, as he had now emigrated. The book was dedicated to the Governor of Pennsylvania, the Hon. W. Denney, under whose benevolence and wisdom, he says, he looks forward to that province becoming the Garden of the Lord and the special care of his Majesty the King and the British Parliament: he had not the least suspicion that within twenty years the American Colonies and the Mother Country, whose interests he believed were inseparably joined, would be at war.

Byron's great chance to distinguish himself came three years after the outbreak of hostilities when France intervened on the side of the colonists and sent a fleet to American waters to prevent the British troops from receiving supplies and reinforcements: he was promoted to Vice-Admiral of the Blue and, in preference to Rodney who was senior to him, he was given command of a fleet that was being sent out to defeat the French and re-establish control of the sea routes upon which, to a very great extent, the issue of the struggle depended. By this time the uncanny perverseness of the weather he so frequently encountered had become proverbial: the seamen had come to dread his command, and he was known as 'Foul-Weather Jack' and 'The Jonah of the *Wager*': whether this was just bad luck or whether it was the working out of some obscure curse he had picked up among the Indians, whose custom it was to call upon the elements to destroy their enemies, it would be impossible to determine. On the 9th June, 1778, he sailed from Spithead with a fleet of thirteen ships of the line and with his flag in the *Princess Royal* of ninety guns. Gale after gale swept down upon him, delayed his passage and scattered his ships. Seventy days after leaving England the flagship arrived alone off Sandy Hook. He found a French fleet of fifteen ships of the line awaiting him there, blocking the way to New York and Rhode Island, so he bore away for Halifax. Slowly he collected and refitted his battered fleet and again put to sea; but again it was scattered by a storm in which two of his ships foundered. Thus the French were left supreme in American waters, and the foul weather which pursued and haunted Byron became an important factor in the defeat of Britain by the colonists.

By the time he had received reinforcements and once more repaired and refitted his ships, the French were threatening the important British possessions in the West Indies: he followed them and got there in time to force them to abandon St Lucia in the Leeward Islands: the town and harbour had already been wrested from them by Admiral Barrington and 5,000 troops under Sir Henry Clinton. He then proceeded with fifteen ships of the line to the island of Grenada which was being threatened by a French fleet, reported to be nineteen ships of the line, commanded by Admiral d'Estaing. With the object of relieving Grenada he hung out the signal for the General Chase, which was the only alternative to forming the conventional line of battle that the strict naval regulations allowed. The French turned out to be greatly superior in numbers, having twenty-seven ships of the line, and also in tactical skill: Byron was not able to bring about a general engagement or to lay his ships alongside those of his enemy, which was the kind of fighting that he and his men preferred. Four of his ships approaching the French line unsupported were badly mauled. When they had fought their way through to the entrance of the harbour they saw that the town was already lost: they were fired on by the defences, and the French flag was flying over the fortress. No doubt if the French had attacked with greater determination, Byron's losses would have been greater as he was encumbered with transports; but Admiral d'Estaing had an objective more important to him than the destruction of his enemy's ships: he wanted to maintain in seaworthy condition a fleet that would give France an overriding superiority in American and West Indian waters. During the late peace the French government, realising that they had lost India and Canada through British control of the seas, had made great efforts to build up their fleet, increase its efficiency and introduce new tactical ideas, whereas the British fleet had been allowed to run down, partly because the Hanoverian kings, unlike the Stuarts, had little knowledge or understanding of naval affairs. Three years passed after Byron's defeat at Grenada before Rodney retrieved the situation by his great victory at the Battle of the Saints, but by then it was too late to save the British forces on the American continent that had been cut off from their supplies and reinforcements.

Shortly after the Battle of Grenada Byron handed over his command to Admiral Parker and returned to England in a frigate. He never went to sea again. Charnock, the naval biographer, says, 'He died on the 10th of April, 1786, with the universal and justly acquired reputation of a brave and excellent officer, but, of a man extremely unfortunate. He married, in August 1748, Sophia, daughter of John Trevanion Esq., of Carhays in the County of Cornwall . . .' The marriage however does not appear to have been one of his misfortunes, though his eldest son, 'Mad Jack Byron, late of the Guards,' must have caused him some anxiety: he married two heiresses in succession and went through their fortunes at a tremendous rate: by the first he had a daughter, Augusta, who married Colonel Leigh: by the second he became the father of Lord Byron the poet, who inherited the title and the encumbered family estates upon the death of his cousin William on active service in Corsica.

Admiral Byron never lost his affectionate regard for his

sister Isabel. She acquitted herself fairly well as the wife of the fourth Earl of Carlisle and the mother of the fifth, and as the hostess of Carlisle House in London and of the huge Castle Howard in the north, but after she had been left a widow, in 1758, she amply justified Lady Mary Wortley Montague's opinion that her inclinations were very gay: she scandalised London society by going off to Provence and living exactly as she pleased: she moved from place to place, usually in the neighbourhood of garrison towns, Nimes, Aix, Montpellier, Beaucaire, dancing all night at open-air fêtes in light dishabille, writing verse, painting sensitive watercolours and enjoying the orange blossom, the fountains and the nightingales: '*Important que cette dame quitte ce pays*' – Important that the lady quits this country, wrote La Marquise du Deffand, influential leader of Parisian society, '*garnison – fréquents repas – fort agréeable à tous les officiers.*' But for the next twelve years she obstinately refused to return to England where there was no place, she said, for older women who didn't play cards. She was still alive when her grand-nephew, the poet, was born in 1788, but her brother, the admiral, had been dead two years.

Lord Byron felt some affinity with his grandfather: 'He had no peace at sea,' he wrote, 'nor I on land,' and the tragedy of the *Wager* left its mark on the narrative poem *Childe Harold* that made him famous, and also on his most important work, *Don Juan*. He always maintained that the outsized Patagonians had really existed and had been truthfully reported. There were some odd parallels in the lives of the admiral and the poet besides their stormy lives and their common interest in the sea: they both had a tendency to retire into isolation, their dogs were their close companions, they shared a great admiration for Spanish ladies, and they both loved their sisters; though Lord Byron's love for Augusta, his half-sister, took a different direction. The dominant characteristics of the admiral, however, are more clearly seen in his second son, George Anson Byron, than in Mad Jack and his descendants. Like his father he went to sea at the age of fourteen. In April 1782, while in command of the frigate *Andromache* in the West Indies, he carried out a daring reconnaissance of Port Royal in Martinique and observed that the French fleet were preparing to put to sea: he brought this news to the British fleet at St Lucia with the result that Rodney was able to intercept the French at the passage of The Saints – small islands between Dominica and Guadaloupe – where he completely defeated them. Thus George Byron to some extent avenged the reverse sustained by his father at Grenada. This son was happily married; and his son, following the family tradition, commanded the frigate *Blonde*: he became Captain Lord Byron on the death of the poet in 1824.

SOURCES

The main sources for this story are the narratives of the survivors, Byron, Bulkeley & Cummins, Campbell, Morris, and John Young:

BYRON. The Narrative of the honourable John Byron containing an Account of the Great Distresses suffered by himself and His Companions . . . London, 1768.

BULKELEY. A Voyage to the South-Seas in the Years 1740–1. Containing a faithful Narrative . . . By John Bulkeley and John Cummins, Late Gunner and Carpenter of the *Wager*, London, 1743.
There is a second edition with a new dedication and some correspondence, published in Philadelphia, 1757.

CAMPBELL. The Sequel to Bulkeley and Cummins' Voyage to the South-Seas . . . by Alexander Campbell, late Midshipman of the *Wager*, London, 1747.

MORRIS. A Faithful Narrative of the Dangers and Distresses that befell Isaac Morris, late Midshipman of the *Wager* . . . n.d.
This narrative begins when Morris and his seven companions are abandoned by their comrades on the Coast of Patagonia.

JOHN YOUNG. An affecting Narrative of the Unfortunate Voyage and Catastrophe of his Majesty's Ship *Wager*, one of Commodore Anson's Squadron in the South-Sea Expedition . . . London, 1751.
There is no author's name on the title page: he reveals his identity only in the course of the narrative.

Other useful sources of information are:

ANSON. A Voyage Round the World in the Years MDCCXL, I, II, III, IV by George Anson Esq; Commander in Chief of a Squadron of his Majesty's Ships, sent upon an Expedition to the South-Seas. Compiled . . . by Richard Walter, M.A., London, 1748.

ANSON. Documents relating to Anson's Voyage Round the World 1740–1741. Edited by Glyndwr Williams, Ph.D. Printed for the Navy Records Society, 1967.

BYRON. Byron's Journal of his Circumnavigation 1764–1766. Edited by Robert E. Gallagher. Published for the Hakluyt Society. Cambridge University Press, 1964.

ISABELLA BYRON. There is a short biography of Isabella Byron, later Countess of Carlisle, in Warren Hunting Smith's Originals Abroad. Yale University Press, 1952.

JOHN CHARNOCK. Biographia Navalis, London, 1794.

DR JOHN CAMPBELL. Lives of the British Admirals. New Edition, 1817.

JOHN MARSHALL. Royal Naval Biography, London, 1823.

ARMADA ESPAÑOLA. (The Official Spanish History.)

ADMIRALTY. Regulations and Instructions Relating to His Majesty's Service at Sea. Third Edition, 1740.

SHELVOCKE. A Voyage Round the World, by Captain George Shelvocke, 1726.

PUBLIC RECORD OFFICE. Adm 36 2986 2988
                      Adm 36 4456
                      Adm 33 390

BRITISH MUSEUM. Original Private and Official Correspondence of Admiral George, Lord Anson from 1744–1762. 3 Vols. Folio 15, 955–6–7. Additional 1846–1847.

An ACT for amending, explaining, and reducing into One Act of Parliament, the Laws relating to the Government of His Majesty's Ships, Vessels, and Forces by Sea. Published 1749.

GENTLEMAN'S MAGAZINE. 1742 1744 1786

ST JAMES EVENING POST. 1745, Burney collection.

THE TOWN & COUNTRY MAGAZINE. A satirical magazine that featured a different liaison every month. In the issue of December 1773 it relates that Admiral Byron in his later years installed his wife's personal maid in lodgings in King Street, Golden Square, where he paid her frequent visits. She is described as well read, and 'Very fair with light eyes, her hair also light, and remarkably beautiful, rather under middle size but proportionately made, a very captivating figure. Several overtures have been made to her but she has rejected considerable sums of money from various quarters so that she may be pronounced the faithful as well as the devoted Betsy G - - - - n.'

This looks fairly authentic, but according to the same article Byron left school and went to sea at the age of seventeen, which is incorrect as he was in the *Romney* from the age of fifteen.

INDEX